ORCH
o
GODS

DAMIEN BUCKLEY

For Jo, Les, Luke & Peter - Thank you!

For Jo, Les, Luke & Peter - Thank you!

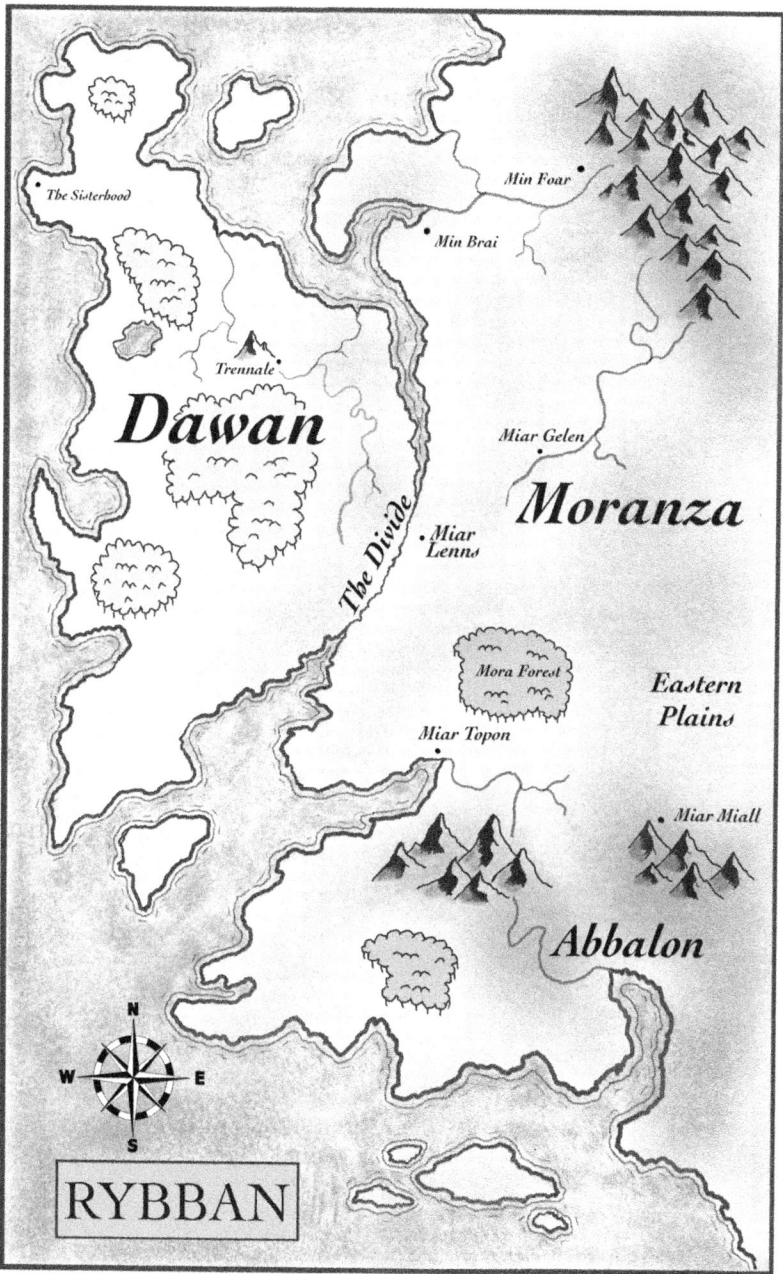

The Sisterhood

Min Foar

Min Brai

Trennale

Dawan

Miar Gelen

Moranza

Miar
Lenns

The Divide

Mora Forest

Eastern
Plains

Miar Topon

Miar Miall

Abbalon

N
W   E
S

RYBBAN

I

HEIST

Liana discovered at five years old that magic hurt. Most children who learned this lesson never touched magic again. She was not one of them. For Liana, the allure and wonder of making objects move without touching them, or creating light with only her imagination, far outweighed any suffering she felt. Even she had her limits, though. Pushing a pin across a table may only hurt a little, but lifting a tamewolf from its bed while it slept would blind her with agony. The one time she tried, the tamewolf—her brother's—didn't seem quite himself after and refused to sleep in her presence again. That was nineteen years ago, and he still refused to forget.

Liana leaned idly against a dirty wall away from the main thoroughfare, waiting. The early moonlight danced across a silver coin she floated slightly above the palm of her open hand. A headache formed behind her eyes, but she didn't mind. She hadn't slept, and the pain helped keep her awake. As she waited, she stared at the orange sky and tried to remember the last time she'd seen a cloud. A long time ago, now.

The ever-present breeze carried through pale and worn out sandstone buildings, ruffling against heavy fabric wind-breaks

1

that offered poor protection against the dust that lived in the air. The city of Miar Lenns cried out for rain, as did most of Moranza. Liana liked it when it rained.

It was almost never dark outside, which made it difficult to hide away from unwanted attention. Twilight lasted less than fifteen minutes per day as the moon passed in front of the unseen sun. That was hours away, the day now only beginning. She watched as passers-by went about their business. None paid her any attention, not so far, at least. Addan was late, and the longer she waited, the more exposed she felt. Finally, he showed.

'Where in all of Rybban have you been?' she hissed. Despite a tatty grey hood obscuring his face, she knew it was him. Addan was slim, but strong, and a little short for a man, but still half a head taller than her. He walked with a slight limp, favouring his left foot. Slight enough for most people not to notice, but she could see it. She had asked him about it once, and learned he'd lost a toe to his tamewolf as a boy. It still hurt after all this time, he'd told her.

'Sorry,' he whispered. 'I thought I was early, actually. How long have you been here?' He lowered his hood, revealing unkempt, mousy brown hair and a small nose that curled upwards slightly at the tip. It looked like he hadn't shaved in days. The rising light of the moon sparkled in his green eyes. She liked his eyes, even jealous if she dared admit it. He was the only person she knew who didn't have brown or blue eyes. Green was unique. She liked unique.

'Long enough.' Her tone sounded harsher than intended, her unease about staying in one place for too long on display.

'If you don't want to do this, we can leave right now and forget the whole thing.'

'You asked for my help and I'm here. Do you want to get the gabbalins off your back, or not?' Liana pocketed her coin and pushed herself away from the wall.

Addan sniffed and looked about warily. 'Yes, Shara, of course I do.'

Shara. That was the alias she used whenever she was out on her own in the city. *If only he knew who I really was.*

Liana couldn't recall the last time she was in this part of the city. Did it always look so... run down? A dishevelled heap of a man, probably homeless, huddled by a gate some distance away, had spotted them and kept glancing in their direction. He was likely no threat, but she didn't want to wait around any longer to find out. Addan's tardiness couldn't become a problem.

It was all his idea, not that she objected. He was heavily in debt, and had run out of time with a gang of gabbalins he'd got involved with. He'd been desperately trying to extricate himself from the hold they had over him, but that meant settling what he owed first. So, he came to her for help. According to him, an old woman—who he had never met before—told him of an artefact the gabbalins would offer handsome recompense for. If he could procure said artefact, the money would be enough to settle his debts twice over. He confessed he was already drunk by the time she introduced herself, so was light on the specifics. He couldn't remember her name, or why she had told him about the artefact either. The whole story sounded far-fetched, which was nothing new, but if even half of what he said was true, she was glad to help her best friend.

'Over the wall, right?' said Addan.

Liana nodded, pulled her own hood tighter over her head, and made for a narrow through-walk running alongside a dry hedgerow thick with dark red and purple leaves. Addan followed behind. Gravel underfoot gave way to untidy brush. Liana carefully stamped on the parched overgrowth, cutting a path through to a grey and yellow stone wall that ran left and right as far as she could see. She looked up. The wall stood almost twice as tall as either of them. The stonework was rough, with several points jutting out far enough to gain a purchase with their hands and feet, if they were careful.

'You go first,' offered Liana.

'If I must.' Addan studied the wall. 'Give me a leg up. If I can reach that rock...'

Liana cupped her hands and lowered herself. Addan placed his foot in her hands and she heaved upwards. He grabbed at his chosen stone with his left hand, missed, and fell to the ground, landing awkwardly. Liana suppressed a laugh. She brushed the dirt his boot had left in her hands off before cupping them again.

Addan's second attempt succeeded. He found a secure purchase with his feet and he pulled himself up the wall and over the top. Liana, starting from a lower stone within her reach, scaled the wall after him. So far, so good.

On the other side of the wall, they found an expensive-looking building that felt out of place compared to most of the others in the area. Stained glass windows decorated otherwise ordinary walls. From their vantage point, it wasn't possible to make out their design exactly, but they looked more detailed than most. To Liana, that meant wealth.

'Who did you say lived here again?' she asked. She kept herself low to the ground with her back to the wall as she studied the building and the grounds surrounding it.

'Dunno. I was told. I can't remember, exactly. What's important is that they're not here. Away in Miar Topon, I think. Until the bridge thing.'

Ah, the new bridge over the Divide. Liana had tried her best to forget about that, and she couldn't be thinking about it now. If Addan was right, then the place was unoccupied, and that was all that mattered.

Liana scanned the area around the building. It was a modest-sized courtyard covered in a thin layer of fine sand gravel. Not so fine it would blow into drifts in the constant breeze, but fine enough for them to leave footprints behind. Six plinths, arranged in a symmetrical pattern, stood proudly in the garden, each with a bust of a man or woman. Presumably they were representations of the Architects, though she couldn't say for certain which one was which. She was relieved to see there weren't any tamewolves or other guarding animals roaming within the perimeter. It was the only thing in the plan they couldn't know for sure. Tamewolves would have alerted anyone nearby to their presence, and the heist would be over before it began.

The next step was to get inside. There was a small door directly opposite them, perhaps twenty paces away. Staying crouched, she crept across the yard towards the door. She told Addan to match her steps to avoid making it obvious there were two of them there. Just in case.

The door was wooden, which surprised her. There wasn't even a metal overplate. 'Who's stupid enough to still use wood?' she asked. Addan shrugged. She ran her hand along the hinged side of the door. The surface was rough and small flecks broke away at the edges under her fingers. Dry rot and age. There wasn't a handle on this side and she wasn't able to feel a locking mechanism for her to manipulate using her magic. She concluded it was disused, and possibly blocked on the other side. She cursed under her breath. They'd need to find another way in.

Neither of the windows beside the door looked like they would open. Given the size of the building, Liana suspected there was at least one other way in, aside from the main front doors at the front of the building. Those doors were visible to anyone who would pass by, so it was out of the question to break in that way. It was an equal decision—left or right? Either side could have another door, or neither, or indeed both. Liana chose right.

She signalled for Addan to follow her as she made her way

around the perimeter. She took care to keep low under the windows as she passed. Even though she believed the house was empty, it was her instinct to remain as invisible as possible. She rounded the corner and caught her foot on a loose stone that had no business being there. If it wasn't for a drainage pipe to grab hold of, she would have crashed to the ground. 'Burn the stones!' she cursed as she righted herself. Addan sniggered quietly behind her, but she did her best to ignore it.

Recomposed, she noticed a small set of railings attached to the wall around ten paces away. A service door. Perfect. The door was set below ground, accessed by six well-worn stone steps. The railings were there to prevent anyone from accidentally falling in, their design favouring function over aesthetic. She crept down the steps and examined the door. Like the first, it was also wooden, but had a brass handle that looked far newer than the door itself. She turned the handle. Locked. She didn't truly expect otherwise, though it was worth a try.

'You're sure you can get us in?' whispered Addan. He was right behind her, almost on her shoulder.

Liana frowned. 'I said I could do it. Now let me concentrate.'

She placed her hand, palm first, over the door lock and closed her eyes. Imagining the mechanism inside, she focused her mind and willed it to turn. Her hand felt hot. Too hot. While pain was enough to stop most from using magic, she had pushed herself to learn how to use it to her advantage despite how much it hurt her. She treated it almost like a challenge; a trial set by the Architects themselves, not that she had believed in them since her childhood. There was a limit to how much pain she could endure, though. Despite years of trying, of researching, all throughout her childhood and into her young adult years, she could never perform more than the simplest thing before the pain forced her to stop. There *was* a barrier, she was certain of that, but *how* to break through it had always eluded her. The lock turned.

The pain in her palm vanished immediately, as if nothing had happened. Carefully, she turned the handle and pushed the door forward. The room on the other side was dark, and it took a moment for her eyes to adjust to the contrast of the light outside. Satisfied the room was unoccupied, she stepped in and beckoned for Addan to follow.

In the gloom, they found themselves in a kitchen. Small, tidy and well-appointed. A large wooden worktable stood in the centre of the room. *More wood*, she thought. *Whoever lives here must be insane.* To her right was a traditional stove that used a self-heating liquid to cook food. A gentle warmth radiated from the top hotplate. In the opposite corner were two doors, again wooden. One she presumed was a pantry and the other, separated by an arm's length of wall, a way out into the rest of the mansion.

Addan helped himself to a hunk of bread on the worktable and took a bite. Liana snatched it from him and put it back. 'We're not here for breakfast,' she said sternly.

'A man's got to eat,' he replied, spitting wet crumbs everywhere. 'There's no harm in taking a bit of bread when the opportunity presents itself.'

'You're always thinking with your stomach.'

Addan shrugged. 'It was stale anyway.'

She ignored him and moved to the door she guessed would most likely lead out to the rest of the house. She was grateful it wasn't locked. The door opened inwards to the kitchen. A flight of stone steps matching the ones outside in both wear and design rose upward into near total darkness. She closed her eyes and concentrated. Within her mind, she created a tiny speck of white light and projected it outward in front of her. Immediately, her head hurt, and she reached out with her arm to steady herself on the doorframe. Burning in her hands was one thing, but headaches were less fun, not because they hurt, but because they made her dizzy.

'Are you all right?' asked Addan.

'It's fine. If I can keep the light as small as possible, I should manage. Let's hope it's not as dark up there.'

The small speck of light, no bigger than a grain of sand, floated in front of Liana. Minute, but bright enough to show the way up the steps. There wasn't a door at the top. Liana climbed the steps, running her hand along the wall as she went. The damp, rough brickwork felt slick underneath her fingers. Her head pounded. At the top was a corridor. It was cold, draughty and dark. She would have to maintain her light for a while longer. Dizziness be damned.

Addan pushed past her. 'We need to hurry,' he said as he tried the handle of the closest door. Locked. He walked farther along the corridor and tried another. It opened. Liana watched as Addan peered through before disappearing into whatever was on the other side. She followed him in. Another dark room. Huge, though. Her light wasn't strong enough to reach the walls. From her right there was a swoosh and a myriad of colours flooded the room. Addan had found a window and pulled open a curtain, the stained glass bathing the room in a vibrant abstract pattern. Liana extinguished her light, and the headache vanished. The dizziness took longer to fade.

The room was long and narrow, with a high ceiling. Huge blue and yellow drapes hung high at equal intervals, each guarding a window to the outside world. A large wooden table occupied much of the centre of the room. Though it could host at least a dozen people, it looked very old and neglected. Its surface was no longer smooth, and the rim had been splintered in several places.

There was only one chair near the table, and again, it was made of wood. As she took in more of her surroundings, it became apparent to her this room was full of neglected and abandoned furnishings. All were combustible, and all were forbidden. She couldn't believe anyone would be so irresponsible. 'Are you sure you can't remember who lives here?' she asked.

'Honestly, no,' said Addan. He was standing near a small chest, examining an ornament of some kind. The object wasn't of any value, and Addan didn't seem impressed with it. He set it back down and brushed dust from his hands against his trousers, creating a small cloud around him that rippled against the outside light. 'Someone important for some reason. I can't remember exactly what she said.'

'How important?' Liana had a sinking feeling within her.

'Important enough to have what we're looking for,' said Addan in a vaguely condescending tone.

Liana stepped through the myriad of furniture and other neglected objects in the room. She picked up a box of a size that fit neatly in her hand. It was carved from marble stone and was square, but with rounded corners. It was heavy, but sounded empty when she gave it a little shake. The sides were all smooth except for the side touching her palm. There was something etched into its surface. Turning it over revealed a symbol expertly carved into the stone. Three circles overlapping in a triangular configuration. She recognised the symbol immediately and almost dropped the box as she hastily replaced it where she found it.

'I think this place belongs to the Tal Valar,' she said, suddenly whispering.

Addan paused. 'That does sound familiar, now you mention it.'

Liana clenched her fists and took a deep breath. 'I'd rather you had—' she stopped still. 'Did you hear that?'

'Hear what?'

'A noise back down in the hall.'

'No, I don't think so...'

Liana shushed him, straining to hear any other sounds. Nothing. Her heart was pounding. It probably had been since

they had entered, but she was only aware of it now. She felt...
excited. She had always liked the tingling in her body she got
whenever she was doing something others would prefer she
wasn't. The danger, the thrill. It had its own feeling deep
within her.

The building was supposed to be empty, or so Addan had
promised, at least. But she was certain there was someone else
moving around in the house, and that was a problem.

She listened at the door for signs of movement beyond it.
Satisfied there wasn't anyone in the immediate vicinity, she
carefully opened the door enough to peek through. The corridor, as best as she could determine in the dark, was empty.

'We're looking for a door with a crack in the frame,' said
Addan, as he exited the room with her.

'What sort of crack?'

'She wasn't specific. A crack is a crack, isn't it?'

Liana huffed, but didn't reply. She created another mote of
light and counted eight other doors along the corridor, each
plated in metal as was proper and legal. Whoever this place
belonged to, it was larger inside than anyone outside would
give it credit for.

Addan moved forward and pressed his ear against the door
nearest to him. 'I can hear snoring,' he whispered. He moved to
the door opposite. 'This one too.'

'So definitely *not* empty.' She glared at her friend through
the tiny bead of light.

'It's not my fault.'

His fault or not, there was no point blaming him. She went
along with his plan willingly, even as something deep inside
her told her it was a bad idea. 'Let's just get what we came for
and get out of here.'

Liana made her way along the corridor, examining each
doorframe for a crack. All were hand-carved stone archways of
identical design. Simple, sweeping lines met at the apex where

a crest had been etched. Each had imperfections and minor damage, but nothing stood out as having a crack that would identify it as separate from the others.

She was ready to give up when she noticed something on the next doorframe. It wasn't a crack as such. It looked more like a gap. A cut in the stone made by a striking sword or axe. She ran her fingers along its edge. It hadn't been made recently. In fact, it looked and felt as though it had been made hundreds of years ago. It *had* to be what they were looking for. She leaned against the door. The thin metal plate that covered the wood underneath was cold, and her breath misted on its surface as she listened for signs of life on the other side. There was nothing. Carefully, she opened the door. It creaked as she pushed. She grimaced at the sound and prayed for it to stop. It didn't, but the opening was wide enough to slide through.

Relief came as she found the room was unoccupied. A chink of light cut the room in two from a small opening in the curtains covering a window. Dust particles danced gently in the brightness. Headache gone.

The room felt cold and utilitarian. A space used for prayer and meditation, and not much else. The light from the window didn't stretch all the way to the walls, merely casting a much-needed warmth on the centre. A rudimentary altar adorned with an embroidered blue and yellow cloth stood at the farthest end away from the door. Several intricate tapestries hung from the walls at equal intervals. Eight of them in all. Each depicted a figure dressed in elaborate clothing. She could only see two in enough detail to recognise the figures as the Architects.

Along the wall to the left stood a long, cushioned seat with enough length to accommodate five, maybe six people. Given her lack of sleep, it looked inviting enough to lie down on, but she brushed the notion aside and focused on the matter at hand. She looked over at Addan and watched him as he rummaged around in a small cabinet next to the window. He picked up something from inside and put it in his pocket.

'What was that?' she asked in a whisper.

'Oh nothing. A few coins is all.'

'Put them back. That's not what we came for.'

Addan sighed and returned the coins. 'I thought, while we're here...' His words trailed away into a muttering under his breath.

Liana nodded, unseen, before continuing her own search of the room. A scraping sound in a dark crevice in the room caught her attention. She turned her head to follow the noise and caught a flash of red in the gloom. She gasped—a small, sharp intake of breath she couldn't control—though not loud enough that Addan noticed. A cautious step closer revealed a metal cage, no larger than two feet square, roughly head height on a pedestal. Within it, on its own little platform, sat a dragon. She recoiled at first, but slowly moved closer. It was the size of a fist—a full-grown adult—and it was watching her with two unblinking black eyes. A long, spiked tail wrapped around strong hind legs flicked cautiously against its perch.

She wanted a better look, so created another light mote. The dragon immediately flapped its winged forearms and screeched a muffled cry. The bars of the cage rattled as the wing tips brushed against them. Addan stopped his search and joined her. The dragon settled back down after a moment, itself adjusting to the light.

'Who would be stupid enough to keep a dragon *inside*?' she whispered. 'Or stupid enough to keep a dragon *at all*?'

'I've never seen one up close.' Addan leaned forward to peer at the creature. Liana pulled him back.

'Neither have I. Not alive, at least.'

The dragon cocked its head as it stared back at them. It had wire wrapped around its muzzle, preventing it from opening its mouth. It looked... *sad*. Liana felt something inside her head. A thought, perhaps even an emotion. A sense of longing.

LOST

She almost felt sorry for it. Almost.

Dragons were feared by all who had seen first-hand the destruction they were capable of. Ordinarily they were exterminated on sight, and it was rare to see one on its own. A single dragon was enough to destroy everything one owned. A swarm of them? Liana shuddered at the very thought. *Keeping* one was not only illegal, it was reckless.

Close up, the creature looked rather innocent. A slender body made it appear so delicate under those red scales. 'How could something so beautiful be so dangerous?' she mused.

'Hmm, what's that?' Addan had lost interest in the dragon and had returned to his search. 'Oh, dirty, verminous animals. Hey, I think I've found something.' He was looking at a statuette made of soapstone set in the centre of the altar.

Liana joined him, leaving the dragon to settle back to sleep. Immediately, the distinct odour of the flame-retardant wash used to protect most fabrics assaulted her nose. It was coming from the heavy blue and yellow cloth that neatly covered the altar. The statuette stood, proudly and on its own, atop a shallow, oblong lock-box made from the same stone. As best as she could tell, the figure was a depiction of the Architect of Life— Eraidor; creator of all things living. Standing around twenty inches high, it was cast in a welcoming, benevolent pose, wearing a simple robe that covered the feet.

'Is that it?' she asked, feeling a little uncomfortable having turned her back on the dragon, caged and muzzled or not.

'Possibly, I don't know. I can't open the drawer, but it looks like what the old woman said it would look like. Can you...?'

Liana knew what her friend was asking. She exhaled slowly before reaching over and covering the small keyhole with her thumb. Closing her eyes, she felt for the lock mechanism with her mind, imagining its workings. There was a momentary stab of pain across the bridge of her nose as the lock clicked.

'Open it,' said Addan eagerly.

The drawer slid forward easily and inside revealed a simple necklace nestled on a pillow of dark blue velvet. Liana smiled as she removed the necklace and held it loosely in her fingers. The chain was made of small, golden rings all looped together. At the bottom of the chain hung a glass pendant. Suspended within the glass was a dark gemstone the size of her thumb that looked purple against the light coming through the window. It was beautiful, though Liana would never bring herself to wear such a thing. She didn't care much for jewellery.

'We've found it,' she said.

Addan stepped closer and made a gentle whistle, showing his appreciation. 'Time to leave then.'

'Time to leave.' She took the necklace and pocketed it inside her tunic before closing the drawer. She looked at the dragon. 'Don't tell anyone we were here,' she said to it. The tiny beast made the hairs on the back of her neck tickle with fear. Then she turned to follow Addan, who was already out the door.

They moved back through the corridor the way they came, quicker this time. She had what they came for and now the priority was to get out as fast as possible. Liana threw up one more tiny ball of light, which floated between her and Addan in front, casting his shadow across the floor ahead. They descended the stairs that led to the room with all the furniture in. Once inside, she extinguished the light as it wasn't needed before realising that *all* the curtains in the room were now open. Someone else in the house was awake, increasing their chances of being caught. She started running, overtaking Addan. He ran too, trying to keep up.

Liana rounded a corner as they headed for the kitchen and crashed into something, knocking it over. No, not some*thing*— *someone!* She couldn't see much in the dark as both she and whoever she had run into fell to the floor. The someone yelped in surprise as the two of them fought to extricate themselves from each other. There was enough light for Liana to catch a glimpse of an insignia on the sleeve of a flailing arm. The insignia was that of the Tal Valar. Someone grabbed her by the hand, pulling her upwards. It was Addan. With his help, she scrambled to her feet and ran with him through to the kitchen and out. She daren't look back at the other man, who was now screaming out at full volume to anyone who could hear, but she found herself laughing. This was *fun*.

They were outside and into bright, painful daylight in a heartbeat. There was no time to stop and allow their eyes to adjust, for there were several voices behind them in the house coming for them. Barking! Liana looked to her left as she ran. Two angry tamewolves were heading in their direction. She glanced over her shoulder for Addan, who was a few paces behind her. 'Hurry up!' she shouted.

The tamewolves, both enormous beasts with long brown-black fur, were getting closer. Close enough to see their white eyes trained on her. She changed direction, now running a diagonal to the wall, trying to keep as much distance between her and the animals as she could muster. As she reached the wall, she jumped and grabbed at a stone on the wall. Addan was right with her, to her relief. He pushed her upwards by her backside, allowing her to get a purchase on the crest of the wall. She hauled herself up, spread herself along the top, and reached down to Addan. He grabbed her hand and clambered up the wall with the tamewolves snapping at his ankles. Over the wall, they both dropped to the ground in a heap. They looked at each other, panting, and laughed. They'd escaped, unharmed, and with their prize.

Liana reached into her pocket, pulled out the necklace, and held it out in front of her. It looked even more stunning in the outside light as it dangled between her fingers. 'What now?'

'I have until the end of the day to give it to the gabbalins. It should be enough to settle what I owe them, and leave some for me.'

Liana had never met a gabbalin, only knowing of their reputation through the stories of others. Every one of them an exile from Abbalon, the neighbouring lands to the south of Moranza. Nobody knew why they were exiled, and no gabbalin has ever revealed that secret, so far as anyone could ascertain.

As she watched the light sparkle on the surface of the gemstone, she wondered what the gabbalins wanted with it. Addan saw little more than its monetary value, a means of paying his way out of trouble. She couldn't ignore the nagging feeling there was something more to it. It was as if it were whispering to her, eager to tell her a secret.

Her thoughts returned to the moment as the shouting and barking on the other side of the wall grew louder, with a greater number of voices shouting alarm. She handed the necklace to Addan. 'Time to get out of here,' she said. 'I will meet you at the usual place before moonfall.'

Addan secreted the necklace away and nodded, then set off back into the streets of Miar Lenns alone.

The thoroughfare was busier now, with dozens of other people going about their business. The moon rose in the distance, heralding the start of a new day, but all Liana wanted to do was sleep. She doubted anyone would afford her that luxury, not today of all days.

Nobody paid her any attention as she walked through the city. Why would they? Her hooded cloak allowed her to blend in with everyone else, but she always carried with her a sense of paranoia in the time immediately after a job. Guilt, perhaps? If she was ever caught, it would be a disaster, and not only for her.

She passed three pairs of Tal Valar patrols as she walked. They didn't give her a second glance as she passed them, but she avoided eye contact anyway. She'd never liked the Tal Valar.

They thought too highly of themselves and policed the city through the veil of their steadfast beliefs of the Old Ways, and the Architects of whose teachings they preached. She didn't believe a word of it, much to the disdain of her mother.

Eventually, she reached a small, plated door set in the rough stonework of the building it protected. A door hidden away around the back. Discrete, rarely used. Locked. She released the lock with only the slightest notion of pain. With the door open, she peeked through and sighed with relief. The room on the other side, barely anything more than a closet, was empty. She snuck in and closed the door behind her. Safely inside and out of view, she removed her cloak, rolled it into a bundle, and tucked it under her arm.

As she reached for the handle of another door opposite, it suddenly opened, making her start. A young girl in a tatty apron and carrying a small pile of rags stood in the doorway. 'Oh,' said the girl with a touch of surprise in her voice. 'Good morning, Princess Liana.'

2

PREPARATIONS

I t was hot within the sandstone walls of the palace. Though the moon had barely begun her daily ascent into the sky, heralding a new day, the halls were already busy. Serving staff, guards, and even the groundskeepers were preparing for the arrival. Cal Tallan marched through the corridors, trying his best to oversee it all.

Everyone moved out of the way to avoid him. Prince Cal Tallan did *not* move out of their way to avoid *them*. He walked briskly. A young girl carrying a metal bucket gasped as she noticed him almost too late, throwing her back to the wall. Water spilled from the bucket, but she narrowly avoided a collision. Cal didn't even acknowledge her.

A man in a less formal version of the dark blue trousers and matching tunic Cal wore approached him from ahead, turned at his side, and walked with him back along the corridor. 'Good morning, Cal.'

The man was only a touch shorter than Cal, with the same slim build. Older though, but Cal didn't know by how much. A few years, maybe. There *was* a hint of grey around his temples, but only in a certain light.

'Shaan, I've told you on many occasions to address me by my proper title when we are in the presence of others.' Cal glanced at him as they walked. No sign of the grey this morning.

'Indeed you have, *sir. However*, I cannot quite get used to it.'

'It's not been a problem in the past.'

'Yes, well, that was *before*.'

More staff moved out of their way as they walked. A few nodded or offered some other acknowledgment, while others avoided eye contact as best they could.

'Have you seen my sister yet this morning?' asked Cal.

'Unfortunately, I have not seen the princess.' Shaan paused briefly. 'However, I understand the word is she was out all night again and is yet to return.'

Cal huffed. 'Liana has no sense of duty or responsibility whatsoever. She knows the importance of today. For a royal, she behaves as though she is nothing more than a commoner. Mother despairs of her and I never hear the end of it. As if I have any sway over her.'

'I quite agree,' said Shaan. 'She is a curious young woman and I have never been able to fathom her. Quite a force of nature, though.'

'You mean she doesn't like you.'

'Hmm, yes. I had hoped we might get along when we first met, but it turns out it was quite the opposite.'

'Quite,' Cal repeated. He turned left along a smaller corridor and up the spiral stone stairs and along another corridor back the way they came, but one floor farther up. He walked briskly and with purpose, as was his manner. Cal was not a man to dawdle. Shaan was one of only a few who could keep pace and not complain about it. Cal stopped at the third door along to his left and knocked. No answer. He knocked again, harder.

'As I say, I am told she is yet to return,' said Shaan as he took position by the door with his back to the wall.

19

Cal kicked the door, leaving a fresh dent in the metal plating. The plating wasn't there for reinforcement, only to prevent fire and thus was little more than a coating over the wood beneath. The dent joined the existing patina as a permanent record of his frustration.

He pulled at the hem of his tunic to straighten it and turned to walk back the way he came. And there she was, standing at the top of the stairwell, paused in mid-step as their eyes met.

'Must you break my door?' Liana said, straightening her back.

Cal glared at her. She looked a mess. Her auburn hair was tangled like a handful of rusty wire, and the dark circles under her eyes told him she had indeed been awake all night. Her clothes—loose fitting green pants and an old shirt that looked made for a man—were filthy, and she had a smudge of something black across her nose. To anyone who didn't know her, she could pass as a slave girl or a common whore.

'Would you look at yourself?' said Cal. 'Have you forgotten the day? You shame this family.' His thumbnail dug into his forefinger as he spoke.

Liana exaggerated a sigh and smiled, which turned into a yawn which she tried to hide. 'Brother, dear, you fret too much. I'm sure everything is in hand. I'm minded not to attend, anyway.'

'Not attend?' Cal looked at Shaan, who raised an eyebrow, but otherwise remained at the wall. 'What do you mean, not attend? This is the most important event in centuries. Your place is at the side of our queen.' He was spitting slightly.

'Another important event, all the fuss and the mess and the noise. It bores me. And you know I hate wearing dresses. Have *you* tried wearing a corset? Believe me, it's beyond torture.'

Shaan was trying not to laugh behind him. 'You can't not... just... mother...' Simmering anger suppressed his ability to speak. Before he could push out a full sentence, Liana had brushed him aside and disappeared behind the door to her room.

'That went well,' said Shaan as he put his hand on Cal's shoulder.

'I swear it's deliberate. Mother says she's only trying to find where she fits in, in the world. I think she does it to spite us. To spite me. I'm sure the Architects themselves must despair of her.'

'Whether they do or do not, her will is her own and even they cannot deny that. Come, you must prepare for their arrival. I will try to speak to her myself.'

'Ha! I wish you well with that.' Cal took Shaan's hand from his shoulder and squeezed it before letting go.

The palace itself was huge by any measure. Cal knew of ninety-seven rooms, not including those of the adjoining outbuildings and follies. He suspected there were more, hidden or lost to time and history. The original structure had to be over a thousand years old by now. Built long before the Division, he knew, not that history interested him much. As he walked at pace back through to the main level—the heart of the palace— he tried not to dwell on his sister, though he couldn't help but dig his fingernails into his palm as he descended the spiral stairs. He shook his head and tried to concentrate on the day ahead. Liana was enough of a distraction herself.

As he reached the centre of the open-air courtyard, a young man with light skin and blond hair approached Cal with alacrity. He wore full Queen's Guard uniform, although it didn't fit him well, particularly around the shoulders. Cal had seen him before. One of the newer recruits who, if he recalled correctly, fell over his own bootstraps during parade exercises on his first day. Cal noticed the boy had correctly fastened his boots as he joined him.

'Pardon me, my prince. The queen requests you speak with her immediately,' said the boy, a little out of breath.

Cal stopped walking and sighed. 'She is in her office, I presume?' *All the way back where I came.*

'Yes, that she is, sir.'

'Thank you.' Of course she was in her office. Unless there was other official business to attend to, that room was where she stayed. She practically lived in that room these days. Alone with her books.

Cal dismissed the young guard who saluted, his too-long sleeve flapping beyond his fingers. Cal closed his eyes and gently shook his head. He made a mental note to have words with the quartermaster about proper attire. Turning back the way he came, he drew breath deeply through his nose and retraced his steps.

The route back through the palace took him past his sister's chambers. He paused briefly at her door before deciding against trying to reason with her again. Instead, he continued along and up another staircase to the queen's office at the very top of the East Tower.

It was the only room at the top of the tower, with a single glassless window opposite the door which offered one of the best views of the city and beyond. He knocked on the door carefully. The plating was old and had separated from the wood beneath and rattled under his knuckles. She didn't answer immediately, which wasn't unusual. Cal expected her to be reading, and as such wouldn't acknowledge whoever was at the door until she reached the end of the particular paragraph she was at.

Through the open window, the moon rose beyond the city skyline. From his vantage point, it filled most of the frame, and its pink-grey hue contrasted against the orange sky. The mother of the Architects and overseer of the entire world. The eminent scholars of Moranza forever argued over how literal or philosophical that definition was. Cal found himself more drawn to the latter, unable to reconcile in his mind how a giant disc in the sky could give birth to a god. Or many gods, for that matter. Nobody had proven the existence of the Architects either, despite the Tal Valar's insistence that there was no other explanation for the creation of the world. To Cal, the moon was simply the moon. It rose in the west every morning, full and bright and pink. And at the end of every day, worn down to a sliver of a crescent, it would set in the east in front of the unseen sun. Even the scholars had no agreed explanation for why that was so.

A voice from with in the office broke him away from his musings. Queen Alyssa called. He adjusted his tunic, straightened his back, and entered the room.

'Cal, my boy,' beamed the queen from behind her desk, peering over an untidy stack of books. She looked like an older version of Liana, except her nose was sharper and wasn't quite as tall. The skin around her jawline wasn't as tight as it was in her youth. Cal wasn't the only one to notice she had lost weight this past year or two. She was dressed, from what he could see of her behind the desk, in one of her casual robes.

'Mother,' he said, bowing slightly. He looked around the room. It was... untidy. His mother was usually so fastidious about keeping everything in its place. The queen's decline into older age was becoming more evident. Or was it something more than that?

Her desk was carved from a single piece of white marble. Intricate shapes depicting flowers Cal had never seen in person adorned the legs and trim. To this day, he couldn't fathom how such a heavy stone found itself in a room at the highest point of the palace, yet there it was. Stained glass in the only window cast a colourful, yet distorted replica of its image across the marble surface like diluted ink on paper. The image in the glass was of Queen Alula—his great-grandmother—in full regalia, surrounded by the Architects as they welcomed her to the next life. There was a small hole in one

23

of the green panels that whistled gently from the wind outside.

'It pleases me to see you already in your dress uniform,' the queen said as she looked over a single-page document.

'Yes, Mother. Unlike my sister, I realise the importance of this day, particularly for you.'

The queen lowered the document to the desk, but didn't set it down. 'Liana has always been... difficult. She gets her temperament from your father.'

He could barely remember his father now, having died shortly before Cal's eighth birthday. He *did* remember him being angry often, though. He didn't think of Liana as an angry woman. She liked to argue, and she was often selfish, putting her own wants ahead of the crown's, but angry? No, not particularly, not unless she was hungry.

'She says she's not attending,' he said. He felt ashamed to say it.

The queen sighed. 'I feared as much. Your sister, she lacks the insight required to realise her place in the world. It is disappointing. Can you not convince her? She looks up to you.'

Cal scoffed. 'She does *not* look up to me. She fights me at every turn, and if she doesn't fight me, then she flat out ignores me. She has no respect for me or this family.'

'Now, that's not entirely true. She's still young enough to be impressionable.'

'Twenty-four is not young. Liana is not a child anymore.'

The queen let go of the document and clasped her hands together, resting her arms on the desk. 'No, you're right, of course. When did you both grow up?' She paused for a moment, thinking. 'Tell her, her queen demands she attend.'

'She seemed quite adamant.'

'So am I,' she said pointedly. It was subtle, but her annoyance showed.

Cal stood straighter before agreeing to speak with Liana

again, unconvinced it would make any difference. Short of putting her in chains, he couldn't think of anything else that would force her to be there. He smiled to himself as an image of his sister bonded to a pillar in the main hall with everyone watching on popped into his head.

'Now,' she continued, 'that wasn't why I summoned you here.'

The mental image vanished, and Cal refocused his attention on his mother. 'Oh?'

'Yes, I wanted to speak with you about Shaan.'

'What about him?' Immediately, he felt uncomfortable.

The queen adjusted herself in her chair. The leather beneath her moaned as she did so. 'I feel he is becoming a little too... influential,' she said in an even tone.

'How do you mean?'

'I mean, he's upsetting the Council with his opinions on how matters are conducted.'

'Perhaps the Council *needs* upsetting from time to time.'

'Perhaps,' she echoed. 'However, it is not his place to do so. I know you are fond of him, and it is not for me to interfere with your... relationships, but I do think he is overstepping the mark. I'm told he's establishing some sort of training ground? Only the Architects know what for.'

Cal shifted his weight from one foot to the other. He knew what she meant, but was under the impression it was on her authority. 'He believes that if we are to open relations with our neighbours, of whom we know almost nothing, then it would be prudent that should they be less than friendly, we have a contingent of men capable of defending ourselves. Indeed you, our queen.'

'Prudent as it may be, he's gone ahead without the agreement or permission of the Council, and quite rightly, they are not at all pleased. And neither am I.'

What do you expect me to do about it? 'Should I speak with him?'

'I would request that you remind him of his place and the protocols we live by. His role is as your advisor. Advisors do not make unilateral decisions about the running of this country. They most certainly do not take it upon themselves to set up, what, I don't know... an army?'

Cal scratched behind his ear. She always made him feel like *he* was the one being chastised, even when the subject of her ire was someone else. She had a point, though. It wasn't Shaan's place to give orders. It wasn't even his role to enact royal instruction at all. Cal had appointed him himself as his personal advisor. How that had come about, he couldn't quite remember now, but he knew it was important to have him around, and the queen had acquiesced to his demand. And now, a little over a year later, Cal would not be without him.

'I will speak to him and see the training ground is dismantled.'

The queen stiffened her back and picked up the document again. 'No, no. His idea is good. Let him continue. I will insist on full oversight by the Council, though. But tell him this. If he steps out of line like that again, I will have him sent to the slate mines in Miar Miall. Am I understood?'

'Yes, Mother.' Cal nodded a bow.

'Dismissed.'

That was it. The meeting was over. The queen returned her attention to whatever it was she was reading, and that was that. Cal nodded a second bow and left the room without turning his back to the queen, as was proper.

As he made his way back through the palace, he found his mind flitting from concern about Liana, to Shaan overstepping his authority—not that he had any authority to overstep—to the arrival of their guests, and a hundred other things. The noise and the bustle of people going about their own tasks reflected the busyness of his own thoughts. What he wouldn't give to find an empty room and lock himself inside until the day was over. To others, he projected himself as a powerful prince who should be feared and respected. Inside, though, he was screaming. He needed to find Shaan.

It took almost half an hour to find him. Not so much because the man wasn't where he was looking, but because everywhere he turned, someone wanted to speak to him. Before he'd had a chance to make it across the courtyard for the second time, he was accosted by Tienn, who was fretting about seating arrangements for the main feast. Tienn was a dusty old man, who by convention was the most senior member of the Council. Deafness had taken hold of him, so everything had to be repeated at least twice. When he spoke, he did with such volume the entire city could hear him. Hyperbole, but that was the oft-repeated opinion of the queen whenever she'd been in his company.

After convincing Tienn to use his own best judgement and telling him that, no, he didn't know if the Dawanii delegation preferred the green seats or the blue ones, the quartermaster stopped him for a word. A man who had eyebrows larger than his more than ample moustache, the quartermaster chose this moment to complain about the lack of appropriate sized uniforms. Cal didn't really take in what the man had to say, but promised to look into it with urgency, but not today, if he didn't mind.

Eventually, he found Shaan talking to a guard of middling age with a proper fitting uniform. The conversation looked serious, but Shaan dismissed the guard when he saw Cal approach.

'Anything I should know about?' Cal asked, trying to look in control and relaxed.

'No, merely finalising guard positions for the arrival. All taken care of.' Shaan held his hands behind his back and positioned himself alongside Cal as he continued to walk.

Cal nodded. 'You've upset my mother,' he said, smiling.

'It would not be for the first time. Or the last. What irks her now?'

'Your training camp. She believes you are pushing beyond your boundaries. Though,' Cal paused briefly. 'I swear you told me she had given you her full backing to the initiative? When I spoke with her, she talked as though she had heard it from the Council.'

'The queen approves of the idea, does she not? The Council too.'

'She does, they do but—'

'Then all is well, no?'

Cal noticed Shaan avoided his question, but with everything else demanding his attention, he didn't challenge it. Liana, uniforms, the arrival. Liana.

'Did you speak with my sister? Please tell me you convinced her to step up to her responsibilities and she will attend after all?'

The pair exited the courtyard and made their way through to the front of the palace and out onto the front promenade. They stopped to watch two stable boys wrangle with one of the strydes as they tried to fasten a saddle. The grey-white bird was having none of it. Cal closed his eyes and exhaled. Strydes were usually of a quiet temperament, though not this one, apparently. Long spindly legs kicked at the dirt as it tried to pull free. Cal had often wondered how they supported their own weight, let alone carry a man on their back. The bird pecked angrily at the stable boys with its large hooked beak as they tried to keep out of reach. With such a long neck, that wasn't easy.

'Alas, her mind is unchanged on the matter. I tried talking to her, impressing the importance of the day, but her disdain for me and the whole occasion was quite clear.'

'I see.'

'I am afraid it got quite heated, and she demanded I leave.

Her choice of language was most unbecoming of a future queen. She slammed the door after me and bolted it. She can be quite feisty when she is tired.'

Several instances of his sister's foul moods over the years flashed through Cal's mind and he found himself agreeing with Shaan. If Liana was tired, anyone would do well to stay out of her way. He nodded. 'Thank you for trying, at least.'

The stryde had bolted and the stable boys had given chase out of sight behind the East Wing. The three other strydes, each with a guard either mounted or by their side, remained calm and even nonchalant about the commotion.

Cal was about to find something to eat when the young guard with the too-long sleeves ran over to them, almost tripping over his boots as he did so. He stopped, out of breath, and placed his hands on his knees. 'Your highness,' breathed the boy. 'They're here. They're early and they're here.'

'What do you mean, "here"?' Cal asked the guard while looking at Shaan for further answers. Shaan shrugged.

The boy straightened up and saluted, his inexperience apparent. 'I mean, they are here at the palace. Less than two minutes' walk. Six of them. No strydes, your princeness.'

Cal rubbed his face in a downward motion with both hands. 'The instructions were to notify us when they had crossed the bridge so our escorts could meet them, and that we would be ready here.' He tried not to shout.

'Yes, sir. I mean, I don't know. I've not seen them myself, only passing on the message, sir. Your highness.'

'Are they at least escorted? Please do not tell me the Dawanii have walked for almost an hour into our country unaccompanied.'

'They mentioned no escort. Only the six. No mounts.'

Cal dismissed the guard, who saluted once more before running off in his dishevelled manner back to his post. He looked to Shaan for answers. 'What do we do now? The queen was due to give a speech to the people as the delegation arrived. It was all planned, all rehearsed.'

Shaan offered a smile and patted him on the back. 'We will have to make the best of it. I am sure the Dawanii will not notice, so long as you do not look panicked when you greet them.'

'I'm not panicking,' Cal said as he tugged at his tunic hem. 'The queen was supposed to be the one to greet them. Not me. She's not even dressed and ready to—'

'A great queen is always ready,' came a voice behind them.

Cal spun on his heel to find the queen standing there in an elegant turquoise dress. Cinched perfectly at the waist and shoulders, and flowing perfectly away from the heel, the dress made her look every inch the queen she was. A delicate tiara, set above her hairline, held her dark red hair in place. Cal bowed, properly, to her, as did Shaan.

'My apologies,' said Shaan. 'It appears our guests are a little eager. Do you wish to be escorted out to meet them as they arrive?'

'No, that's quite all right. I would still like to address my people first. Have my guards greet them and ask they hold their position while I take my position. Cal, would you please be so kind as to escort me to the balcony?'

Shaan bowed again, shallower this time, before making his way through the main gates. He took a small contingent of guards with him. Five of them, Cal noted. With Shaan included, he was matching their number.

Cal took his mother's hand as she offered it to him, and they both made their way to a small stairwell that ascended to a box platform overlooking the grounds immediately outside the perimeter wall. The platform was used by both the monarch and her representatives, as required, to address the people of Miar Lenns. The last time Cal had stood in the box was exactly a year ago when the queen announced the building of the new bridge between Moranza and Dawan. He himself had never spoken to the people in this way. Protocol stipulated he never would.

The box was simple and had no decoration within it, though the royal banner adorned the outside. At least Cal hoped it did, and that someone had the foresight to make sure it was the correct way up this time. Short of leaning over the balcony to check, there wasn't another way of telling. He and the queen stepped to the front together. The queen waved with her left hand. Cal kept his hands by his sides. Protocol.

Below on the main road that ran parallel to the wall was a modest gathering of ordinary city folk. A few hundred, Cal guessed. Not as many as he would have liked, but it did look like there were more than last year. He looked farther into the distance where Shaan and the Queen's Guard were holding position with the Dawanii. They were too far away to see what they wore other than dark attire. The young guard was right— no mounts.

Queen Alyssa spoke. 'One year ago to this very day, I stood here before you, as I do so now. I spoke of how the Architects came to me in a dream to tell me now is the time to reunite our great country with our neighbour now known as Dawan. Nine hundred and forty-seven years ago, we were one country. A country at war with ourselves. A war that culminated with the greatest calamity to befall us.

'The Division will forever be remembered as the darkest day in our shared history. And since that day we have lived as two peoples, neither knowing the other. A year ago today, the Architects came to me and said it is time to mend this division and to build a bridge and invite our lost brethren home. And that is what we have done.

'I pay tribute to those of you who worked tirelessly to build this new bridge, and we remember all those who lost their lives in the process. It wasn't easy, I know. Nothing in life worth doing is ever easy. But now, after almost a thousand years, we will start a new chapter. A new era of peace and prosperity between our two peoples hoping one day we will be truly reunited.

'Today, we welcome our first honoured guests and we hope to reconnect with our forgotten brothers and sisters and forge a new family together. For Dawan and Moranza. Reunited!'

There was a ripple of applause from the crowd, but it was far from enthusiastic. Cal had been privy to the reports that the bridge project had never been popular. When the first attempt collapsed, killing more than twenty people, there were calls for the work to be abandoned entirely. He had echoed those calls himself. Not only because of the loss of life, but also for the cost. The queen, supported by Shaan and a small number of the Council, insisted the bridge was completed.

'How was it?' the queen asked as she smiled and waved at the crowd. The applause had stopped, and the fringes were already dispersing. There were a few boos amongst the gathered, and one man was particularly vocal in his protest, his words muffled by distance.

'Positive, on the whole, I think. You were most eloquent. I hope you are proved correct, and this is the start of a grand future. The Architects know this city needs prosperity.'

'Yes, yes,' she waved away his words. 'Come, now let's meet our guests.'

Cal sighed as he took his mother by the hand and escorted her down and out into the city. Guards flanked their sides to keep the people at a safe distance. Ahead, Shaan was already returning, with the delegation following behind.

The first thing he noticed about the Dawanii was their attire. All six were wearing furs. Not loose like a shawl or cloak, but cut and fitted tight like a soft armour. Four were female; two at the front and two more at the rear, with two men in the middle. Three of the Queen's Guard flanked their left, the remaining two with Shaan on their right.

All six had painted hair. A stripe of burnt red running from their right temple going backwards. A thinner stripe of yellow ran from above their left eyebrow, again in a backward line to the neck. They carried no weapons. In fact, they appeared to have nothing in the way of personal effects at all. Cal wondered if they'd left a wagon, or another of their party at the bridge with their belongings.

He couldn't tell which of the six was their leader. There were no badges or insignia on their clothing to mark a rank or otherwise. Aside from their gender, there was nothing to distinguish one from another. His mother's history books, covering the time before the Divide, were light on detail. He recalled reading somewhere that the land they occupied belonged to a number of small communities that shunned the established rule of Moranza. They preferred to live apart from the rest of society. The Divide ultimately granted them that wish. A thousand years later and those communities have given themselves their own name and identity. Dawanii—the Children of Dawan.

As the delegation approached, the guards broke away and fell in line behind the receiving party. Shaan took up a position beside Cal. If he had any thoughts on first impressions, his face didn't show them. The group of six stopped in perfect timing with each other around ten paces away.

'We bid you good welcome to our great city,' said the queen, addressing the two Dawanii at the front.

There was no reply.

The queen repeated her greeting and added a shallow bow with her hands held flat together in front of her.

Again, there was no reply. None of the six moved or even acknowledged they'd heard her words. The queen looked at Cal for help, but he was unsure what he could offer. He wondered if they expected to be addressed by a man. He took a step forward.

'May I, Prince Tallan, also extend an honoured and humble welcome to you. My mother, the queen,' he gestured to her, 'has been looking forward to your arrival for a long time.'

Silence. The six all continued to stare straight ahead, unmoving. Whispers rippled through the crowd of onlookers, sharing in the confusion.

Cal leaned towards Shaan. 'Any ideas?' he asked discretely.

'I am at as much of a loss as you are.'

'Didn't they speak to you when you met up with them? Surely one of them must have said *something*?'

'I am afraid not. I assumed they wished only to speak to her majesty.'

'What do we do now?' asked the queen, her head turned towards Cal. She looked flustered, but only a little—enough for him to notice and no other.

Before Cal could answer, the two Dawanii women at the front knelt down, their eyes still focused ahead. The two at the rear did the same. The two men in the middle remained unmoved.

'Some kind of ceremonial greeting?' the queen asked.

Cal shrugged.

Then, movement. Without a sound, the two men reached into a hidden pocket at their waist before throwing their arms forward, pointing at the queen in one swift, synchronised motion. Nobody, including Cal, realised what had happened at first. Not until there was a scream from a woman in the crowd a second before the queen fell to the ground.

The Queen's Guard reacted first, raising their spears and swords, surrounding the group of Dawanii who remained motionless, exactly where they were, with the two males still pointing at where the queen stood.

The scream from the woman in the crowd spread like a contagion through the rest of the gatherers and most fled from the area. Awkward silence had descended into chaos in an

34

instant. Cal didn't know what to do. He stood frozen, his bottom lip quivering as words failed him. Guards continued to surround the delegation. It was Shaan who Cal heard next.

'Execute them!' shouted Shaan. The guards hesitated. It wasn't his place to give orders to them. They looked to Cal. It shouldn't be his decision, either, but with the queen fallen and his sister absent... in that moment of panic, he nodded. Somewhere inside him, something broke as he condemned them to die.

There was a flurry of motion from the Queen's Guard, and although he couldn't see the deed from where he was standing, Cal knew the lives of all six had been taken. Not a one of them cried out or made a sound of any kind.

Finally, he gathered his senses enough to rush to his mother's aid. He crouched down beside her as she lay face down in the dirt. Blood had pooled beneath her dress. He turned her over as carefully as he could, revealing two identical black knives protruding from her stomach. Her eyes were still open, but the life within them was already gone.

3

THE BRIDGE

Liana regretted not taking a bath before she left the palace. Her original plan was to sneak home, get a little sleep, then clean herself up before sneaking back out again. She hadn't planned on telling Cal she wasn't joining him and their mother for the Dawanii arrival. She hadn't planned on speaking with him at all, but he *had* to be outside her chambers at the moment she reached the top of the stairs.

And then there was Shaan. The skinny weasel of a man who had worked his way into her brother's favour—and his bed— almost from the day they met. Almost. When Shaan first arrived at the palace, he was particularly interested in *her*. She took an instant disliking to him. She didn't know why, exactly. Sometimes you can *not* like someone through no apparent fault of their own. Time had proven her instincts correct, though. Cal, however, fell in love with the man. Fool.

After she locked herself in her chambers to avoid further argument with her brother, Shaan had talked her into letting him in. She had no intention of opening the door to him, but he had mastered the art of persuasion, and she was too tired to push back.

'I need to sleep,' she said as she walked away from the door and sat down on her bed. She tried not to look directly at him as he entered and closed the door behind him. She picked at the dirt under her fingernails.

'Why do you hate your family?'

She turned her head sharply to look at him. 'I don't hate my family. Why would you say such a thing?'

'Your disregard for your role within the royal household seems a good place to start. You sleep all day, go out all night like a common vagabond. I am told you have been neglecting your responsibilities with the Council, not to mention your neglect of your appearance.'

Liana unconsciously covered her hands at that last remark. *Defend myself or attack?* 'Who are you to lecture me?' *Attack.* 'You may have favour with the prince, but I remind you *I* am the heir, and I ask that you remember that.'

Shaan sniffed. 'If one were to *act* like the heir, then—'

'You are not my mother, nor are you even my advisor. I ask that you leave.' She sat straighter on the bed, glaring. Shaan's expression was entirely neutral. She hated that about him. He offered no hint of emotion one way or the other.

'I will indeed leave. I bear no ill against you. As you rightly say, you are the heir. Your brother and the queen would prefer that you attend today. I do not need to remind you how important this event is for her. However, you must do what you feel is right. I know you seek more than what these walls can offer. There is a whole world beyond this city, and I understand how attractive that can be. Live as you choose, Princess Liana, but choose wisely.'

'I'll think about it. Now, if you wouldn't mind, please leave.'

Shaan bowed and left without another word between them.

She had tried to sleep after that, but her bed felt uncomfortable and she couldn't settle. The housekeepers had replaced the bedsheets with fresh ones and she disliked the smell of the fire retardant dip they were washed in. A rotten egg-like smell heavily disguised with perfumes, it took at least two days for it to become bearable.

After an hour, she gave up on the idea of sleep, changed her clothing—dark, comfortable pants and a heavy cotton shirt— and snuck out of the palace. It wasn't hard. Everyone was too busy making preparations. She'd thought about giving in and attending, like the dutiful princess they all wanted her to be. That thought lasted less than a second. The day would proceed just as well without her as with her.

It was still a long time before moondown, but she knew where she would find Addan. He, at least, would offer no lectures about responsibility. He didn't even know her true identity. Except he wasn't there. The tavern, which to her was barely more than a large hole in the ground under one of the poorer living complexes in the city, was empty. Too early in the day. The gruff, sweaty man tending bar claimed not to have seen Addan. He knew who he was, though, and Addan owed him money.

Even though sleep called to her, she didn't want to return to the palace. So she spent the day wandering the streets of Miar Lenns. It made her feel like she was one of the common people and not their future queen. Depending on which part of the city she was in, if folk discovered her true identity, she would either be embraced or murdered. Opinion on the royal family had been polarised for as long as she could remember.

A stranger to the city would get lost quickly. All the buildings were the same sandstone colour—except for the scorch marks—and there was no sense of intention as to where they'd been built. Most roads and pathways were not in straight lines, and turning a corner would often lead to a dead end or back where you started. It was always dusty and the wind always blew. Scarves often covered mouths and noses, and cowls obscured the eyes as the men and women underneath looked at the ground as they walked.

The city was anonymous, if you wanted it to be. Especially in the south-west quarter where Addan lived. There was no money here, no prospects. Not since the dragons ravaged it all. For the people who lived in these parts, there was no hope of rebuilding, for it would all be destroyed again when the next swarm came in from the desert. Liana didn't like to think about it, but she knew these people lived in fear of them. *She* lived in fear of them. The thought of the one she had seen earlier still made her feel uneasy.

A single bell chime danced on the wind through the streets. Liana looked up to see the moon had reached its apex, divided perfectly down the middle, equally light and dark at the same time. The bell at the top of the tallest tower in the city marked mid-day. When she looked back down again, two men wearing black robes with their hoods lowered stood before her. Tal Valar. How anyone could tolerate wearing such heavy clothing in this heat was beyond her.

'Forgive me,' said Liana, believing she had got in their way. She made to step around them, but one raised an arm to block her path. A tall, light-skinned man with yellow hair and searching eyes, and one finger short of a full hand. She tried not to stare at it.

'Forgiveness is something one should ask of themselves in the presence of the Architects,' he said. The other, a darker man with a tiny scar above his lip, nodded along without a word. 'Have you done something that requires forgiving?'

'No, I, uh, was merely being polite. I was admiring the moon, so maybe I wasn't looking where I was going.' *Don't draw too much attention to yourself. Stay calm.*

'Ah yes, Mother is truly a wonder as she watches over all of us. Watch you as she may, it is wise for a young lady such as yourself to watch out for others as you go about your day.'

'Yes, of course. I will be more careful. I apologise.' She offered a small bow in deference, hoping it was enough to let her go on her way.

'See that you do. May the Architects guide you and keep you safe.'

'Keep you safe,' echoed the second man.

There was a brief pause where all three stood there. To Liana, it felt like an hour until the two men stepped round her and left her behind. She exhaled, grateful for no further inquisition.

Her lack of sleep was catching up with her, so she decided to wait in the tavern for Addan to arrive. If it were still quiet there, she might be able to take a small nap in a corner. Unfortunately, sleep would have to wait.

She could hear the shouting inside before she'd started on the steps that led into the tavern. If she hadn't had recognised Addan's voice shouting, she would have come back later still. *What trouble has he got into this time?* She paused briefly at the top of the steps before continuing down just as there was a loud crash from within.

It took a moment for her eyes to adjust to the relative darkness. Addan was slumped against a broken table, nursing a bloodied nose. Standing over him, at less than five feet in height, were two gabbalins. Both had pale grey skin with darker mottled patches, black hair that grew in sporadic tufts, and pointed ears that would otherwise be too big for any human. They had nothing that would be considered a nose, nor any real muscle. Typical of gabbalin stock, they were little more than ashen skin stretched over bone. Despite their frail, gaunt features, only a fool would take them for being weak. They both wore human clothes that were way too big; their pants held up only by string.

'Shara,' said Addan when he noticed her. 'Help me up, would you?'

'The female will not interfere,' said one of the pair. His voice crackled and vibrated as he spoke. A gabbalin trait.

'What's going on?' asked Liana. She looked around the room. Aside from the barkeep, who kept his distance, there wasn't anyone else there. Pale green liquid pulsed gently inside transparent glass orbs, which were scattered randomly around the establishment. The thick and sticky liquid, called chaulk, didn't offer as much light as a candle flame, but was considered far safer. Tables were all made of regulation plated wood, and were long past their best. Around each table were a number of stools or chairs. They were also made from plated wood, but only to the bare minimum standard.

'These... gentlemen... are here for the necklace.'

'Yes, we came to collect what is owed,' said the second gabbalin, his voice a touch higher in pitch than the first.

'So, why haven't you given it to them?' Liana scratched her arm. The whole point of stealing the necklace in the first place was to settle what he owed to the gabbalins. And now he was holding out on them. She made to help her friend to his feet, but the gabbalins blocked her way.

Addan propped himself up on his elbows, groaning in pain. 'These aren't the right gabbalins.'

'The male one has the artefact and he will surrender it to us.'

'He said it doesn't belong to you,' said Liana.

'I will only hand it over to Granx personally. As agreed.'

The gabbalins grunted and then hauled Addan to his feet. One slammed a fist into Addan's midriff, while the other rifled through his pockets.

'Where is it? We will take what is owed.'

Liana pulled at the closest one's shoulder, but she was pushed away. She managed not to lose her balance. *They really are strong.* She looked at the barkeep, silently willing him to intervene, but he simply held up his hands as if to say, "I'm not getting involved."

When she looked back at Addan, one of them had their hand at his throat. Without thinking it through, she pounced on the gabbalin, threw her arms around his neck and tucked her legs around his tiny waist. The gabbalin released Addan before twisting and writhing to force Liana off. She held firm as she swung about on his back. She was the larger of the two, but it was as if she weighed nothing. She refused to let go, even when she noticed the ripe smell of his body odour. She gagged, but held firm.

Addan seized the opportunity and swung for the second, connecting fist with jaw. The gabbalin barely flinched. Mayhem descended and within seconds, all four had gone to the floor and were wrestling each other. In the fracas, Liana took an elbow to the mouth. She didn't see whose elbow, but the blood tasted the same either way.

Neither side gained an advantage, with both pairs evenly matched. They traded blows and chokeholds. But then Liana found herself pinned to the dusty floor, held down by the shoulders. She scratched at the gabbalin's face, but she was stuck. They were *so strong*. And then she was free. Something had pulled the gabbalin away from her. Addan was to her left, still grappling with the other one, so it wasn't him. She scrambled backwards, forcing herself to sit up. What had happened?

Liana wiped the sweat from her face and saw an unfamiliar figure standing there. *A woman*. Huge! The woman had the gabbalin by the scruff of the neck, held aloft, his legs kicking wildly. Liana watched on as the hulk of a woman prized the other gabbalin free from Addan. The two gabbalins hung in the woman's grasp like a brace of rabbits, but screaming like a pair of pigs.

Helping Addan to his feet, Liana watched as the woman carried the gabbalins up the steps and out. She returned a moment later empty-handed, with a satisfied look on her face. The woman was as big as any man she knew, bigger even. Liana herself stood only as tall as the woman's waist, and nobody could accuse her of being short. She wore a well-tailored shawl over broad shoulders made from an expensive fabric. Soft, but angled, cheekbones sat beneath dark eyes, possibly blue— though it was hard to say for sure in the poor lighting. Her sandy blonde hair was pulled back and held in a tail, comple- menting a pale complexion.

'Thank you for your help,' said Liana.

'Your gratitude is welcome, but unnecessary,' said the woman. She stepped forward and righted the broken table as if it were made of paper. 'My name is Dess.'

Liana introduced herself by her alias, and Addan who seemed somewhat intimidated.

The barkeep had found his backbone now the gabbalins had gone, and was grumbling about the damage to his fixtures and fittings. He was a sweaty man with a double chin and wild eyebrows. Liana didn't like him.

'Dun spose you're payin' for the damage?' he asked, looking particularly at Addan.

'Ask the gabbalins. I didn't start this.'

The barkeep grunted and shook his head.

'We will have drinks, though.'

'Marks first. You owe 'nuff already.'

Addan rummaged in his pockets. Liana knew he didn't have any money, so she produced a handful of coins herself and set them on the bar top. 'Three ales.' She looked at Dess for confir- mation she would partake. Dess nodded once, slowly. 'And whatever is left, put towards the damage.'

The barkeep eyed the money briefly before sweeping it away, satisfied, and replaced it with three mugs of brown liquid.

Liana handed one of the mugs to Dess and invited her, with

43

Addan, to a table in the far corner away from the bar and the ears of the barkeep. There was something about the woman that compelled her to know more about her. At the very least, she wished to thank her properly for saving them from the gabbalins.

'Where are you from?' Liana asked. She sipped her ale and winced at its warmth. She could feel her bottom lip getting puffy. That would take some explaining to her mother later.

'Everywhere and nowhere. I am merely a traveller, passing through.' Dess spoke with a carefree demeanour and tone.

Liana studied the woman, as she liked to do occasionally. Dess had the appearance of a young woman, in her mid-twenties maybe—the same as her—but there was something within her eyes that made her seem far older. Experience? Perhaps. Or maybe she'd spent too long in the harsh desert heat of the Eastern Plains. What Liana did notice was she didn't drink her ale.

'What's that supposed to mean?' asked Addan.

'It means she's not Moranzan.' Liana looked at Dess for affirmation. She nodded.

'Whatever. Doesn't matter to me. Glad you turned up when you did, though.' He massaged his shoulder while rotating it.

'Do you often find yourself in trouble with other people?' Dess asked.

Addan laughed nervously. 'Only the ones I owe money to.'

'And money is important to you?'

'Everyone needs money, don't they?'

'Perhaps,' said Dess. 'Money is not everything. Other things have value, do they not?'

'Like what?'

'You value your life, I am sure. Hopefully, you value the lives of others around you, too? Opinions are of value.'

'Yeah, yeah, I get it. What's your point?'

Liana watched the conversation move back and forth.

Money wasn't important to *her*. Well, not in the same way. It wasn't even until she began sneaking out of the palace and met Addan that she'd actually seen a coin.

'My point is, I would very much like to see what the gabbalins valued of yours that saw them attack you so.'

Addan's hands immediately went to his lap under the table. 'How do you know about that?'

'I know about a lot of things.'

'Yeah, I bet you do. You're not having it.' He paused. 'Unless you can pay more than what the gabbalins were willing to.'

'I am not one for carrying money,' said Dess.

'Then it's not for sale.'

Dess turned to Liana. 'Do you know what it is that you have stolen, the two of you?'

Liana blinked in surprise. How did this woman know so much? Not only about the necklace that she couldn't possibly have seen, but that they had stolen it too? She shifted in her seat. 'Have you been following us? Spying on us?'

'Nothing of the sort. What your friend carries calls to me. I suspect you have felt something similar, have you not? That it is not what it appears to be on face value.'

'It did feel rather warm to touch,' she confessed.

'May I see it?' Dess asked. 'Please.'

'No chance,' said Addan.

Liana felt a compulsion to please the woman, to agree, to acquiesce. It was an odd feeling, but whatever it was, Addan evidently didn't feel it, too. 'No harm in showing it to her,' she found herself saying.

Addan sighed and reached into his pocket, and pulled out a small cloth bundle. He placed it on the table in front of him and held it close, guarding it.

Dess leaned forward a little.

'Show her then,' said Liana as she nudged him in the leg with her own.

Reluctantly, Addan pulled back one corner of the cloth to reveal the necklace. He didn't let go.

'What you hold there, young man, is a piece of life itself. A remnant.' Dess looked at Liana. 'It calls to you, does it not? It is why you stole it.'

'We stole it because we were told the gabbalins wanted it,' said Liana. She didn't deny that she felt a pull to it. 'We stole it to help Addan clear his debts with them, nothing more.'

'But when the moment came, you could not surrender it to them, could you?' said Dess.

Addan nodded.

'How do you know all this? Who *are* you?' Liana demanded.

'Let me say only that it is *fate* that brought you here. Fate took you to the artefact, and it is fate that will determine what comes next for you. Your life, your *destiny,* can change in an instant.' She snapped her fingers on her final word.

For a brief moment, everything went white and there was a ringing in Liana's ears. She felt dizzy. When her surroundings returned, Dess was gone, and so was the necklace. She looked at Addan, who was rubbing his eyes, trying to focus himself. He realised the necklace was gone just after she did.

'That thieving *bitch!*' he said. He heaved the table away from him, the legs scraping loudly against the floor, and ran for the exit.

Liana followed behind, stopping to ask the barkeep if he saw anything, but he only shrugged and muttered something about money. She found Addan outside the tavern entrance, pulling at his hair, looking in all directions, pacing, trying to see which way Dess went. He grabbed at a random passer-by—an old man in a raggedy shirt—demanding if he'd seen her. The old man wailed in protest at being accosted and shouted at. Addan let the man go.

'Calm down,' she said, pulling him to a stop.

'I knew I couldn't trust her. I *knew* it. Now what am I going to do?'

She didn't have an answer for him. But then, in the distance, the back of a head of someone taller than anyone else around. *Could it be her?* She pointed. 'There!'

Addan followed her arm and, without a word, darted off in pursuit. Liana shook her head and ran after him, weaving in and out of other people trying to mind their own business. He was faster than her. She tried her best to keep the head she thought to be Dess in view, but it wasn't easy. Eventually, she caught up with Addan, who had stopped running, their target lost.

Then he started running again, in another direction. Had he found her? She ran after him, but her legs were burning and she found it difficult to keep up. *I want my bed!* Again, Addan slowed, losing sight of Dess for the second time. This pattern repeated itself several times until they both found themselves outside the city limits, exhausted, and no closer to catching her.

Outside Miar Lenns, there was little cover to hide behind. Ahead, a lone figure walked in the direction of the Divide and the newly completed bridge. She had never seen the figure run, but for all their own running to catch this person, there always remained quite a distance between them. Though she hadn't seen a face, she knew for certain it was Dess, given the sheer size of the woman.

'Can we stop for a moment?' said Liana. Her breathing was laboured, and she took the opportunity to rest on a nearby rock.

'We can't lose her now,' Addan protested.

'Look,' she pointed, 'there's nothing else around. We can watch her from here for a bit. I'm tired of running.'

'But...'

'Besides, what are we going to do if we catch her? You've seen how strong, how *big*, she is. She picked up those gabbalins as if they were nothing.'

'I don't care. I *need* that necklace.'

She knew he was right. They couldn't simply steal another one. It was unique in every way. But something still didn't sit right with her. How did Dess know they had it? Did it actually belong to her? For her, finding the answers was almost as important as retrieving the necklace itself. Dess spoke of fate, and that single word resonated with her somehow.

Liana and Addan both agreed there was little point in running—for now—not so long as Dess remained in view. They had no idea if she knew they were following, but it was reasonable to assume she did. It had crossed Liana's mind that Dess was deliberately allowing them to follow, as if she was leading them somewhere. Playing a game with them. For all she knew, she could be imagining it all, considering how sleep deprived she was. She imagined being in her bed right now. She shook it off and kept walking.

It soon became clear Dess was heading specifically for the bridge. The Divide stretched for miles in either direction and there was nothing else but scrubland around this far outside the city.

'Do you think she's from over the Divide?' asked Addan.

It was a reasonable question. She had never seen someone from the land now known as Dawan before; no one had, not in almost a thousand years. She *was* human, and yet she looked unlike any other woman she knew. 'You could be right. Why else would she be heading there? We may have a chance here— the bridge is guarded.'

The new bridge—the only bridge—between Moranza and Dawan was a monumental feat of engineering. It took a full year to construct and was the largest project the city had undertaken in many lifetimes. Liana had visited it once before, when she accompanied the queen and Cal midway through construction. That was months ago, and back then, it still didn't look like a bridge. Not that she had much of a chance to see it. Protests over the large human cost had cut the trip short.

Many history books told of the Divide, and the war that ended with its creation nearly a millennium ago. What they didn't agree on was *how* the Divide came to be. The texts curated by the Tal Valar spoke of a great battle between the Architects and the ground beneath them split asunder. Other volumes—the ones preferred by most scholars—state it was merely a groundquake. Either way, that cataclysmic event brought about the end of the war and split the land in two. Moranza has been at peace ever since. No written knowledge exists about the fate and the history of Dawan.

And now there was a bridge. As it came into view in the distance, almost an hour's walk from the city, Liana couldn't help but be impressed by its scale and splendour. Built from a combination of sandstone and marble, it had an archway at either end decorated with intricate carvings. The arches stood some fifty feet high. Liana thought they were a little too grandiose and unnecessary, but the queen had insisted on the design be completed exactly as it was shown to her in her dream. Addan was less impressed, and she could sense his unease as he looked on. Then she remembered. He had been one of the hundreds that built it, at least until the day the first iteration collapsed, killing his brother, and a score more. She placed her hand on his shoulder and squeezed gently.

Close enough to the bridge, they took up a position behind a small pile of rubble—a mixture of rock types left over from construction. They watched Dess approach the four Queen's Guard positioned at the bridge entrance, but they were too far away to hear anything that was said. There was little doubt Dess had seen them at least once on the way up, but the guards didn't need to know they were there.

'What do we do, sit here and wait?' asked Addan.

'The guards won't let her cross. As big as she is, I doubt she could subdue all of them. So, she'll have no choice but to turn back. Then, we will confront her and demand she hand over the necklace. If she causes any trouble, we can call on the guards for help.'

Addan pulled a face that said he wasn't convinced. It wasn't foolproof, but it was the best plan she could think of.

Liana looked into the sky and at the waning moon above the city behind them. It wasn't long until it would set and the brief period of darkness would be upon them. Every day, the moon would pass in front of the sun as it dipped below the horizon and would block out the light. Once per day, the world would darken for almost a quarter hour. It was a time called twilight, and for most people, it meant the end of working and time for the day's main meal. As Liana watched the faceless smile head for the hidden sun, she felt hungry and forced silent a yawn with the back of her hand.

As the moon set, the forever breeze cooled and the orange skies took on a purple hue that darkened quickly. In the distance, the sound of a single bell-ring from the Moonwatch Tower rippled through the air. The end of the day. Liana glanced upward and watched as little tiny specks of light appeared in the sky. She had often wondered if those dots were always there, hidden by the light of day, or if they only came when it was dark. Whatever they were, and wherever they came from and went, Liana had loved looking out for them ever since she was a child.

The bridge looked far more imposing in the dark. The archway towered above the guards like an ominous shadow. The four guards stood in pairs on either side of the archway. When they saw Dess, the inner two broke position and blocked the way with their spears crossed. Liana could hear one of the men speak, but couldn't make out any specific words. If Dess spoke back, Liana couldn't hear her at all.

It looked like there was a brief conversation happening

before Dess took a step forward. The guards responded with a more aggressive posture. The two outermost guards had rounded on her from behind and pointed their spears right at her. None of the five moved any farther. The lead guard spoke again. And then the oddest thing happened.

Dess raised her arms upwards in a slow, smooth motion and held them aloft. The guards, all four of them, withdrew their spears, turned around, walked to the arch walls... and laid down as if to go to sleep. Liana looked at Addan and his face showed as much disbelief as hers likely did.

'What in the name of all the Architects happened?' asked Liana. She rubbed her face and looked again. Spears on the ground, the guards were lying down. Three were prone on the dirt and the fourth had his head propped up on the stonework at the bottom of the wall.

Dess lowered her hands, looked over her shoulder directly at where they were hiding, and then walked over the threshold and into Dawan.

As the darkness of the fleeting night melted away, Liana considered what to do next. Addan made the choice for her by breaking cover and running for the bridge. She huffed and pushed herself after him, her legs stiff after being crouched for too long.

The guards *were* actually asleep. It had crossed her mind that they might have been dead somehow, but one of them was definitely snoring. She considered trying to wake them, but thought better of it, as it wouldn't benefit either her or Addan. She felt a touch envious of their slumber, though.

Dess was already out of sight. Daylight had fully returned and Liana could see the full length of the bridge—some three hundred paces—and it was empty. Pristine. New. The choice was simple, and that was to follow Dess if they were to retrieve the necklace. Either that or go home and forget the whole thing. She looked at Addan as he stood there, gazing across the bridge.

It was no choice at all, really. Yet, she hesitated. Following Dess meant she would leave Moranza for the first time in her life. She had always yearned for true adventure, but now, in the moment, something held her back.

She looked back at Miar Lenns, her home. It looked so small and lonely. She thought about her mother and Cal. They would be entertaining their guests right about now. The first Dawanii to cross the bridge where she now stood. She had been obliged to be there herself. It wasn't the life she wanted. She turned her back to the city, and with her best friend, walked into Dawan.

4

A CRY FOR HELP

First impressions of Dawan were that it looked much the same as Moranza. Beyond the bridge was a blend of hilly scrubland where barely anything of use grew. Of course, Liana and Addan stood less than twenty paces away from the Divide. Time would tell how different this country would *actually* be. It did feel colder somehow. Perhaps she was simply looking for differences and her mind was playing games. Maybe she needed sleep.

There was no sign of Dess. Whatever game she had been playing on the way here from the city, letting them follow without catching up, was clearly over. It was hard to see too far ahead, though. In all directions, the ground sloped upwards. Liana decided walking straight ahead was as good a direction as any.

She pressed forward, leaning into the steep incline as she walked to what she thought was the peak. Instead of a similarly steep incline downwards on the other side, the ground simply ended. Dirt crumbled beneath her foot on the final step, and if it wasn't for Addan's quick reflexes, she would have fallen to her death. Though not as deep as the Divide behind them, the cliff edge they found themselves at towered over a dense forest. Liana had never seen so many trees in one place before.

A stunning vista stretched for miles ahead below them, and the forest filled half of it. In the far distance, there was what looked like a white desert with an occasional mountain peak to break up the horizon. She was wrong. Dawan was *nothing* like Moranza. As best as she could tell, there weren't any signs of civilisation. Nothing that looked like it could be a city or even a town. Everywhere looked natural and unspoiled by humankind.

'I think maybe we should head home,' said Addan after a minute or so of gazing at the scenery.

'Home? Why? We can't give up now. We need to find Dess.'

'And how are we going to do that? Look.' He swept his hand across the landscape. 'How are we supposed to find her in all of this? If there's even a way down.'

'There must be. She couldn't have just disappeared.' Liana stepped away from the cliff edge and looked for a path or other indication of a route down.'

'She could have jumped.'

'I doubt that very much.'

'Or fallen.'

'We need to find a—' Liana broke off as something rustled in a nearby hedge to her right. *Was Dess spying on us?* 'I know you're there. You may as well come out.'

There wasn't a reply. For a minute, everything was still aside from the gentle waving of leaves in the perma-breeze. Then there was more rustling. She followed the sound until she could see where it was coming from and took a couple of steps closer to it.

'This isn't funny,' called Addan. 'Give us back the necklace and we can all go home. Forget we ever met.'

Liana exchanged a questioning glance with Addan. He shook his head. Then she pointed at him and then to the left of the hedge, and to herself and to the right side. He knew what she meant; she didn't need words. She held up her hand with three fingers, then two, one. At the same time, they charged at the bush to flush out whoever was hiding behind it.

There *was* something there, but it wasn't human—it was too small. Liana caught a glimpse of something white run out from underneath the overgrowth, but she was too slow to catch it. Her pants snagged on some bramble and by the time she'd extricated herself, whatever it was had gone. She looked at Addan, who shook his head.

Something behind him caught her eye. And there it was, sat only ten paces away, was the most beautiful creature she had ever seen. A white furry animal with a grey beard and large bushy tail looked back at her, its mouth open and panting gently. It had bright bronze eyes and black flecks at the tips of its ears. It was too small to be a tamewolf and—if she wasn't imagining it—the fur had a soft, rippling blue glow to it, like fire.

Liana tapped Addan's arm with the back of her hand and pointed. 'Look!'

He turned and saw the animal. It didn't move or flinch. 'What is that?'

'I don't know,' she said, but something in her mind nagged at her. She felt like she *should* know what it was.

'Do you think it's dangerous?' He crouched down and held out a hand to it, but it just looked at him.

A word came to Liana. Something she'd read in a book. She couldn't remember where or when. 'Cinderfox,' she whispered.

'Huh?'

'If it's what I think it is, they're not meant to be real. I remember reading a story when I was young, a child's fable, I think. "Fur of fire and tail so white." It *has* to be a cinderfox!'

'It is dangerous?' he asked, withdrawing his arm.

'I don't think so. I don't know. It was only a story and I can't remember how the rest of it goes.' She took a cautious step forward. 'Hello little one,' she whispered.

The cinderfox tilted its head to one side, yawned, and then turned away and ran off into the thick brush.

Addan snorted. 'I guess not then.'

Liana walked in the direction it went.

'Hey, where are you going?' asked Addan.

'Well, it had to have come from somewhere. Maybe it'll lead to a way down.'

Her theory was right. After pushing through the thicket, she found herself on a rough path leading in a downward direction. The path, barely more than a meandering line of patchy grass and weed, curved down around the top of the cliff edge. The cinderfox was long gone, and aside from a few colourful insects here and there, they were alone.

Eventually, they found their way to level ground. She looked back and regarded the rough face of the cliff they had come from. The sheer surface was rough and yellow, dotted with plenty of outcroppings and jagged edges. To her, it looked like a fun and challenging climb to the peak where they had come from. *Another time, perhaps.*

The way ahead, farther into Dawan—farther from all she knew—was nothing but trees. Whenever she'd left the city before, it was always east. Hunting meant laying traps for dune rats and other small animals that preferred living underground. Never had she travelled west before. It was like another world. It seemed more alive, more inviting, and it smelled different, too. The perfume of a myriad of wild flowers carried on the breeze. Small bushes and unfamiliar plants were scattered around among the trees. She watched as small yellow and black insects flew in and out of tiny white flowers. Beautiful little bundles of winged fluff going about their lives. *The world must seem so huge to them.*

'What now?' said Addan.

She rolled her shoulders and puffed her cheeks. 'We keep going, I guess.'

It was difficult to see the sky through the canopies of the trees. There was no moon as a marker to help keep a sense of direction. Knowing where the moon was meant it would have been easier to keep a sense of direction as they progressed through the forest. Without it, she tried her best to keep the cliff directly behind them and walk in a straight line. Not an easy feat when walking around trees that stood in their way. She tried to make a mental note of anything that could mark their way. Fallen branches, a dip in the terrain. A stream...

Water! The shallow flow of a brook meandering through the trees crossed their path. Until that moment, she hadn't realised how thirsty she'd become. Neither she nor Addan had thought to bring any kind of provisions with them. Exploring a whole new country had not crossed her mind when she had left the palace.

They both ran the last few steps to the water's edge and fell to their knees with a splash. They cupped their hands and drank freely. Liana had never known water so cold before. She smiled as the coolness of the liquid spread through her chest, not caring how wet her legs were getting.

With her thirst quenched, Liana looked up from the water to the other side of the brook and gasped. Sat on a rock with toes dipped in the water was Dess. 'I don't believe it.'

'Hum, what?' Addan hadn't noticed. He looked where she indicated and immediately pulled himself to his feet and waded through the water towards the woman. At its deepest, the stream was barely ankle deep, but he almost lost his footing near the middle. 'Hey! I want my necklace back.'

Liana followed, though wasn't inclined to run through the water. Dess didn't look as though she was getting up.

'It took you long enough to get here,' Dess said nonchalantly. 'What do you think of Dawan? Pretty is it not? Come, sit for a while.'

'I need that necklace,' demanded Addan. He stopped short of leaving the water, but kept a distance between him and Dess.

Liana ignored the chill in her feet as she joined her friend. She tried to decide what sort of game this woman was playing with them. First, she helps. Then steals, then runs—but lets them follow. Now, she waits and watches. Why?

'You do not need. You may desire that what is not yours, but to need is not the truth.' Dess produced the necklace from a hidden pocket and let it hang on her fingers.

'I *do* need it. I need to repay a debt. You stole it from us and I want it back.'

'Stole. Now there is a word. You *stole* it yourself, did you not? And the man you stole it from, stole it himself, also. This remnant has been stolen so, so many times now. Who did it belong to originally, do you think?'

Liana narrowed her eyes as the woman spoke. She wanted to help her friend, but didn't know how. Short of rushing the woman and snatching the necklace away... She decided that wouldn't work. 'Are you saying the necklace is yours?' she offered.

Dess looked at the piece of jewellery in her hand. 'Of sorts. I suppose you could say it once belonged to me. Or perhaps I belonged to *it*. Together, yes. We belonged together.'

Belonged. Past tense. Liana was developing a headache at the same time as losing the feeling in her toes from the cold water. She was growing tired of Dess toying with them. She sloshed through the stream and onto the dry ground, keeping ample space between herself and Dess. Addan stayed where he was in the water. *Good, now she couldn't see us both at the same time.* 'Who does it belong to now?'

Dess shifted on her rock to look at Liana. 'Everyone and no

one. The stone at the end of this chain is a remnant of the Origem, and as such, it has no owner.'

That's right, keep your attention on me. 'Why did you let us follow you? You could have disappeared into a building somewhere and we'd have never found you. But you let us see you. Let us come after you to the bridge.' She paused for a moment. *The guards.* 'And what did you do to the guards? Why did they fall asleep?'

Dess chuckled. 'Those men are unharmed, are they not? As I said when we last spoke, violence is no answer, so they were merely encouraged to rest a while. As for you, well, your journey began long before you found this remnant. Long before you could possibly comprehend. Fate brought you here and brought you here for reasons beyond your reach. I mean you no harm, little one, but I do mean you to be here.'

Liana tried not to move her head or give any indication she could see Addan slowly edging towards Dess. She wanted to keep her talking, but the woman was talking in riddles. *Little one?* Patronising, too. Dess wanted her to follow, and yes, as she thought about it, she *wanted* to follow her. Not only to help her friend as she'd promised, but something else compelled her to come. She made the choice to be here. *Didn't I?*

'We,' continued Dess, 'all have our role to play in the world. I know mine, but do you know yours? You were born into your life, but you reject it. Oh, how you reject it. You yearn for something *more*. Your time has come, little one, your—'

Addan snatched at the necklace and the chain snapped. The glass shell, along with the chain, fell from its binding and struck a rock jutting out above the shallow waters. The glass shattered, and the stone broke in two, both halves landing in the water. He swore loudly. Dess barely reacted. She simply looked down at him, her arm still aloft, holding a small piece of the gold chain.

Liana tensed, unsure of what would happen next. Her

thinking was if Addan had been successful, he would have bolted and she would run after him. But now she only watched on as he scrambled in the water for the broken pieces. It was too late to run.

'One has become two, but there is only one of me and two of you,' said Dess. She lowered her arm with a sigh and stood up from her perch. 'A piece each. A gift of fate, you might say.'

Liana opened her mouth to speak, but words failed her in the moment. Addan stood up with a broken half in each hand. He passed her one of the pieces. Immediately, it grew hot as purple light shimmered deep within it. There was something peculiar about the gemstone, and she could hear whispering again, like it was trying to communicate with her.

The warm feeling grew quickly into an intense heat that felt like it was searing her flesh. She instinctively tried to drop the stone, but it stayed in her hand, attached somehow. As she tried to pull it with her other hand, the stone vanished, leaving only a black mark the size of a bean in the centre of her palm. She yelped in pain and tried to shake the feeling away.

'What happened?' asked Addan. He examined Liana's hand as she held it by the wrist, and then looked at his own stone, then back at her.

'I don't know.' She looked up at Dess. 'What did you do?'

'My part here is done,' said Dess. 'For now, at least.' Then it happened again—an instant of white light, as if the world stopped for a heartbeat before continuing on.

Dess was gone, nowhere to be seen. Liana couldn't find her off in the distance this time. Something told her there was no point in searching for her again. She watched Addan retrieve the remains of the necklace from the water and pocket it. The gold would still be worth selling on its own.

The pain in her hand faded. The mark, however, stayed, even when she tried to rub it off with her finger. It was barely more than a smudge. She was more annoyed that the stone had disappeared than the pain it had caused. It felt more like the pain she experienced when using magic, not the kind she felt when she cut herself or banged her head. She looked at Addan and wondered why his hadn't done the same.

'Is yours not burning your hand?' Liana asked.

'No. It's cold. Really cold, now you mention it.' He held it out to her, offering. She refused to touch it and took a step back.

Her mind wandered off into nothing for a moment, as if trying to recall a memory too far out of reach. She looked back at Addan. 'Well, I guess there's nothing else for it now but to go home.'

'And then what? I've broken the necklace. The gabbalins will want my head when they find out.'

'We'll figure something out, but we can't stay here, can we?'

Addan muttered something she couldn't hear, but there was a nod of agreement in there somewhere. Liana splashed her way back across the stream. She wondered how long it would be before her wet feet blistered. Addan followed, but neither of them walked with purpose or urgency. She herself was too tired and her mind was so consumed with Dess's words she forgot how hungry she was.

After what she supposed was an hour of walking, she realised they should have made it back to the cliff by now. Instead, there were only endless trees, and none of them looked familiar. She stopped and circled on the spot, searching.

'We're lost, aren't we?'

'Uh huh,' she conceded.

Addan slumped to the ground and sat with his legs tucked underneath him, his arms resting loosely on his knees. 'In that case, I'm resting here for a while.'

She didn't argue with him. Resting was a good idea, but she didn't feel inclined to sit down herself. She stretched out the muscles in her arms and legs. For the first time since leaving the palace, she felt worried. What if they couldn't find a way back?

There was no food here, nothing to forage. The trees were tall and didn't bear fruit, and there wasn't even so much as a mushroom on the ground. They would either succumb to hunger or exhaustion. Probably both. She screamed.

'Are you done?' Addan said when she ran out of breath.

'Done? Yes, I'm done. I'm done with being tired and hungry. I'm done with being lost. And cold. And wet. None of this would have happened if—'

'If, what? If I hadn't pissed off the gabbalins? If I hadn't broken the necklace? This isn't all my fault, Shara.'

'I didn't say it was.'

'You didn't have to. But I... shit. Shara, *don't* move.' Addan carefully and slowly pulled his weight around until he was crouched on his toes.

'What?' She looked at him and noticed a fearful look in his eyes. He wasn't looking at her, but somewhere beyond her. And then came the growling—a low, quiet rumble—not far behind her. She spun on her heels and saw immediately what Addan had seen. In between two trees was a direwolf staring back at them. It looked like Cal's pet with long grey-black fur, but its eyes were wild and yellow. The beast's posture warned it was ready to attack at any moment, hackles raised and deadly teeth on display as it snarled. Liana froze, her arms held out a little to the sides.

'What do we do?' whispered Addan.

'I don't know!' Her heart was thumping. She daren't take her eyes off it. Their stares locked together. Should she run? Run where? There was no way she could outrun a direwolf, even when she wasn't exhausted. What other choice was there? Which way then? Away? Left? Right?

She could go *up*. That might work. She looked for the closest tree that she could reach and climb. To her left, away from the direwolf, was a skinny pine tree. It had a low enough branch that if she judged it right, she could get a purchase on and reach relative safety. She talked through her idea to Addan, telling him to follow on the count of three.

'Three!' She dashed for the pine as fast as she could and leapt up to reach her chosen branch, but it snapped under her weight and she crashed to the ground as Addan came up underneath her, taking him down too. They scrambled free of each other, but they were out of ideas and out of time. The direwolf had closed the gap between it and them. It didn't charge. Step by step, it moved closer, stalking low. Growling. Liana closed her eyes and held Addan's arm and squeezed tight.

She waited for death, but it never came. Cautiously, she opened one eye. The direwolf was still there, but its attention was no longer on them. She breathed, opened her other eye and looked. And there it was, locked in a standoff with the direwolf, the cinderfox. Was it the same one? It looked bigger, much bigger, almost the size of the direwolf itself. The white fur of the cinderfox was awash with a bright blue fire, more fierce than she'd witnessed earlier. The big brush of a tail swung aggressively behind it.

The two animals circled around, their eyes fixed on the other. Liana pulled Addan away and behind some foliage. She wanted to run, but she *really* wanted to watch and see what happened.

The direwolf broke first and ran at the cinderfox. They threw themselves together, growling and snarling. The white animal sank its teeth into the direwolf's neck. It howled in pain. They wrestled back and forth, each taking the advantage before succumbing to the other and then back again.

Blood spilled from each, with red smears more apparent on the white fur than the black and grey. The sound they both made as they fought was visceral, primal. Either could win this fight still. The direwolf squealed under another bite to the neck and the pair separated, but only for a moment. The cinderfox leapt forward for the final, killer attack. It tore at the direwolf's throat and the wolf cried out and then fell silent. It was over.

The cinderfox stood proudly over its dead foe and looked at Liana and Addan, its mouth open, panting, dripping with blood. It seemed pleased with itself. The blue fire that flowed through its fur settled from a roaring flame to little more than a faint glow. It lowered its head as if to bow to its audience of two, turned and padded off into the forest.

Liana laughed. Not through humour, but at the relief of realising she could easily be dead right now. The direwolf was a sorry sight. She couldn't help but feel a little sad for it, but only briefly. She had grown up hearing many stories about the sheer strength and ferocity of these animals, and had even seen a few in her younger years. They were the most dangerous beasts she'd ever known. Until today, when she witnessed a supposedly mythical animal tear it apart like it was a stuffed toy.

Once she had gathered her thoughts, she remembered they were still lost. How many more direwolves or other dangers were out there, waiting? After this latest incident, she had even less of a sense of direction. When they left the stream, she led them both in what she thought was a straight line with the water right behind her. She didn't feel as though she'd wandered off course, but yet the cliff never came. Now? She couldn't tell which way they'd come from or were headed.

'I say we go this way,' said Addan. He pointed in a random direction.

'Why that way?'

'Seems as good as any. It all looks the same now, don't you think? I'm not going to wait around here and get mauled to death. We have to come across *something* eventually, right?'

It was as good as anything she could think of. He was right. If you don't know where you're going, you may as well follow your nose. 'Fine. Come on then. At the very least, let's find something that we can use for shelter. I need to sleep.'

Addan nodded. 'Food, too. There's got to be something worth eating around here.'

Their surroundings continued to be nothing but endless trees and foliage. They must have walked for another hour at least, but if she didn't know any better, she wouldn't think they'd walked far at all. It *was* getting colder though. Everything else was the same. Except...

'Can you smell smoke?' she asked.

Addan stopped and exaggeratedly sniffed at the air. 'No, I don't think so. Wait, hang on, maybe. Yes, I do smell something. I think it's coming from that direction.' He pointed a finger to his right.

Liana walked after him. The smell of smoke grew stronger, but it didn't smell like how burning wood would smell. It was... sweeter? Like burnt sugar, almost. After a few dozen paces, the ground, which until now had been largely flat, began to slope downward. A few paces after that, they found themselves at the edge of the tree line. Ahead, there was the smoke, and beneath the grey billowing clouds, a fire. Not a wildfire—a handmade fire with a ring of large grey and brown stones encompassing it. And then she noticed the people. She counted five, all stood with their heads bowed, by the fire on the far side, except for one who was kneeling. A sense of relief washed over her.

'What are they doing?' asked Addan.

'It looks like they're praying.' Liana studied the Dawanii below. She'd not met one before and saw immediate differences from her own people. Their hair was a mix of white on one side and black on the other, except for the one kneeling who had a red stripe instead. Probably painted, she considered. They all wore thick fur clothing, similar to a poncho or shawl, but cut in such a way it was hard to tell if it was clothing or a natural covering like an animal. Only their faces and arms gave away the truth.

'There's more of them,' Addan said. 'Behind the fire, there's buildings, I think. It's hard to tell.'

He was right. On the far side of the clearing, hidden within the trees, were several small wooden huts. In front of them, a number of Dawanii stood watching the prayers around the fire, but otherwise weren't taking part in any discernible way.

A cry of pain snapped her attention back to the ones around the fire. The four standing were chanting, while the one kneeling—the one crying out—was holding his arm in the fire. Liana watched on in horror. *Why would anyone do such a thing?* And then she noticed the man—barely more than a boy— wasn't simply holding his arm out. He was reaching for something.

A few seconds later, the young man fell silent. He was speaking now, but she couldn't hear the words clearly enough to understand them. Pulling his arm out of the flames, he held aloft a rock he'd plucked out of the fire. Liana had seen nothing like it.

'How crazy is that?' remarked Addan.

'Isn't it!' she said. 'They're very strange people, but we're going to need their help if we're going to find a way out of here.'

In that moment, she felt a sharp, stabbing pain in her hand and gasped. She couldn't help it. The pain radiated from the dark smudge on her palm. If she wasn't imagining it, she swore it looked bigger. She picked at it with a finger and the pain subsided back into nothing.

Somewhere over to their left was the sound of a snapping branch. They froze. Were there more Dawanii they hadn't seen? Liana squinted as she tried to find the source of the sound, but couldn't see anything out of the ordinary. She looked back towards the Dawanii near the fire. They had also heard the cracking sound and were doing the same as her—looking for the origin. *They weren't expecting anyone else there either, then.*

Another snap. Closer this time. *More direwolves?* No—it

wasn't an animal. There was a voice, whispering. And another. Definitely people, possibly more Dawanii, meaning they were surrounded. She glanced at Addan. He looked worried.

The voice again, male, raspy, somewhere to her left. 'I see something up ahead.' There was no mistaking the distinct vibration in the voice. Gabbalins.

'We need to get out of here,' she whispered. Addan nodded. His eyes were wide, alert.

There was a rustling in the undergrowth. A foot. And another. Then a mottled grey arm holding what looked like a club. *What were they doing here?* It was a stupid question. She already knew the answer. She looked over at Addan. He had seen them too, and was keeping low to the ground, perfectly still, perfectly hidden.

Liana spotted a way past the gabbalins, but as she went to make a run for it, one of them hollered and pointed to the Dawanii in the clearing. The Dawanii yelled, sounding their own alarm. Liana shuffled backward through the brush and watched. There was no sense in her revealing themselves. One of the Dawanii, who looked much older than the rest, picked up a fist-sized rock and hurled it at the advancing gabbalins. It struck one of them in the chest, making it squeal.

The first of the gabbalins had already reached the fire, a crude wooden weapon raised above his head, ready to attack. He brought it down in one quick motion at the Dawanii closest to him. He missed, barely. Liana was certain the Dawanii stood no chance, but the weapon seemed to have been brushed aside, like it had glanced off an invisible shield. The Dawanii man pushed outward with his right hand. Untouched, the gabbalin fell backwards to the ground, dropping his weapon as he landed.

Liana felt she had to do something. She realised the gabbalins were only there for her and Addan. Why they felt the need to attack an innocent people, she didn't know. She stood up and shouted at the gabbalins, at anyone who would notice her. No one did. There was too much screaming and shouting for anyone to notice her behind them.

'What *are* you doing?' hissed Addan.

'I'm not going to hide here and watch.' She ran forward as two, then three of the Dawanii fell at the hands of their attackers. One of the gabbalins was hurled clear over the fire, launched by an unseen force, and landed against a tree a dozen or so paces away. *What is going on?* Sixteen Dawanii became ten, then seven. More than half their number fell to the onslaught. There seemed to be a higher power helping to defend them; an invisible ally fighting on their behalf, but it was not enough.

She had counted no more than five gabbalins to start, but now there were only two. She had screamed the whole way down the slope into the clearing, begging for everyone to stop the madness. Nobody listened.

Another Dawanii man fell dead as she reached level ground. Despite their greater number to begin with and their valiant defence, they were no match for the gabbalin invaders who were nothing short of relentless in their pursuit for blood. She considered what she knew about gabbalins. While they *did* like a fight, and were often involved in criminal activities in the city, she'd never heard them to be capable of such savagery. As exiles from their own country, they were grateful for any kind of food and shelter on offer, simply wanting to get on. *They were exiles for a reason, though,* she thought.

'Stop!' she screamed as loudly as she could. It worked. The two remaining gabbalins stopped their attack and turned to her. One she recognised from their altercation at the tavern, the other she did not. The three remaining Dawanii shrank back, unsure, frightened.

'Give us the necklace,' snarled one of the two. Drool spat through jagged, rotting teeth.

'I can't,' she said. 'It's gone. Broken.'

'Lies!' said the other, the one she recognised.

'It's true,' said Addan. He pulled out the pieces of necklace from his pocket and held it out for them to see.

'Bah! Worthless now. Your debt shall be repaid with your life. Hers too.'

'And what of these people? They owe you no debt, yet you slaughter them anyway. Why?' Liana asked.

'They attacked first.'

She looked around her. The one who had thrown that first rock lay bloodied and broken near the fire. 'He was frightened, and rightly so,' she spat.

'And? Makes no difference to us,' said the one with the bad teeth.

From nowhere, one of the last Dawanii rushed at the gabbalins. In that moment, she watched as Addan took his opportunity and shoulder-charged the familiar one. Liana didn't know what to do with herself as she watched the four fall to the ground, wrestling with each other. To her right lay one of the gabbalin corpses. It still held on to a crude, elongated knife. It wasn't quite a sword, but looked deadly nonetheless, as proven by the Dawanii blood smeared along the metal. Without taking her eyes off the gabbalins, she crouched down and retrieved it.

She ran to the melee and went to strike with her new weapon, but hesitated for fear of accidentally hitting Addan. The Dawanii somehow got to his feet. He didn't have a weapon. None of them had had weapons of their own, she realised now. Seizing an opportunity, she swiped her blade at the gabbalin engaged with the standing Dawanii. She struck her target, though it barely scratched his arm, and he took no notice of her or the injury.

'Save me!'

Liana spun around, looking for who spoke.

69

'Save me!' the voice repeated. She could only see one other —the older Dawanii man who had thrown the first stone, and also had presided over their ritual. There should have been a third, the younger one with the red hair, but he was nowhere to be seen. The old man was doubled over near the fire. His fur clothing was bloodied, and he was clutching at his middle, trying hard to protect a wound in his abdomen. She stepped closer to him.

'Save me!'

She looked back at the fight in time to see the familiar gabbalin strike a fatal blow to the Dawanii man. Addan was on the ground, holding his own against the other, raining punches down on the grey-skinned enemy. It was two against one, though. She didn't know what to do. She wasn't a fighter, and definitely didn't know how to use a sword, or knife, or whatever it was she was holding.

So, she did the first thing that came into her head—she threw the weapon at the standing gabbalin with as much strength and precision as she could muster. The blade flew through the air and landed with a thud in the gabbalin's chest. He groaned and fell to the ground. She had never killed before and she immediately felt a knot in her stomach.

'Please, save me! Help!' The call came again, more desperation in their voice. Liana looked at the old man, at Addan, and then the old man again. She decided she wouldn't be much help to Addan, but if there was a chance to help the Dawanii, she would regret not at least trying.

'Help me.'

She was looking at the man as she went to him, but as she heard the plea, his lips didn't move. The words *did* come from him, she was sure of that, but it felt like they were pushed inside her head instead of actually *hearing* them. She ran to him, her legs buckling underneath her as she rounded the fire. Exhaustion finally catching up with her.

'Save me.' A whisper now.

Liana almost had to crawl the last few steps to him. She was close and the old man reached out an arm to her. She glanced back at Addan. He was in trouble. The gabbalin had the upper hand. She couldn't help him now. It was too late for her to change her mind; too late to go help her friend. 'Run!' she screamed at him. 'Get help!'

Addan managed to scramble to his feet and ran from the gabbalin, up the slope and into the trees. The gabbalin gave chase, but Addan got a good head start. She hoped that would be enough.

Liana looked back at the stricken old man, the life draining from his eyes.

'Save me!'

Deep inside, she felt an urge, a compulsion, to help this stranger. It was unlike anything she had experienced before. She was being drawn to him. Out of all the Dawanii there in the clearing, why this one? She dragged herself closer until she was within reach of him.

She felt his laboured breath on her face, but didn't know what to do. How could she save him? The blood was oozing from him, warm and sticky to her touch. Then, a pale blue mist blurred her vision. Coming out of nowhere, it felt warm, almost comforting. It engulfed her.

'Thank you,' said the voice. It was the last thing Liana heard before she passed out.

5

LOST

Addan ran through the forest without turning back. He ignored the scratches to his arms and face as he fought against the sharp branches and brambles in his way. He felt guilty leaving Shara behind, but it was better to have that last gabbalin chasing him than turning on her. Fight or flight—that's what his father had once told him. You either stand your ground and fight like a man, or you run and accept the shame that comes with it. There was no shame in running this time, though. He had tried to fight, he really had, and he almost won, but they were armed and he wasn't. He was scared, but that's not why he ran.

His feet dragged as he stumbled his way through the overgrowth. The gabbalin must still be close behind him, but he didn't want to stop running, not yet. His mouth was dry, and it took every effort to stop himself from retching. An acidic aftertaste of an empty stomach caught in the back of his throat. He had to keep going and could only hope he was running in the right direction.

Fight or flight. What was he doing? He couldn't abandon Shara. What sort of coward did that make him? He stopped running. His lungs were burning, and he ached all over. Without any momentum to keep him moving forward, it was all he could do to remain upright. He *had* to go back for her. First, that meant confronting the gabbalin chasing him.

Addan turned back the way he came, scanning the forest for his grey-skinned foe. There was no one there. Had he outrun him by that much? Gabbalins were as quick as they were strong and should have been right behind him. Nothing. *Shit! Had he broken off his chase and gone back for Shara?* Panic set in and he went to throw up, but nothing came. He brushed himself down and ran back. In less than two steps, something slammed into him from the side, sending him crashing to the ground.

He caught sight of a flash of grey skin as he tried to wrestle free. The gabbalin was on top of him. With considerable effort, he managed to extricate himself.

'Can't let you escape,' grunted the gabbalin.

'Look, Granx, it broke. I'm sorry. I'll get you what I owe you, I promise.' Addan pulled himself to his feet and tried to put some distance between them.

'Gone beyond that now,' said Granx, as he produced a blade. 'Can't let you escape, can't let you live.'

Addan hobbled backward, unarmed. His right leg burned with pain, reminding him of its damage. He told everyone he'd lost a toe to a tamewolf when he was a child, but the truth was worse than that. A truth he promised he would share with no one, ever. 'I'll give you whatever you want. I don't want to fight you.'

Granx spat at the ground and tossed his dagger back and forth between hands. It was clear he had no intention of bargaining. He sprang forward and swiped the blade in a back-hand motion across Addan's chest. It didn't connect. A test.

Addan had to disarm him somehow. He was handy in a fight, one that only involved fists and a lot of alcohol, at least. Here, he had no weapon of his own and no drink to numb any pain. He feinted forward, trying to induce Granx to come at him. It worked. The gabbalin lunged with his blade. Addan sidestepped out of harm's way and grabbed Granx's wrist. In one swift motion, he twisted Granx's arm up behind his back and cracked his elbow into the back of the ash-coloured skull.

The gabbalin squealed in a strange vibrating tone, but didn't drop the knife. Addan had him immobile, though, and continued to hit his opponent in the head until he relented. Granx's legs fell from underneath him, and Addan let go. Instantly he realised that was a mistake as the gabbalin twisted on his knees. The blade sliced into Addan's thigh. It wasn't a deep cut, but pain burst through his leg and he screamed out. He managed to stay standing and successfully avoided a second swipe.

As Granx missed, he lost his balance and leaned forward. That was Addan's opportunity, and he took it. He threw himself onto the gabbalin and reached for the knife as he landed his full body weight on top of him. The two wrestled in the dirt, Addan pulling hard on the knife, twisting, pushing, until... Granx gave out a groan and his body relaxed. Addan felt warm, sticky blood oozing down his hand and arm. He pushed free of the gabbalin as it twitched in the dirt, the dagger hilt protruding from its chest.

Addan fell back and sat in the undergrowth. He laughed with relief, grateful to still be alive. His body ached, and the cut to his thigh burned with pain. His own red blood seeped through his pants. He could probably walk on it, but he needed to rest a little while first. Shara couldn't wait, though. He had to get back to her. A hundred count—that was all the time he would allow himself to rest. Then he would find his way back to her. Somehow.

When his count reached one hundred, he took a deep breath and forced himself to his feet. His legs had stiffened in the time he'd taken to rest, and it took a moment to walk them loose. He retrieved the dagger from Granx's corpse. The hilt was made of a winding pattern of gold and silver, but the blade itself was blue steel. Expensive, most likely stolen. He wiped the blood on some leaves and tucked it into his belt.

He set off in what he hoped was the right direction, back to the clearing with the fire. How long had he been running from Granx? He figured no more than ten minutes, even though it felt like hours. If he was sensible and methodical and didn't walk for too long in his chosen direction, he was confident he would find her. After walking enough distance without finding anything, he doubled back until he reached the gabbalin corpse, then chose a new direction and tried again. On the third attempt, he found the clearing.

There was an eeriness hanging in the air. The fire had faded to little more than smouldering ashes and there were dead bodies everywhere. Most of them were Dawanii, with a gabbalin mixed in here and there, but none of them were Shara. She wasn't where he had last seen her—with an older man, if he remembered right.

He found the old man propped up against a rock on the far side of the fire. He was dead, his chest wet with blood. Why had she gone to him specifically? Why help them at all? That was her way, though. If she could help someone, she would. How many times had she got him out of trouble? He'd lost count.

'Shara!' he called. Aside from the gentle crackle of fading embers and a bird or two high above him in the trees, there was only silence. He called her name again. And again. Nothing. The lack of a body gave him hope. As far as he could remember, she hadn't been injured in the fight. It was reasonable to presume she had gone looking for him. He hadn't been away that long, though. If their roles were reversed, *he* would have waited. That was a lie, though. He *hadn't* waited, he hadn't stayed. He ran. She told him to run, and he did without a second thought. He kicked the dirt in disgust with himself. *Coward.*

Behind the clearing were several oddly shaped structures. He had spotted them when they first found the clearing. He'd presumed them to be huts, but as he looked at them now, they appeared to have been sculpted from the trees themselves. Stretched out walls, with loose brush covering their tops. It was as if someone had taken hold of a tree trunk and *pulled* it into this new shape. He'd never seen anything like it. Each building —if they could be called that—had a heavy animal skin hanging over an opening like a door.

Addan called Shara's name again. Still, there was silence. He pulled back the skin covering the entrance to the dwelling closest to him. It was dark inside. 'Hello?' he whispered. Outside, he'd shouted, but it didn't feel right to shout into someone's abode. There wasn't anyone there.

He checked the other dwellings and found them empty, too. He didn't even find anything that resembled belongings. No clothes, no tools, no beds. Nothing. No clues inside or out. No clues as to Shara's fate anywhere. He had no other choice left— find his own way home and pray to the Architects she was safe and they had simply missed each other along the way.

There wasn't even any food in this—whatever it was— encampment. A rabbit had hopped by in the distance a while ago, but it was gone before he remembered they were edible. He hadn't seen another since. Searching the corpses yielded nothing, except a renewed urge to throw up. Any hope of some dried meat or other morsels of food went without success. 'Maybe I should have died here too,' he muttered.

'You know, you should not tempt fate.'

Addan snapped his head upwards, surprised to hear another voice. He looked around and saw Dess standing not three paces behind him. She looked different somehow, but it was definitely her. 'Am I glad to see you,' he said. 'Though you shouldn't sneak up on someone like that.'

'Why not?' Dess walked past him and examined the scene

around them. 'Oh dear, what a sorry sight this is. It saddens me to see so much death in one place.'

'Gabbalins, they must have followed us from Moranza and when the Dawanii saw them, they attacked each other.' He paused. 'Have you seen Shara? She was here, but there's no sign of her.'

'Shara. Is she your friend? I am afraid I have seen no one else here. Not alive, at least.'

Addan frowned. 'You know she is.'

'I know not of your friend.'

'Dragonshit. You led us here. You talked to her not two hours ago.'

'Ah, you are mistaking me for someone else.' She ran her hand through the remnants of the fire, plucked a fist-sized stone from the ashes, examined it, and then tossed it back. Tiny flecks of hot ember scattered into the air.

'I don't think so. Don't piss me about, Dess.'

'Oh bless, you must believe me to be my sister. I must apologise for I am not her and she is not me. My name is Yra. I am one of three. Dess is another. Mo is our third, but I have not seen her in such a long, long time. If you meet her, do tell her I miss her.'

Addan didn't know what to say, and wasn't sure he believed her. It seemed too much of a coincidence. 'If that's true, then why are you here now?'

'I like to help people, if I can, and you definitely look like you are in need of help. Your leg, I see it is injured.'

He looked down at the red sticky patch on his thigh. 'I'll live. I've had worse.'

'Ah yes, your impediment. I see that too. I cannot do anything about that one. Too much time has passed. I *can* help with the new one, if you would allow.'

He took a step back at first in an unconscious move. 'What are you going to do?'

'There is no need for alarm. I only wish to help.' Her voice was soothing, but had an undercurrent of authority. 'Now, lower your pants.'

'Huh?'

'Wounds, I can heal. Clothing, I cannot.' She turned and scooped a handful of the still glowing ash from the dying fire.

'Wait, what are you going to do with those?' He was halfway to lowering his pants and took another step backwards, lost his balance and fell on his backside with a groan. *How are those ashes not burning her hands? Who is this woman?*

Yra made soothing sounds like one would do to a small animal or child as she came and knelt down beside him. 'This will not hurt, I promise,' she said as she cupped the hot ashes in one hand and slapped them down on the wound in one swift motion.

Addan closed his eyes and screamed in pain before realising there was none. Tentatively, he opened his eyes. Yra had already stood up and returned to the fire. He looked down at the wound. The blood was gone and all that remained was a long, thin black line where the cut had been.

'The discolouration is permanent, I am afraid. Nothing I can do about that. Consider it a reminder of how lucky you are. If that were allowed to fester... You may pull your pants up.'

'Lucky is not something I feel right now.' Addan stood up and rearranged his clothing. 'Can you help me find Shara?' He looked at her pleadingly.

'Alas, I cannot. People are... difficult. Your friend must follow her own path, and if that path is not your own, then fate will take you another way.'

'Can you at least tell me which way is Moranza?' Going home was his best option now. Shara could be anywhere. He was already lost, and if he tried to find her by wandering around aimlessly in this forest, he could only make his predicament worse.

'Ah, now that I can do for you,' Yra said cheerfully. She put her hands together and blew gently into them. When she opened them, a soft ball of green light hung in the air. It looked very similar to the light Shara could produce, only stronger. 'This will show you the way, though I warn you, be quick, for its strength will not last forever.'

'Will you not come with me?' He tried not to make it sound desperate, but safety in numbers always sounded like a good thing.

Yra shook her head. 'We all have our own paths to walk and my path does not follow yours, in the same way yours does not follow your friend's. They may cross occasionally, as ours does here. They may even cross again in the future. Who knows? For now, it is goodbye. Follow the light, now, and be on your way.' She smiled, bowed slightly, and then walked into the forest.

Addan was alone again, save for the ball of light, which swayed gently from left to right in the air. He had tried to see which way Yra went, but she seemed to walk behind a tree on one side, never to emerge from the other. She was gone.

'Well,' he said to the light as if it were alive, 'show me the way home.' The light continued to sway. It wasn't until he took a step towards it that it moved in any proper direction. The light led the way, always staying a steady distance ahead. If he stopped, so did the light. If he ran, the light moved at the same speed.

As he walked, he found himself talking to the light as it zipped around the trees and thick brush showing him where to go. 'This is all my fault. And I shouldn't have let Shara get involved. How was I supposed to know the gabbalins would follow us here? Why am I talking to you? It's not like you can understand me, is it?' He talked almost the entire way through the forest. It was preferable to silence, because that would mean he had to admit he was alone. He didn't like to be alone, not for long, anyway. Is that why he encouraged Shara to help

79

steal the stone with him? Not that she needed encouragement —that woman would do anything he suggested if it involved an element of danger. Her real life must be so dull, but she'd never let him see that side of her. And he'd learned a long time ago not to ask. He trusted her, and she trusted him. *I've let her down this time, though.*

As he tried to shake off his self-pity, he realised the area ahead of him looked familiar. The light had taken him all the way back to the bottom of the cliff and the path where they found that curious fox creature. Instantly, he felt like a heavy blanket had been lifted from him. He was no longer lost. The light seemed to realise as it faded into nothing, its job done.

'Thank you,' he said to the air. There was nobody to hear him.

The bridge looked different from the Dawan side and it took Addan a few moments to realise why. The arched entrance looked unfinished. No, unfinished wasn't the right word. It simply wasn't up to the same standard of design as the Moranzan end. There were no elaborate carvings in the stone, and if he had to guess, wasn't as tall either. He appreciated good design and expert stone craft, and this wasn't it. Not that it mattered now—he was home. Almost. He tried to block out the painful memories the bridge offered him and pressed forward.

Once he was around two-thirds the way across, he noticed the guards ahead. They were no longer asleep and were back on sentry watch. They hadn't seen him coming from behind as they watched over the city ahead of them.

As he approached the far side, he had a decision to make. Either engage with the guards and tell them how he came to be on the wrong side. That *would* be awkward to explain, but they would know if Shara had somehow made it here herself. If not, he might be able to persuade them to help find her. The alternative was to run as fast as he could through the archway, past the oblivious guards and down towards the city before they knew what was happening.

He weighed up his options, but in the end, he decided he was far too tired to run.

With a deep breath, he pulled himself tall and crossed the threshold with the manner of someone who had every right to be there. 'Good day to you, gentlemen. I'm looking for my friend. Have you seen her?'

All four guards turned on the spot towards him. The one to his far right was startled enough to let go of his spear, with the sharp end hitting the guard next to him on the shoulder before falling to the ground. The young guard hurriedly retrieved it, surrendering his dignity as he did so.

'Stay where you are and tell me how you got up here,' said the guard closest to Addan on the left, pointing his spear at his chest. The man was tall, well-built, and looked older than the other three. It was reasonable to assume this one was in command of the unit.

'I mean no harm,' said Addan, slowly raising his hands.

'Could be Dawanii,' said the guard who had dropped his spear. He had a shaved head, which made him look older than he probably was, and wore a vague, wispy beard on his chin.

'Doesn't look Dawanii,' said another guard. All four now had their spears trained on Addan.

'I promise you, I am not from Dawan. I'm from the city,' Addan nodded behind them.

'He could be lying,' said the bald one. 'We ain't let anyone across since it opened and there ain't any other way over, is there?'

'Speak the truth, boy,' said the leader. 'Your life depends on it.'

Boy! The man looked barely a year older than him. 'We snuck across the border when you were, ah, distracted. We were attacked by gabbalins, and my friend and I got separated, and now I'm trying to find her. Have you seen a young woman, about this high, reddish hair and brown eyes?'

'Gabbalins!' two of the guards said simultaneously, then spitting on the ground.

'We ain't seen no girl and ain't seen no gabbalins either. I say he's full of shit, sir.'

The leader narrowed his eyes. Addan could almost feel the man's stare burning through him. 'I'm not sure if this is some sort of prank or scam of some kind, but I do believe you're not Dawanii, and you're definitely not gabbalin. If you know what's good for you, you'll take this as a warning and be on your way.'

This wasn't going as Addan had hoped. He hadn't ever had cause to interact with the Queen's Guard before, but first impressions were they weren't as bright as the stories told, and seemed unwilling to listen. Still, they were marginally better than the Tal Valar. They would exhaust you with their preachings and *then* ignore what you had to say. If the guards weren't willing to help, and if they were truthful when they said they hadn't seen Shara, it meant she was still in Dawan somewhere. He *had* to find her, and he would do it alone.

'I have to find my friend,' Addan said, turning around to head back to Dawan. Before he'd taken two steps, he found his way blocked by spears.

'We can't let you do that, lad. Strict orders not to let anyone cross,' said the leader.

'But I've already *been* across. Let me through. I have to find her.'

'I said no, lad.' The lead guard used his free hand to grab Addan by the shoulder, face him towards the city, and gave him a shove.

'Please,' said Addan, as he stumbled to remain upright. 'I have to—'

The guard shoved him a second time with more force.

Addan fell to the ground, flat on his back. All four spears pointing at his face.

'All right, I get the message,' he said. He pushed one of the spears away. It was a stupid and dangerous thing to do in the heat of the moment. He was relieved when the guards withdrew enough to allow him to get up.

It was over. He was defeated. He felt cold and numb. There was nothing else he could do now except trudge his way to the city.

Shit!

6

AFTERMATH

It took Cal a few minutes after waking up to remember his mother was dead. For a brief while, everything was as it should have been. Then the new reality caught up with him. Liana was queen now, but she hadn't been seen since she shut him out of her room yesterday. After the initial turmoil following the assassination, he'd had one of the guards fetch her, but she wasn't there. Nobody saw her leave, and as far as anyone knew, she hadn't returned. He'd asked Shaan to wake him if she returned while he slept. Shaan had not woken him. The old queen was dead, and the new one was missing.

He sat up in his bed and wiped the sleep grit from his eyes. Emotions oscillated through his mind. Sadness, anger. *Fear.* What now for this country? For this city and his family. For him? He closed his eyes again and wept.

After a deep breath and a count of ten, he forced himself out of bed. Feeling his way in the dark, he found the curtains and threw them open. He winced as the new day burst into the room. It was still early—the moon was only now beginning to rise above the skyline. The bell must have chimed already, but he didn't remember hearing it. It likely woke him, though.

His bedchamber was sparsely furnished. A bed large enough to accommodate two people, a copper fronted wardrobe and a silver-plated wooden writing desk. The desk was a masterpiece of design, and far more lavish than he would have chosen for himself. It had been handed down through many generations and bequeathed to him by his late father. A rug, handmade by his grandmother, covered a decent amount of the stone floor. It was his favourite possession, despite it having worn thin with age.

There was a knock at the door. A short man with a receding hairline and a stoop entered without invitation. Cal hoped it was Shaan and his shoulders dropped when he saw it wasn't. The man carried a metal tray with Cal's morning meal. Toasted bread, some tea, and a small bowl of berries in various shades of greens and reds.

'Thank you. Please set it down on the bed, however, I don't feel that hungry this morning.'

'Very good, sir. Though I *do* recommend you eat at least some of it. Today will be a very... trying day, I feel.' The man's voice was quiet and soft.

Cal looked again out of the window and ummed in agreement. 'Liana?'

'Alas not, sir.'

'When are the dukes arriving?' In the absence of Liana, the Council, led by Tienn, had taken charge in the immediate aftermath. Tienn had sent messengers to Cal's cousins in Min Brai and Min Foar to inform them of the news and summon them to the city. Cal had tried to insist that as the only member of the senior royal family currently present, he should be the one making decisions, but he had been talked out of it. He relented —for the time being.

'I understand one of them is already here, and the other will arrive presently.'

'Have them wait in the reception hall. I will make my way

there when I'm ready. Please see to it they are made comfortable.'

'Sir, the Council has already made the necessary arrangements.'

Cal sniffed. 'I see. That will be all then.'

'Very good, sir.' The balding man left the room and closed the door behind him without making a sound.

Alone again with only his thoughts, he sat down on the edge of his bed and picked at the bread. It was over-toasted, but he liked it that way. He sipped his tea and ate two of the berries. Green ones; he didn't like the red ones. Despite never eating them, and on many occasions informing the staff he didn't like them, they brought him a bowl equally full of both green and red fruit every morning. He suspected someone in the kitchen didn't like him. He picked up one of the red berries and squashed it between his thumb and forefinger, and watched the sticky juices dribble down his hand and wrist. The juice stained the cuff of his white nightshirt.

He stood up, forcing himself away from the triviality of disliked fruit, and tried to focus on what lay ahead for him. He pulled his nightshirt off over his head and picked the blue fluff gathering in his navel. *Why was it always blue?* A slight paunch was developing around his waist. He stood straighter to disguise it, for no one other than himself. *Trivia. Concentrate. Get dressed. Be the man people need you to be.*

From inside the wardrobe, he pulled out a fresh black shirt, tunic, and pants and put them on, wrinkling his nose at the smell of the fabric. He combed his hair backwards until it was neat and straight before pulling on a pair of black leather boots. He was ready to face the day. Physically, at least. Mentally, he only wanted to shut out the world and stay in his room.

He almost had his hand on the door handle when there was another knock. He opened the door to find Shaan standing on the other side.

'Before you ask,' said Shaan, 'there is still no sign of your sister.'

'Does anyone outside the palace know?'

'Not yet, though I would not imagine it will take long before word spreads. If the people of the city realise they are without a queen, it could become a problem.'

Cal nodded in agreement as he closed the door behind him. The palace halls were quieter than yesterday. Not simply because there were fewer people about, but those who were in the corridors were in no mood for chatter and small talk. His favourite tamewolf, Star, was waiting for him outside his room, as he often did, and followed dutifully at his heel. Star was an old boy these days at nearly twenty years old and his age was showing. He was unsteady on his hind legs as he walked, and his long grey coat hid the scrawny body underneath. Star was more loyal than any man Cal had known, and he loved him.

The meeting hall was at the back of the palace. It was a cold room with damp walls frequented mostly by the Council. Cal had little cause to visit the room himself. He didn't much care for the Council. He found politics rather boring and best left to those who were actually employed to run the city. He often wondered if he'd have paid more attention to the machinations if he were heir and not his sister. Perhaps not. As a son of a queen, there wasn't really anywhere for him to go. Had he have been a cousin, a duke, he would have been given his own land to manage somewhere else in the realm. As a prince, he was simply expected to... be. And he resented it every day of his life.

The room fell silent as Cal, followed by Star and Shaan, walked in. The chattering and murmuring from within the room stopped as soon as they saw him, all except one—a small man wearing red. He had blond hair that looked more gold when matched against the colour of his tunic.

'... but of course, we are all very well aware he is more than just a friend, if you follow my...' The man stopped mid-

87

sentence, not because he saw Cal, but on account of the man seated next to him jabbing him in the ribs with his elbow.

The blond red-clothed man stood up awkwardly. His chair toppled backwards and clattered against the stone floor, the sound echoing off the bare stone walls. All the other men who were not already on their feet stood up. Tienn was there, of course, along with five other Council members. With Cal and Shaan, that made seven in total, plus Star, who padded off to a corner for a nap.

Cal motioned for them all to be seated as he took up the chair at the head of the table. Then everyone waited for the blond man to right his own chair and settle down while everyone stared at him with impatience.

Tienn was the first to speak. 'On behalf of all of us in the Council, may I offer our condolences for your loss.' He was so *loud*. The others all nodded with whispers of concurrence.

'Thank you, all. Now, would someone *please* explain to me how in the name of all the Architects was this allowed to happen?' demanded Cal. He looked at the faces sat around him at the table. They all looked in his direction but were avoiding eye-contact.

'We are at a loss, sir,' said a thin man with even thinner white hair. His eyes were cloudy with cataracts. Cal knew him as Scoble, the Queen's Chancellor. 'The Dawanii had not previously shown any inclination towards violence.'

'Who was our envoy to Dawan? Who met with them and arranged their visit?'

The blond man in red tentatively raised his hand. 'That would be me, sir. I was in charge of the party who first met with the Dawanii.'

Cal didn't recognise the man, and first impressions weren't the best. 'What is your name?'

'I am Humbold, sir. Duke of Min Brai—your cousin— though it has been many years since we last met. You were still a boy back then. I have experience with trade negotiations, and the queen requested me specifically.'

'Ah, yes indeed. Very well, tell me what you know.'

'When the bridge was completed, the queen ordered a small group of us to travel into what she called the Lost Realm, as per her vision. We reported back five days later, having found a small village in the south. Despite some quirky mannerisms and a proclivity to paint their hair, they came across as friendly. If I may say so, even a little *backward*.'

'And you did nothing to antagonise them. Inadvertently insult them, perhaps?' said Cal.

Humbold shook his head. 'No, sir. I thought the meetings we had together went very well. And they were very keen to come here to meet us.'

Something didn't sit right with Cal. 'So what went wrong?' He turned to Shaan. 'You met them when they reached the palace. Did anything seem out of place then? Did they say anything to you?'

Shaan leaned forward in his chair and waved his hand, elbow resting on the table. 'Aside from their early arrival, everything seemed in order. Six delegates as agreed. No apparent weapons. No provisions, either, though. I did think that a little strange. You would think they would have brought *something* with them. We searched their bodies, and aside from the two daggers, they carried nothing with them.'

The mention of the daggers took Cal back to that moment. The image of the six Dawanii standing before them was perfectly clear in his mind. He saw them reach inside their clothing and pull out the blades. Everything slowed down for him. He wanted to yell. He wanted to stop them, but he was powerless. The daggers flew forward from their hands and met their target in the blink of an eye. He forced his mind back. Before the blood, before the blades. He remembered their silence. The blank expressions on their faces as if there was nothing behind their eyes. He shivered.

'Sir? Are you all right?' shouted a voice.

Cal shook himself back into the room. The deadly scene returned to memory. He looked up. Tienn was trying to get his attention. He sat up in his chair. 'I'm fine.'

'Might I ask?' came a new voice from the end of the table. 'Where is Princess Liana, uh, I mean, the queen, Liana?' The voice belonged to another old man with as many wrinkles on his hands as his face.

Cal knew the man. His name was Furan, deputy to Tienn. As he looked at all the faces, it dawned on him how *old* they all were. Every member of the Council had to be approaching a hundred years old. His mother allowed these withering old farts to run her country. The parallel between the crumbling walls of the palace and these ancient advisors was not lost on him. *If I were queen...* he thought.

Cal looked at Shaan, who shook his head. 'We don't know. We have guards looking for her. We *do* have guards looking for her, right?' Shaan nodded silently.

'Have we heard from Queen Liana yet?' shouted Tienn. Furan leaned into Tienn and spoke. Tienn nodded in understanding. 'Most irregular. Most irregular indeed. That girl will be the death of us all.'

'The question is,' said Shaan, 'what do we do now? We have no queen. Our city, no, our *country,* has been attacked at its very heart. How do we respond?'

'Respond?' asked Cal.

'You cannot let this act of aggression go unanswered.'

All the other heads around the table nodded in agreement.

'Of course not, but it is not my place. Liana is the queen, even if she is not aware of it. Our first priority is to find her. Someone must know where she is, surely?'

A young man in Queen's Guard uniform entered the room.

Cal recognised him as the boy with the ill-fitting sleeves. It appeared the quartermaster had provided the lad with new attire. The boy saluted to everyone in the room before approaching Cal, saluting again. 'Sir, my humble condolences, sir. It's about the princess, queen, princess, Liana. Queen Liana.'

'You've found her?' asked Cal. The other men leaned forward in their seats, eager to hear what the boy had to say.

'Yes, sir. They believe so, sir. The Tal Valar report a woman matching her description, sir, with another man, sir. Yesterday, in a tavern by the tower. Fighting with gabbalins they were, sir.'

'Gabbalins?' gasped Tienn.

'Yes, sir,' the boy said, addressing Tienn. He turned back to Cal. 'The Tal Valar say, sir, she was last seen leaving the city in the direction of the new bridge, sir.'

'Alone or with this... other man?' Cal asked.

'I'm sorry, sir. The Tal Valar didn't say, sir.'

Cal thanked and dismissed the young guard, who bowed— several times—backward out of the room. Cal shook his head and rolled his eyes. Someone on the other side of the table stifled a snigger. He didn't see who.

'So, she's gone to Dawan,' said Furan. 'Why, in the name of all the Architects, would she do that?'

'The bridge is guarded,' stated Shaan. 'They would not have allowed her to cross.'

'Yesterday,' Cal mused. 'Was this before or after the Dawanii arrived, do you think?' He wasn't addressing anyone in particular. Nobody could give him an answer.

'It's a sorry state of affairs,' said Tienn loudly.

The youngest of the Council—still far older than Cal— spoke for the first time. 'This *affair* risks spiralling out of control.' His voice was gravelly and uneven. Cal remembered his name was Mett, but not what position he held within the Council. Huge earlobes, though. 'I propose that until she is found, the Council takes full charge of the city. We cannot descend into disarray. We need stability. Continuity.'

Everyone else around the table nodded in agreement. Not Shaan, though. 'Though he is not heir, Cal is still of royal blood. The Council should not have full autonomy.'

'I, uh, well,' fumbled Cal. Ever since he was old enough to understand his place in the world, he wished he would someday rule the country. That feeling only grew stronger as it became more evident that Liana didn't share the same ambition. But now, in this moment, it didn't feel right to him. He didn't feel ready to be a leader. It wasn't supposed to be like this. *Where is she?*

'Are you suggesting he should fulfil the role of queen in her absence?' asked Mett.

'A man cannot be queen,' said Scoble, almost laughing at the very notion.

'I did not say he should be queen,' said Shaan. 'I meant, I am of the opinion that the Council should not have unfettered authority.' His words were met with grumbles and the shaking of heads.

'We don't even have a word for a male queen. Throughout history, the Architects have always seen to it there is a female heir, and upon her mother's death, she shall be queen,' shouted Tienn after Furan caught him up on the parts he hadn't heard.

'The gabbalins are ruled by a man, if one could call him that,' interjected Humbold. 'As far as I can fathom, they have something akin to a royal family, and the man is known as king.'

Cal's mind was racing. 'I need some air,' he said, standing up. Everyone else stood up with him, the sound of chairs scraping echoed off the walls. 'I won't be long.'

Before anyone could object or say anything else, Cal exited the room and made for the nearest door that would take him outside the palace walls. He found himself in the garden. It was a large oval space in the middle of the palace grounds. A single tree, a moon-cedar, stood proudly at its centre. Around the perimeter ran a narrow pathway. The walls themselves were decorated with detailed carvings of figures, each representing one of the most revered and well-known Architects. Despite the high walls, the wind reached even here. The breeze felt good as he closed his eyes, head facing towards the sky.

After a few minutes, he took a deep breath and opened his eyes. Before him stood the carved stone likeness of Tieri—the Architect of Wisdom. She was depicted as a beautiful, yet elderly woman, with long hair that flowed to her waist. The artist who sculpted her was clearly talented. Her eyes did indeed seem to convey true wisdom as she looked down upon him.

'How can this be right?' he asked of her. 'Is this what you wanted? Yesterday, the world was as it should be. My mother was full of hope, her dream fulfilled. Today, you have taken that away from her, from all of us. Why? Tell me.

'The Tal Valar preach of your benevolence, your kindness. They teach us to be good people and to do your will and to follow you without question. Well, *I* question you! I demand to know *why!*' He fell silent for a moment, in thought. 'And what of my sister? Where is she? I pray you let her come home safe. I pray you give her the wisdom to see sense and take her place as queen. Because...

'Because I cannot begin to think what will become of us otherwise.' He wiped away the tears welling under his eyes. 'Ha. Look at me, standing here talking to a stone wall. Talking to *myself*. If mother saw me now, she'd laugh. She'd tell me to be a man and stop with the self-pity.'

'She would likely give you a slap for good measure, too.'

Cal turned to find Shaan standing behind him. 'How long have you been there?'

'Oh, not long.' With a wry smile, he opened his arms and stepped forward.

Cal immediately relaxed and accepted the hug from him. Right there, then, everything felt *manageable*. 'Do *you* have any words of wisdom for me?'

Shaan pulled back and took Cal firmly by the shoulders. 'You need to be strong. With Liana missing, the Council are positioning themselves to govern. You cannot allow that to happen.'

'We'll find her though, won't we? She'll show up as if nothing had happened. Then she will be queen.'

'Cal, you know as well as I do, she is not fit to be queen,' Shaan said, releasing his grasp. He moved his hands behind his back and slowly walked around the garden, looking at each of the Architects in turn. 'She does not even *want* it. She is irresponsible, immature. Not like you. She is not good for this country. Not as she is. Your mother had hoped Liana would grow into her responsibilities. Maybe with another decade or two...'

'So you're suggesting I take over as, what was the word Humbold used? As king? How would that even work? No man has ever ruled Moranza. The people wouldn't accept it and nor would the Council. By the Architects, the *Tal Valar* would be outraged.'

'The Council must not be allowed to take charge, either. These are difficult times, Cal, and you have one chance to make your mark. You need to go back to that room and show them you mean for the Tallan name to continue ruling. You need a demonstration of strength.'

'What sort of demonstration?'

'Retaliation against the Dawanii.'

'What sort of retaliation?'

'They attacked us, so it is only right and proper we attack them.'

Cal didn't like where this was going. 'You mean, invade Dawan. No. I won't.'

Shaan sighed with a frown. 'They killed the queen. They killed your mother.'

'I know, but you are talking about *war*. We don't have a proper army. We haven't needed one since the Division.' Cal paused, tapping his finger to his lips. 'We destroy the bridge. No more Dawanii threat, no war, no more killing.' It felt like an excellent solution to the problem and his spirits lifted. He stood taller and looked at the Architect of Peace, depicted on the wall as a curly-haired man wearing nothing but a sash.

'We cannot destroy the bridge.'

'Why not?'

'Not while there is a chance Liana has crossed into Dawan herself already.'

Cal's shoulders slumped. A sense of frustration washed over him and he found his anger at his sister renewed. 'I won't go to war. My priority is to find Liana.'

Silence fell between them both. Cal was grateful Shaan didn't push it any further, but he knew that change was coming. Whether Liana would take up the throne or not, things would never be the same. As he looked up at the Architects, he wondered what his role in the world would be from now on, and the more he thought about it, the more he felt taken by the idea of being the one to rule.

'Do you think they really do watch over us?' Cal said eventually.

'The statues?'

'Don't be obtuse. The *real* Architects.' He took Shaan's hand in his and held it tight. 'The Tal Valar say they are all seeing, all knowing. I wish I knew what was to come. What to do.'

'The Architects are many things to us all. Do they watch over us? Maybe. Are they all knowing? That, I cannot answer.'

'I wonder if they look like these sculptures. Personally, I

don't think they do. I've seen sketchings in my mother's books and some of them look nothing like these.'

'They are an *interpretation*, I would say. It is more about... what they represent.'

'That one has your nose,' Cal joked, pointing at the carving of the Architect of Ruination—a stern looking bearded man with accentuated muscles. The artist had him holding a staff originally, but the top section had weathered away with age.

'I feel as though I should be offended. Come, the Council are still waiting. Remember what I said.'

The members of the Council were still sitting in their respective seats, talking amongst themselves when Cal and Shaan returned. Scoble was writing something down and closed the metal protective plates around the paper when he saw them enter. They all fell silent as if to hide a conspiracy.

Tienn spoke first. 'We have all concurred that in the absence of Queen Liana, that it be wise that all matters and decisions of state be properly executed and otherwise decided upon by the Council.' He looked at the others who all nodded back in agreement.

Cal hadn't even taken his seat properly. He exchanged glances with Shaan before rising to his feet again. 'Is that so?'

'We advised your late mother on all manner of matters. She placed her trust in us to assist in ruling over Moranza. Therefore, the prudent way forward is to keep a certain... continuity. Once the new queen is safely located, we're certain she will wish us to guide her reign in the same vein as your mother did.'

'No,' said Cal. His tone was sharp, direct. Authorial.

'Pardon me?' said Scoble, pulling the metal folder closer to his chest.

'The late queen, my mother, gave the Council too much latitude. She was too obsessed with her books to see what's been happening in the real world. The city is falling apart. This *palace* is falling apart and I say no more. You serve your own interests over those of the people. I will not stand for it. I am taking back control for this family. I may not be heir, but I am of royal blood. Until our new queen returns, all decisions will come through me. Is that understood?'

He could feel the heat in his face and his blood was pumping. He watched the look on their old wizened faces, the colour draining from their cheeks. It felt *good*. He looked at Shaan, who was smiling approvingly.

'I, ah, well, this is most irregular, I, um...' said Tienn, who definitely heard what was said *that* time.

'I said, is that *understood?*' Cal leaned forward with palms on the table for added effect. It worked. Shaan was right, the world needed to change, and that started with him. His first priority was to find his sister, and quickly. The longer she was missing, the more unstable the situation would become. 'I want every guard out looking for Liana. Please see that the Tal Valar are informed and tasked with the same. I want her found by the end of the day. Do I make myself clear?'

Every one of the Council nodded in wide-eyed awe, dumbfounded and intimidated. He liked how that felt. He doubted if any of them had been stood up to like that. Change was in the air and it terrified him, but that was a secret only for himself.

7

AN AWAKENING

I t took a while for Liana's eyes to focus when she woke up. It felt like she was... moving. As if she was being carried. No, not carried. Her surroundings were a blur—moving shapes of green and white. The wind was much colder than she was used to, and the ground beneath her felt rough and uneven. Whatever she was on jostled her, and every bump vibrated through her entire body. She rubbed at her eyes with the backs of her hands, forcing them to see. Concentrate. Focus! Slowly, the fog lifted. Her mind felt heavy, like something was pushing down on it from the inside.

It was as though she was riding on the back of a carriage, such was the discomfort. Turning her head to the left, she was surprised to see she was barely three fingers off the ground. More surprising was that the ground was dusted with snow. The sky above her, from what of it was visible through the trees, was dark. It wasn't the same as the dark right after moonset; unfamiliar and more... mauve. She turned her head to the right, and there, walking alongside her, was a cinder-fox. Startled by the sight of the animal, she shifted away from it instinctively and fell into the snow. She scrambled backwards to put some distance between them. It stopped, sat down on its hind legs and watched her, mouth open as if smiling.

Whatever it was she'd been carried on came to a stop a dozen paces ahead. It was a crudely put together bundle of tree branches laid flat like a bed of sorts. Her vision was still a little hazy, but there was definitely someone at the other end of a rope attached to the ride.

'She wakes!' said the figure. The voice sounded young. Not a child's voice, but not an adult either. A young man, almost still a boy. He sounded pleased.

Liana's head was pounding. 'What happened? Who are you?' She didn't know whether to be more wary of the cinderfox or the boy. She tried to keep both in her sight, which wasn't easy.

'I am not hurting her. She will not be afraid. I see. I see her being chosen. She is important.' The boy approached her. He had a wide smile and wild dark hair, half of it painted red. His eyes were almost copper and just as bright. He wore a dark grey, well-fitted fur coat and leggings like the ones the—

'Dawanii,' she said, looking around hurriedly to see if there were others.

'Yes, and I am not hurting her. I am happy as you are no more asleep. One turn of the moon, you will slumber. Too much sleep and I will worry.'

'You talk funny.'

'I will help you from the bad men.'

Bad men? What bad men? Am I in danger here? As far as she could tell, they were alone. Only her, the boy and the cinderfox. She wondered if it was the same one that saved her and Addan from the direwolf, but decided it couldn't be, as it was much smaller. Although...

'The bad grey men will attack us and we will fight back. I will hide, as I am scared. You want to save the holy man. You

99

will not save him.' The boy's smile melted and his eyes looked sad.

And then she understood. He was talking as if it were the future, but he was describing what had happened. That was the last thing she remembered—trying to save that old man's life. If she interpreted the boy's words correctly, she had failed. She slumped backwards on her elbows. It was only then she realised how cold, and wet, the ground was.

'The old man died then,' she whispered.

'You will not save him, but you will save *him*. I shall see.'

'What does that mean?'

The boy offered his hand to help her stand up. His left hand. She noticed he was protecting the other, as though it were injured. Then she remembered. This young man was the one who had put his hand in the fire, screaming in agony. It was a sound she would never forget. She accepted the invitation and pulled herself to her feet. Immediately she felt dizzy, and it took a minute to steady herself with the help of his arm. She caught a glimpse of his injured hand. It didn't *look* burnt. She'd seen skin burns before—red, angry and often with peeling skin. It looked unharmed. Except. Except there was a mark on the palm. It was a strange circular wound of blackened skin with a red edging. She realised it was painful for him. She reached out with her own hand, gesturing for a better look, but he pulled it away.

'I'm sorry,' she said softly. 'My name is Liana. What's yours?' For now, it was probably better not to mention she was anyone of importance.

'Uehan,' he replied proudly.

'Ew... eh han,' she tried.

He shook his head with a giggle. 'Uehan.'

'You an.'

'Yes, my name will be Uehan, and you will be Liana. I will be happy to meet you.'

'And who is your friend?' She nodded toward the cinderfox, which was still sitting in the snow, watching her every move.

'She will follow Liana from the camp. She will stay with you. She will think you special. Protect you.' Uehan stroked the cinderfox behind the ears, which she seemed to enjoy. The gentle blue flame in her fur danced under his fingers.

'Does the fire not burn you when you do that?'

He chuckled and shook his head. 'What you will think as fire will not be fire. Energy. You will touch it and it will be cold.' He gestured for her to touch the animal.

Uehan was right. It *looked* like fire, albeit blue and not the yellow and orange flames she had always known. However, it was as he said—cold. It felt like nothing more than running her hand through the wet steam of a hot bath. The flames wafted and gave way between her fingers as she ran her hand carefully along the cinderfox's back. The fur was softer than she'd expected; more akin to a baby rabbit.

'Does she have a name?' Liana asked. The cinderfox licked her arm. She was falling in love with the creature, which surprised her a little. She'd never had a close bond with an animal before, and didn't have a pet as a child. That was more her brother's thing. He'd always had a few tamewolves, as their father had done, but she'd never really taken to them.

'You will choose a name. The cinderfox will follow Liana. She will be hers.'

She had never given anything a name before. Sure, she'd come up with a few rude names for Cal when she was younger, but this was different. It seemed like a lot of responsibility. After pondering for a moment, she said, 'I will call her... Ember.' The cinderfox cocked her head to one side, as if approving of her new name.

'Come,' said Uehan. 'We will go now.'

Liana's thoughts snapped back to her situation. She was alone with a stranger and, somehow, a new pet. Only the Architects would know where she was, or how far that was from home. She didn't feel as though she was in any danger, for the time being at least. And this young man, Uehan, was taking her somewhere, presumably to his people. Would she be safe there? She knew nothing about the Dawanii. *Well, I always wanted a real adventure, so I guess this is it.* "Be careful what you wish for," her mother had once told her.

She wondered if she should feel scared. Was that the normal thing? She thought about Addan and hoped he found his way back to Moranza and escaped that last gabbalin. 'Where are we going?' she asked.

Uehan was already walking. He'd abandoned the sled he'd used to pull her along with. She supposed it was redundant now she was awake and able to walk on her own. He wasn't carrying anything else, as far as she could tell. No supplies. No food or water. He said nothing, simply waving his good hand, beckoning her to follow.

They walked through the forest along a path that appeared to have been walked by many others before them. Ember kept up, barely a step behind her. The air grew colder the farther they went, and the sky was *still* dark. If it wasn't for the contrasting white of the snow, she likely wouldn't be able to see much at all. It was only then, as she was paying more attention to her surroundings, she noticed the trees themselves had their own light. Yellow-white spots wrapped around the trunks, spilling onto the ground and foliage around them, glowed gently as they walked. Only the closest ones, though, as if as a reaction to their proximity. The trees farther ahead, and the ones behind, appeared normal. Closer inspection revealed the spots to be insects, their bellies glowing as if lit by a fire within them. Hundreds of tiny bugs, all reacting to their footsteps as they walked, lighting the way. Liana smiled to herself as she took in the novelty.

She pulled her arms around her chest, trying to keep warm

as best she could, but she couldn't stop the shivering. Uehan didn't look cold at all, not with his layers of fur. She concluded that because of his attire, it was always cold here. She looked at Ember with jealous eyes. Oh, how she wished for fur of her own. Dawan was nothing like back home. The only thing the same was the wind. Here, though, it stung her face and made her eyes water.

The heavy feeling inside her head wouldn't go away. The fogginess she had felt when she first came to had passed, but it still felt like something inside was pressing on her mind. She tried to find the last thing she could remember. The old man lying near the fire. The voice! There was a voice. "Save me," it had said. And then nothing. No—not nothing. Something else. She fought hard to remember that last moment. Blue. Everything turned blue, and then to black. *What happened?* Frustration gnawed away at her. Her right palm itched as she tried to think, and she scratched at it with her thumb.

'Can you tell me what happened when the...,' what did he call him? 'When the holy man died?'

'You will not save him. I will see you save *him.*'

'What does that mean? I don't understand.' She wasn't only frustrated with herself. She looked down at the cinderfox. 'I don't suppose you know anything? Ember simply kept on walking.

The farther they went, the darker it got. The sky lost its purple hue, and the canopies of the trees lost their definition in the darkness. Birds had stopped singing, and she wondered how long it had been before she'd noticed. Uehan wasn't much of a talker, though he did like to hum as he walked. Strange melodies that didn't appear to have any structure or rhythm to them. She couldn't tell if they were actual songs, or if he was making it up as he went. Every time she tried to press him on what happened to her, he only repeated the same words over and over. In the end, she gave up, resigned to following him wherever he was going.

'Can we stop for a while?' she asked, reaching the end of her stamina. It felt like they had walked forever, and she was both hungry and cold.

Uehan turned to her and shook his head. 'We will be arriving.'

She bent over, resting her hands on her knees. *How much farther?* The dizziness was returning and her head felt so, so heavy. 'I need to rest.'

'We will be arriving. You will see.' He pointed ahead, jabbing his finger with a pleased look on his face.

'Do you mean we *have* arrived?'

Uehan nodded vigorously, still pointing ahead.

She felt a sense of relief which helped her shake off the dizziness enough to find the strength to move forwards. If they had truly reached their destination, she could surely manage a few more paces. She willed her feet to carry her on. Uehan must have noticed her struggling as he came back and tucked his head under her arm, helping her to stay upright for the last few steps.

Liana was unprepared for what she saw. The woodland gave way to a vast network of strangely shaped buildings of varying sizes stretching out in front of her, nestled at the foot of a mountain that almost touched the sky itself, with sharp twin peaks surrounded by a ring of wispy cloud. Stone and wood were fused together like the patterns in marble. No two structures were the same. Some of the wooden ones looked like the trees themselves had been melted and then moulded into liveable dwellings.

Above her head were countless more, blown out of tall trees like bubbles, all interconnected with precarious rope and wood walkways. The buildings, if that was the right word for them, continued for some distance up the side of the mountain.

'Is this where you live?' she asked.

'I will live here.' She took that as a "yes."

As they walked slowly through what appeared to be a central thoroughfare, with Uehan still supporting her, she noticed a growing number of residents all trying to get a look at her—the stranger in their midst. She'd never seen a Dawanii before she crossed the bridge, so she reasoned they had never seen a Moranzan before either.

Some stopped and stared. One or two ran away back into the hut they'd come out from. Above, one stopped in the middle of the rickety walkway to observe the sight below. Several small children approached, curious and eager. One of them pulled on her shirt and laughed. It was almost mocking, in a way. Every one of them wore the same snug-fitting furs. A simple, loose shirt must look odd to them, especially given how cold it was here. She shivered as she thought about it.

She was feeling uneasy. Not through fear, but self-conscious of being the centre of attention for so many people. If she had to guess, more than a hundred pairs of eyes were upon her. Of course, being a princess and heir to the throne meant she drew her fair share of attention during public events back home, but never to this extent. It was always the queen who everyone admired, and she was content with that. Here, though, all the attention was hers, and hers alone.

Through the noise of dozens of voices around her, one broke through clearer than the rest. *'Can you hear me?'* It was only a whisper, but it was distinct from all the others. She recognised it immediately—it was the same voice she had heard in the clearing; the one asking to be saved.

'Can you hear me?' came the voice again. She looked around for the source, but found nothing. None of the Dawanii looked like they were talking *to* her or trying to get her attention. They were all only interested in the spectacle of her. None of them

were all that bothered by Ember, though. Cinderfoxes weren't novel here, it seemed.

She allowed Uehan to guide her along the path carved by well-trodden snow. The gatherers moved out of their way as they progressed. The Dawanii all looked quite similar to each other. There was no discernible difference in their attire, aside from the naturally varying patterns of their furs. Much like her own people, there were a multitude of skin colours, though most of them were paler, on average, than most Moranzans. Their hair was their most unusual feature. All without exception had exactly half their heads dyed a bright red. Some the left half, others the right side. Their natural hair colour appeared to be a light brown, allowing for some variation. She wondered what cultural significance the colouring had, and how strange her own single-toned hair must seem to them.

'*Can you hear me?*' The voice again. It was almost as if it were *inside* her head. Her mind could be playing games with her. Starve a person and drive them insane, someone had once told her. She couldn't remember when she last ate.

'*Can you hear me?*'

'Yes, I can hear you,' she offered.

'I was not going to speak,' said Uehan.

'Sorry, I wasn't talking to you.' There was no other reply from the voice.

Uehan directed her left at a junction and up the steps of a dwelling slightly larger than the ones either side of it. The walls were curved, bowing outwards. The lower part was mostly stone that looked like it had been stretched up from the ground like you would with wet clay. Gradually, the stone turned to wood in a haphazard way. Liana shivered, and her head pounded as she tried to take it all in. Uehan pushed away an animal skin covering a gap in the wall like a curtain over a window, and led her inside, leaving the growing audience to continue with their day. Ember was still by her side.

The first thing Liana noticed was a roaring fire at the far end of the room. Its warmth filled the air, and it looked so, so inviting. She released herself from Uehan's arms and almost ran to the flames. Fire was something she had learned to fear all her life, but she was not afraid of this one. It called to her, welcoming her away from the cold outside. She fell to her knees on a small patch of rug by the hearth and held out her hands, the flames almost licking her fingers as they danced on the burning wood.

The feeling in her hands slowly returned. She started to sway from side to side. Her head pounded as the icy feeling in her bones subsided. It felt like her mind was being stirred with a giant heavy spoon, like soup in a bowl. A yelp from behind her snapped her back into focus.

'Three moons gone by! Where have you been? And who is this stranger in my home?'

Liana shuffled on her knees away from the fire to see who the voice belonged to. A broad, short woman stood near a table with a rag hung over her shoulder. Her hair had the same colouring as Uehan's, though tied back behind her ears. She wore a dark grey fur with flecks of white, cut at the elbows showing thick forearms. She did *not* look happy.

'I will find the girl and bring her home. She will try to save the holy man, but she will fail,' he said, hanging his head forward. He was standing in front of the woman, a good head shorter than she was.

'Oh no, no, no! What have you done?' The woman grabbed him by the shoulders in distress, crushed him against her bosom and then held him out at arm's length again. She stared into his eyes, her own showing great worry.

'I shall take the Branding. I will allow the Architects to choose.'

'You silly boy! Why? Why would you do such a thing? You know it is forbidden. This was not your path. Now look at you.'

107

She turned to Liana, glaring. 'Is this you? Did you do this to him? What are you doing in my house? You are not Dawanii! Who *are* you?' Her face grew more flushed with every question.

'I, ah, no.' Liana struggled to find the right words. She thought it best she stood up away from the fire, just in case she needed to run. Her legs were stiff, and she rose awkwardly.

'I shall help her,' protested Uehan. He fought against the woman, trying to push himself free. 'She will save the holy man. She will save *him*, and I shall help her.'

His words did little to calm her.

It then became apparent to Liana that his way of speaking was not the norm for these people. The woman's reaction told her something was wrong with him.

Another figure appeared through the doorway. It was another young man, perhaps a little older than Uehan. The resemblance between them was evident. Brothers. A family, though no sign of a father figure yet.

'Why are you shouting?' asked the newcomer, scratching his head. He didn't immediately notice Liana as she stood uncomfortably near the fire.

'Your brother. Your irresponsible brother had taken the Branding, and it's broken him.'

'Uehan, in the Architects' name, that right is mine!' he shouted, his turn to be angry now. He stormed over to Uehan and grabbed the hand with the burn on it. 'The Brand of Foresight. Why would you do this?'

'I shall allow the Architects to choose. I will see beyond.'

The brother threw Uehan's hand, letting it drop to his side, and turned away. He looked right at Liana. She had never seen such anger.

'Who is this?' he demanded, his breathing heavy.

His demeanour made her feel uneasy. As far as she could tell, the only way out was through the same door she came in through, and the three of them were blocking the way. She took half a step back. 'I'm sorry. I don't wish to intrude. Uehan there saved my life. He brought me here. I would have been lost otherwise.'

The brother's posture relaxed slightly. Ember yawned with a tiny squeak as she watched on from near Liana's feet.

'Do you know what happened to him?' the woman asked.

'Yes, but I'm not sure I understand it.'

The woman must have sensed Liana's apprehension. 'Please, do not be afraid. If you speak the truth, then you are welcomed here as a friend. Your companion there,' she indicated Ember, 'would not be by your side if you meant us harm.'

Liana was invited to sit down at a table near the wall to her left. It looked ever so slightly off level, and shaped rather than cut. Four basic wooden chairs with low backs were tucked around it. None were plated, she noticed, and they didn't look comfortable to her either. She did as she was directed and took the seat nearest to her. Ember followed and laid down at her feet.

Their home was simple and sparsely furnished, with the fire as the only focal point. There were no paintings or tapestries to decorate the walls which looked the same inside as they did outside. There was a food preparation area in one corner with an array of utensils made of copper. Various cuts of vegetables, only a few of which Liana recognised, lay on a wooden bench.

The woman took up another chair and smiled for the first time. It was a weak smile, one forced to hide her pain. 'Now, tell me what you saw.'

Liana took a deep breath and recounted everything she could about what she saw until the point where she blacked out. She only briefly described the deaths of both the gabbalins and the Dawanii, deciding that such a level of detail wasn't required for her story. Uehan, who remained standing with his brother, nodded throughout. The woman listened without interruption until she finished what she had to say.

The woman said nothing for a minute or so. The only sound was the gentle crackle of the fire behind them. She briefly closed her eyes and lowered her head contemplatively. 'Thank you for sharing with us. My name is Helela, and this is my eldest son, Aranan.'

'Hello,' Liana replied, unsure how else to respond. She'd already introduced herself by name at the start of her story and fought the uncomfortable urge to do so again.

'What you bore witness to,' said Helela, 'was our most sacred of ceremonies. Sadly, it was unsanctioned. Uehan is not the eldest child, thus he was not permitted to undergo the Branding.' She looked at her son. He looked ashamed and didn't make eye contact with her. 'Only the first born in each family may participate in the Branding if they so choose. He has stolen that choice from Aranan. If he survives, he will be punished.' Her voice grew quiet on those last few words.

'Survives?' repeated Liana. Her eyes widened as she looked at her new friend with worry.

'The Branding is a delicate ceremony, only performed by our most high-standing and wisest elders. Uehan chose to undergo the ritual illegally and performed by people who are little more than charlatans. As you can hear from the way my son talks now, his mind is broken.'

'I'm not sure I understand.'

'He stole my birthright,' said Aranan. 'And he will most likely die because of it. He chose the Stone of Foresight. It grants the gift of knowing what is to come, to see the future. In return, as tribute, he surrenders his eyes to the Architects. Yet he can still see, and now he is trapped in his own past, foreseeing only what has already been. It will slowly get worse and his mind will burn inside him.'

'That's awful. Can't you do anything for him?' Liana asked as she looked at Uehan. She had barely known him, but she felt bad for him.

'It is not for us to decide. It is in the hands of the Architects now. They will determine if he is worthy of the gift he has *stolen*.'

Liana nodded slowly. The Architects were revered in Moranza almost universally. The Tal Valar ensured that. People prayed to them, either as routine, or in times of great need—or both. There were places people would gather to offer gifts and ask to be blessed or forgiven for their wrongdoings. The Tal Valar encouraged humility before the Architects, but even they had nothing even close to a Branding ritual. From what she had seen with her own eyes, and what this family was telling her, it sounded horrific.

'I should really go now,' she said. 'It is clearly a bad time for you, for your family, and I am intruding. If you would please have a map of some kind, so that I may find my way back home. I'm sorry to say I have rather lost my bearings.'

'You must stay,' said Helela. 'You are witness. You must testify to the elders. If there is any hope for them to help my son, they will first need to hear you tell your story.'

Liana thought for a moment. There wasn't any reason for her *not* to stay. Her head still felt heavy, and she was still tired. *Perhaps I'm coming down with a cold.* 'I guess I could stay for a while. Might it please be possible to have a little something to eat or drink? My head feels...'

'Are you unwell?' asked Helela.

'Since I woke up in Uehan's company, my head... I can't describe it, really. It just feels...'

'She will not save him. She shall save *him*,' said Uehan softly.

'I don't know what he means,' said Liana. 'He keeps saying things like that, and it bothers him.' There was a flash inside her head, like the zap of an eel. A sudden burst of pain, only for an instant, leaving only the dull heavy feeling that persisted. Her attention was drawn to Aranan. He was standing behind his mother and brother, arms folded across his chest. Looking at him, she felt something, in the single moment after the flash. An intense notion of... anger? No, that wasn't it. Loathing—she felt *loathing* from him, not for her but for Uehan. It was a strange sensation, one that almost felt like she was inside *his* head. And then it was gone. The mental image faded away like a dream half-remembered.

'Look—she's lost all the colour in her cheeks,' said Helela. The woman bent down in front of Liana and touched the back of her hand to her brow. 'You're burning up. I believe you require one of our healers.' Helela turned to Aranan and told him to find one at once.

Liana wanted to protest, but had too little energy left to argue. Aranan grumbled under his breath, but did as he was asked. His brother only stood in the middle of the room, uttering words to himself over and over.

Aranan returned almost as soon as he'd left, so far as Liana could tell. Maybe it was longer than that, she wasn't sure. Behind him were at least four other people, perhaps five. The fog in her vision returned, and their shapes blended together a little. One of them was definitely much shorter than the others. He seemed to be missing some hair. She could tell that much. A streak of brown over one ear, red over the other. He was balding. Liana was fighting hard to concentrate. The man spoke some words she didn't understand and then cupped his hands around her ears. She tried to pull away, but his grip was tight.

Amid her struggling, she felt as though something was being forced into her mouth, yet there was nothing there. The short man still had his hands firmly on the side of her head, but something was making her gag. She became aware of a bitter taste at the back of her throat, like she'd swallowed something rancid. The bitter taste evolved into a feeling, a warmth, which spread to her chest and radiated outwards through her body. A moment later and the fog in her eyes and the heaviness in her mind abated, but not completely. Her muscles relaxed, and she stopped struggling.

The bald man hummed briefly as if satisfied, stood up and took a couple of steps backwards. 'This will work for now, however, possibly not for too long. I can't say for certain. I have to say, I am relieved it worked at all on someone such as... her.' The man had a nasal tone to his voice, which did little to mask his smugness.

Liana pulled herself straight in her chair, suddenly conscious of the number of eyes all looking at her. She felt like one of those fish her mother kept in a glass box in her study. It was not a comfortable feeling. 'What did you do to me?' The bitter taste lingered on her tongue.

The man simpered and said, 'it's for the best you do not know. It would probably do you more harm than not.'

'Where did she come from?' asked one of the others. A woman, aged somewhere between her and Helela, Liana guessed. The woman had delicate features with a hint of age lines around the corner of the eyes that became slightly more pronounced when she smiled.

'She comes from the Old Land,' said Helela. Liana hadn't heard it called that before.

'I am from Moranza.'

Helela tilted her head to one side a little. 'Yes, the Old Land. This is Dawan, the New Land. Once, we were all as one. A long time ago. And then came the Great Separation, and we became two. The calamity of our ancestors, a dark time of our past.' She paused for a moment, thoughtful, and then smiled. 'We are cousins then, I think.' The others gathered around her all nodded agreeably. Then, in unison and without a word said, their attention turned to Uehan.

Liana watched the bald man hobble over to the young man, who was still muttering to himself, oblivious to the goings on around him. The man pulled Uehan down to his knees and, with his hands on the boy's shoulders, and examined him as if checking for lice. He manhandled Uehan, pushing and pulling his head this way and that. Prodding, poking. There was no protest or objection. The boy simply stared ahead, uttering his words over and over.

'Yes, yes... huhum. It is as I thought. His Branding has gone wrong. Terribly, terribly wrong indeed.'

'Can anything be done?' asked Helela, wringing her hands, her knuckles turning white.

The animal skin door slapped loudly against the wall, which made Liana start. Aranan had left without saying a word.

'I'm sorry to say, but no, I don't think there is. What is done cannot be undone.' The man said, leaving Uehan to his madness.

'What about completing the Branding? Is that something we can do?' asked Helela. She went to her son and pulled him in tightly to her.

The gathered people huddled close together and talked amongst themselves. Liana watched on from her seat, unsure if she should do anything. She decided to stay quiet and observe.

The huddle broke and the woman with the smile spoke first. 'The consensus is, it will not save him.'

Helela made the tiniest of sounds, almost a squeak, her eyes becoming wet.

'However,' the woman said. 'Leaving him as he is will no less benefit him, either. Therefore, we have concluded that it is for the best that we try.'

Uehan briefly stopped his uttering, seemingly taking in what he'd heard, but his expression changed. He went from docile child fool to frenetic insanity in less than the blink of an eye. He stormed over to Liana. She pushed herself back in her chair, such was the speed of his advance. He stopped short of her and leant in and looked her right in the eyes, his breath hot on her face. Her heart pounded. She wasn't able to escape.

'You have chosen!' he shouted at her frantically. 'The storm comes and the girl will die. He cannot save her. He cannot save them all. He walks alone, and she will save him. Her life is given, else all is lost!'

Liana was frozen still, her hands gripping the seat of her chair. The boy was frightening her. The healer moved forward to intervene, but the boy had stopped shouting. Uehan stood up straight and stared at the wall behind her, his face vacant and expressionless.

And the girl will die.

8

DRUNK

There is a fine line between falling asleep when you're tired, and passing out from sheer exhaustion. Addan woke, screaming from a nightmare. A hundred Queen's Guard attacking him, killing him as punishment for failing Shara. He felt as though every one of those hundred spears burrowing into his chest were deserved. It *was* his fault. He had to do something to help, but what? His only way to her was blocked, and now his face was known to the guards. There had to be another way.

He was unsure how long he'd been asleep. He wasn't rich enough to own a timepiece, so had to rely on the moon to keep track of the day like the majority of people. There was the bell of the Moonwatch Tower, of course, but that only rang out three times a day. It wasn't so much of a problem if one kept to a proper routine of work, but he didn't even have that at the moment. He'd never felt so tired. He was almost certain it was only the next day, but for all he knew, he could have slept for three days or longer.

He got out of his straw bed and stretched out his aching body. The black scar on his thigh proved he hadn't dreamt it all.

He massaged the still-painful gnarled pink and brown scar that ran from his ankle up to the back of his calf, behind his knee on his right leg. It never hindered him too much, but was a permanent reminder of how reckless childhood could be.

His home was a single room with next to nothing else in it except for his bed and two other sets of clothes. Once, they had been expensive and well-tailored. Now, they were old and nearly threadbare, and he lacked the money to replace them. He no longer had a job, not since the incident with his brother, but at least he didn't have to share his home with anyone. He'd lived that life. Twenty other men and women to a larger room, all fighting over the tiny amount of space they tried to call their own. They were the truly poor; barely one foot above the destitute.

His room was one of around forty others in a complex behind a tavern. All of them were single occupancy, filled with all manner of people. He knew of stoneworkers, like he used to be, farmhands and even a librarian. They all mostly kept themselves to themselves, unless they were in the tavern. So long as you had money, everyone was your friend there. He pulled out the broken chain and piece of gemstone. As his hand trembled, he examined the chain and decided it wasn't worth enough to settle his debts. *How much would the stone be worth now?* Nothing, most likely. The chain would buy him a few drinks, though, and a drink felt like a good idea right now. He fashioned a new necklace from an old leather shoelace and hung the stone around his neck. A reminder of Shara.

The tavern was partially underground. Carved out from the dense sandstone almost as an afterthought when the complex above had been built. There were other rooms above the tavern reserved for travellers and patrons who found themselves too drunk to find their way home safely, if at all. Those and the rest of the complex were owned by the same man, and that man owned the tavern.

Addan carefully descended the steps and was met by a throng of people. If it were this busy, that meant it was after the third bell, he decided. Nobody seemed particularly drunk, so it wasn't too late in the day either. Over on the right was the performers' area, home to four women playing a gentle melody. A song he'd heard a thousand times before. He hated that song, but the woman singing the words was at least in tune.

The bar was to his left, with the owner behind it busy serving drinks to thirsty customers filling the eight seats that lined it. The rest of the room was a mix of full and nearly full metal-plated tables of an octagonal design, with several alcoves along the far wall. These alcoves were, more often than not, occupied by men looking to make a little extra money on the side, sometimes even legally, and valued a little more privacy.

'You're still behind on your rent,' growled the man behind the bar when he saw Addan approaching. He was a tall, scrawny man with greasy hair and greasy skin to match. He wore a simple white shirt with the sleeves rolled up. It was speckled with wet beer stains and something else, but Addan didn't want to know what.

'Yes, Yawl, I know. I've been distracted lately. I'll settle up with you soon, I promise.' He squeezed himself between two sweaty men sat on stools to reach the bar. 'I'll have an ale.'

'Only if you have the money. Behind on your rent, and also on your tab.'

Addan sighed and pulled out the broken chain from his pocket, and placed it on the bar. The bar top was made from a pale soapstone that reflected what little light there was around the room. 'It's all I have right now.'

Yawl examined the chain. 'Half your tab and one ale. Take it or leave it.'

Addan nodded reluctantly and the chain disappeared into Yawl's pocket before serving a tankard of dark brown ale.

He sat and stared at his drink. He held the tankard with

118

both hands and watched as the bubbles frothed and burst at the top. His hands were always steadier when holding something. Conversations rattled on around him and he paid no attention. Shara was the only thing on his mind. No matter how he looked at it, there was nothing he could do for her. It pained him to think that he might never see her again. His mind kept churning over the same thoughts, repeating themselves in his mind, gradually getting worse with each pass.

After an hour, he'd still not touched his drink. He wanted it, yet didn't want it. He continued to stare, the bubbles long having faded away. In his mind, she was dead now. The worst-case scenario his mind taunted him with. Eaten by a direwolf. Attacked by more gabbalins they hadn't seen. Fallen down a hole in the ground. He even considered a swarm of dragons burning her to death. He couldn't stop his thoughts. The tankard wobbled in his hands as he brought it to his lips. The liquid was warm and bitter. He swallowed half of it, and then the rest. He didn't want it. He set the tankard down too hard and the handle cracked between his fingers.

'You'll have to pay for the breakage,' Yawl said.

The man didn't miss a trick, did he? 'Add it to what I owe, and I'll have another ale.' Addan barely looked up.

'No money, no ale.'

Addan sniffed and shook his head. He was out of money and out of ideas. What now for him? He didn't care. He stared at the empty tankard and continued to ignore the noise around him.

'... and another ale for the lad, here.' The tail end of a sentence that barely registered with Addan, but when a fresh tankard of ale—with a full complement of bubbles—slid his way, he looked up.

Sat beside him was a man old enough to be his father. With a beard more grey than brown, and thick hairy arms resting on the bar, the man nodded once. Addan had never seen him before, but gladly accepted the drink from this stranger. 'Thank you.'

'Looks like you needed another.'

Addan offered half a smile. Reaching for the tankard and taking a mouthful was a lot easier than the first. Too easy. 'I'm unable to buy you one in return.'

'I didn't expect you to. Simply the kindness of one stranger to another. The name's Joeh.'

Addan gave him his name and thanked him again for the ale. Yawl watched from the other side of the bar, making himself look busy and uninterested, but Addan knew that look. He shifted in his seat towards Joeh so Yawl was out of view.

'I lost my friend,' Addan said, unprompted. Something compelled him to talk to the man. 'I don't know where she is, or if I will see her again. My own fault. I should never have let her get involved, or got mixed up with the gabbalins, or stol— I mean, ah, I don't know. It all got out of hand.'

'We all have our regrets,' said Joeh. 'I'd wager the queen regretted building that bridge in the end.'

Addan frowned. 'How do you mean?'

'Well, she's dead, i'nt she?'

'Since when?' Addan's eyes widened, and suddenly his self-pity was forgotten.

'Been living under a rock, have you?' Of course Yawl was listening. *Nosey bastard.*

'I've been... busy,' said Addan.

'Terrible business,' said Joeh, looking glum. 'She, the queen, that is, made this big speech in front of everyone. How she invited the Dawanii to the palace. Anyway, they came, right, and you know what they did? They stabbed her to death, right in front of everyone!'

'Burn the stones! Is that true?'

'True enough,' said Yawl. 'Rumour is the prince had a hand in it.'

'Dragonshit,' said Joeh, spilling some of his ale in his beard. He wiped it away with his other hand. 'What makes you say something like that?'

'I hear a lot of things in this room. Word is, he seeks the throne for himself.'

Joeh let out a big belly laugh and slapped the bar. 'Ridiculous. Who's ever heard of a man as queen? Leave the entertainment to the music girls, barkeep.'

Addan listened in disbelief. Why would the Dawanii want to kill the queen? Did Shara know? How could she? *Today couldn't get any worse.* He sat in stunned silence and listened to Yawl and Joeh talk over him about politics and the true nature of why the bridge was built. He tuned out when Yawl began talking about the labour used to build it. Too many terrible memories.

He drank his way through his ale, and as he found the bottom of the tankard, he felt a tap on his shoulder. He turned in his seat and found an angry-looking gabbalin staring at him, arms folded.

'Where's Granx?'

'Sorry, I haven't seen him,' Addan said. He tried to swivel back to the bar in his seat, but the gabbalin grabbed his arm to stop him.

'Lies. Where is he?' The gabbalin was taller than most, and this one looked like he'd actually eaten occasionally. There was definitely some flesh around this one's bones.

'I told you, I don't know.'

'Is there a problem here?' Joeh had stopped his conversation with Yawl and sat up tall on his stool. He cut an imposing sight, but the gabbalin didn't show any sign of feeling intimidated. Quite the opposite, in fact.

'Stay out of this, *friend.*' His vibrating voice carried through the tavern enough to dull the chatter of the other patrons. The quartet of musicians continued to play in their corner.

'Have you looked in the brothel? He might be there with your mother.' It was deliberately provocative, and he didn't know why he said it, but he did so with a grin, nonetheless. Those within earshot clearly enjoyed the insult. The best entertainment was always free and impromptu.

The gabbalin took offence. Why wouldn't he? He snarled and spat at the floor before producing a small blade with a design now familiar to Addan. 'Say that again, I dare you.' His tiny red eyes burned with rage inside their hollow sockets.

'Does she charge you, your mother, or is there a family discount?'

That was enough. The gabbalin launched himself at Addan, but Joeh, now standing at his full height—which was considerable, and hidden well when seated—pushed the gabbalin back out of reach of Addan.

Addan, emboldened by his new protector, pulled out the knife he had retrieved from Granx's corpse and held it in such a way that the gabbalin would be in no doubt what it was. Yawl squealed from behind the bar, deploring the impending violence, begging for calm.

'See! Lies! He has stolen his blade. Where is my brother, pink-skinned scum?' He stood ready to launch another attack, but he kept glancing at Joeh, as if weighing up his chances.

'Your brother is dead. I took this knife from his rotting corpse. Unless you wish to meet him in the next life right now, leave me alone. My debt to your brother does *not* pass to you.'

The gabbalin cried out, a raw, rumbling sound of pure emotional pain. He threw himself forward with arms flailing at Addan, trying to connect, but Addan ducked out of the way and came up behind, landing a punch in the gabbalin's side. He didn't want to use the knife, not if he could help it. The gabbalin twisted back, but before he could retaliate, Joeh took hold of him in a headlock with one massive arm and relieved him of his blade with the other.

Addan wanted to move in with another punch, but Joeh shook his head as if to say "enough now," to which he relented. After fighting to breathe, the gabbalin eventually stopped resisting and promised to leave if he was released. Joeh let go, and true to his word, the gabbalin ran out of the tavern as fast as his legs could carry him.

'This isn't over!' were the gabbalin's last words before disappearing into the city above.

The normal hum of the tavern returned a few seconds later. Addan knew at least some of them would have enjoyed witnessing a full-scale brawl, but they would settle for the minor scuffle it was, thanks largely to Joeh.

'I appreciate the help,' said Addan.

'No bother, though I would have stepped in for anyone against those dirty creatures. There's too many of them in the city nowadays and I don't like it. Most of them are thieves and all of them stink.'

Addan nodded, but wasn't sure he entirely agreed with the man. He had known one or two decent, well-meaning gabbalins, but it *was* only one or two. For whatever reason, they had all been outcast from their own country and were trying to get by as best they could wherever they could find a place to call home. The sad fact of the matter was, very few were willing to offer them work, so they often resorted to crime. Some of them were even quite good at it, in his experience.

Joeh offered to buy him another drink. Part of him really wanted to say no, he shouldn't, but who turns down a free drink or two? Especially when you can't afford your own. He politely hesitated in his acceptance, not wanting to appear too eager. The stranger was friendly enough, though he wondered if there was something else about the man; something to be wary about. Yawl set down a fresh ale in front of him and he soon forgot his concerns.

By the fifth drink, Addan and Joeh had talked and laughed

about a whole range of topics. These included women, of course, which made him think of Shara. The gabbalins and how they were ruining everything, and why they never talked about their home country, Abbalon. They argued over whether the bubbles in the ale were actually good for your gut, and reminisced over good days past when everyone had work and money in their pocket. Joeh had money. Enough for ale, at least.

'Of course,' said Joeh, unsteady on his seat. 'The *real* reason we cannot see the sun is because it stopped moving. *Some* even believe it used to rise in the skies, like the moon does.'

'Don't be... don't be ridiculous,' Addan replied. 'It would burn us all alive, surely.'

'I swear on my life and may the Architects strike me down right here, right now if I'm lying.' Joeh looked up at the ceiling with his arms open expectantly. Nothing happened. 'See? What I tell ya?'

Addan chuckled and downed the rest of his ale. He wasn't sure if it was the room moving, or him. He decided it was the room, most definitely the room. And the chair. And Yawl, too. Both of him. 'Maybe the Architects didn't hear you. That music is very loud.' He looked over at the quartet and shouted. 'Hey, why don't you play... you play *Song of Stoneses and Rains.*'

'I think you mean the *Rain-song of the Everstone*,' said a new voice. A young man with expensive clothes and well-groomed hair had taken up an empty seat next to Addan and Joeh.

'Yes,' Addan said. 'Play that one. I like that one.' He waved a dismissive arm at the musicians when they ignored his request.

'Terrible business with the queen, don't you say?' said the new man.

'Aye,' said Joeh quietly, disengaged.

'My friend here,' said Addan, slapping Joeh on the back, 'says the Dawanii did it. Not very... nice of them.'

'No, indeed not. My name is Wann. Pleased to make your

acquaintance. I would offer to buy you both an ale, but it looks like you've had enough already.'

'No, no. I think I can manage one more.' Addan belched into his hand, which brought up a mouthful of ale. He forced it back down again. 'Maybe you're right.'

'Quite. If it were true that it was the Dawanii, it would mean war, of course.'

'War? Who with?' Addan asked, his concentration waning by the second.

'The Dawanii,' said Joeh. 'There's been no war here in a thousand years. Not even with the gabbalins, though I'd like to see them try.'

'The last war ended with the Divide, of course. A rather abrupt end, so the story goes. No way across for either side, no war. Instant peace, and everyone got on with their lives for all this time,' said Wann.

'And now there's a *bridge.*' Addan stabbed at the bar with his finger on each syllable.

'Now there's a bridge,' echoed Wann. 'Our illustrious queen had to build herself a bridge. And now she's dead. If that doesn't lead to war, I couldn't possibly imagine what will.'

'We don't have an army,' Joeh pointed out. 'How can there be a war without an army?'

'Rumour has it the palace is looking for volunteers,' said Wann quietly.

'Volunteers for the Queen's Guard?' asked Addan. Something brightened somewhere inside his head.

'Ha! Not likely,' said Wann. 'The Queen's Guard are the best of the best.'

Addan held back a laugh. In his opinion, the calibre of the Queen's Guard was rather overstated.

'The word is,' continued Wann, 'they're forming a militia, of sorts. Need to up the numbers. There's not enough of the

Queen's Guard on their own for a minor battle, let alone an entire war. Expendable folks, that's what they're after.'

'You're talking nonsense,' said Joeh. 'I've heard no such talk of war. You're stirring shit.'

Addan tried to listen to the two men argue back and forth for a while, but his head was filling with fog. He wondered if he should move out of the way and let them get on with it, with their fists, if it came to it. He went to pick up his tankard, but had forgotten it was empty.

'Of course, you wouldn't last half a day in battle,' sneered Joeh.

'Nor would I want to. I have my business to attend to. Besides, a tailor such as myself is likely to be in demand, on account of making all the uniforms.' Wann's tone was indignant.

'I think I shall b... bid you gentlemen farewell,' said Addan. Stuck between two men in the middle of an argument was no place to be, and he decided it was unlikely he'd be offered any more ale. He thanked Joeh and bid Wann well and left them to their opinions.

'Rent!' Yawl's voice carried well above the din of chatter and music. Addan simply raised a hand in acknowledgment as he fought with the steps leading out. He didn't remember them being so uneven.

The air outside was a welcome treat compared to the stale mix of alcohol and sweat behind him. He closed his eyes and breathed deeply as the wind ruffled his hair. And then he threw up, but that didn't matter to him. He had a plan. Probably not a good plan, but he had one nonetheless.

9
ATTACK!

Helela had refused to let Liana leave once all the commotion had calmed down. The kindly woman insisted on providing her with a meal and a bed. Liana was grateful for both. The meal was a simple broth with some meat of unknown origin and what she hoped were potatoes. Whatever it was, it was a welcome feast for someone who hadn't eaten in, she didn't know how long now. As best as she could tell, she had left Miar Lenns only two days ago, and even then she'd missed her morning meal. Life took a turn, as her father was fond of saying when he was still alive.

The bed, while simple, was more comfortable than her own, or maybe it only seemed that way. The pillow smelled of wildflowers and she fell asleep the moment she closed her eyes. And then the dreams started.

It was dark at first. There was no moon and no sky. There were no walls, floor, or ceiling either. She was standing on something; she was sure of that, but there was no ground beneath her feet. There was nothing except her. And then the world lit up, and she found herself in Miar Lenns. She recognised the Moonwatch Tower, but everything else seemed different somehow. It was bigger. *Busier.*

Buildings swirled around her as the scenery changed, as though she were flying. It was definitely her city, but it had changed. The palace looked nothing like how she knew it. There was an entirely new wing on the east side, except it didn't look new. It looked old, weathered. Battle-beaten. Below her in the streets, fires raged and people screamed, attacking one another with weapons of metal and wood.

Some of those embroiled in the fighting wore uniform, that of the Queen's Guard, though there were many more of them than there should be. The Queen's Guard numbered fewer than twenty, but she could easily count a hundred or more if she tried. This was her home, except it wasn't. The same, but at the same time, not.

The city fell away beneath her farther still until the fighting men looked no larger than insects. She could see all the way across the Eastern Plains, and almost glimpsing the hidden sun itself. She turned around and looked the opposite way, towards Dawan, where in the waking world she knew herself to be. A loud noise pummelled her ears as the ground tore itself apart from corner to corner below her. A great chasm ripped through the land, kicking up rocks and dust towards her. And then everything faded away.

In seconds, she found herself back in complete darkness. No walls, no sky, no light. Nothing again except her.

She called out. 'Hello?'

Silence. She tried to walk, but it didn't feel like she was moving. There were no shapes or points of reference, but she could still see herself. There was simply nothing. A void. Emptiness. She felt both warm and cold at the same time.

There was a voice. 'Can you hear me?' it asked. She recognised it immediately.

'Who's there? Yes, I can hear you.'

'Who are you? *Where are you?*'

Silence again. It was definitely the voice she'd first heard from the old man. She tried to turn, searching for where the voice came from, but there was still nothing. And then there was a rush of air; she was falling. Falling into nothing and *from* nothing. A banging sound. No, not banging—knocking. She opened her eyes.

Liana woke, back in the unfamiliar bed that smelled of flowers. Sweating, her bedding and pillow sodden. The knock came a second time. Someone was at the door.

'Come in?' she ventured, her mind still stuck somewhere between awake and asleep. The door opened inwards with a gentle creak.

'Good morning.' It was Helela. 'I didn't wish to wake you too early. You looked like you needed plenty of rest.'

Too early? It had only been a few moments since she had closed her eyes. *Hadn't it?*

'I've saved you some food. All the best of it has gone already, but I'm sure there's something you will like.' Her accent had a musical cadence, and was unlike any of the accents Liana knew back home. It had a disarming quality to it, regardless of the words spoken.

She propped herself up by the elbows. 'Thank you. Is Uehan all right?'

'As well as a boy with a broken mind can be,' the woman said, her brow furrowing. Her pain and worry were obvious. 'He's resting right now. Once you have eaten, I will take you both to see our elder, Orratan. He will see what can be done for him, and perhaps determine what ails you as well.'

Liana didn't feel unwell, exactly. She didn't really know how she felt. The foggy feeling had gone, which she put down to being tired and hungry. Now, though, there was a heavy feeling that lingered within her. She decided it wouldn't do any harm to humour Helela and meet with this Orratan.

'I've left you some clothes. I believe they will fit you well enough,' Helela said. She pointed at a pile of fur at the bottom of the bed. She then left Liana alone, closing the door behind her.

Liana got out of bed and picked up the clothes. The fur, the purest black, was softer than any clothing she'd worn before. It was much lighter than she had expected. She removed the damp, sweat-laden clothes she'd slept in and pulled on the leggings, which were fashioned from some sort of leather. They were a little loose around the thighs, but tight at the ankles. *Close enough*, she thought. The black fur coat fit her almost perfectly. There were no buttons; it simply slipped on over her head like a second skin. She doubted an expert tailor who'd taken her precise measurements could have done any better. The sleeves ended halfway down her forearms. The entire outfit was *so, so* comfortable. No new shoes, though, she noticed. Her old brown and dirty boots would have to do, but it was a shame they looked so out of place with the rest.

When they left the house—the three of them, plus Ember, who had slept outside Liana's room the whole time—Liana was surprised to see numerous people gathered outside, hoping to catch a glimpse of the stranger who had come to town.

'She will not save him. She shall save *him!*' shouted Uehan between all the other words he had been muttering to himself. There were a few gasps of concern when the boy shouted. They seemed to know something wasn't quite right with him.

Liana was much more clear-headed than she was when she first arrived and was able to take in more of her surroundings. It was hard to miss the mountain as it towered over the settlement. The half-moon of mid-day was framed by the snowy double peaks. An interesting sight to behold as she had known nothing taller than the Moonwatch Tower before now. It looked a different colour here, the moon. She had never seen it look so pink before. It *was* the same moon. She was almost certain of that.

Her eyes followed the peaks down the rocky slopes. Small, abstract-looking wooden structures stood clustered together, almost merging with the rock they nestled on. These dwellings grew larger as she continued her gaze downwards until they met the tree line at the bottom and poured out into the space around her.

Many of the buildings looked as though they had been grown from the trees themselves, and pulled into shape. *I didn't imagine them, then.* The rope and wood walkways and gantries hung neatly between a mixture of oak and fir, and some other types she didn't recognise. It looked possible to walk around the entire circumference of the settlement without ever putting a foot on the snow-laden ground, if one so wished. She could see the occasional Dawanii walking along the walkways as they stopped every few steps to cut something from the branches. Fruit, possibly.

Helela had allowed her to take in the view, but eventually reminded her they should get moving.

'Do you know what they will expect of me?' Liana asked, still looking around and finding new things to notice.

'He will wish to hear your story. After that, I cannot say. No harm will come to you, so do not be afraid. You are quite safe here as our guest.'

'She will save him,' murmured Uehan. Ember squeaked a yawn every time he said that phrase, almost as if it were a reply.

A substantial number of curious men and women followed them as Helela led them along a path towards the mountain. It made her feel a little uneasy, but the woman didn't seem perturbed by their presence, so she simply went along with it. One or two of them tried to ask questions of her, but Helela told them to mind their own affairs. She would have loved for

Addan to be here with her. He would have been amazed by it all, just as she was.

Eventually, they came to a building that looked different from the rest. Larger, and more stone than wood in composition. It still looked like it had been pulled from the ground itself somehow. Liana guessed it was some kind of communal place, like a tavern, maybe. Heavy animal skins covered a doorway, much like all the other structures.

A grey-looking man with long, flowing grey hair—half painted in red, though not as recently as most—emerged from behind the animal skins. He wore the same furs as all the others, with the addition of a long, dark grey fur cloak that fell beyond his feet, trailing behind him. He stepped clear of the doorway and smiled through wrinkled blue eyes.

A second person, a woman, stepped out from behind, hidden by his cloak. She was far younger than him. Liana's first guess was she was his daughter, or perhaps more likely his granddaughter, such was their appearance.

The man stepped forward, arms open, welcoming. He took Helela by the hands. Neither spoke, only looking at each other in the eyes. Liana could see the woman's pain showing through. The man looked at Uehan as the boy mumbled away. He shook his head before releasing Helela's hands. Then he turned to Liana.

'Welcome to Trennale, our humble home. I am Orratan, elder of our people. I trust you will feel comfortable during your stay with us,' said the younger woman as she stood a little to the side and barely a step behind the old man.

Liana was confused, but said, 'thank you,' to her.

'Please,' she said. 'You are to address Orratan directly. I merely speak his words on his behalf.'

'He's mute and unable to speak,' whispered Helela softly, leaning closer to Liana.

'Oh, I see,' said Liana. She looked at Orratan directly. 'Thank you. Helela has made my stay so far most comfortable.'

"Please, come inside," said Orratan.

Liana followed behind Helela and Uehan. Ember kept up, barely a few inches away from her feet. The cinderfox had quickly made herself her new best friend.

The inside of the building was warm and elaborate. She was wrong. It wasn't a tavern at all. It had all the decoration and furnishing befitting the residence of a leader. It wasn't as grand as the palace, not in size, at least. Tapestries of abstract design hung on the stone walls, with more of the same on the floor. They reminded Liana of the stained glass windows she was accustomed to at home. Instead of transparent glass that let light through, vibrant colours and skilled craftsmanship gave a sense of light where there was none. There were no actual windows in this room. The only light came from small thin candles that gave the tapestries the illusion of movement as their flames flickered gently. The back of Liana's neck tightened when she looked at the naked flames, so she did her best to pretend they weren't there.

Orratan led them to a smaller chamber at the back end of a hallway. A small, simple desk made of a pale wood filled most of the space. Orratan sat himself down behind it and his companion took a standing position behind his left shoulder. There were more tapestries on the walls, hung on either side of the only window, which was more of a rectangular hole as there was no glass. A rug on the floor reminded Liana of the ugly ones her grandmother used to spend many hours weaving. She hated those things and were always scratchy on her feet if she forgot to wear shoes whilst walking on them. No other chairs, she noticed, taking in the detail. She, with Helela, Uehan, and Ember, crowded together in the only remaining space by the back wall. Evidently Orratan didn't have company in this room often.

"Now, tell me what happened to the young man," said Orratan through the woman.

It would take Liana some time to get accustomed to this new way of communicating. She recounted her story once again, remembering to look at Orratan himself. The man listened without interruption as she spoke. Occasionally he would nod, but he mostly looked concerned.

"Is this true?" he asked Uehan once she'd finished.

Uehan still seemed to understand what people said to him, but there wasn't any sense to his replies. He just repeated the same thing over and over. His tone suggested he may have been trying to answer the questions put to him, but the words never changed. Liana had noticed he was getting more agitated as time went by, though.

'Can you do anything for him?' asked Helela.

Orratan lowered his head a little and closed his eyes in thought. "It's a terrible thing, what he has done to himself. Ordinarily, he would be punished severely for breaking with centuries of tradition. There are reasons—good reasons—why the Branding is only performed in the proper manner, and that only the eldest child may participate. The results are rather evident, wouldn't you say?" Orratan snapped his head up and stared at Uehan with a narrowed brow.

Liana watched Orratan and the young woman as she spoke for him with interest. Was she really speaking on his behalf? His actual words? It was hard to tell. Telepathy was something she'd only read about in children's stories.

'So his mind is lost, then?' said Helela, quietly.

"I didn't say that. If there is to be any hope of restoration, he will have to submit to the Branding a second time. It will then be the Architects's decision—and theirs alone—whether they wish to spare him."

'Sorry,' said Liana. 'I don't really understand. What is the Branding, exactly?'

"You have already seen a... how shall I put it... a crude version of it. It is our most important ritual, which has been part of our way of life for hundreds of years. Only the first-born may participate. Boy or girl, it matters not. When they reach adulthood, they must choose whether or not to participate. They are asked only once, and they may not change their mind once decided.

"Not only does it come with its own danger, as demonstrated by the young Uehan here, there is also a high chance of death."

'It can kill you?' asked Liana, her voice a little more high-pitched than intended.

'Kill is perhaps not the right word,' said Helela.

'But you can die. What's the difference?'

"When a person undergoes the Branding, they submit themselves to the will and judgement of the Architects. They look in to your very being and they decide your fate. They will bestow a gift on them, but there is an exchange for that gift. Nearly half are chosen by Aelene, the Architect of Death herself and are welcomed to the next life."

'Half?' Liana's eyes widened. 'Why would anyone choose to do this if they had as much chance of dying as... as flipping a coin? I wouldn't even consider it.'

"We embrace death, as Aelene embraces us all. Every soul in this land will meet her eventually, even you. That is the way of things. It is an honour and a good way to transition to the next life. Very few would wish to die old, frail, possibly in pain from a cruel disease our healers cannot cure. Or even to die in a violent manner."

'And if you don't die? What are the gifts you mentioned?'

"There are six other gifts once can receive. The first is immortality. The Architect of Life searches inside you and, if chosen, will forbid Aelene from taking them. For as long as

135

there has been the Branding, there has only ever been one to receive this, the greatest of gifts."

'Where are they now?' Liana asked with interest. She wondered what it would be like to live forever. Exhausting eventually, she thought.

'Nobody knows,' said Helela. 'It was a long time ago, long before our lifetimes. Even their name is lost to living memory.'

"The remaining five gifts are bound to our senses. For example, I received the gift of thought. It is limited, but it allows me to communicate with others without a tongue. It also means I can ascertain if another is truthful or hides behind deceit."

Ha! I was right. Self-congratulation quickly disappeared when she wondered if he could read her mind. 'That's a rather fortunate gift to have when you cannot actually speak.'

Orratan chuckled silently. "Ah, as I said, each gift comes as an exchange. The tribute I gave for my gift was my voice. I have also not fully enjoyed a good meal since my Branding, since I can no longer taste anything.'

She didn't know whether or not to feel bad for the man. It was a lot for her to take in at once. 'What was Uehan's gift meant to be?'

"It would seem, had the process not failed as it did, he would have the gift of foresight."

'To see into the future, you mean?'

"Correct, young one. Unfortunately, he is trapped in his recent past. To him, he is seeing the future. In reality, he speaks mostly of what has already passed, with barely a brief insight into what is to come. His mind is unable to reconcile these differences. If that cannot be undone, or completed, he will go insane at best. Or die."

Liana couldn't help but keep asking questions. She was horrified, yet keen to know it all at the same time. 'What is his tribute? What does he give in return?'

"I told you. The senses are the tribute."

She thought about it for a moment, then it came to her. 'Blindness. But he can still see, can't he?'

"Indeed, that is exactly right. Truthfully, he would be blind by now. It takes a little time to manifest, but not this long."

Uehan was rocking gently back and forth on his feet, never silent.

'He keeps saying, "I will not save him, I shall save him." Do you know what it means? I assume the first him refers to the old man I tried to save, but I couldn't, according to him. When he could still make sense, at least. But, who is the other "him"?'

"I do have a theory. It's possible that—" The door burst open, interrupting them.

'Attack! Attack! We're under attack!' shouted a man, before running off. Liana couldn't quite turn around fast enough to get a look at him.

'By the Architects! Have they returned? Twice in only ten moons!' cried Helela. She hurriedly grabbed her son by the arm, ready to lead him out of the room.

Liana didn't know what to do. Ember howled, circling herself, agitated.

'Come, we must leave here,' said Orratan.

'What's happening? Who's returned?' shouted Liana as she was jostled through the door by the others.

There was a crashing sound from outside, mixed in with screaming and shouting of Dawanii voices. Helela opened the main building door to chaos. The entire population was in a panic. People were running in every direction. A woman, screaming, was frantically trying to navigate her way through the crowd to a small child that was standing in the middle of the thoroughfare, crying.

'We need to get to the caves,' shouted Helela, pointing at the mountain with her free hand. She was still holding on to Uehan, who looked only vaguely aware of his surroundings.

Most of the people were running towards the mountain. Liana had to move out of the way of a man charging past to save herself from being bowled over. A low-pitched whistle came from above her. She looked to see where it was coming from in time to see a shard of ice the size of a small knife slam into a hut roof on the other side of the path. The wood splintered, with debris thrown into the air, leaving a perfectly circular hole in the roof. The sound of a second crunch of wood breaking echoed in the wind behind her. She ran, following everyone else. What she saw next made her stop still.

In the air above the city, a dark, swirling mass streaked back and forth as it created strange, mesmerising shapes in the sky. It pulsed, and it turned as it moved, blocking out the light of the moon behind it. She didn't realise what it was at first. It was only when another ice shard shot past her from right to left did she see the dragon that had created it. Then another, and another. Dozens of tiny winged beasts darted around overhead, creating the panic on the ground.

It may have been a trick of the light, but Liana swore they weren't red like the ones she knew from back home. Not the same as the one she had found in the cage. These were slightly bigger, but not by much. And if she had to guess, they looked more of a blue colour. She ducked as one swooped low near her, screeching as it flapped its wings.

She looked back at the cloud as it meandered around the mountain and then she saw its true nature. Hundreds, if not thousands, of the tiny beasts were swarming the skies, almost as if they were as one. She knew dragons swarmed, and had witnessed such an event once or twice in the past, but it looked nothing like this. The dragons she knew were erratic, clumsy even. Their fire was the destroyer of lives, of towns and cities, but never did they behave in the way this swarm did. She couldn't help but watch in awe, even as they wrought havoc around her.

Liana wasn't the only one not running away from the danger, though. It didn't register with her at first, such was the spectacle she was witnessing, but there were some Dawanii who were standing their ground. She watched as one, a girl roughly her age and build, threw rocks at the winged terrorists —except that wasn't what the girl was doing. Liana paid closer attention. The girl looked like she was summoning the rocks from the ground and hurling them into the air with magic. Like the way she herself could make small objects like coins move without touching them. Liana was stunned at the sight. She knew how much it hurt to move even a pennymark an inch. What agony was this girl enduring to make heavy rocks fly—at speed—into the air? The girl didn't look in any sort of pain, and wasn't alone in her actions, either.

Ember barked and pushed into Liana's leg, breaking her attention away from the girl in time to see another dragon diving in her direction. There was barely enough time to throw herself to the ground out of its path. She thanked the cinderfox and pulled herself to her feet, only to find her arm grabbed by an older man she'd not seen before. He shouted at her and pulled, trying to get her to run with him to safety with the others. Something inside her told her to break free, to stand her ground. To help, somehow.

Throwing stones in the way the girl was doing was beyond her ability, but there was nothing stopping her from helping in the old-fashioned way. She picked up the nearest rock she could find—a rough silver-grey stone slightly larger than her fist— and searched the sky for a target. She spotted a pair of wings up ahead and threw the rock as hard as she could at it. She missed. Undeterred, she tried again. Her aim was better the second time, but still she was unsuccessful. The Dawanii girl had noticed her by the third attempt and smiled at her before turning her attention back to the matter at hand. The girl had no trouble herself, finding her mark every time. Liana watched as the girl's stone struck a dragon in the head and watched it fall in a spiral and thump into the ground.

There were fewer people around now, with most of them having made it to wherever their place of safety was. With the screaming lessening, Liana could hear the swarm-cloud itself as it danced in the wind. It almost had a voice of its own. She should have felt terrified, but somehow wasn't. The last time she'd seen a dragon swarm, the feeling of horror stayed with her for a week, and she didn't sleep. This time? She felt nothing like that. She was calm, focused. Almost mesmerised.

She felt a sharp pain in her right hand, as if a needle had been pressed into her palm. She yelped in surprise. As she looked for the cause of the injury, she saw the black smudge. And she remembered what happened back with Dess. Somehow, she had forgotten about that. The smudge had grown and now appeared to have small lines growing out of the edges. It looked like an oddly shaped spider flattened against her skin. She heard whispering again.

Dragons continued to swarm the skies, darting and weaving in and out of trees and people as they either fled or tried to fend off their attackers. Liana couldn't find any more stones within reach to throw at them, so looked for the nearest place to take cover. As she ran, she slipped on an icy patch and stumbled to the ground. Cursing to herself, she turned and looked up at the dragons. Three, no four, were flying right for her.

Instinctively, she held up her arms to shield herself from their attack. The sharp, stabbing pain in her hand spread until her whole hand felt as if it were on fire. And then a flash. A bright white-purple light filled her vision. Pain seared through her skull, unlike anything she had felt before. A thousand dragons all cried out at once, and then it was silent.

Carefully, she opened her eyes. The cloud was retreating

behind the mountain. Any dragons that had been closer had already flown away. Whatever had happened, it had worked. The threat had gone, as had the pain. She looked at her hand. The strange spider-like mark persisted.

It took her a moment to realise that everyone remaining around her, including the girl, was staring at her. She looked up at them, expecting to see relief that the attack was over. What she really saw was horror.

'What? What's wrong? Why are you looking at me like that?'

'She wields the forbidden power!' shouted a man, pointing.

'She is torn!' cried another. A woman this time. The crowd was working itself into a frenzy. People were shouting at her, and it was more frightening than the dragons.

'I don't understand,' she said. 'I didn't do anything.'

The angry mob was closing in on her and there wasn't anywhere to escape to. Ember was crouched beside her in a defensive posture, growling and barking at them as they shouted. Liana was sure one of them threw a stone at her, bouncing off her shin. But then a gap opened up between two women, and a friendly face appeared. It was Orratan. He held out his arm to her, but he looked far from happy to see her. Liana took his hand and the crowd, reluctantly, likely out of deference to Orratan, allowed her to leave with him.

Clear of the baying mob, Liana thanked him. Orratan silently mouthed some words while making gestures with his hands. He didn't need his companion to convey his anger. He turned from her, walking away, but beckoning her to follow.

'What did I do?' she said to Ember. The fox only blinked in reply.

Behind her, the crowd who had witnessed her apparent crime was following. Liana quickened her pace to catch up to Orratan. He was leading her back to his place. Helela and Uehan were already there waiting for them. Uehan was clutching at his own hands, pacing back and forth. He was still talking to himself and getting more agitated as time passed. When he noticed Liana, he grew louder and pulled at his hair. Helela was trying her best to calm him down, but nothing was working. Orratan's companion was the last to arrive before he led them back inside out of harm's way.

Within the safety of the building, Orratan grabbed Liana by the hand.

'Hey!' she complained as she fought against him.

"Show it to me," he demanded through his companion.

'Show me what?'

"Your hand. Show me your hand."

Liana huffed before holding out her arm, palm face up.

"Where did you get this mark?"

It was a good question, one that Liana hadn't prepared an answer for. Nobody had asked her about it until then. 'It's only a burn. I was given a stone, and it disappeared, gone.' There was no confidence in her voice.

"Lie!"

The regret was instant. She had forgotten he was telepathic, though she was uncertain how far that power went. *Did he already know the truth?*

"I was given the stone—'

"No," interrupted Orratan. "That's not quite the whole of it, is it? Do not try to hide a lie behind a half truth."

Liana resigned herself to be honest with the man. She took a breath, trying to quickly find the least worst choice of words, when the now familiar voice inside her head said, *'be unafraid. Tell him. Trust him.'*

'We stole the stone,' she said, dropping her head forward.

"Stole it from whom?" Orratan turned her hand over in his, examining it against the light, tracing the dark mark with his thumbs.

'I don't know, exactly. We took it from a house I think belonged to the Tal Valar in my city.'

Orratan nodded, acknowledging she was telling the truth, but he didn't seem satisfied. "Do you know where *they* obtained it?"

'I'm sorry, I do not.'

"You knew it was there. You went there to search for it specifically, no?"

'In part. I was helping a friend. We stole it to help him pay his debts. Then it was stolen from us by another woman who led us to Dawan, then she gave it back to us, in a way. Then it vanished in my hand. It was all very strange.'

Orratan nodded again, though looked solemn. "I'm afraid you must leave now. You cannot remain here with us. It is far too dangerous. *You* are too dangerous."

Liana blinked with surprise. 'Leave? Have I done something wrong? What do you mean, dangerous?'

"I suspect the artefact you stole was a remnant of the Origem. A power so great it cannot be wielded by any man —or woman. We have seen before how such power consumes all life." He took hold her by the wrist again. "See how it is spreading inside you? I'm sorry. We cannot help you. You must leave at once before you become a danger to us all."

A danger to all? She gulped as she digested his words, still unsure of their gravity. *So that's it then. The adventure ends here. Time to go ho—* A blinding flash of light tore through her mind. She screamed and held her head with both hands, trying to fight the feeling it was being ripped apart.

Uehan shouted. 'She will not save him. She shall save *him*! He is saved! The Architect of Life is saved. The Architect of Life lives on! The Architect lives on through her! She has saved him. The Architect is... *within!*'

Liana watched—through her agony—Uehan fall to the

floor, motionless. Helela dropped to her knees beside him, shaking him, trying in vain to rouse him.

Orratan looked at Uehan, then looked at Liana. He clasped his hands over hers and stared into her eyes. He pulled back away, causing her to stumble back a step.

"He speaks the truth!"

10

A SECOND CHANCE

The pain in Liana's head faded enough to regain some semblance of normality. Something *had* changed inside, though. The heaviness in her mind that had been there ever since she tried to save the old man had moved. There was a sense it had spread throughout her body, like she was wearing a heavy suit, but on the inside.

'Will he be all right?' she asked, looking at her friend on the floor. His mouth was moving ever so slightly, telling her he wasn't dead. Not yet, at least.

Helela, tears running down her cheeks, was trying her best to comfort him. The woman who spoke for Orratan simply stood there, stoically, ready to speak when necessary.

Orratan's attention was still on Liana. She could almost feel the thoughts racing through his mind.

'Please help him,' cried Helela.

His attention snapping away from Liana, Orratan turned to the boy. "I fear he doesn't have long." He turned back to Liana. "Please, you mustn't let him die. You must forgive him. He is young, a good boy. Please don't punish him for his actions." The man was right up in Liana's face. She could see the emotion in his eyes, though his lips didn't move; the female voice behind him conveying every ounce of his concern.

Liana's brow furrowed. 'I don't know how to help him. I'm sorry. I don't know what you expect me to do.'

"Not you—Eraidor. I speak to the Architect inside of you."

She stepped back, raising her hands, waving. 'Hang on a moment. There's nothing *inside* of me. I don't know what Uehan meant, but he's wrong. There is only me, there has only ever been me and there will always only be me.'

"Falsehood!"

To Liana, the Architects were little more than a myth. She respected those who believed in their teachings, and learned at a young age not to contradict the Tal Valar when they preached their parables and stories. But that's all they were to her— stories. Yet, here she was, in a foreign land, whose people were clearly more fearful and respectful of the Architects than the most ardent of the Tal Valar. And they claimed one such Architect was *inside* her. Yes, there *was* a strange feeling inside her, but that couldn't be anything other than an illness of some kind. A flu, maybe.

'I promise you, I don't know what I can do,' she protested.

"You must ask him to help us. Help Uehan."

'I don't know how to.' *What am I saying? Do I believe him?*

"Try!"

Liana panicked and tried to think her way through the problem. She raised her arms in the air and said, 'please, oh Eraidor, great Architect of Life. Please save this boy, and do not allow him die.' Her words weren't insincere, but there wasn't any genuine conviction behind them either. She didn't know what else to do and felt ridiculous. She thought she heard laughter inside her head.

And then Uehan coughed and opened his eyes.

Liana sighed with relief, along with the others. Even Orratan's companion relaxed a little.

'I don't think I had anything to do with that,' Liana said.

"He is still gravely ill. We must prepare him for the Branding at once."

'What about me?' Liana said, realising her timing might be a little inappropriate. 'Am I still to leave?'

"You must stay now. You are too important. The Architect of Life chose you and I need to understand why, and what this means, and how it is connected to the artefact. So many questions. Dangerous questions. Dangerous for us all. Dangerous for you, too. Yes. But Uehan *must* be the priority at this time. Please, help him up and follow me."

Liana and Helela both took an arm each and hauled Uehan to his feet. Despite his small stature, he was heavier than he looked. With one arm supported over each of their shoulders, they carried him. He was barely conscious, his feet dragging along the smooth stone floor. They followed Orratan and his companion through an animal skin door at the back of the building.

A short walk through a corridor, they came to a huge circular amphitheatre. It was an open-air section of recessed land, with a towering sculpture at its centre. There was no snow here. Around the perimeter were dozens of giant statues of men and women. Their bases looked like everything else made of stone—as if it had been stretched out from the very ground itself. These rough bases gradually became smoother as they went up until the shapes became recognisable as bodies. Each statue had to be at least twenty feet tall, and all were equally spaced apart in a circle, all facing the imposing centrepiece.

The sculpture itself stood almost as high as the statues. Three spiralling arms curved into each other, twisting into a point at the top, though not quite touching each other. Each arm had an array of symbols carved into their surface that Liana had not come across before. The structure towered over everyone, a sight equally as imposing as the statues that watched over it. Each inside edge of the three arms glowed a gentle purple, though Liana couldn't see where the light came from.

Encompassing the triangle was a circle of smooth, black stone, built up to roughly knee-height. On one side was a gap large enough for someone to walk through. Within the circular wall was a smaller stone ring, at least an arm-span across, set on a loose shingle base. Inside the circle lay seven fist-sized spheres made from dark grey stone, all identical to each other.

Orratan requested Uehan be placed close to the gap at the outer circle. Liana and Helela carefully set him down. He appeared to have enough strength to keep himself upright, but he was muttering again, quieter than he had been.

A thought appeared in Liana's mind. 'The Branding,' she said.

"Yes. This is where, and only where, the Branding ritual is performed. The one you saw was a crude version, unsanctioned and dangerous. Ordinarily, this sacred place would be filled with family and honoured guests to witness their son or daughter make their greatest, most honourable choice. The Branding ritual takes time to prepare, particularly for the one participating. Alas, we do not have that luxury now."

'How often do you perform the ritual?'

"As often as is required. Whenever a child reaches adult-hood, they have the right to choose."

Like a birthday banquet, but without the food and drunkenness. Something inside her head seemed to agree with her. It was only a feeling more than it was a thought or words, but the feeling was making itself known more strongly.

Orratan hobbled quickly around the stone circle, periodi-cally bending down to do something Liana couldn't quite see. He did this four times before seeming satisfied. All the while, his companion simply stood there, never helping, doing nothing other than speaking when required to do so. Orratan gestured for Liana to come to him.

"These stones are what make the Branding possible." He picked up one of the spheres and handed it to her. It was heavy, really heavy, and extremely cold. "Turn it over."

Liana did as asked, flipping the sphere over into her free hand. Carved within the surface of the stone was a symbol. She'd not seen it before, but it looked similar to the burn mark on Uehan's hand. This symbol had two lines through it.

"The Orb of the Mind." He held out the palm of his right hand, revealing a mirror image of the symbol melted into the flesh. He took the sphere from her and placed it to one side. He then selected each of the others in turn, showing her the symbol and briefly explaining its meaning. Sight, hearing, touch, taste and smell. All the five natural senses and their respective gifts.

The sixth sphere, he told her, was the Orb of Immortality. "Of course, this is the one almost all wish for, but that wish always seems to remain unfulfilled."

'Except for one, you said.'

Orratan nodded. "Except for one. *If* the stories are to be believed, of course."

That left the final sphere—the Orb of Death. The symbol resembled the crescent of light on the moon just before it would disappear behind the horizon, along with three diagonal lines that looked like claw marks.

'So, it's a random choice, which one someone picks?'

"Yes. But also, no." Orratan said pensively. "The choice is not made by the participant. The Architects search the very soul of a person and present their offering to them."

'I still don't think it very fair the most likely outcome is this one,' she said, handing back the orb.

"Life is rarely fair. Life is also short. Our passage to the next life is determined by many things. To have the privilege of being chosen by the Architects and welcomed to their realm is a precious thing indeed. Death should not be feared, nor should it be desired. Aelene is a friend who will meet us all in good time, and we should not be fearful of that."

Orratan selected the Orb of Foresight from the pile next to him and replaced it in the circle, leaving the others where they were. He stood up, clapped his hands and the ring ignited with a pale violet flame. It was small at first, but steadily grew until it engulfed the entire circle, its light filtering up through the spiralled arms, merging with the light Liana had noticed before.

Liana instinctively pushed herself backwards out of harm's way, but she felt no heat from the fire. In that moment, seeing Uehan putting his arm into the fire when she first saw him all made sense to her. 'Shouldn't all the orbs be in there? If it is a choice he has to make, I mean.'

"That choice has already been made. Something went terribly wrong that first time. If he is to have a chance to save his life, he must undergo the ritual again and retrieve the same orb. Now, help me bring him forward."

With Helela's assistance, Liana lifted Uehan up to his feet once again and place him in a kneeling position in the gap of the outer circle. The boy was delirious, and it was a struggle to keep him from falling headfirst into the flames. Liana had to remain behind him, holding his shoulders.

Orratan stood on the opposite side of the circle and raised his hand. His companion remained positioned behind his shoulder. "Our great Architects, I pray you hear me now. This child seeks your favour, your light, and your strength. We ask you to grant him completeness of your divine gift and accept his tribute in your name."

More words followed, but it was in a language she didn't know. She could only watch as the flames pulsed, growing dimmer and then brighter, larger.

Orratan stopped speaking and then looked to Helela.

With her help, Uehan reached into the fire. He screamed. Liana turned her head away, eyes closed tight, as if feeling his pain for him. When the screaming stopped, she looked up to see the fire gone and Uehan holding the orb in his hand. Liana was about to let go of his shoulders, but he suddenly went limp and the orb fell from his grasp and rolled away.

'It didn't work?' asked Liana, looking at Orratan and then Helela.

"It is uncertain. He will need to rest now, and we will know when he wakes."

'How long will that take?'

Orratan shrugged. "Two, possibly three moons. Maybe more, maybe less."

Liana wasn't convinced, but could only defer to his experience. She helped once more to carry the boy back to Orratan's abode. Helela wanted to take him home, but Orratan insisted he made his recovery where he could be on hand should it be needed.

Something nagged at Liana throughout the ritual—that "something" inside her. There had been no time to really process the meaning or implication of what Uehan had said. Now the immediate danger to his life had passed, she thought about nothing else. Ember kept rubbing against her leg as if to offer comfort. Liana stroked the back of the cinderfox's neck, still in awe of how the blue flame rippled within the fur. She wondered if there was a connection between the animal and the ritual somehow.

'I want it out,' she said to Orratan. 'Whatever it is inside me, Architect or otherwise, I want you to remove it. Can you do that?'

"If only it were that easy."

Helela stayed with Uehan in a room Orratan had provided for him. Orratan then led Liana back through the building.

When she realised he was about to take her outside the front way, she pulled his shoulder to get him to stop.

'I can't go out. They'll still be there, waiting for me, for what I did to the dragons.' There were a number of voices on the other side of the skin curtain, confirming her fear.

"It isn't what you did to the dragons. I'm certain they are grateful you stopped the swarm. It's the danger you pose because of the Origem itself."

'That's the same thing. If I go out there, what's stopping them from hurting me? Chasing me out of the city, or worse.'

"My dear child. Do you think so little of me that I would allow you to come to any harm?" He reached for the curtain, but she stopped him, putting her hand on his arm.

'I don't know you. And you were ready to cast me out less than an hour ago, were you not?'

"Ah, but everything has changed since then. You have been chosen and I must find out why. This... predicament... is without precedent, and I must know what it all means."

This is insane! But what choice do I have? 'You guarantee I'll be safe?'

"You have my word. I will speak with them and they *will* listen."

She relinquished her hold on the door and allowed Orratan to open it. There weren't as many people outside on the steps as she'd expected, but there were still enough for her to feel intimidated. Behind them, work had already begun clearing up after the dragon attack. Men and women she'd seen handlessly throwing stones at the creatures were now moving rubble and broken wood with the same magic, alongside others who carried impossibly heavy rocks in their hands as if they were nothing.

Orratan raised his arms and motioned for the gatherers to be silent. It took a few moments, but the calls for the stranger in their midst to be punished or expelled eventually subsided.

"I understand your fear of this young woman, but I insist that no harm is to come to her. No harm will come to you either. Of that I promise. She will stay here as my honoured guest. Be mindful that she comes from the Old Lands, and as such, does not know our ways. Our beliefs. Let us not forget, she *did* stop the attack. The dragons will return, so I urge you to return to your homes. Rebuild them, or help your fellow brethren to rebuild theirs. These are my words and they shall be heeded."

One of the crowd—a younger man—managed half a syllable before Orratan interrupted him.

"These are my words and they *shall* be heeded."

There was reluctant murmuring between them before, in unison, they said, 'those are your words and we shall heed them.' One by one, the crowd dissipated.

Orratan looked at Liana. "My word is law here."

'Are you their ruler?' She felt her question a little crass, but she was still trying to understand these people and their ways.

"Ruler? No. Not in your sense of meaning. Dawan is built on wisdom and experience. The young look up to the old and they respect them. Reaching an old age is a privilege not everyone lives to see. There are many young people, but not so many of us elders. It's the Architects' way of natural order. The elders of a community will always have the final word."

Liana considered this and then said, 'and you are you the oldest of this place?'

"Ah, it's amusing to me that you ask me this particular question at this particular moment. I am not the oldest. There is another, far older than I, and we are to meet her now."

He had said, "far older" which surprised Liana. To her, the man already seemed pretty ancient. She didn't dare ask his age.

The Dawanii, though now not getting too close to her, were still paying her a lot of attention as Orratan led her and Ember back towards the mountain. It was mostly wary staring, with the occasional whisper between themselves. There didn't appear to be any malice, but there was definitely caution in abundance.

As the ground grew steeper, soft snow-encrusted dirt faded into hard mountain rock. Liana noticed a series of winding step-ways cut into the mountain face. These followed the natural crevices, leading the way to more hand-built platforms that supported more dwellings. Before long, the steps were barely less than vertical. She looked at the peaks and guessed they were a third of the way up at this point. She hoped they weren't going all the way to the top.

Eventually, and not really all that farther above the platforms, they came to a cavern entrance. Orratan invited her to enter, but informed her that Ember had been requested to remain outside. The cinderfox protested in her own way and reluctantly took up a spot in the centre of the opening, looking down over the city. Liana stopped to look at the vista herself. It was mostly snow-capped trees beyond the city, with a massive lake to her right. It was almost black. Gentle waves rippled in the breeze, reflecting the light of the waning moon as it danced on the water. There was nothing obvious that could help her work out which way was home.

The inside of the cave had quite a low ceiling, which forced Liana to crouch. Orratan and his dutiful companion were both shorter than her, so had an easier time avoiding hitting their heads on the rock. Ahead was a flickering orange glow. A fire.

The tiny passageway opened out into a modest-sized room, large enough for her to stand fully upright. Despite her aversion to naked flames, the fire was small and inviting. A thin trail of smoke rose upward, drawn into a small crack in the rock-face. By the fire was the smallest person of adult age she had ever seen; a little ball of fur with a woman's head on top of it. Her face had more lines than the rings of a cut-down tree. Eyes sunken far into her skull, but twinkled with life. Her hair was thinning, though still coloured in the Dawanii way.

'You took your time,' said the woman, not looking up. She moved in a shuffle around the fire, poking at it with a stick made from both wood and a dark metal twisted together. It appeared to have once been part of a larger piece, such was the design of it. A staff, perhaps.

"One arrives only when they are ready."

'I didn't mean *you*. I meant the girl.'

Liana raised her eyebrows. She wasn't expecting that.

'Let me get a good look at you.' The old woman turned to her and poked her just as she had poked the fire.

'Ow, please stop that.'

'She's not what I expected. Not at all.'

Liana dared not move her feet, but followed the woman with her head as she shuffled around her. Her request for the poking to stop was not granted.

"Liana, this is Nalla. *She* is our eldest, and wisest of our people."

'It is nice to meet you,' Liana ventured. *Manners were always free,* her mother had taught her.

'Yes, I suppose it is.' Nalla looked up at her.

As Liana met her gaze, she noticed one of her eyes was whiter than the other—cloudy. *Maybe it's the light.* She made a conscious effort not to stare.

'It appears you have found yourself in quite the situation, young lady.' Nalla finally relented with the stick.

'Yes. I, ah, mean, well... I don't really know what my situation is, exactly.'

'You tried to save the man's life. *Why?*'

Nalla indicated for Liana to sit on the ground, which she did. Even with her backside on the floor, the old woman barely reached as high as her chest. She wasn't a dwarf. Liana had met some of those before. Nalla would make any dwarf feel tall. Her right eye still looked cloudy at this angle, so it definitely wasn't the light. *Was she blind in that eye? Another Branding gone wrong, maybe?*

'He needed my help. I could see he was injured.'

'Yes, yes, but *why?* What was it that made you go to him?'

'He was calling out to me. He said, "save me",'

'Are you certain of that? Think. Picture him in your mind. See yourself going to him. Tell me what happened.'

Liana closed her eyes and cast her mind back to the clearing. 'I heard the man calling first before I saw him, but...'

'Yes, yes, go on. But *what?*'

'But the voice didn't seem to be his own. I could hear the words, but his mouth didn't move.'

Nalla leaned forward. 'Good. You went to him, you felt drawn to him.'

'Yes, it was strange. I crawled over to him. There was a lot of blood. So much blood. There was nothing I could do to save him. I tried, really I did.'

'And then...'

'And then nothing. I passed out.'

'No!' snapped Nalla. 'There was more. Concentrate. Create the image in your mind of the moment before you passed out. Tell me what you saw.'

Liana, her eyes still closed, furrowed her brow as she willed herself to remember. Nothing. There was nothing before. She opened her eyes and sighed. 'I'm sorry, all I remember is it went black and when I woke up, I was somewhere else with Uehan.'

"Search for the truth within you. It *is* there and you *can* reach it. Bring it out."

'Blue,' she said tentatively. 'There was a blue light, right before—'

'There was something within that light. Tell me what you see.'

She shook her head, closing her eyes tight again. 'A shadow. A ghost, I think. I saw it leave his body. Then it vanished. No—it didn't—it moved into... me!' Her eyes blinked open. She could feel sweat running down her forehead, her breathing heavy.

'You see it now,' said Nalla triumphantly, waving her stick around her head, hopping from one foot to the other.

'So there is something inside me, after all?'

'You already know. You have always known. You could feel a presence within you. I simply needed to show you. To help you remember.'

'But how did *you* know?'

'I am very old and very wise. There is nothing you can tell me I haven't already witnessed myself.'

'How do I get this... the Architect... out of me? I don't want to have them inside me.'

'I'm sad to say it isn't that easy,' said Nalla quietly.

"Tell me," said Orratan. "What do you know of the Architect of Life?"

It had been such a long time since Liana had heard the Teachings. As a young girl, she had been forced to learn at least a basic understanding of many subjects and disciplines. Her parents had provided her with the best governess Miar Lenns offered. A stiff, no-nonsense woman who called herself Mistress. Liana hated her completely. She'd almost forgotten the vile old woman until now. Though, "old" meant she had probably been close to the age Liana was now.

'The Architects created the world. Thera was the Architect of the mountains, seas, and the very ground we stand on. Father—the sun—gave us light, but is forever distant and unseen. Mother—the moon—watches over us, giving us the days. Eraidor, the Architect of Life, was the creator of all peoples and animals. Everything that breathes.' It was almost a perfect recital of the first part of the First Teaching.

Nalla nodded with approval. 'What do you know of the curse of Eraidor?'

She had a very vague memory of such a story. 'I think... a

thousand years ago, Eraidor and Sarratenian were at war with each other. I can't remember why. Maybe something about the Divide? Sarratenian was banished and has not been seen since. Eraidor... Eraidor was forced to live among his people, his favourite of all his creations. His curse was that no matter what happened to his people, he would be powerless to help and could only watch from within. Through war, disease, famine. He had to suffer through their eyes.'

Orratan was clearly impressed. "That's almost correct. There may be hope for you yet."

Liana frowned. 'I still don't understand what this has to do with me.'

'Eraidor was trapped within a man, and forced to watch from inside. A bad, bad man who did many unspeakable things. He was chosen for that very reason. Wholly unaware that he lived with a god inside him, he killed and fought and stole. Eraidor could only watch on in pain, powerless to intervene.'

'That sounds awful. Was Eraidor ever freed from his curse?'

'No. When the man eventually died, Eraidor hoped he would be released, but another host was found for him. Over time, he learned he could choose who to... inhabit, I suppose, passing from one to another, but only at the moment of death.'

Liana's eyes opened in realisation. 'Eraidor was in the old man, and he died, so Eraidor came to me next.'

Nalla and Orratan looked at each other knowingly.

'So that means... Eraidor is a part of me until I die?' She shuddered at the thought. 'I don't want him. There must be another way.'

'There is no other way. That is his burden, and now also yours.'

Liana sunk to the ground, defeated. A tear rolled down her cheek. 'I didn't ask for any of this. All I wanted was a bit of adventure, to be away from my tiresome life. I'd rather be the princess they want me to be than live the rest of my life knowing someone else is there, knowing my every move. I'll go insane.'

"It is curious, though."

'I see what you're thinking,' said Nalla.

'What? Thinking what?' Liana lifted her head, but still had to look down on Nalla.

"Why is it you can feel him within you? The history explicitly says the host is unaware, always. That is part of the curse. You are not meant to know he's there."

'Yes, it does go against everything we know. The Teachings are not completely accurate all the time.'

"I have never known them not to be."

Nalla paced around the cave, occasionally waving her stick in the air, as though writing something on imaginary paper. Eventually she stopped and turned to Liana. 'You must seek counsel with the Sisterhood.'

II

FIRE

C al barely remembered his father's funeral. It was almost fifteen years ago when Alhen Tallan fell ill whilst on a foolish expedition through the Eastern Plains to see the hidden sun with his own eyes. Many an adventurer had travelled east hoping to catch more than a glimpse. Most turned back when it grew too hot to travel any farther, their prize elusive.

Dehydration had got to him first, and he was brought back to the palace by his entourage, but he developed a fever, which brought about the madness. He was dead within three days. Cal was only nine years old; Liana, a year younger.

Everyone in the city, so Cal was told, came out to pay their respects. The queen had commissioned a full ceremonial funeral, which included a procession of the body through the streets. It's what Alhen wanted, and so it was ordered.

Cal could remember the words of sympathy and condolence spoken to him by so many people. He remembered the flowers, the singing, and the prayers spoken by the Tal Valar. They promised him his father would be safe in the next life with the Architects, and that they all would watch over him. What Cal could not remember was the lighting of the pyre itself. His mother said he *was* there to see it, but there was a hole in his memory of that moment and it frustrated him. He vowed to himself he would remember this one, this time. For his mother, the queen.

He stood, undressed from the waist up, staring out of his bedchamber window, looking over the city. The near half-moon of the late morning cast the cityscape with a golden light. How long had it been since he'd seen rain, now? According to the farmers—too long. Since the queen's death, he had been inundated with requests for an audience. Everyone from farmers seeking answers about an impending drought, to representatives of the slate mine workers in Miar Miall wanting better conditions and pay—they all made demands of him. He was tired of it. It had only been two days since she died. His sister and Dawan were more important right now.

'I thought I would have more time,' Cal said.

'We all thought we would have more time.' Shaan was behind him, choosing an appropriate shirt for him to wear. 'Indeed, I would say that we did not really consider how much time we had either way. Your mother was in good health for her age. There was no reason to believe we would arrive at this moment so soon. So... unexpectedly.'

Cal turned away from the window. Shaan held up a black silk shirt with a formal cuff and collar. Cal nodded. 'I'm not ready for this.' He took the shirt and put it on, pulling his arms through the sleeves.

'They will wait until you are ready.'

'No, I don't mean the funeral. I meant everything else. I'm not strong enough, not wise enough. My mother, now she *was* a wise woman. She always knew what to say and when to say it. More importantly, she knew when *not* to speak.'

'And you are her son. You have your own strengths, and yes, weaknesses, too. But, you also inherited your mother's intelligence. You will have a grasp of matters before you know it.'

'I hope you're right.' Cal struggled with the buttons on his shirt. They were made from polished black stone and were a tight fit for the holes they paired with.

Shaan stepped forward, almost toe to toe. 'Here, let me.' Shaan fastened the remaining buttons and then, with both hands, smoothed out the fabric over Cal's chest before resting his hands on his shoulders. 'A shirt worthy of the new king.' Shaan smiled and kissed him.

'Thank you. Though, while there is still hope of finding my sister, I'd prefer you didn't refer to me that way.'

'As you wish. Now, shall we go? The queen may no longer be here to care about your tardiness, but I'm sure the strydes are growing impatient.'

'That's not funny.'

The order of the day was a procession through the streets of the city. The queen's body would be carried from the palace to a pyre that had been built—as they had been for generations—in the centre square of the city, overlooked by the Moonwatch Tower. There, she would lie until the bell chimed for moonset when the last ceremony conducted by the Tal Valar would take place.

Cal walked through the palace corridors and hallways with Shaan by his side. He was mindful to walk somewhat slower than his natural pace, which was more of a march few could keep up with without breaking into a light canter. The halls were deserted, in much contrast to the usual hustle of people going about their duties. They would all be outside in the grounds, save for the kitchen staff who would be preparing for the banquet that after-moon.

As the pair stepped out into the open courtyard, everyone gathered and fell silent. Even though it was expected, especially today, Cal disliked the abrupt ending of conversations whenever he appeared in front of people. It made him uncomfortable.

He looked around, scanning the faces as they all watched him. 'Still no word about Liana?' he asked Shaan.

Shaan shook his head. 'Alas not. Concern is growing over her whereabouts. If she were still in Miar Lenns, she would surely have heard of the queen's passing by now.'

'If she had, then she would be here. For all her disdain of this place and her role within our family, she would have returned if she had known about...'

'Hmm. I agree. The Queen's Guard are still searching for her. It is most likely she is in Dawan. For what reason, I cannot fathom, and we have a contingent across the bridge looking for her there. If there is any word, I promise you will be the first to know.'

Cal sighed before stepping forward to greet the line of staff who had assembled to pay their respects. He stopped before each one in turn, offering his hand to those wishing to shake— or kiss—it. Fifth in the line was Tienn. Even in his finest clothes, the man still looked untidy.

'Your majesty,' shouted Tienn, lowering his head briefly. 'May I say once again, you have my condolences in these sad times. The queen, your mother, was the best of women.'

'Thank you,' said Cal, noticing the slightest of scowls on Tienn's face directed at Shaan. The man was still clearly unhappy about being put in his place. Today was not a day for political manoeuvring, so Cal smiled and ignored the glare. He moved on down the line. Thirty-five men and women, all of them palace staff of various rank and status, each offered their condolences in turn. Finally, he made it to the carriage carrying his mother's body.

The carriage was open-topped, with two wheels, one on each side. They looked new and far too big for their purpose, standing nearly as high as Cal was tall. The carriage had been freshly painted a dark blue—the queen's preferred colours. Cal had yet to decide if he was keeping the same colour for himself, should his new title be made permanent, or choosing a new one. It was irrelevant to him right now, but the chancellor had asked already, mostly out of an interest in the financial cost. He always was a tight bastard, in Cal's opinion.

Two strydes were harnessed to the front of the carriage. Both were black, with additional white feathers adorning their headwear. In front of them were twelve Queen's Guard, all in their dress regalia, filed and standing to attention in pairs.

Cal was to follow immediately behind the carriage with Liana. That would have been the correct order of affairs. In her absence—which was growing more conspicuous among the general population now—it was agreed Cal's great-aunt Millesen would stand in. Stand was a misnomer as she was too old and frail to walk, even with a cane. So, one of the servants had to push her along the route in a wheeled chair.

Cal was dreading the small-talk he would have to make with her. She didn't like him much and took every opportunity to throw an insult or jibe his way. To his relief, when the servant lined up next to him with her, she was asleep. She was strapped to an old plated dining chair with four pram wheels attached to the legs. Makeshift handles had been awkwardly attached to the back support to aid the pusher in moving her. The straps—leather—Cal surmised, were there to stop the poor woman rolling off onto the ground. She had a line of drool down her chin which dripped onto a black crepe dress that had bunched up around her armpits. *There had to be a better way of helping the immobile get around,* he thought.

Shaan was behind Millesen next to Tienn, which Cal found slightly amusing. Behind them were the other senior members of the Council, followed farther behind by the rest of the staff in descending order of importance. At the very back was a solitary cleaner on hand to clean up any stryde mess.

With the procession assembled, a horn played a solemn tune to herald the commencement of the funeral march through the city. The double gates ahead swung open. As they came out past the palace walls into the streets, Cal was heartened to see so many people had turned out to pay their respects to the late queen. Some threw flowers at the carriage as it progressed, whilst others gently applauded the memory of their monarch, as was custom. Most simply observed in contemplative silence. That silence was interrupted when one of the strydes screeched and flapped its wings in distress, unseating its rider. The whole procession ground to a halt.

Call couldn't immediately see what was happening, but he could hear a man's voice shouting. 'May the Architects condemn you and all your family to damnation!'

Commotion rippled through the gathered crowds. Cal broke his position to get a better look at what was happening. Shaan stepped forward to hold him back. 'Best you don't get too close. Remember your position now,' he warned.

'Nonsense. I wish to see what is so important that they need to interrupt a royal funeral.' Cal pulled his arm free from Shaan, but before he made another step, something soft thumped into his chest. He looked down to find his uniform splattered with... 'shit,' he said, grimacing at the smell attacking his nose.

Shaan doubled his efforts to get Cal to retreat to a safer position, but he wouldn't have it. He walked briskly, pushing his way past Queen's Guard, and the encroaching crowd, who were also itching to catch a glimpse of whoever was responsible for the interruption. Two members of the Tal Valar charged with keeping order had the man restrained—albeit with difficulty—by the time Cal reached him.

'Who dares disrupt the queen's funeral in this manner?' demanded Cal.

The restrained man was well dressed, even if the clothes did look years past their best. Grey hair covered his ears and his brow was sweaty. 'You should all be ashamed of yourselves.' The man spat at the ground.

'Ashamed?' Cal repeated. 'Of paying tribute to my mother. *Your queen.* Before we release her to the care of the Architects in the next life? It is you who ought to be ashamed.'

'Ashamed of letting this once great city, no, *country*, fall to ruin.'

Cal looked at Shaan quizzically, who shrugged his shoulders in return.

'Tell me your name, sir,' said Cal.

'Brannon,' he growled, trying to break free from the Tal Valar's grasp. He was a big man, but not big enough to overpower two others at once.

'Why do you believe the city is in ruin? It is my understanding the city has been prospering of late.'

'Prospering *you*, maybe, but you don't see the hardship suffered by the real people. You all sit in your fancy palace, in luxury, eating your fancy food. I've not eaten in four days now. My family is starving. Our entire district is on its knees, and you do nothing. Nothing at all to help.'

Cal patiently listened to the man. 'I sympathise with your plight, I really do. That being said, whatever your grievance is, you must agree this is not appropriate?' He indicated to the carriage behind him.

'How else was I to get anyone to listen? I've tried to speak through the proper manner, but all that happens is we are turned away.'

'That is still no excuse.' Cal looked at the Tal Valar holding the man. 'Please take him away and ensure he is given a good meal.'

An elderly woman standing a foot or two away from the spectacle tutted her disapproval. Her sentiment spread out in her immediate vicinity, but didn't escalate, to Cal's relief.

'He deserves proper punishment,' said Shaan.

'Perhaps. If what the man says is true, then I will need to know what is happening in my country and not ignore problems.' As apprehensive and unprepared as he was, Cal felt determined to do what he thought was right—especially in front of hundreds of other people. Being perceived as uncaring, or worse, a tyrant, was not an image he wanted. With his sister still missing and the prospect of war with Dawan weighing heavily on his mind, he didn't want to escalate any civil unrest. If war *was* coming, he would need his people standing with him.

Millesen was still fast asleep as everyone resumed their positions to continue with the procession. There wasn't much Cal could do about the mess on his uniform. He carefully brushed off the worst of it and did his best to ignore the smell. If Liana could see him now, she would laugh, no doubt.

If one were to walk briskly from the palace to the Moon-watch Tower, it would take less than ten minutes. The procession march was markedly slower, and the entourage arrived at the open grounds at the foot of the tower half an hour after they had departed.

The road, lined with hundreds of people on each side, opened out to reveal the pyre. It was unusual—illegal, in fact—to have such a large amount of wood in one place. Thus, the pyre stood isolated and proud some fifty paces from anything else. The tower was closer to a hundred paces away. If it wasn't for centuries-old tradition, the final burning of the queen's remains wouldn't take place at all. There had been a petition by the Council after the death of the previous queen to have her body buried rather than cremated. Queen Alyssa had overruled them, and insisted that when the time came, she too would be sent on to the next life by fire, and not condemned to rot away in the ground like some kind of animal.

And so, every precaution was taken. The whole area had been sanitised of anything that might be combustible, and a cordon erected in a giant circle that encompassed the tower. Even the carriage wasn't permitted to enter the cordon. The strydes were pulled to a halt at the end of the road and everyone in line behind the carriage filtered around to a designated area separate from the rest of the crowd, where they could watch the final moments of the ceremony.

Cal *did* remember his father's funeral, after all. A lost memory had returned, and he remembered standing in almost the same spot those fifteen years ago. He now had a clear image in his mind of him standing next to his sister, holding her hand as the flames engulfed the body of his father. He remembered the intense heat on his cheeks, even though they were quite a distance away.

He held that memory in the moment as he watched the four members of the Tal Valar take Queen Alyssa's body—wrapped tightly in pristine white silk cloth—and carry her solemnly to her final resting place. Underneath her body would be a narrow sheet of metal. He knew from asking her about it when he watched his father's body being moved from carriage to pyre. This facilitated the body to be carried and yet be all but invisible to anyone other than the four carrying her.

As her body was laid to rest, Cal looked to the moon as it made her final descent between two rows of buildings to the east. As much as the city was built with little thought to practicality or aesthetic over the centuries, there remained a clear line of sight running from west to east with the tower at the centre. Thus, the moon's path across the sky could be seen from here at any time of the day.

There was still a short while to go before the moon crest passed in front of the sun, bringing about the brief spell of darkness when the pyre would be lit. It was a well-choreographed period of calm and reflection. The lead Tal Valar figure stood close to the pyre and read from his metal-bound book of prayers. Cal cared little for their religious preaching, but he somehow found comfort in the man's words as he bowed his head and reminisced over easier days now passed.

His thoughts were interrupted by a commotion over on the opposite side of the cordon. The Tal Valar priest continued his reading at first, in an attempt to ignore the distraction, but he soon had to stop as whatever was happening became too much to continue.

'What is it now?' hissed Cal. Was this day not to go as planned? Which of the Architects had cursed him so?

'I am uncertain,' said Shaan.

'Am I not allowed to lay my mother to rest in a dignified manner? I could do without more stryde shit being thrown about.'

The silence of the crowd was washed away by inquisitive chatter as it rippled around the perimeter until it sounded like any other normal day in the city. Cal, feeling his anger and frustration rise, pushed his way past Tienn, who, thanks to his deafness, was rather oblivious to what was going on, and marched across the square to the source of the noise.

Before he'd made it past the pyre, there was a scream from a woman. 'Dragon!' she cried. 'He's got a bloody dragon!' There was a lot of pushing and shoving in the crowd and within seconds there was a gap where people had moved out of the way. Left standing alone was a sheepish-looking man who found himself with nowhere to run or hide.

The woman's voice came again, anonymous in the immediate vicinity of the isolated man. 'I seen it. He's got a dragon! Run for your lives!'

Cal, now flanked by Shaan and several Queen's Guard and a number of Tal Valar, made towards the man, who was hiding something small within clasped hands. The man was short, overweight, and unkempt. There was a look of panic—no, of desperation—in his eyes.

'Step back!' shouted the man. 'Step back or I'll release it.'

It was enough of a threat for everyone advancing on him to stop still. A guard carefully moved forward alone, his arms outstretched, his palms facing the man. 'Now, don't do anything rash,' he said calmly.

'I mean it. Get away. I'll speak with the prince only.' The man jerked his hands forward, threatening to release whatever he was holding.

Cal exhaled through his nose, counted silently to three, and stepped forward, motioning to the guard to resume his former position with the rest.

'I didn't mean to. I didn't want... No one was supposed to see,' protested the man. 'I'm sorry, I truly am sorry.'

'Is it true what the woman says? Do you have a dragon?'

The man nodded. 'I do, Your Grace. I thought she was well hidden, but someone must have seen it. I'm sorry for spoiling the funeral. She's my pet, see?'

Cal could hardly believe his ears. A *pet*? Who in their right mind would keep a dragon as a pet? 'All dragons are illegal. You must know that?'

'I do, sir, I do. I didn't mean to have one. It's just that I found it injured, and it was only a baby and I couldn't bring myself to be killing it.' The man hung his head. 'So I kept it.'

The crowd around him was growing restless. Some had already chosen to flee the area, a sentiment shared by many others as word spread around the circle. Cal sensed that pandemonium could erupt at any moment. He looked back at Shaan for answers, but none were forthcoming.

'You realise you have placed everyone here in danger, don't you?' Cal said, trying to keep his voice even.

'I'm sorry, sir. It was not my intention. Not my intention at all. Just wanted to pay my respects like everyone else.'

Something caught Cal's eye, high on a building to his left. A shadow. He looked up to see what it was, but there was nothing there. He looked back at the man, who was becoming increasingly agitated. 'I need you to listen to me carefully. I want you to walk towards me and keep those hands nice and tight. Then I will have two of my guards escort you away from here to somewhere safe, away from everyone else, and you will surrender the dragon. Do you understand?'

The man shook his head. 'I can't. She's all I've got. You can't take her away from me.'

'I'm sorry, you have no choice. Will you do as I ask?'

The man shook his head again and withdrew into himself, pulling his hands closer to his chest. 'I can't. I *won't!*'

What happened next was all a blur to Cal. From nowhere, another man in the crowd broke through and charged at the man. He pounced, and they both crashed to the ground. From the clasped hands emerged a tiny red dragon which bounced and rolled forwards before finding its feet. It stretched its wings and looked around with wide, black eyes. For a few seconds, everything was calm. The dragon looked so innocent, and everyone else around froze.

And then mayhem descended upon them all. The owner of the dragon reached out from his prone position to grab the animal, but he was too far away, and the weight of the man on top of him had him pinned. Those closest to the dragon screamed and hollered in fear. The rope cordon broke as people scattered in all directions. The noise was incredible.

As the Queen's Guard sprang into action to contain the situation, failing desperately, Cal remained still, his eyes locked with those of the dragon. Then, in an instant, the tiny beast took to the air. Cal watched as it soared upwards, its tiny wings lifting it into the sky above. It flew right before circling back around, and then it spat.

Small globs of liquid came from the dragon's mouth like water at first, but within seconds, they burst into little balls of fire that rained down on the people below. Cal counted four fireballs before he found the wherewithal to run for cover himself.

The dragon cried out as it swooped low past the tower. It

was a high-pitched sound that, on its own, didn't sound threatening. Until that cry was answered by another high up on a nearby roof. And then another.

By now, Shaan, Tienn and the others were being rounded up by several of the Queen's Guard so they could be led away to safety. Cal followed along with them as instructed by the guard closest to him, all the while watching the sky. One dragon became three, then seven, and then too many to count. Dozens, if not more, all flying above, all spitting at the ground below. A rain of fire fell on the city square. Within minutes, the pyre was alight. Dozens of little individual fires amongst the pile of wood merged into one. Cal knew at that moment the funeral was over.

As he fled, he pulled his coat up over his head to protect him from the fire. He could smell the fire-resistant wash within the fabric and hoped it was adequate for its purpose. With the others, he withdrew from the square towards the palace. He looked back at his mother as she disappeared behind the flames and wondered if she would still be carried into the next life with the Architects. Would they still accept her, even though the ceremony was not completed? He hoped they were as true and good as the Tal Valar proclaimed.

The dragons continued their terror above as the moon blocked the sun and the sky went dark. Only a shower of fire offered any light at all.

12

GABBALINS

C al wrestled with the cloak of his dress uniform as he stormed through the palace gates. It was too long, and it caught on his heels as he walked. One courtier had tried to assist him with the removal, but he brushed them aside, insisting he could remove his own clothing. In his haste, he tore the left lapel where the cloak was fastened. There was no point saving the other lapel after that, so he yanked the damned thing free and tossed it to the ground as he made his way inside.

There was to be a feast immediately after the funeral, had everything gone to plan. He wasn't hungry now, even though he'd not yet eaten since he woke up. Serving staff were still making final preparations in the Great Hall when he entered. They looked surprised to see him standing at the entrance. The moonset bell, which was supposed to have heralded the lighting of the pyre, had only just sounded in the distance. He needed to find somewhere quieter, somewhere to be alone.

He initially sought refuge in the Architects' garden, but he didn't feel comfortable having all the stoney faces of the gods staring down on him, so he went to the Council's meeting room. He could be alone there, for a short while, at least. The Council members were old, slow. It would take them time to find him, should they choose to look. He slumped down in his mother's chair at the head of the table—Liana's chair, now—and banged his head on the table, deliberately.

'That will do neither you, nor the table any good.'

Cal looked up to see Shaan had followed him in. 'I want to be alone.' He paused. 'No, in fact, I want to go back to before those bastard Dawanii came into *this* city and killed my mother.'

Shaan sat down in the seat next to him and rested his arms on the table. 'What is done is done. You need to show strength now. Hiding away in here will not do. You are the king and you need to act as such.'

'I'm not the king, and I'm entitled to be angry. The city is falling apart, the people are restless and I cannot even see that my mother has a proper funeral. I mean, dragons! Who in their right mind keeps a dragon?' He looked up at Shaan with hot eyes.

Before Shaan could say anything in reply, Tienn, Scoble, and the rest of the Council shuffled into the room.

'Terrible business. Terrible indeed,' said Scoble as he took his seat.

'I wish to be alone,' said Cal.

'Nonsense,' said Furan. 'You should not be alone today.'

'Those dragons are a blight on our city,' said Scoble, shaking his head. 'More must be done to eradicate them. Can we not even lay our queen to rest without them...'

'Destroying everything?' interjected Shaan.

'Precisely,' Scoble said. 'That being said, the outcome was the same.'

'Meaning?' said Cal.

'The pyre did burn, did it not?'

'Before the Architects could hear the prayers. Who's to say

they will accept her to the next life now? For all anyone knows, they could have turned her away. And then what? There is a reason why things are done the way they are. The way they have always been done,' said Cal, restless in his seat.

'Your Grace,' said Furan, 'I find it hard to imagine the Architects would refuse to accept the Queen of Moranza into their care simply because a dragon... how shall I put it... took care of matters a little early. However, if it pleases Your Grace, I shall seek reassurances from the Tal Valar that all will be well for her.'

'Terrible business, these dragons,' shouted Tienn. 'We should seek advice from the Tal Valar. I fret for the queen in the next life.'

Cal gave Shaan a look from the corner of his eye. *Oh, how to be old, deaf and oblivious to everything around you.*

Ceron, one of the younger members of the Council—though still old enough to be Cal's father—entered the room looking flustered and joined them at the table. 'Apologies, Your Grace. I was unaware there was a meeting.' The man was overweight, breathless, and wore an unruly beard that hid his mouth.

'Neither was I,' said Cal, inviting the man to sit down.

'I do bring news regarding Princess Liana, though.'

Cal shifted in his seat, straightening his back. The others—except Tienn, who was still tucked away in his own world without sound—did the same, eager to hear what Ceron had to say.

'Alas, it is not *good* news. We believe she *is* in Dawan. The guards at the bridge reported a man from the city trying to cross the bridge, not two days past. The day *they* came.'

'What does that have to do with my sister?'

'That's just it, Your Grace. They say the man claimed he had already been across the bridge and he sought their assistance to find a girl who'd gone missing. The description the man gave matched the princess. All nonsense, of course. The guards insisted that no one had been over the bridge since the Dawanii came to us, but even so. It's the only event of note we have to report. There's been no sighting of her within the city. Both the Queen's Guard and the Tal Valar have searched all the places she is likely to be.'

'So you believe this girl who has supposedly gone—unseen —into Dawan is Princess Liana?' asked Shaan.

'It isn't for me to say what I believe or not. It is all we have to go by presently.'

'What of the man? Where is he now?' Cal asked.

'Alas, he was sent on his way by the bridge guard. They did give a description of the fellow, but unfortunately it fits what half the men of the city look like. Though...'

'Though...?' echoed Cal.

'Though, the man did also mention gabbalins, but we're uncertain what that could mean, Your Grace.'

'It all sounds rather far-fetched,' said Scoble. 'A sighting of a girl, who may or may not be the princess—'

'No sighting, Scoble. Nobody claims to have seen this girl,' said Ceron.

'All right, a man, who we can't identify, claims he was in Dawan—with a girl—who *he* described her similarly to the princess, except the guards stopped him from crossing. And also gabbalins are involved? Preposterous.'

'I agree,' said Furan. 'Any gabbalins in Moranza are mere outcasts from their own realm. There's no reason Princess Liana would have cause to know them, or be in their company.'

'That we know of,' said Cal quietly. 'She spends too much of her time in the city, and I have no idea who she sees or what she does.'

'I'm hungry. Where is all the food?' Tienn demanded.

'The feast preparations should be complete by now. There isn't anything else we can do for Princess Liana right now,' said Scoble. 'Not unless there is any further news?'

Cal drummed his fingers on the table, then dismissed the Council. 'I will follow behind presently. I would like a few moments alone to gather my thoughts.' He motioned for the old men to leave, which they duly did. One by one they filed out of the room, except for Tienn, who had to be led by the arm by Scoble. 'That includes you too, please, Shaan.'

Shaan had remained in his chair and didn't move at first, following Cal's request, but eventually, he did as he was asked. 'Do not be by yourself for too long. Solitude benefits no one.'

'I won't be long.' He offered a smile to his friend, which was enough to satisfy him. Shaan bowed, as he always did, when he left the room, leaving Cal with only his own company.

The room felt colder with nobody else in it. He leaned back in his chair and stared at the ceiling. There wasn't a lot to look at. It was just as plain as all the others in the palace. Pale sandstone brickwork with metal support beams. He was unsure if they were solid metal or only plated. He suspected the latter. Despite this being home to the Tallan family for nearly thirty generations, it had not been built with all the finest materials a family of their status should expect. The Tal Valar, on the other hand, they had money and all the trappings that came with it. A fact that never sat right with him.

His parents had taken him and his sister when they were still children to a ball in honour of the senior ardent's one hundredth birthday. He remembered very little of that night, and the ardent himself was probably long dead by now, but he could still picture the most exquisite and expensive tapestry on one of the walls there. It was a depiction of all the Architects together at the gates to the next life, as they watched over the people below. Thousands of hours must have gone into that piece of artwork. There was nothing so grand here in the palace now, and he doubted there ever had been.

He wondered if the gabbalins had similar tapestries in their country. Did they pray to the Architects also? Or did they follow a different religion? That was hard for him to imagine, as he sat there alone, thinking about it. Very little was known about the gabbalins, mostly because they didn't like to interact with outsiders.

There had been a number of diplomatic attempts over the centuries by his ancestors to open trade routes and the like, but each time they had been rebuffed. Indeed, even the few of them who had been exiled from their own homeland refused to talk about what it is like there. The Moranzans called their country Abbalon. That wasn't its true name, but that wasn't forthcoming either. It was as if every one of them had taken an oath of secrecy about where they come from. An oath so sacred they even hold on to it as outcasts from their own. Strange creatures, the gabbalins, in more ways than one.

An idea popped into Cal's mind as he thought about his grey-skinned neighbours. The man found at the bridge, who may or may not have seen Liana, also spoke of gabbalins. There *had* to be something in that, he thought. It was too much of an odd incident, and it played on his mind. If his sister *was* in Dawan, and the gabbalins had tried to get across the bridge also, there had to be a connection. But what?

He thought about tracking down the man. Impossible, with only a vague description given by the guards, who were next to useless at the best of times. But the gabbalins—they were easy to distinguish. How many of those lived in the city? There couldn't be that many, surely? Cal thought about having the Queen's Guard round a few of them up and bring them here to the palace for interrogation. To what end, though? Would they even talk if they knew anything? Probably not.

Another thought entered his head. Could he? No, that was stupid. Too risky, but risking what? He *was* the ruler now, even if only temporarily, and he could do what he liked, couldn't he? There wasn't anyone to stop him. They would all be in the Great Hall, eating and drinking; celebrating the life of the late queen.

If he were to go out into the city himself, he could ask around. He could find out if anyone had seen his sister. If he dressed like one of them, acted like he *was* one of them, it might work. He figured many wouldn't talk to the Queen's Guard, nor to the Tal Valar. Indeed, that's probably why they have had no success so far. It was a great idea.

Getting out of the palace unseen was easy. Liana managed it most nights, and more importantly, he knew how she did it. He'd seen her sneak out once or twice. That was a while ago, though, back when he didn't really care what she got up to, as it didn't affect him in any way. Finding an appropriate change of clothes wasn't difficult either. He left the meeting room and walked through the palace grounds, making a mental note of who he saw and where. Aside from a scullery maid and two stable hands, there weren't too many others around. Dressed in his uniform, he drew no suspicion. The prince was going about princely business. The maid and the hands all stopped and bowed to him as he passed, as they would always do, but he felt a buzz as they did so. His heart beat faster and he suddenly realised why his sister did it. It was thrilling to do something that others would disagree with. He felt excited and guilty all at the same time.

He stole a pair of plain pants, a cap and a well-worn grey shirt from the palace laundry room and changed into them. He couldn't find any appropriate footwear, so his own boots would have to do. They were too shiny, too polished, so he took a dirty gardener's shirt from the unwashed pile and rubbed some of the mud onto his boots. Except it wasn't mud. His nose wrinkled and his eyes watered when he realised it was actually stryde shit. *Too late.*

Once he was satisfied with his attire, as best as he could manage in the moment, he skulked back through the grounds to his sister's secret exit. His heart was racing now, and he decided he didn't like the feeling it gave him. Though he now understood why Liana liked her secret journeys outside the palace, he knew it wasn't something he'd get accustomed to himself.

Aside from the funeral, he'd never been outside the palace on foot before. If there were an engagement that required his attendance, usually at the behest of the queen, travel to and from had always been by carriage. It was also the first time he'd been in the city on his own. It took him less than five minutes to decide he didn't like it.

It was too noisy for a start. There were people everywhere. They were loud, swore often, and there was a smell in the air that offended his senses. The collective scent of a thousand unwashed bodies clung to the wind as it whistled through the streets.

The question was, where to look for his sister? He had no idea where he was going as he wandered through the city. No idea where anything was, or even *what* the city had to offer. A myriad of shops offered an array of goods such as clothing, food and the like, but it all meant very little to him. He'd not had cause to exchange money for items before. If he wanted something, he'd simply ask one of the serving staff for it and some while later, they would return with said item.

He decided his best option was to look for a gabbalin and ask them if they knew of his sister. Then he realised he hadn't thought this through at all. What was he supposed to say? "Good morrow, my fine fellow. Have you seen a woman with red hair and looks a lot like the princess?" No, that wouldn't work at all. On top of that, he was lost. He'd planned to keep the towers of the palace in view, to keep his bearings, but most of the surrounding buildings were tall enough to obscure his view in any direction. It was a bad idea, and in less than half an hour since he left, he decided enough was enough and to find his way home. For that, he'd need to ask for directions.

'Pardon me, miss. Which way is it to the palace?' he asked

the closest person to him. It was an elderly woman who walked with a stoop. She ignored him wholly, not even looking in his direction.

The second person he asked grunted something he didn't understand. The third, another woman, sniffed deeply and winced at the smell. She then retrieved a copper coin from the pocket of her cloak and pressed it into his hand. 'May the Architects bless you,' she said before carrying on her way.

Cal looked at the coin in his hand. It was a pennymark, bearing the image of his grandmother—the queen before Alyssa—on one side and the Tallan crest depicting two strydes fighting inside a crown on the reverse. He didn't know what to do with the coin.

He walked a little farther, money still in hand, and then he caught sight of something ahead, turning a corner down a narrower path. It was only a glimpse, but it was unmistakable —the pointed grey ears of a gabbalin. It was the first one he'd seen outside of sketches in textbooks. There weren't all that many in the city, and none were employed by the palace. It wasn't the done thing. He followed those ears.

The side path weaved between overbearing buildings and Cal found it difficult to keep the gabbalin in view. Despite being away from the main thoroughfares of the city, the cut-through was still busy, mostly with people walking in the opposite direction to him. They jostled by, often rubbing shoulders unavoidably. Most were polite, with a "pardon me" exchanged as they brushed by, but others weren't so friendly. Cal decided he didn't like mingling with this part of society.

He followed the gabbalin for a while before he eventually lost him along a left turn. When he rounded the corner himself, there was nothing there but an empty alley. There were no apparent doors or further turnings for the gabbalin to disappear behind or into, and there were no other people around now, either. He'd lost him. He'd lost himself too, and he found his mouth now suddenly dry, as he didn't know what to do next.

He gave up and walked back the way he thought he'd came until a scrawny grey hand appeared out of nowhere from an unnoticed alcove, grabbing him by the sleeve. 'Why you following me?' The voice at the end of the arm was scratchy and vibrated on each syllable.

Cal's heel skidded in the dirt as he turned in surprise to the one who had accosted him. 'Remove your hand from me at once.' His voice didn't hide his panic. He couldn't recall anyone ever manhandling him in such a manner.

'Not until you tell me who you are, and what business you have spying on me.'

He had to make a decision and make it fast. Reveal himself as the prince, or lie and give a false name. In the second he had to think, he decided on the latter. 'My name is Venn. Forgive me, I wasn't following you, and I do not wish to cause alarm or concern.'

'You *were* following me. Heard your footsteps as soon as I walked off the market road. See.' He rotated his ears back and forth in the same way a cat would, demonstrating his auditory prowess. 'So I ask you again, *friend*, why are you following me?'

'I'm looking for a friend of mine. She's gone missing and there was talk of her associating with gabbalins in the area.'

'Talk, eh? You humans are all the same, aren't you? Any word of trouble, or law breaking and your instinct is to blame us. I tell you now, *friend*, I have seen no girl, and I've done no associating either. You would do well to walk away before there was, perhaps, an accident. If you understand my meaning.'

The right thing to do would be to walk away and try to get back to the palace. If he did that, though, he'd be no better off than when he'd left. The gabbalin was acting rather defensive. Too defensive maybe? This grey man, whether he was involved or not, was the only lead he had, and he wasn't about to squander this chance.

'Are you threatening me?'

'Threat? No, not at all. Merely a warning, is all. You take care now.' The gabbalin didn't move. He only stared Cal directly in the eyes, as if daring him to push further.

Cal refused to back down and be cowed by this grey-skinned creature. This was *his* city. It was *his* sister who was missing. He grabbed the gabbalin by the throat and spun him round, pinning him against the wall. He was surprised how light this fellow was, easily holding him up so his feet were well clear of the ground.

The gabbalin thrashed about, making gurgling noises. 'Put me down!' The vibration in his voice was more pronounced under duress.

'I'll let you go when you've told me all you know about my missing sister, or when I'm satisfied you're not involved, as you so claim.'

'How would I know who your sister is? Who are you? Release me at once or I'll...'

'Or you'll what?'

The gabbalin continued to thrash and wail, struggling to break himself free. And then he stopped and grinned.

The sudden change confused Cal. 'What's so funny?'

The gabbalin said nothing. He just... cackled and looked beyond Cal as though there was something more interesting behind him.

There was a scraping noise, and before he had time to register what it was, or even react, he felt a sharp, searing pain in his shoulder. The gabbalin fell from his fingers to the ground, the shock of pain forcing him to release his grip on the creature.

Something had struck him, and in the mere instant it took him to realise that, Cal found himself pulled away from the gabbalin and thrown to the dusty ground head-first. The sharp gravel cut into his bottom lip and he tasted blood.

He rolled onto his back to find three shadows bearing down on him, the brightness of the sky behind them obscuring their features. One of them was the gabbalin. He figured that much. All he could do was try to scramble backwards, but there was nowhere to go. He was cornered, surrounded. No way out.

'Wh... what do you want?' Cal whimpered. He wiped at the trickle of blood with the back of his hand. Although there wasn't much, and it didn't really hurt, being injured at the hands of another surprised him.

'We don't take kindly to others getting into our business,' said one of them. The voice vibrated. So definitely gabbalin. Deeper, though, which meant it wasn't the one Cal had accosted. That little grey man hadn't been alone, and now Cal was outnumbered three to one.

'I only wish to find my sister. Your business is no concern of mine otherwise.'

'Is that so?'

'I say we kill him right here, take whatever he has on him,' said the third voice.

Those words sent a chill right through Cal. He tried desperately to pull himself to his feet, only to be shoved back down against the wall. He had to find a way out. Find a way to escape. *Why did I leave the palace? I'm such a fool.* He fumbled around for the coin he was given and, with a trembling hand, offered it up to his assailants. 'Take it, it's all I have.' The coin fell from his fingers.

As one of the three bent down to retrieve the coin, Cal saw an opportunity. If he was to get out of this situation unscathed, it was now or never. Using the wall as a pushing off point, he lunged forward and threw his weight into the gabbalin before it had a chance to react. Both of them crashed to the ground in a heap.

With the gabbalin weighing so little, it was easy to over-power the creature—at first. Cal had him pinned to the ground and landed a punch to the gabbalin's face. That was all he managed, though. The other two had come to their senses and realised what was happening. Before Cal could hit his target a second time, he found himself overwhelmed by all three of them. Punches and kicks rained down on him. All he could do was pull himself into a ball, curled up in the dust and dirt, protecting himself as much as possible. The light around him turned from burnt orange to purple.

Purple? This is it. I'm to die here in the streets like a vagrant. And then the beatings stopped. Through blurred vision he saw the gabbalin figures back away from him, away from... something else. Someone else.

Cal heard voices, vibrating voices. Submissive and fright-ened. Scampering, running, and then nothing. They were gone, and he was still alive. Sore, but alive.

'The city is no place for a prince to be out on his own,' said a voice.

Cal knew that voice. It was Shaan's voice. He was sure of it. He opened his eyes and looked up, using one hand to shield away the light to better focus on the silhouette standing over him. 'What are you doing out here?' He coughed away a mouthful of sand.

'I should ask you the same thing. What possessed you to leave the palace unaccompanied?'

'I couldn't stand by and do nothing. I had to try to find Liana myself.'

Shaan extended his hand, which Cal gratefully took, pulling himself to his feet. His ribs ached, as did his back and shoulders. All in all, he'd got away lightly. He stretched his limbs to make sure everything worked as it should.

'Gabbalins are scurrilous vermin who are best avoided. You should count yourself lucky they did not kill you.'

'I think they know where Liana is. I swear one of them knew something.'

'Whether they do or do not, leave it to the guards and the Tal Valar to investigate. Not everything needs to fall on your shoulders. Come. Let me get you back to the palace.'

Cal gladly accepted Shaan's arm to lean on as they walked back through the city. Though there were no obvious signs of injury, his right leg hurt when he tried to put weight on it. He was surprised to find he'd made it not fifty paces from the perimeter wall of the palace grounds.

'I would suggest you get yourself cleaned up before you make your appearance in the Great Hall. Everyone is expecting you,' said Shaan as they neared Cal's private chambers.

'I think I should sleep.'

'You need to maintain appearances for the sake of everyone else. You cannot hide away, nor can you shut everyone else out.'

Cal punched at the metal plating of his chamber door and screamed. 'How could I have let those gabbalins get the better of me like that? They're nothing. I am the Prince of Moranza. How *dare* they attack me?' All the pain inside him gave way to a rage he could barely control. He screamed again and flung the door open hard enough for it to clatter against the wall inside the room.

'Calm yourself. Do not let your temper get the better of you,' said Shaan as he followed him into the room. He closed the door behind him.

'Why should I be calm? I'm angry, Shaan. Angry! Angry about my mother dying. Angry for Liana disappearing without a care in the world. Leaving me to face everything. I can't...' he grew breathless through his vitriol. He kicked the copper bedpan across the room, uncaring if it was empty or not.

'You have every right to be, but you need to control yourself. All this rage inside you, you need to focus it. Use it in the right way. The world is now at a precipice. A dangerous moment in history that will define this country for years to come. This new world requires strength. Leadership. The people of this city will need someone to look to, and as it stands, that someone is you. Now is the time to be strong. Channel all that anger in the right direction.'

Cal sat on the edge of his bed, panting. He wiped at his mouth, checking for more blood. There was none, though his lip did feel a little swollen. Nothing permanent. 'You believe we should strike back at the Dawanii.'

'What I believe is not important. You must consider all the options and come to the correct conclusion yourself.'

'May the Architects damn you, Liana,' he shouted at the ceiling. He took a deep breath and looked at Shaan. 'I do not wish to start a war. Not until I am certain there is no other option.'

'If that is what you wish.'

'I cannot sit around and do nothing, though. How many men do you have at your training camp?'

'Five, six hundred. Maybe more. Why?'

'I want you to take fifty into Dawan. I trust you, and I know you'll do what you can to find her and return her here safely. Go to the Dawanii. Find her if you can, but deliver a message to them. Tell them that while we do not wish for war, we will defend ourselves.'

Shaan nodded, bowed, and left without another word.

13

SOLDIER

Addan loved her, Shara, ever since he first met her nearly two years ago. He had never told her she saved his life that day. She didn't love him back, of course, and probably never would, but that was fine by him. He didn't need her to love him back. He knew who she really was—the Princess Liana. He figured that out in a few days, but decided to keep it to himself, even from her. Now, she might be dead, or at least in a lot of trouble, and it was all his fault. Again. Trouble always had a way of finding him. Maybe it was the drinking. Maybe it was his brother's death. That *was* his fault, for sure, but even when he was trying his best, things always had a habit of going wrong for him.

He would die for Liana, and he wondered how long it would be before he would have to prove it. Signing up for the militia seemed like a good idea at the time. Again, the drinking made everything look better than it was. Even so, it was the only thing he could think of that stood any chance of success in finding her.

The reality wasn't like anything he had pictured in his head. He didn't know what to expect, really. A brand new Queen's

Guard uniform with perfectly fitting boots and a gleaming sword. A sense of pride and belonging. A purpose. Instead, he found himself in a barren field to the south of the city with nothing more than mould-green fatigues, a tin mug and the company of nineteen other men who probably had the same picture in their minds.

He wasn't given a weapon of any kind. Not even a stick. None of the other men looked like the sort of people he would usually want to associate with, but they were all forced to share the same large canvas tent that looked ready to collapse at any moment. Addan lay on his cot—a thin piece of fatigue-coloured cloth stretched over a flimsy metal frame—and watched the peak of the tent sway in the wind. Sometimes, he regretted life. This was one of those times.

The man in the cot next to his own, almost within arm's reach, was sitting upright picking his toenails. He had dark brown hair, thick arms, and really hairy feet. The bottom half of his left ear was missing. Addan wondered how, but was too afraid to ask. He watched as the man tore off a piece of a toenail, using his fingernails to scrape a starting point, pulling off a sliver. The man examined it up close before using it as a toothpick. Addan shuddered and rolled over.

The smile of a young man—too young—looked back at him from his own cot. 'What's ya name?' He couldn't have been more than fourteen or fifteen. He had messy light blond hair which hung over a lazy eye that looked inwards at his nose. There was no muscle to him and his fatigues were too big.

'Uh, Addan.'

'I'm Milo. Good 'ere innit?' He looked genuinely thrilled to be there.

'If you say so. I'm not sure I'd agree.'

'Why not?' Milo sat up, swinging his legs round to face Addan. 'Free food, free clothes, *an'* they payin' us good too.'

Addan stayed in his lying position, eyeing up the boy. 'It may be free, but it isn't what I'd call food.'

Milo shrugged. 'I'm not fussy. Food's food. Much more than what I'm used to, anyway.' He looked beyond Addan, raising an eyebrow at the sight of the other man. 'Can't say I've ever eaten me own toenails, even when I've been starvin'.'

There was a grunt from behind Addan.

'What did you do before here?' Addan asked.

'Beggin' mainly. Living on streets, makin' the best of what I 'ad. They were 'ard times.'

'I see.' Addan understood now. As grim as it was here, it was a big upgrade for the boy. If he were destitute like him, he'd sign up too. As he considered this, he realised he was no better off than his new friend. It was all a matter of perspective.

There was a clanging noise from outside the tent. Metal against metal, which meant it was meal time. Milo sprang from his cot and grabbed his mug from underneath. It was only when Addan stood up next to him he realised how short the lad was. Milo looked up at him and squinted a grin before falling into line out of the tent. Addan could feel the hot toenail breath on the back of his neck. He shivered. He couldn't help it.

The tents were all lined up with each other perfectly. "Precision and order," the induction commander had told him. Addan liked precision and order. It differed from the rest of the city, and he appreciated it. He told himself it might not be so terrible after all. That was a lie.

Across from his row of tents was the larger food tent. Everyone called it "the mess" but he found it to be as orderly as all the others. Hundreds of men filed in through one side of the tent, received their meal before leaving via the opposite end.

It was Addan's second meal since signing up—still drunk— the day before, and was surprised to see it was the same slop as the first time. He hadn't liked it. It was a swirl of brown and grey, with lumpy bits. It reminded him of the bottom half of milk after it had been sat out for a few days, but not as offensive on the nose.

'Do you have any other options? I'm not keen on this one,' he said, holding his mug back out to the man on the other side of the serving table.

'You hear this?' said the server to anyone close enough to hear him, struggling to contain his laughter. 'He wants something *different*! Would sir care for a menu? Some wine to wash it down, perhaps?'

'I was only asking. No need to be rude about it.' Addan felt offended just before feeling like an idiot.

'Bugger off,' sneered the man.

Addan glumly stared at his food as he made his way out of the tent. No sooner than the moonlight met his eyes had he felt something catch against his foot and he landed chin-first in the dirt. His mug spun away from his hand, the contents spiralling into the air. He rolled over to see the toenail man standing over him before sniffing and walking away without a word.

Addan dragged himself to his feet and retrieved his mug. There was only a mouthful left at the bottom, and his stomach growled in protest. He tried to go back into the tent, but was stopped by one of the supervisors.

'One mug per recruit.' He was tall, broad, and had a face that dared you to pick a fight.

'But I lost mine over... I was tripped up...'

'One mug per recruit. No exceptions.'

'But...' Addan's shoulders dropped in defeat.

'Back to your tent, recruit.'

He did as he was directed, trying to scoop out whatever was left of his meal with his fingers. Somehow the dirt on his hands from his fall improved the flavour.

'What 'appened?' asked Milo, who was already back on his cot.

Addan was about to tell him what happened when he

caught the stare of "Toenails" and thought better of it. 'I fell,' was all he said.

'That's dumb luck.' Milo shook his head sympathetically. 'Would ya like some of mine?'

'I'm fine. Thank you. I wasn't that hungry anyway.' Addan watched as his new friend shrugged before gulping his slop in one go, leaving behind a gooey smile.

Addan noticed, looking around the tent, most of the other recruits looked rather downtrodden. Many of them had been here longer than him and had already settled, willingly or otherwise, into the routine. To him, it felt more like a prison camp than an army barracks. All of them had volunteered. *Hadn't they?*

The clanging of metal from outside the tent rang out again.

'Trainin',' said Milo.

When Milo said "training", Addan had thought it would be practice sword fights or duelling with staves. Instead, he found himself forced to run laps around the encampment. He didn't like running. Folk should only run if they were being chased, and not simply for the sake of it. Before he'd barely made it around the perimeter once, his lungs were already burning. Somehow, he had to make it round another nine times before he was allowed to stop. The only thing that kept him going was seeing he wasn't the only one struggling. He dug deep within himself and forced one leg in front of the other. He reminded himself he was doing this for Liana and kept her at the front of his mind with every step. He imagined her there with him, willing him onwards. It worked. Three laps. Four. Then he watched Toenails pass out with exhaustion a little farther ahead. Addan couldn't help but snigger to himself.

He was one of the last to finish, but he *did* finish. The supervisor overseeing the training gave him a simple nod. Exhausted, Addan wanted to collapse to the ground, but seeing as no one else had done so, he fought against the urge and tried to remain standing. Somewhere deep down, he knew there was more torture to come. He was right.

He was grateful he wasn't the last one to finish, as it gave him some time to rest. The poor soul who *did* finish last—a middle-aged man with too much weight around his waist—had no such luck. The moment he crossed the finish line, the supervisor called for the recruits to gather before issuing instructions for what came next.

What followed was a series of exercises, ranging from press-ups, pull-ups—on a rusty bar that cut into his fingers—and rope climbing for no reason he could discern other than getting to the top and back down again. Three times. Of course, he realised these exercises were designed to break the men. Make them ready. It wouldn't matter much in the end. If they were going to war, most of them were so far past their prime, they wouldn't last very long, in his opinion. He was determined not to be one of those men. He climbed, he pulled, and he pushed, with his imagined version of Liana cheering him on. He did everything that was asked of him. When it came to the evening meal of yet more slop, he did not complain.

The thin material of the tent—some kind of hessian, he guessed—did little to shield the outside light when it came to sleeping. As with everyone else he knew, he preferred drapes over the window of his lodgings to block out the near-perpetual light. Somehow, it was easier to sleep in total darkness. He was so tired after the training, he should have fallen asleep quickly, but he couldn't. He closed his eyes and imagined being in his own bed, in the dark. The chorus of snoring, farting and other unworldly noises and smells in the tent shattered any illusion he was alone. So he laid there—awake—watching the peak of the tent sway in the wind.

He must have dozed off at some point as he felt someone shaking his shoulders, trying to get his attention. It was a supervisor. He was a spindly man with unmanageable eyebrows and a split in his lip beneath the nose. Addan hadn't seen him enter the tent, let alone stand over him like a tame-wolf wanting breakfast. The man forced him to get up out of his cot.

'Training.' The man spoke with a slight lisp. It was only a whisper, but to Addan it felt like shouting. It seemed like a useful talent to be able to be loud and quiet at the same time.

'What's going on?' Addan forced his stiff body to move.

'Now!' The supervisor was older than him and wore a sorry attempt at a moustache that did little to disguise the split lip. It was a different colour to his wild eyebrows—more red and less brown, as if it had its own anger issues. His uniform was the same shade of green as the recruits', though his was properly fitted and less worn out. His shoulders were adorned with lapels, with one gold stripe on each. Addan didn't know what the stripes meant. Some had only the one. At least one had three. It seemed important for him to know that he, and all the other recruits, had none.

Addan got out of his cot and shuffled his way out of the tent. The supervisor had woken nine others to join him, including Milo. He noticed they were all ones who had performed well in the training exercises earlier, most of them better than he had done. And their reward was *more* training. Why did it feel like it was a crime to do well here?

'Do you know what this is about?' he asked Milo, who was standing directly in front of him.

'Nope. Excitin' though innit?' The lad's enthusiasm knew no bounds.

The supervisor led the ten of them away from the main camp to an open area that had to be at least a mile square. It wasn't only them out in this field, he noticed. Other supervisors had chosen and gathered their own sets of ten and were assembling at different spots across the space, with plenty of distance between each group. A simultaneous private training session for each team. Addan counted twenty groups, including his own. Two hundred men.

Once they were all lined up, the supervisor introduced himself properly. 'I am Lieutenant Makkel and I will be your new sub-leader. You have each been chosen, as you have proven yourselves to be the least pathetic of a very sorry bunch.'

'Chosen for what, exactly?' asked a man with brown hair at the end of the line. Addan was third in the row and couldn't see who asked the question, but he was tall enough to see the hair.

'Advance party. Our esteemed commander has taken it upon himself to go to Dawan at moonrise. He has requested two hundred men to accompany him and the Queen's Guard to determine if we are to go to war.'

The assembled line of men looked at each other, many surprised at the mention of war so soon.

One man in the middle raised his hand. 'Sir, I am not ready for war. I wish to resign and go home.'

Makkel marched slowly along the line from one end to the other and back again, not directly looking at his charges. 'Nobody is truly ready for war, not unless they are insane, fool-hardy, or both. While clearly this news has come as a surprise to us all, you *did* sign a contract for one season each. That contract shall be honoured by each and every one of you.'

'Yes, but,' said the man in the middle. Addan turned his head a little to see who the coward was. It was a red-haired man with a sharp nose and a trembling bottom lip. 'I've been here only one day. Honestly, I didn't think we would *actually* go to war, I—'

'You thought this was be a wonderful opportunity to make a little extra money while having a nice little vacation down here.'

The man didn't reply.

'As I was saying, you have been chosen, along with all the other reprobates you see on this field, because we have numbers to make up. Of course, it would have been ideal to provide you all with more training before the situation, shall we say, escalated as it has, but we shall have to make the best of it.'

There was a pile of sticks close to where Makkel was standing. Addan hadn't noticed them until the lieutenant picked one up. The stick was smooth, straight, and as long as his arm.

'Now, who here has any experience with a sword?' Makkel asked, spinning the stick in his hand. It made a swooshing sound as it cut through the wind. Nobody said anything. 'None of you? This is... disappointing.'

Addan saw the lack of enthusiasm of his peers. He'd had a little practice with a sword, a long time ago, now. Even then, that was only for an hour or two when he apprenticed with a blacksmith. The apprenticeship itself only lasted three days before he got himself fired for trying it on with the blacksmith's daughter. That was back when he was young and stupid. These days he was a little less young and clearly still stupid, considering where he was standing now.

If no one else was going to put themselves forward, he thought he may as well have a go. If he was lucky, he might be rewarded with an extra mug of slop. It seemed logical to him, so he stepped forward.

'Ah! We have a volunteer. What is your name?'

'Addan, sir.'

'Consider yourself a master swordsman, do you?'

'No, not exactly, sir.'

'Be exact, lad. Vagueness and imprecision will probably get you killed.' Makkel was still swinging his weapon, left and right, trying to be intimidating.

'I was apprentice to a blacksmith. He showed me how to hold a sword. A long time ago now, sir.'

'Very well.' Makkel tossed him the stick. He caught it by the "blade" end. 'Not a good start, lad. If that were a real sword, you would be on the way to the infirmary.'

'Yes, sir.' Addan wondered if they really had an infirmary. He grasped the stick at the "correct" end and turned his wrist, getting a feel for its weight. It felt exactly like the stick that it was. The only other sword he'd held would have been heavier and definitely more intimidating.

Makkel picked up another stick from the pile and took a readying stance, stick held in front with both hands. 'Show me what you can do.' The other nine watched on with gleeful interest.

Addan took a deep breath and mirrored Makkel's stance. *They're just sticks. If this goes wrong, at least I won't get hurt.* He stepped forward and swung at the lieutenant. Makkel moved backwards out of the way.

He swung again, this time he was blocked by the other stick. The impact vibrated through his arm and into his shoulder. Before he could ignore the pain, he found himself on the defensive. Makkel came at him fast. From the left and then from the right, attack after attack. Addan defended the first blow successfully. The second knocked the stick from his hand. He held his hands up in front of him instinctively to block a third strike, but it never came. And then he saw the sky, his legs kicked out from underneath him. Makkel stood over him, his "sword" pointing at Addan's nose. Mocking laughter rippled through the small audience.

Makkel sighed and allowed Addan to stand up. 'Again,' he said, retaking his attack posture.

Addan performed worse than the first time. His backside was in the dirt again before he'd even started. Twice more, by which time the others were all in hysterics. Each time, Addan got himself up, dusted himself down, and went again. He was determined to show his worth, however little that may be. *This is for Liana. Remember that. This is for her. This is all for her.*

He closed his eyes and raised his weapon. He tried to remember the paltry amount he had learned from the blacksmith. It wasn't much at all. A fire burned within him and he attacked. His stick met with Makkel's, but this time, he kept his footing. He struck high at Makkel's head. He missed, and he rotated his body, carrying through the momentum.

Makkel countered with a left swing aimed at Addan's waist. Blocked. *It's working!* He spun on his heels, bringing his sword —*it's not a stick, it's a sword*—across from right to left, slamming it into Makkel's shoulder. Makkel stumbled, trying to keep his balance. *He had him!* Addan forged forward, going in for the final attack, but Makkel dodged right at the last moment. Addan had nowhere to go but down, crashing into the dirt. *Shit!* It was defeat once again, but the jeers and laughter behind him had given way to cheers and applause.

'There's hope for you yet,' said Makkel, out of breath, and helping Addan to his feet. 'That's enough for now.'

Addan wanted to keep going, his blood pumping through him, buzzing with a newfound energy. 'One more time.'

'No. Return to the line.' Any sense of amiability in Makkel had given in to stern authority. 'You are all to pair up and practice amongst yourselves. Choose your partner and take a stick. Begin when ready.'

Addan wasn't surprised when none of the others wanted to pair with him, having witnessed him *almost* win against Makkel. Except Milo.

'If ya promise to go easy on me, I'll fight ya,' said the lad, blowing a tuft of blond hair out of his eye-line.

Addan nodded and smiled, tossing his new opponent his stick. He then fetched one of the remaining ones from the pile and backed away into an open space where they weren't likely to be in anyone else's way.

'Ya're really good,' said Milo as he waved his stick around haphazardly before dropping it.

'I lost every time.'

'But ya nearly won that last one.'

'Nearly isn't good enough. If it were a real sword fight, I'd be dead.'

Milo wrinkled his nose in thought. 'I guess.'

The other four pairs were hacking at each other with their makeshift swords with little sense of form or forethought. Addan didn't really have much of an idea what he was doing himself, but the little knowledge he had told him they wouldn't last long in an actual battle. Though maybe only a few minutes less than himself.

Taking a different approach, Addan taught his young opponent the correct way—as best as he could remember—to stand and how to hold his weapon properly. He then took Milo through the same, and only, lesson he'd had with the blacksmith. Each step in slow motion. Milo thought it was hilarious, but did as he was instructed.

The ten men practiced until they were told to stop. Addan didn't know how long they had been training, but it felt to him the opportunity to sleep further before moonrise had long since passed.

'I'm sorry to say,' said Makkel, 'you all need far more training and practice than you have been given. This programme was meant to take a month, but alas, your time has been cut short. The prince will arrive here at moonrise and he will lead you all to Dawan.'

The prince is coming here? It surely meant war, but instead of feeling afraid, Addan's heart lifted. He would be going to Dawan, so it wasn't such a daft plan after all.

Makkel continued. 'Return to your tent. Get what sleep you still can, but it won't be much. Addan, on account of you being the least worthless of this group, you will be company leader.'

'What does that mean?' whispered Addan to no one in particular.

The man to his immediate left replied, 'it means you'll probably die first.'

199

14

INVASION

Addan found himself looking forward to his morning slop. He wasn't sure whether it was the prospect of seeing the prince arrive at any moment, or the comfort of knowing what he was getting and thus spared of any disappointment. Once his tin mug had been filled, that first sip reminded him there wasn't really all that much to get excited over. The grey, gloopy food slid down his throat like dragon shit on a window.

Naturally, Milo seemed to enjoy his slop as he'd previously showed. That boy was far too eager for everything. Nothing got him down. Addan had been like that too, once. When he found himself old enough to pay taxes, the eagerness and energy of life was slowly chiselled away with each passing year. Being on the city streets should have worn down a lad's enthusiasm, but not Milo. Of course, being a beggar meant he was exempt from taxes by default.

Word had already spread through the rest of the camp about the late night sword practice for the selected few. Most were grateful for not having their sleep interrupted. Some, including Toenails, weren't happy at all, and didn't try disguising it. Toenails had taken it upon himself to clean out his mug on Addan's bedsheet.

'Ain't like you're needing it, are ya?' he said, spitting on the floor. It was the first time Addan had heard him speak. For all his height and breadth, the man had an oddly feminine voice.

'It's not as if we volunteered,' said Addan. He left it at that, not wanting to pick a fight so early in the day. Brawls were fine when your head was already obliterated by alcohol, but sober and common sense intact? No, thank you.

A supervisor entered the tent with a bundle of blue material. It was one of the younger looking men on the official city payroll, not the one who had led their training last night. Addan and his fellow tent-mates watched as the man proudly handed out what turned out to be royal blue coloured tunics to the chosen ten.

'Put these on and assemble outside,' the supervisor said as he handed out each tunic.

Addan wrestled with the sleeves, but once it was on, he found it fitted rather well. Toenails grunted with disapproval and spat again. Turning away in disgust, Addan glimpsed an angry red stripe of a scar across Milo's back before it disappeared under his new uniform. Every scar tells a story, and that one must be awful.

Makkel was waiting for them outside the tent. Addan was the last one out, but not far behind enough for Makkel to pay any attention.

'Your designation for this mission is Company Nine,' said Makkel, appraising each man in turn with an air of contempt. 'You are to proceed to the weapons tent over there, and you will be furnished with your swords. Please try not to injure yourselves with them. You won't get paid if you're dead.'

One man stifled a giggle. Addan didn't know his name, though he was sure he would learn them all soon enough. Not that he'd remember most.

Makkel marched up to the man, nose to nose. 'Enjoy yourself while you can,' he sneered. 'War is no laughing matter.'

The swords were all the same basic design. Functional, but cheaply made. There were no decorations or embellishments, only a small strap of leather as a grip and a thin disc of metal as a cross-guard. Addan felt a little disappointed somehow. He chose the closest one and picked it up. It was much lighter than he expected. Swords looked like such heavy things, but it barely weighed anything. He turned the blade over in his hand, getting a feel for it. As much as he wasn't an expert, it didn't feel well-balanced. It looked cheap, and it felt cheap. The others were doing the same, some clearly taking their cue from him. A tan-skinned man with long curly brown hair somehow thought it a good idea to run his thumb along the edge of his blade. The pain and dripping blood came as a complete surprise to the man. Addan shook his head and smirked. At least they were sharp.

'Something to say?' said the bleeding man.

'Oh no, not at all. I'd be careful though. Swords can be a little bitey.' Addan was on thin ground here, and he knew it. This man was a whole lot less of a threat than Toenails, though.

'I'd watch your mouth if I were you.'

'What's your name?' Addan asked.

'Jonn.' He was sucking his thumb, trying to stop the bleeding.

'Well, Jonn, I'll bear that in mind. I'm Addan.'

Jonn sniffed and tended to his wound. They all knew Addan had seniority over the rest of them, for whatever that was worth. Only Milo was happy with it. One was enough to start. Addan hoped the rest would come around in due course. He tucked his sword into one of the leather scabbards provided and left the tent. It slapped into his thigh as he walked, which would take a little getting used to. It made him feel different.

Stronger, maybe. Half of him still regretted the drunken decision to sign up. The other half only thought of Liana.

A horn sounded on the far side of the barracks, coming from the main gates. Addan's attention was pulled in its direction. He squinted, trying to see across the distance to catch a glimpse of the prince arriving. Makkel ordered Company Nine to fall in and take position with the other companies in the centre of the camp, ready for presentation.

In position, Addan watched—with his peripheral vision— the six strydes with their mounts approach the far end of the line up by Company One. None of the men dismounted. All were in Queen's Guard uniform except for the one. Leading the front was a man dressed all in black, contrasting with the white stryde he rode.

Addan wasn't certain the man in black was the prince. It had been a long time since he'd seen what he looked like. The only time he'd seen him was during the last royal funeral procession. He tried to remember how long ago that was. Twelve years, maybe? The prince would have still been a boy back then. They were about the same age now that Addan thought about it. The prince's name eluded him. He knew it, but it was hiding somewhere in a deep crevice of his memory. Carl? Kial? Something like that. It would come to him, eventually.

The strydes slowly carried the men past each company. Addan felt nervous. Was now the right time to say something to him about his sister? Or should he wait? As the procession reached Company Nine, Addan had opened his mouth, ready to speak, but something made him stop. Addan was almost certain the prince had brown eyes, but this man had blue eyes. Was this not him? He frowned, confused, which drew further scrutiny from the man in black.

'You there,' he said, pulling his stryde to a stop.

Shit! 'Yes, Your Grace,' said Addan. He forced himself to stand straighter.

'Your Grace? Sir, I believe you are misinformed. I am not the prince, nor should I be addressed as such.'

Then who are you? 'Forgive me, sir. I have not had the privilege of meeting the prince before now. Naturally, when we were told he was coming here this day to lead us into Dawan, and seeing your good self dressed apart from the others...'

The man smiled. 'A logical, but flawed, assumption. I am Shaan, senior advisor to the prince. I stand here in his stead. He has decided it is more beneficial to the people of the city he remain here.' Shaan pulled his stryde away from the gathered troops a few steps before addressing them all. 'I will be leading you all into Dawan myself. I am to meet with their leader for negotiations. You have all been selected to accompany me as a show of strength, nothing more.'

Addan relaxed a little. He wondered what the man meant by "negotiations". For money? Land? For all the rumours of impending war, he was grateful he was about to embark on a mission of peace and diplomacy.

'We depart at moonrise,' said Shaan. He led the other men on strydes away, ignoring the other eleven companies he'd not yet appraised.

Makkel hurriedly stepped forward, taking charge. 'Well, you heard what he said. Moonrise. Fall out for final preparations.'

The horizon to the west was looking lighter, meaning the moon wasn't too far away from making a new appearance. All the companies broke their formations and merged into one. Final preparations turned out to mean taking a piss if one was needed. Addan declined, hoping he wouldn't regret it later. He asked the closest man, a tall fellow with a neat scar below his bottom lip, if he knew how long it would take to get to their destination. The man simply shrugged.

In his naivety, Addan had hoped for strydes to ride on, or at least carriages to ride in for the journey. However long that would be, it would be quicker if there was transport of some kind. He fought back a look of disappointment when Makkel told them they would all be on foot, save for the men already on their strydes. Addan's damaged leg had already been under enough strain of late, and it was hard to shrug off the nagging pain it caused him. What other choice did he have now but to keep going? If he was lucky, his new boots wouldn't give him blisters, adding to his discomfort.

Shaan led his new troops from the compound right on schedule. Addan could almost see the top of the moon nudge the sky before the horizon merged with the trees. Each company stayed within its own ranks as they marched, but there was little sense of order among them. Instead of neat files of men, to anyone watching on, it would look like random patches of bodies meandering through the countryside away from the city into the surrounding hills.

By the time the moon was in full view, the silent march had broken into conversations between various men in some of the companies. Addan took the opportunity to try to get to know more about the ones he'd been grouped with. Milo, never without a smile on his face, had barely left Addan's side since they'd left. To Addan's right was a muscular man with a greying beard and long hair tied back in a tail.

'What's your name?' asked Addan. He'd not seen the man speak before. He was one of many of them who didn't seem too likely to pick a fight or quarrel with anyone else. Addan was wrong about that.

'Piss off, rich boy.'

Addan was taken aback by the reply, losing his walking rhythm for a step or two. 'Rich boy? I'm not rich. What makes you think I am?'

'Saw you sign up. I were right behind you. Good clothes, talk proper. I figure, why would someone like you wanna get involved with this?'

'I wouldn't consider my clothes to be good. I'm no nobleman.'

'Bet you went to school though, yeah?'

'What's that got to do with anything?'

'Rich folk go to school.'

'I can assure you, I'm not rich. Rather the opposite, in fact. I owe a lot of money to a lot of people.'

'Rich folk can owe money just as well as poor folk,' the man grunted. He stayed quiet for a minute as they continued their march. 'Tobin. My name's Tobin.'

'Addan.' He offered his hand, but Tobin didn't take it.

'Most of 'em think ya rich,' said Milo happily. 'I thought ya're rich, too.'

'Is that so?'

'When ya live on the streets, beggin' an' such, anyone with their own roof an' not worryin' about bein' hungry is rich to them.'

Addan thought about what the boy was saying. For most of his life he'd never gone a day without a meal. Nor had he been forced to sleep without shelter. True, he'd come close on both counts a number of times, especially in the last year or so. He was a lot poorer now, but that was all of his own making. He got by, barely. Taking occasional work for the gabbalins and other unsavoury residents of the city helped him get by most of the time. He still had his lodgings, as meagre as they were. For him, life wasn't *so* bad, all things considered. Plenty were far worse off than he was, and some of them walked beside him here.

'Tobin were on the streets too, like me,' said Milo.

'Born to it,' said Tobin. 'Mother was a whore. Never knew

my father. Spect the only money he ever spent on me was when he paid her to lie on her back.'

'Not shy, is he?' Addan said to Milo quietly. Milo kept on smiling.

'She died when I were young. And I've been making me own way ever since. See him over there?' Tobin nodded at the man diagonally to his right. 'Pol, his name is. He used to be rich once, like you. Never paid his taxes, though, so he ended up like us. Everyone here is down on his luck, one way or other. Except you. Best I know, you're the only rich one among us. Some are wondering why that might be.'

Addan felt a flash of heat on the back of his neck, feeling rather uncomfortable. 'I joined up because a friend needs my help.'

'What friend? Owe them money too, do ya?'

'Not that sort of help. She's in trouble. Well, I think she's in trouble. Possibly. Anyway, I joined because I need to find her.'

'A woman, eh? Spose we all do mad shit for women. Well, just remember the company you keep. Don't be thinking you better than us and you probably won't get hurt. Probably.'

'Oh, I won't.' *How am I supposed to lead this group and also not have them think I'm better than them?*

The two hundred men continued to march, though at times it was more of an amble. The bridge between the two countries looked smaller somehow when they marched across it. Maybe it was the number of men and women crossing it all at the same time. To Addan, it felt different, less intimidating.

On the other side, it didn't take him long to realise they weren't following the same route he and Liana had taken. Instead of continuing west, for the first hour or so they progressed almost parallel to the Divide in a northerly direction before a natural valley steered them deeper into Dawan. The scenery looked much the same to him, though. Rough foliage became rough woodland with uneven terrain. He had to assume Shaan and the other men on the strydes knew where they were going, not that he saw any of them with a map.

As they walked, he spent more time observing the other men in his company. It took most of the morning before he realised one of them was a woman. With no difference in the uniforms they had been provided, it was hard to tell. She kept short hair and had a muscular frame that hid most of her womanly features. That was either a deliberate effort on her part, or pure ignorance on his. Addan had not heard her speak until she questioned the parentage of one of the other men and challenged the man to a fight right there and then.

Addan knew of six women in the complement of two-hundred soldiers. There were probably a few more like the one in his Company. Ones who were content with everyone else assuming they were a man.

The men on the strydes must have sensed he was hungry because, without a hint of warning, they ordered a halt. The word "food" spread through the—was it an army? He couldn't think of a better way to describe them, even though they were nothing more than an undisciplined and disorganised group of people who were desperate enough to want an escape from their old lives.

One rider pulled free a sack attached to his saddle and, from within it, handed something out to each recruit in turn.

'What's he doing?' asked Addan to Tobin.

'Rations.'

'Do you mean food? We're not getting that slop?'

'Not sure you noticed, but they ain't carrying a barrel of slop on them strydes.'

Addan was about to ask if he knew what was on offer when he got a clearer view of what the rider was handing out. 'Biscuits?'

'Biscuits. Not very satisfying, and you'll likely be preferring the slop, but they's easy to carry.'

The man with the bag eventually reached Company Nine and Addan gratefully accepted his meal with a "thank you." The rider ignored him. The biscuit was a thick, greyish brown rectangle with a lumpy texture. As he turned it over in his hand, he had a feeling this meal was nothing more than dried out slop cut into individual portions. Carefully, he bit into a corner. The biscuit was so hard and dry he had trouble chewing it and felt like a tooth would break at any moment. Any vestige of saliva in his mouth was sucked away by the biscuit, and before he was even half done, he was begging for water.

'Where's your bladder?'

'What bladder?'

'Back at the camp when they ordered final preparations, you were meant to collect one and fill it with water to carry.'

Addan rubbed his face with his free hand. 'When they said bladder, I thought they meant empty it.'

Tobin laughed, nearly choking on his own meal. 'I've heard it all now. Bloody rich boy.'

'Here,' said Milo, holding out his own bladder. 'Ya can 'ave some of mine.'

Addan accepted the water, thanking what was probably his only true friend there. He was careful not to drink too much, so as not to appear greedy. As he handed the bladder back to Milo, he noticed Shaan had taken his stryde to an area slightly raised from the rest of the field they were in and was now facing the troops. He called out for attention.

'We are drawing close to our destination. Now, I know you have all been told we are on a mission of negotiation and diplomacy with the Dawanii on behalf of your prince. However, this is not the case.'

A low murmur rippled through the companies. Confusion echoed back at Shaan. He continued.

'As you know, the queen was murdered in cold blood. We invited these people into our great city and their first act was to strike her down for all to see. It was an act of savagery never before witnessed and a tragedy for us all.'

The murmur grew louder. Confusion gave way to agreement.

'This *murder* was an act of war against our country. Not only has our queen been slain, her daughter, Princess Liana, has been taken prisoner by these bastards.'

Prisoner? Addan looked up at Shaan with surprise. That meant they'd had word about her. They knew what had happened and that she hadn't made it home. *Was this a rescue mission, then?* His heart lifted.

'We will not stand by and let this happen. If we do not take action this day, then only the Architects themselves know what may befall us. Your own mothers and sisters may be next. We cannot simply stand and wait for the fight to come to us. We are to go to them. To war. To fight. We do not march this day for diplomacy. We march to demonstrate our strength. Our power. We take the fight to them!'

The low chatter had turned into a roar. Addan felt a rush of energy throughout his whole body. While it seemed all those around him were shouting and cheering their approval, he felt nothing but dread. The remaining half of his meal fell from his hand and he felt light-headed. *War?* This felt *wrong*, and there was nothing he could do about it. He clenched his fist, if only to steady his nerves. He closed his eyes and focused on what brought him here in the first place—Liana. He had to save her, he owed her that. Lest he be seen as an outsider further, he joined in the cheers and cries for war.

As the cheering and chanting continued, Shaan's stryde squawked and flapped its immense wings, as if calling for attention. Shaan held his sword aloft and his army fell silent. He ordered everyone to follow as they made their final approach to their destination. Addan kept pace with the others. The slow march thus far had turned into a slow run. His heart raced as though he'd ran a mile at his fastest pace. Even Milo's ever-present smile had faded.

Eventually, the untrodden grass and undergrowth turned into a barren and dusty path that led towards a large settlement. Under the direction of the riders, the two hundred recruits fanned out into a line, hidden behind a row of trees that separated the woods from the first buildings. Addan looked ahead. It was too small to be a city, perhaps more of what he would consider a large village. Dozens of buildings, mostly made from wood, scattered into the distance. They were of a bizarre construction, as if they grew from the trees themselves.

It was very different to home. Very little was made of stone here. It all looked so natural, as if all the structures had been created organically and not by man. And there was a lot more thought to how everything was laid out. It looked tidy. Clean. He spotted a shallow river winding its way through the buildings. He followed its path with his eyes and noticed a strange structure on the far bank. It was tall and narrow, with four wings that turned slowly in the wind. He'd never seen anything like it. The hollering of those around him brought him back and reminded him of why he was there. He was disappointed he likely wouldn't learn of the building's purpose.

'Are you ready to die this day?' asked Tobin. He drew his sword, grinning. He looked as though he had been waiting for a day like this his whole life.

Shaan addressed his charges again. 'These people, these savages, do not yet know we have come. Soon, they will learn of our arrival and they shall know the same pain that we felt when they killed our queen.'

The army cheered.

'For the Architects are surely on our side this day. The side of righteousness. The side of victory. On my order, make yourselves known. Show them the consequences of their actions. They must bear—'

Shaan was interrupted by the sound of a horn echoing in the air. It was coming from within the settlement.

'They have seen us! The time has come. We will free the princess and return home victorious! Charge!'

Shaan led the way, his stryde galloping down the slope towards the river. The other five riders followed immediately behind. The noise of two hundred riled up soldiers rang out over the village. Scared birds fled from their branches, the sound of their wings like a round of applause. Addan swallowed, drew his sword, and ran.

Deep inside him, it felt wrong. Every sense and sinew screamed at him to stop, to turn around and run away. He couldn't. He was caught in the wave of men carrying him along. There was no other way but forward. He thought of her and why he was there. He might only be moments away from seeing her again, and that was enough to keep him going. He ran.

He had barely made it fifty paces before he saw the first body. The bloodied mess of a Dawanii man lay prone in the dirt. Then a second, and a third. None had weapons. Most of his company had split up—as had they all—and now they merged into one large force streaming through streets and pathways in all directions. Milo was ahead of him. He decided to keep the boy close to him. Out of all the people in this attack, he didn't want to see him hurt.

The sound of horns continued to reverberate around them, mixed with shouting and agonising cries as bodies fell. Addan had not yet killed. Twice he came close, only for another of his comrades to claim the kill for themselves. He rounded a corner just as a large rock crashed into the ground a few steps ahead of him. *Where did that come from?* Then another landed behind him. He looked up but there was no one there, not that any one man would be capable of throwing something that heavy.

When he looked back down, an ageing Dawanii man was right in front of him, screaming. He had a bloody gash on his forehead, matting a mix of brown and painted yellow hair. Addan lunged forward with his sword, but something blocked him. There was nothing there *to* defend his strike, yet it felt like his sword hit an invisible wall. He stumbled. The man shoved, and Addan fell to the ground. He scrambled to his feet, but his foe had already run for his life.

He was relieved to still have eyes on Milo, who was only a little way in front of him. The lad had claimed his first life, though through luck rather than judgement. The boy had taken a glancing blow off a woman running for safety. Milo had spun on his heels, his sword skewering an already injured Dawanii who happened to be in the sword's way.

Addan progressed deeper into the village. The bodies of the fallen were scattered on all sides. Most were Dawanii, but a few wore the uniform of Moranza. He recognised the corpses of two men from his own company. Their bodies weren't bloodied, nor were there any obvious signs of stab wounds or other injuries. They were simply dead. He daren't enter any of the houses, unsure of what might lie behind those doors. Others on his side weren't so shy about breaking through them.

He turned round the next corner along a wider pathway between the trees and buildings. Milo had gone that way first. *The boy is brave. I'll give him that,* he thought. As he cleared past a tree blocking his view, he almost tripped and fell over the body of one of the strydes. It was brown, so not belonging to Shaan. Its rider lay crushed and motionless under the animal.

There was an acrid smell of smoke. He looked up to see one of the huts burning. His mind flashed back to a time when he was a boy. His neighbour had made a wooden table—forbidden, of course—and within two days the neighbour's house was gutted by a fire started by a dragon. The only survivor was the stone shell of the building.

The orange flames licked at the wooden structure. Black smoke choked the air, trapped by the canopies of the trees above until they too burned. There were fewer people running now, and the sound of screaming faded. Addan stopped running and stood between two small huts that overlooked a main concourse. He surveyed the havoc before him. Despite the untold number of dead and dying, he wasn't responsible for a single one.

Someone grabbed him by the shoulder. He turned, sword ready, only to see Tobin's face before him. He was dirty, sweaty, covered in blood that wasn't his own, and had a look of sheer enjoyment in his eyes.

'Is it over?' Addan asked, pushing Tobin's hand away.

'Aye, seems to be. Few stragglers, but they barely put up a fight. Easy. Rather unsatisfying, if I'm honest.'

'There shouldn't be *anything* satisfying about taking a life.'

Tobin shrugged. 'If you say so.' He walked off.

Addan found Milo not far away from him. He was still very much alert, wary of any more Dawanii coming his way.

'I got one of 'em,' the boy said, his smile as wide as ever.

'Good for you.' It wasn't meant as praise.

'Did you get any?'

Addan shook his head. Milo looked sad for him, but he only felt relief. He had an uneasy feeling in his stomach as he looked around. *Not one weapon.* Yes, somehow they'd thrown huge rocks in their direction, but the Dawanii were otherwise unarmed.

'Did you see any of them with weapons? Swords, knives, anything?'

Milo said nothing at first. He squinted with one eye, thoughtful. 'I don't think so. Why?'

'Surely if these people were even half the threat Shaan claimed them to be, they would have weapons, don't you think?'

'I guess,' Milo said nonchalantly.

The fire didn't appear to be spreading and was burning

itself out. The leaves above were charred, but the trees didn't catch somehow. He was grateful for that. Through the remaining flames came the silhouette of a man on strydeback approaching their position. It was Shaan. Addan noticed the man didn't have a mark on him. Not a scratch. He didn't have Liana with him, either.

'You have all done well,' Shaan said as he pulled his stryde to a stop beside them. 'I do believe we are able to claim this as a victory.'

'Yes, sir,' said Addan quietly, not wishing to be contrary right now. 'If I may, have they found the princess?'

'No.' His tone was flat, indifferent. He looked at Addan as if he recognised him, but he said nothing else before kicking the stryde to move on.

To his left, came the sound of quiet moaning. He motioned for Milo to join him as he followed the sound to a pile of splintered wood—damage caused by the attack. He found a Dawanii man, pale-skinned beneath a tight fur coat, lying awkwardly against the debris. The moaning continued, intermittent and barely audible. Addan placed his fingers on the man's neck. He'd been shown once, by an old uncle who worked occasionally as a surgeon, how to feel for movement under his fingers. Addan felt nothing except cold skin.

'Dead?' asked Milo.

Addan nodded, but there was still a faint whimper somewhere close. He crouched, not making a sound, and signalled for Milo to do the same. There was nothing at first, then, there —under the broken wood and rubble. He heaved the corpse aside and pulled the rough broken planks away until he found who was making the noise. There was a hand, a small hand. He quickened, and with Milo's help, he pulled it all away until he uncovered a child. A girl. She couldn't have been more than ten or eleven years old and was badly injured. Her face was bruised and dirty. Tears mixed with blood covered her cheeks.

'It's all right,' said Addan, trying to free her from the last of the wood. 'Tell me your name.'

The girl tried to answer, but she was unable to speak, on the cusp between life and death.

'I'm going to get you out, you hear me?'

Addan hefted the final wooden beam from her chest and then he saw. A swell of nausea rose within him as he found the fatal splinter of wood—almost as thick as his arm—protruding from her abdomen. The wound pulsated with blood. There was nothing he could do except try to comfort her, talking to her softly as she faded away. Hot tears streamed down his face as he held her hand. It was in that moment he realised that this wasn't war. There was no threat here. It was a massacre of innocents.

He stood up and screamed. An angry, frightened scream. He wanted to run, run all the way back home without stopping or looking back, but his legs wouldn't work. He stood in the middle of the broken village and cried.

Then someone barged into him, knocking him to the ground. Looking up, Tobin loomed menacingly over him. 'What's the matter with you?' He was carrying a cloth sack, bulging with something metallic clinking within as he moved.

'Why?' asked Addan, forcing himself to his feet. 'Why did we attack? There's no threat here.'

'Not anymore there ain't.' Tobin shook his sack with a grin, rattling its contents. 'Just a few mementoes.'

'I want no further part in this.'

'Ha! Are you forgetting your contract? I can cut you down right here if you want. That's the only way out now. Shaan wants us to set camp here. He's going back to Miar Lenns for more men before we move onwards. This is only the start, friend.'

'Set up camp? This is not our place. So much death and

destruction and you want to live in it, surrounded by the bodies of *children?'*

Tobin shrugged. 'It's only for a day or two.'

Addan walked away, unable to suffer the man's unabashed glee. It was a mistake signing up. He knew that now. Yet he still thought of Liana. *Must I really trade the lives of the innocent to save her?*

15

TORN

The twins, Eelan and Haal, were a curious pair. Liana had so far found them to be amiable and intelligent, if not rather young. She guessed they were barely any older than Uehan. Nalla insisted they be the ones to guide her on her journey to the Sisterhood. 'The wilderness can be a dangerous place,' she had said. Liana thought that meant more dragons, but Nalla implied there were other dangers out there. Though, she wouldn't be drawn on what, exactly.

The Sisterhood were located, in Nalla's words, "on the very edge of darkness itself." Liana had already learned that "dark" meant "cold", so was grateful when Orratan presented her with a hooded fur cloak to complement her already warm-but-not-quite-enough clothing. She had also been given a pair of gloves made from the softest leather she'd ever seen or touched. They were so light it was easy to forget she was wearing them. The tips of her fingers were very grateful. He'd also found her a soft, yet sturdy pair of leather boots. Everything about her looked Dawanii now, except for her hair.

It would take nearly two days to reach the Sisterhood,

which meant more walking. A lot more walking. Liana had asked if they had strydes to ride. Their dismay at the notion that animals were used to ride on surprised her—not that she'd seen any strydes or other similar-sized animals. Much of their surrounding land was used for farming. She'd noticed huge open fields full of grazing cattle and several species of small four-legged animals she didn't recognise. All were too small to ride on. So, they left on foot, the four of them—the twins, herself, and the ever-faithful Ember. There was a fifth member of the party, of course, though she wasn't in any hurry to meet them.

She was grateful for the company, mostly to have someone to talk to, but also because she had no idea where she was or where they were going. At this point, she wasn't sure a map would be a lot of help to her, either. 'Have you been to the Sisterhood before?'

'No,' said Eelan. 'This is our first time. The Sisterhood is a very sacred place, and you need a very special reason to go there.' He, like his brother, was half a head taller than her. Both had broad shoulders, broader than you'd typically see in such young men. Narrow waists, though, she noticed. The only discernible way of telling them apart was Eelan had a small scar on his left eyebrow, which meant the hairs ran out before completing their trail over the brow. They were both equally pale, with eyes almost perfectly black. In the right light, though, she could see they were actually the deepest of dark blues.

'How do you know where to go?' she asked.

'All Dawanii know where the Sisterhood is,' said Haal. His tone was flat, as if his statement was as well known as "the moon is round."

'What is the Sisterhood, exactly?' Liana was struggling to keep pace with them. If they kept it up, she'd soon have to ask them to slow down, but she didn't want to appear weak. She'd grown tired of being made to feel that way by her brother. It only made her more determined to prove herself to everyone, even if it wasn't always necessary.

'You'll see soon enough,' they both said in perfect unison.

She smiled at the novelty of their synchronicity. 'Are you able to read each other's minds?'

'No,' said Haal.

'We have not taken the Branding, so we have no gift yet,' continued Eelan.

'After this journey we will come of age, and we will take the Branding upon our return. You may bear witness, if you wish.'

'Yes, we would like that.'

Liana was pleased to hear they expected her safe return to the city. 'I would be honoured,' she said, breaking into a light jog to catch up. Ember kept by her side, however fast or slow she went.

After what really felt like a week of walking through dense forest, carving their own fresh pathway in the snow, the twins stopped. In reality it was barely an hour or two after moonset. The twins removed the leather satchels they each carried and set them down next to a large fallen tree that lay broken to the right of their path. The glowing insects on the trees around them that had lit the way faded in the absence of movement.

The tree wasn't a recent felling, perhaps several years old. Liana knew little about trees, as they were more scarce in Moranza, but she could tell it wasn't fresh.

Behind the giant log, now their feet weren't crunching in the snow, she could hear the gentle trickling of a stream.

'We shall stop and rest here until moonrise,' the twins both said.

'You'll hear no argument from me.' She brushed off some of the snow on the log and sat. It didn't seem to impress the boys, so she stood up again.

'We need wood for a fire,' said Eelan as he plucked a large twig from the snow. He waved it in her direction before running to forage for more.

'No rest for the already exhausted,' she said to Ember. She swore the cinderfox laughed at her. 'Oh, be quiet. I don't suppose you want to help too?' She raised an eyebrow when Ember snuffled in the snow and produced a stick in her mouth.

It didn't take long for the four of them to gather enough wood together for a modest fire. Liana looked at the arrangement of sticks, surrounded by a circle of small rocks to prevent spreading. 'I have a question,' she said. 'How do we start a fire out here?'

Ember seemed to know the answer. She padded over to Haal, who petted her before pulling a small tuft of fur from the scruff. The cinderfox didn't flinch at all. The tuft glowed with its blue flame in Haal's hand. He crouched down and pushed the tuft into the pile of wood. The soft blue hue flickered within the twigs and branches and grew brighter. The new fire slowly changed colour until it was a familiar orange with all the warmth it promised.

Liana held out her hands, feeling the heat through her gloved fingers. Before the thought of her sitting down had barely entered her mind, Eelan handed her a black knife made from a single piece of reflective stone, and a dead rabbit from one of the satchels. 'What am I supposed to do with this?' She already knew, but the words came out anyway.

'Fur doesn't taste good,' said Eelan, grinning.

'No, I suppose not.'

The twins and Liana set about skinning a rabbit each. With no idea what she was doing, and as much as she tried to copy their technique, her rabbit ended up looking like it had been mauled by a direwolf. She didn't much care for the taste of rabbit. She found the meat tough and the bones too small. It was, however, all that was on offer, so she was grateful.

The twins' meals were already cooking by the time she was done with the knife, the meat browning in the fire. It *did* smell good. With her rabbit eventually mounted on a stick of its own, she placed it alongside the others and allowed her mind to drift into the flames.

'Can you hear me?' said a voice. *The* voice.

'Yes,' she whispered. 'I can hear you.' The orange of the fire faded away until there was nothing but black.

'Wonderful! It has been so long since I have had anyone else to talk to. A very long, long time.' The voice sounded emotional.

'Are you really Eraidor, the Architect of Life?' She felt something pull on her shoulder. The darkness gave way to the orange light.

'Your rabbit is on fire.' It was Eelan, nudging her back to reality.

'Hmm, what? Oh goodness!' She grabbed the end of the stick holding her meal and pulled it from the fire. She blew hard repeatedly, trying to extinguish the burning animal, but it didn't work. Panicked, she drove it into the snow. The rabbit hissed and the snow around it melted.

The twins roared with laughter.

'It's not funny,' she said, examining the charred remains of her meal. 'It's ruined.' She tossed it aside.

Both boys offered her some of their own rabbits, again in unison. She took the meat reluctantly, but with gratitude. Ember helped herself to the twice dead, discarded rabbit and tore into the blackened flesh.

'What happened?' asked Haal, once the excitement had calmed down. 'You looked... empty. We couldn't rouse you.'

'Empty? What do you mean?'

'We're not sure. You were there, looking, staring into the fire, but there was nothing in your eyes. Empty is the best way we can describe it.'

She felt a sudden chill down her spine. 'I was here, looking at the fire, then it all went black. I heard his voice. Eraidor. I could hear him.'

'What did he say? Could you see him?' asked Eelan excitedly. They both leaned forward towards her.

'I don't know. Nothing. You pulled me back before he said anything.'

Together, the boys both sat back again, identical disappointment on their faces. 'The Sisterhood will help you,' they said.

For the rest of the meal, they all sat in silence. Liana wasn't sure what to say to them and felt more than a little awkward. She wondered in they felt the same. Then, one of them spoke.

'Tell us about your home,' said Haal.

She smiled as that one simple word transported her back, in her mind, at least. 'What would you like to know?' It was the first time since waking up with Uehan anyone had asked about *her* directly.

'What's it like there?'

'Much warmer than here. We don't need to wear furs. The sky is bright almost all the time, and our homes are made from stone, not wood. There aren't many trees there. Which is for the best, I suppose. We have dragons, like you have, except their spit sets fire to everything.'

'That sounds horrible,' they said.

'Oh, it's not *horrible* at all. It's just different. My family are the rulers of our country. Well, my mother is.'

'Is she your eldest?'

It seemed such an odd question to her until she thought about how they lived here in Dawan. She smiled and gently shook her head. 'No, she *is* old, but not *the* oldest. It's hard to explain now I think about it, but we have one family who are the leaders of our people. There is my mother, who is the queen. When she dies, then I will be queen.'

'That is very strange to us,' said Haal.

223

'Yes, very strange,' agreed Eelan. 'You are not old. Only the oldest in our city decides for our people. Each community has their own elder. If they die, it is not their children who lead us. It is still who is the oldest. We value wisdom and experience above all else. The eldest are the wisest, so we trust in them.'

'If you knew some of the old men advising my mother, you'd be proven wrong on that,' she said, giggling a little.

The boys looked confused. 'The old are *always* wise,' they said.

She was intrigued. The more she learned about the Dawanii way of life, how it contrasted from Moranza in almost every conceivable way, the more it appealed to her. If she had been born in Dawan, she would not be a princess. She would not have such great expectations placed on her from an early age. There would be more freedom to choose. Would she choose to take part in the Branding? Maybe. The high chance of death put her off, though. She decided to ask the twins, to try to understand.

'Why would you choose to participate in the Branding if there's a good chance it will kill you?'

'Why would we *not* choose? It is a great honour. Not everyone is given the opportunity. Our sister, she will never be Branded, no matter how much she wishes for it,' said Haal, between chewing the last remains of the meat from a small bone.

'Yes, I understand *that* part. But, aren't you scared? To die? You're so young. To sacrifice potentially decades of life, for what? And even if you *don't* die, you could go blind, or deaf.'

'She doesn't understand,' they both said.

'You're right, I don't. Let's take you both, for example. Almost half who are Branded will die, correct?'

'Yes, that is the way of things.'

'Then, mathematically speaking, one of you will die. The other will then have to live without the other for the rest of their lives. You both have such a close bond, anyone can see that. Why risk losing that?'

'To die is not to stop living,' said Eelan. 'This life here, now, is only one part of our journey and we are only here for a short while. Aelene, the Architect of Death, will choose only those who are worthy of their honour in the next life. For her to choose us to walk with her is the greatest privilege.'

'As opposed to what?' she asked.

'Sometimes Aelene doesn't choose. If a man were to kill another, or if a woman dies fighting a dragon, then Aelene did not choose them. It is not part of her plan. Of course, she will come and look after us in the next life, but we are not honoured in the same way,' said Haal.

'Aelene chooses only the most worthy,' the twins said together.

'So, only the first born would ever be considered worthy?'

'Of course,' said Eelan. 'Why would they not be?'

Liana sat back, trying to take it all in. There was a certain logic to it all, she supposed, but it was a flawed logic. Who was she to argue, though? They accepted it so freely, without question or fear. There was something to admire within it all, even if the whole concept made her feel uneasy. To her, and most Moranzans, the Architects were more of an idea. A representation of morality. Their Teachings were a guide on how to navigate your way through life, while also respecting the lives of others. There were those, of course, who didn't believe in the Architects at all, claiming everything was only random. She leaned more towards that idea, especially since she became old enough to form her own opinions independently. That has all changed now, if the Dawanii were to be believed. *Something* was in her head, after all. Unless she was going insane.

Ember, who had curled up and fallen asleep by Liana's feet, sprang awake and growled at something in the gloom behind the twins. Liana snapped alert. 'What is it?'

225

The demeanour of the twins shifted. Quickly, they both stood up and turned to where Ember was looking, drawing their knives. 'Quiet,' hissed Haal. Both boys stood perfectly motionless. Ember's growl became low and quiet; her posture, ready to leap forward.

Liana didn't know what to do with herself, so she crouched down next to the cinderfox, prepared to run in any direction if needed. Something was out there in the dark, but what? A dire-wolf? Dragons? Other people? She was about to open her mouth to speak when a small ball of purple light flew past and hit a tree beside them, exploding in a wheel of sparks. 'What was that?' she asked, trying to hide any hint of fear in her voice.

'Torn,' said the twins.

'What's torn?'

'Dangerous. We need to leave. Now!'

Two more balls of light came their way. One whistled past Liana, only an arm's length away. The other hit the fire, scattering the burning wood in all directions. Ahead, a feral cry echoed through the trees. She froze on the spot. The twins snatched up their satchels and ran. Ember reared up and pushed Liana with her front paws. Liana broke her trance and followed the boys.

Somehow, she became separated from the twins in under a minute and was unsure in which direction they had gone. It was darker here than she'd ever known, and it was disorientating. At least Ember was still by her side. All she could do was trust the cinderfox and keep with her. She sidestepped a tree stump, barely keeping herself from tripping over it. As she looked back up ahead of her—still running—a dark figure appeared from behind a tree.

It was taller than her, by quite a margin. It looked human, but something was... off. Its left shoulder hung lower than the right as if dislocated. Its whole body was distorted, like it had melted somehow. The fur clothing it wore was nothing more than rags that exposed bare flesh. Its skin glowed faintly purple. The creature's veins were alight, rippling, as if a fire was raging within the flesh. Two equally purple eyes stared out of a misshapen head topped with wild white hair. The creature screamed and it was anything but human.

The creature reached out for Liana, but she dived into a roll before straightening into a run, away from whatever *that* was. A purple bolt of light slammed into the soft ground ahead of her, followed by another, and another. More screaming rang out through the forest like a call to the netherworld below. *Where were the twins?* She had to find them. And then she fell, cutting her forearm on a rock as she landed awkwardly. Ember stopped beside her and tried to nudge her to her feet, but she was winded and unable to stand. It took every effort to roll onto her back, in time to see the creature bearing down on her less than ten paces in front. It ambled slowly, unsteady, towards her. Ember positioned herself between Liana and the attacker.

As the man-like creature approached, closer and closer, Liana watched in wonder as Ember grew in size, reacting to the threat before them. The cinderfox stood now, as large as a dire-wolf, as large as when she first saved Liana's life. Ember launched at the creature ahead, going straight for the throat. The beast fell backwards, crying out in pain as the cinderfox ravaged it, but somehow it broke free and rose to its feet. From her prone position, Liana lost sight of the creature in the gloom, and Ember soon after.

A few seconds later, to her left, the sound of snapping wood. She turned her head, still unable to pull herself up. The melted man was coming her way. She shouted to Ember for help, but no sound came from her mouth. Liana tried again, but her voice was gone, the air still absent from her lungs in the fall.

'Call to her,' came the voice from within. 'Use the bond between you. Call to her in your mind.'

Liana closed her eyes and willed the cinderfox to come to

her aid, trying to picture her new friend answering her. Something crashed to the ground beside her. She opened her eyes to see the man-creature right beside her, face down. Ember standing on its back, looking very pleased with herself. As Liana breathed in relief, she was hit with the worst smell she'd ever known. Like rotting meat, but well beyond rotten. She gagged and coughed. Slowly, she found the energy to push herself away from the corpse.

And then she saw a friendly face. Two faces. Haal and Eelan were looking down at her. *Was it over?* She relaxed a little. 'Where in the name of all the Architects did you go?' she croaked, forcing the words from her lips as she regained the use of her lungs.

The boys helped her to her feet. 'We're sorry. We thought you were behind us. As soon as we realised you were not, we came back.'

Ember had returned to her smaller size, now that the threat had passed. Liana gingerly crouched down and thanked her for saving her life. 'Could you *really* hear me call you?' Ember simply blinked and squeaked a yawn.

'We are sorry if you thought we had abandoned you. We would not do that. We have an oath to protect,' the twins said together.

'What was that... thing?' Liana gagged again. The smell lingered.

'It was a Torn. They used to be like us, but they touched the Origem, and it consumed them,' said Haal.

'The Origem made it like that?'

'Yes, it is why they were all so angry when you used the power of the Origem against the dragons. You were not permitted. The Torn were not permitted. The power eventually destroys the part that makes them human,' said Eelan with a soft, grave inflection.

'So, you're saying, because I held that stone, I will turn into one of them?'

'Yes. The power of the Origem is everything. It must not be touched in this way.'

The thought of turning into one of those creatures terrified her. She removed her glove and looked at the dark mark on her palm. *Was this mark the beginning? Was she dying?* The back of her neck tickled in the icy breeze. 'Are there many of these Torn? Will more come for us? Are we even safe out here alone?'

'Nobody really knows. It is unusual to find one alone, and this far into the forest. All the stories say they live in the south, away from others. It is possible to live your whole life without seeing them. Torn do not like to be seen,' said Haal.

'So I am just unlucky, then?'

The twins cocked their heads. 'We don't know that word. Come, we cannot stay here now.'

Liana tried to explain what luck was, but they didn't seem very interested. They kept close to her now as they walked, slower, not letting her out of their sight. She stretched out the pain from her back, and her forearm was bleeding, though it didn't hurt enough to worry her too much. She tried her best to ignore the mark on her hand, silently praying the Sisterhood would have a way to help her.

The farther west they walked, the darker it became until the sky was almost black. Eventually, the trees ended and Liana saw her first clear view of what felt to her was the edge of the world. The snow-covered ground stretched for miles out to the horizon. Above, in the sky, were thousands of tiny specks of light—far more than she'd ever seen before in the brief hint of darkness after each moonfall. Most of them were white, but occasionally she would spot a blue or red dot among them. Some even flickered gently as they hung in the air.

'It's beautiful,' she said. 'I've never seen anything quite like it.'

'We agree,' the twins said, standing either side of her, looking at the sky also. 'You can see the Architects themselves in the stars.'

She wasn't sure what they meant by that. *Was each fleck of light really an Architect? Surely there can't be that many of them. There must be thousands up there.* 'What am I looking for? I don't understand.'

'Constellations,' said Eelan. 'Some of the brightest stars represent different Architects. Let us show you.' The twins each found a long stick. Haal stabbed at the fresh snow in front of Liana, making holes in precise places. Eelan did the same. Liana was amused by the spectacle.

Haal pointed at the sky. 'See that red star there?' Liana nodded. 'And you see the big white one below it? That's these two here.' He indicated two holes in the snow with his stick. 'Now, look at the stars and find the other three I've marked out.'

Liana compared the snow holes to what she observed above her, pointing out what she found as she went. 'I still don't see any Architects,' she said with only a small amount of frustration.

'Watch.' Haal used his stick to draw lines between the holes until they formed the outline of a crudely shaped human. 'See? This one is Aelene.'

'Oh I see now! How clever. Who is that one?' She pointed at the figure Eelan had drawn next to Aelene.

'That is Sarratenian, Architect of Ruination, and this one is Esper, Architect of Music.' said Eelan.

Liana was fascinated. The shapes and lines all seemed a little arbitrary to her, but she appreciated the imagination and was more than happy to imagine with them. 'Where is Eraidor? In the stars, I mean.'

The twins pointed out all the stars, adding them to their map in the snow, along with several other Architect representations. The map was coming along well until Ember walked through the middle of it, making her own "stars" with her paws. Both twins were miffed, but Liana saw the funny side and laughed.

'We can rest here for a while,' said Eelan, admitting defeat to the cinderfox. 'We will be safe enough here.'

'You're certain of that?' said Liana.

'The Torn do not like to venture from the forest. They won't bother us here,' said Eelan.

'It will soon be moonrise. I promise it will be the best one you'll have seen,' said Haal.

'And then we will continue to the Sisterhood,' they said together.

'Is it much farther?' Liana tried not to sound like she was complaining.

Eelan pointed off into the distance, a little to their right. 'Can you see the blurry red light there? That is the Sisterhood.'

It still looked terribly far away, but Liana was pleased it was at least in sight. There was no fallen tree to sit on here, and the snow was at least a hand-span deep, possibly more. The boys seemed content to stand or mill around in small circles, talking between themselves. Ember remained, as always, by her side. Liana was becoming rather fond of the cinderfox. It was more loyal, more well-behaved than any tamewolf she'd known. And if it were at all possible, more *human* than some of *those* she had known.

Desperate to sit down and rest for a while, she walked back to the nearest tree and used her feet to clear the snow around her until she had a circle large enough to sit in. The ground beneath was rough and solid, with frozen shards of grass and brush protruding in intervals. Satisfied with her effort, she removed her cloak and placed it in the middle of the circle and sat, giving her sore feet a much deserved rest.

She looked out over the icy vista. It was so peaceful. The wind, while still present, seemed more gentle. If it wasn't so bloody cold, she might stay there forever and lose herself in the stars. Ember had curled up over Liana's feet in a light sleep. Liana stroked the soft fur, letting the cool blue flames ripple through her fingers.

The near silence gave her the opportunity to reflect in the past few days. She examined the cut to her arm and grimaced when she realised how deep it was. Blood had soaked into her glove, though the cold had stemmed most of the bleeding. *That will leave a scar.* How many times had she come close to death now since arriving in Dawan? Twice? Three times if she included the dragon incident. Any rational person should be terrified enough to beg to be taken home back to the safety and comforts of their normal, perhaps boring, lives. Liana, though scared at times, found her adventure thrilling. Every time her heart raced, pumping hot blood throughout her body, reacting to a new danger, she wanted more. It was becoming like a drug to her, an addiction. Now there was calm, a stillness, even in the wind, and she ached for more danger. And that scared her more than any Torn or dragon, but not as much as the stone's power. She wrapped a corner of her cloak over her gloved hand and tried her best not to think about it.

Ahead, where the ground ended, the edge of the sky gradually lightened. The stars closest to the horizon faded into the pale pink light seeping up towards them. A new day, a new moon was dawning. The leading edge of the celestial body was barely visible, yet it was already brighter than she'd ever seen it before, contrasting against the black void behind it. As it rose, it seemed bigger. Ordinarily, if someone stood ten paces in front, with the moon directly behind them, their head would just about eclipse the sphere, save for their ears. This moon was bigger than that, maybe by a pace or two closer in perspective.

The moonlight wasn't its own, Liana had learned as a child, merely a reflection of the light of the hidden sun. In Moranza, the perpetual daylight made little difference to how bright the moon was and its influence on the world. Here, at the edge of the world where even the sun didn't reach, the moon lit up the land as if it were the sun itself. It was beautiful. Liana stood up, eyes closed, allowing the moonlight to warm her, filling her with energy.

'Mother will watch over us now,' said the twins. 'The Sisterhood calls you.'

16

COUNCIL

While it, of course, still hurt him, the initial pain and grief of losing his mother had passed, and Cal now saw the world around him with more clarity. What had been several restless nights with little sleep gave way to a new obsession over all that was wrong in the city and what he could do to improve it. The thought of war still made him shudder whenever it crossed his mind, but he conceded it might be the new way of life.

It had been almost a thousand years since the last war, and there were very few books remaining on the history of that time. Some had been destroyed in various dragon incidents over the years, while others were simply lost. Cal had asked Tienn to find whatever remained and bring it to him. Cal sat at his mother's old desk and looked at the one and a half books Tienn had given him and sighed.

The intact volume was titled "*A true account of the Divide as told by Wawn Tallan*". The other only comprised the back half, and the title was unknown. Neither offered much help. As best as he could understand, the Tallan name stretched all the way back to before the Divide. The incomplete text referred to another party, though the exact name had been lost. A second family vying for the rule of Miar Lenns and the whole of Moranza, long ago.

The centuries between then and now, according to his mother's texts, were uneventful. There were mentions of minor skirmishes between Moranza and Abbalon to the south, though none in the past two hundred years.

He found three paragraphs on a civil war between Min Brai and Min Foar, which had lasted a century itself. The texts didn't mention the victor, but he knew Min Brai was the larger of the two cities today, so reasoned they probably won.

Cal sighed, closed the book, and tossed it on the desk. He wondered if the Architects really were responsible for the Divide, all but cutting Dawan off from the rest of the world. Was it punishment or protection? The books didn't say either way. He thought about his sister. If Shaan returned with her safely, war might be avoided altogether. He closed his eyes and prayed to the Architects that it be so. All his life he'd ignored his gods, but lately he asked for their help or forgiveness—sometimes both—several times a day.

He opened his eyes as the door creaked open. Shaan entered the room and closed the door behind him. 'Hello, my friend.'

'You've returned!' Cal jumped from his chair, rounded the desk, and threw his arms around Shaan. He took a deep breath and forced himself to let go.

'I have, though my stay is sadly a short one.'

Cal stepped back a little, giving Shaan some room to breathe. 'Any sign of Liana?'

'I am afraid to say it appears Liana has been abducted and taken to their largest city. We arrived at one of the outer settlements, ready to talk with them, to offer peace. Alas, we were attacked almost immediately. We had no option but to fight back. Diplomacy failed in the end. Many were killed, including some of our men, who all fought bravely, I must add.'

235

Cal's head swam. He sank back in his chair. The news was far worse than any outcome he'd thought of himself.

'I have instructed the village to be turned into a base of operations,' Shaan continued, 'bridging the gap between our city and theirs.'

'Any prisoners?'

'None I am aware of. Any who did not die likely fled. If that is the case, then word will reach their leaders of our presence. I have only returned to inform you and ask for more men.'

'We are at war, then.'

'We are at war.'

Cal drummed his fingers on the desk. He was lost, deeply conscious of his own inexperience. 'What do we do now?'

'I suggest we increase our numbers at our new base to begin with. There are only five hundred more at the barracks, most of which have only very basic training, which, despite our initial victory, is woefully inadequate.'

'There hasn't been a war in nine hundred and forty-seven years.'

'Forty-six.'

'You get my point?'

'I do. We will have to do our best with what we have, but we *do* need to increase our numbers.'

Cal sighed. 'That will *not* be easy. If you'd witnessed the day I've had, you'd know the people are not at all happy with the idea of war.'

'They need to be presented with a choice—either stay and do nothing, protest for the status quo, and risk the lives of every man, woman and child here if Dawan launches a full attack. Or they can stand up for what they hold dear and fight.'

'How will this all be paid for?'

'Is it not Furan's responsibility to oversee the finances?'

'As it turns out, he seems to be lacking in that respect. I've discovered there are sizeable sums of taxes going unpaid, for only the Architects know how long. There's no money to pay the soldiers. The city is crumbling on its foundations, and I don't mean figuratively.'

'The new recruits are only paid at the end of their contracts. Given we are on the brink of war, it may not be necessary to pay *all* of them, if you understand my meaning?'

'Do you really value the lives of others so poorly? Lives who are standing up willingly to protect others? Sometimes I feel I don't know you at all.'

'Of course, I value the lives of others. Of everyone. I was merely being... pragmatic.'

Cal glared at his friend through his eyebrows, showing his unease. 'There's really no other way?'

'To rescue Liana, if she is indeed still alive? No, I do not believe so. We have tried diplomacy and good will twice now, and it has only ended badly.'

'Fine.' Cal, elbows on the desk, rested his head in his hands. 'Conscript anyone left in the prisons who is not a danger to others. Put out another call for volunteers from everyone else. I won't start forcing free men and women to fight unless there are no other options.'

'Also...'

'Also what?'

'I thought you might consider leading the troops yourself. A demonstration of your willingness to fight for your people may encourage more to voluntarily join the effort.'

'My place is here. I'm not a fighter.'

'Very few of us are. Not one soul in all of Moranza has battle experience.'

Shaan was right, but now wasn't the time to leave the city. 'Who would stand in my stead if I were to go to Dawan? My mother's advisors are already proving themselves less than competent.'

'Tienn has the most experience.'

'He's too old. Far too old, and almost blind. And deaf.'

'True, but in the same manner, he is too old to fight. I am sure if you left him with clear guidance for how you wish everything to be run in your absence, he, with assistance, would prove adequate.'

Cal thought about it. *Could I really survive in a war? Is it the right thing to do, to lead from the front?* 'What if Dawan invaded the city and I'm not here to defend it?'

'There is only one way in or out of Moranza, and therefore, easily defended. Taking the fight to them is sensible, which we have done and are doing.'

'If only Liana hadn't gone to Dawan, we could simply destroy the bridge and both countries would continue as they have always done. Damn that sister of mine. Why couldn't she simply do what was expected of her?'

'Perhaps that is exactly it. She is a free spirit. To conform is not her nature.'

'Evidently.'

Neither spoke for a while. Shaan offered his arms, but Cal was no longer in the mood for physical contact. He stood up and moved to the window. Outside, the city looked duller than usual. Maybe it was the clouds in the sky obscuring the moon, their shadows drifting over the buildings. More likely, it was only the way he felt right now.

'I need to think about it some more,' Cal said eventually.

'Take your time, but do not delay too long. I shall return to the training camp and see that our numbers are increased.'

Cal nodded, dismissing his friend. Alone again in the office, he slumped back into the chair and exhaled. He thought back to when he was a child, playing swords with his sister. Back then he was eager to fight, to injure, to kill, but that was all pretend. The playful imagination of childhood when you thought you were invincible and could live forever. As an adult, it becomes more about self-preservation, being more balanced and sensible. As Cal sat, staring blankly at the bookshelf behind their protective glass panels, he longed for the old carefree days he once had.

In a moment of self-reflection, he wondered if he'd have noticed how rundown the palace—and the city—was becoming if he'd spent less time playing and more time showing an interest in politics. Things wouldn't be *this* bad, would they?

A knock at the door snapped Cal from his daydream. 'Come in,' he said. He'd been practicing a more authoritative voice recently, but wasn't sure if it suited him. The door didn't open. 'Enter!' he shouted.

The door opened and Tienn stepped in, catching his sleeve on the doorknob as he closed the door behind him. 'Bloody thing,' he said to himself.

Cal stifled a laugh. 'What can I do for you?' he said, straightening his posture.

'I saw Shaan as he was leaving the palace. He said you wished to see me?'

'He did, did he?' Cal tried not to act too surprised. *He's forcing my hand.*

'He, ah, said you wish to discuss something. Something important.'

Cal invited the old man to sit in the only other chair in the room. He remembered his mother inviting him to sit there himself on many occasions. It was far more comfortable than the one he was currently in, but it was too unsophisticated for use by the monarch when a guest should be asked to sit in the more decorative chair.

'Shaan says we will soon be at war,' said Cal softly.

'Hmm?' Tienn cupped his hand to his ear.

'I said, war is coming,' he stated, louder.

'Indeed, sir. I have been appraised of matters.'

Cal nodded. 'He has suggested it would be better if I were to

239

lead from the front line, rather than remain here in the city. I wanted to seek your opinion.'

Tienn raised his eyebrows and drew air deeply through his nose, which made him cough. Once he'd settled down, he said, 'and what is your view?'

'I'm uncertain. This is all moving too fast.'

'I think that man has too great an influence on you. I'll forever wonder what it is you see in him.'

'I love him, and I trust him, although he does seem keen on war. It wasn't a side I thought I would see in him, but until recently there's been no thought of war at all. By anyone.'

'Liana didn't, I mean, *doesn't* like him.'

The correction in tense did not escape Cal, but he didn't acknowledge it. 'She used to. When he first arrived here, they seemed quite fond of each other.'

'Hmm, they were, weren't they? I never did find out the reason behind her sudden cooling towards him.'

'Jealousy, maybe? Of me, I mean. I asked her once, and she denied ever liking him at all.'

'It's possible. I can't say I've ever been fond of him myself. I've been clear on that, and it's not out of jealousy, I can assure you.'

Cal smiled. 'Indeed.' He paused. 'Should I go?'

'Who would look after your affairs here?'

'He suggested you as it goes.'

'Hmm?'

'You!'

'Pah! Barely two days past and he was pressing you to cut our influence entirely. Now he proposes the opposite? Be wary of that...' He trailed off mid-thought, before adding, 'besides, I'm too old. There's too much to do for someone such as myself.'

'You are more knowledgeable in the day to day running of

the palace. It would be only until Liana is safely returned, which, Architects willing, won't be long.'

'And if you were to... how shall I put it... *die?* Who would be the monarch then? It's not as though you have an heir, nor with... the way it is... will there ever be an heir.'

It was a good point, one which had never entered Cal's mind before. 'Then what shall be the difference if I died tomorrow or in a hundred years? As you rightly say, I will have no heir.'

'The *difference* is if you died tomorrow, the whole bloody country would fall into chaos. In a hundred years, we'd have time to prepare.'

'Would a hundred years be long enough, you think?' Cal smiled. He stood up and walked around the room, stretching his legs. He hated sitting for too long at a time. His father had always sat, and he'd grown fat because of it.

'The point I am trying to make,' continued Tienn, 'is the country needs *certainty* at a time like this, and that is what a ruler should represent.'

'Then you don't think I should go with Shaan.'

'You must do what you feel is best, young man. Your Grace.'

Cal thanked Tienn for his time and allowed him to leave. He opened the door for him to avoid any further entanglements with the fixtures and fittings. Closing the door, he was again alone with his thoughts. He looked at his big empty chair. 'What would *you* do, mother?'

Of course, there wasn't anyone there to reply, but he closed his eyes and tried to imagine what she would say if she were still alive, still sat at her desk.

She would say, 'your first duty is to your country.'

'Yes, but should I go and fight, or stay and protect?' Cal asked.

'In an ideal world, one would do both.'

'How can I be in two places at once? I am not an Architect, merely a man. And a man who isn't ready for this burden.'

'Readiness comes from within. We would all wish for more time to learn, to prepare, when we face uncertainty. Success comes from determination and persistence. Draw upon the experience you already possess, and rely on those around you to help guide you the rest of the way.'

'I wish you were still here, mother. Why did you have to go so soon? I need you.'

Cal opened his eyes, hoping, willing his mother to be there, but he was alone. He walked to the desk, tucked the chair underneath it neatly. He'd made his decision, and the chair wasn't needed.

17

INTRODUCTIONS

E ven as they approached, Liana still didn't know what the Sisterhood was. Nalla said the experience was different for each who sought an audience with them, whatever that meant. The vague red light in the distance slowly turned into a small hill. At the top of that hill stood a strange stone abomination of a building. It looked as if a small child had taken a handful of clay, squashed it between their fingers, made a few holes representing windows and doors, then called it a finished masterpiece—only bigger. This artful structure was surrounded by four pillars, also made of the same gnarled, dark stone. They curved inward at the top like clawed fingers. It was from these stone claws the red light emanated. Access to the building was via an uneven, winding line of steps carved into the hill surface.

'You must go alone from here. We are not permitted to come with you beyond this point,' said the twins. 'Ember will remain with us as well.'

Liana wanted to say something in reply, but didn't see any point in arguing with them. She indicated the steps as though asking for approval. The boys nodded and waved her on.

'We will wait here for you,' said Haal.

As she climbed the first step, it struck Liana that there was no snow here. Looking back beyond the boys, the snow had ended a hundred or so paces back. *Why hadn't she noticed that?* The stone steps were dry, very well-worn and much steeper than they appeared. There were twenty-three from bottom to top.

The final step opened out onto a large marbled platform on which the building and the pillars stood. The red glow made the air feel warm, yet uninviting. On the marble floor were many symbols and shapes etched into its surface. She didn't recognise them, nor did she expect to as her eyes followed the lines and curves to a large, irregular open archway that didn't look sound enough to hold the wall above it.

The strangely sculpted building rose into the sky. It was old, misshapen, and looked impossible. There were many windows on the walls, but no two were the same. She likened the eclectic open holes in the stonework to the eyes of a monster looking down on her. Slowly, she walked across the floor. Instinct made her try to avoid stepping on the etchings as best she could, but that wasn't always possible without leaping over them.

'Welcome, Liana. Daughter of the Old Lands,' said a woman's voice, breaking the silence.

It *was* silent here. There was no wind. There was something eerie about this place, something playing with Liana's perception. It was harder to focus, to remember, to notice.

'Hello,' Liana said tentatively. She turned around, trying to see who was speaking, yet there wasn't anyone there. *Wonderful! More invisible voices inside my head.*

'Your arrival is expected. Please come this way.'

'Which way?'

Near the doorway to the temple stood an old woman wearing a crimson fur robe that flowed from shoulder to ankle. She had shoulder-length grey hair with only a small streak of amber colouring running backwards from her right temple. She matched Liana's height almost exactly. Light blue eyes looked out from shadowed recesses, distracting from the age lines on her face.

The woman smiled at Liana before turning towards the misshapen temple entrance. 'Come,' she said.

Liana followed through the archway, which leaned a little too far to the left. It didn't feel safe to her. In fact, the entire structure looked as though it should have collapsed decades ago. She had given little thought to what the inside would look like, but there should at least have been a ceiling. Instead, as she gazed upwards inside the temple, there were only the stars. Small fires burned in their own alcoves in unequal distances around what once could have been a great hall. The floor was made from marble, like outside, except in thousands of small pieces, creating a mosaic. If there were a pattern to it, she would have to look at it from above to see what it was. There were steps that led somewhere upwards, although they didn't look at all safe to climb. The hall was otherwise empty, except for four other identically cloaked figures standing in a wide circle at the centre.

'Please, join us. Stand in the middle.' The woman pointed to the centre spot with a long fingernail.

Liana complied, trying to look at each of them without making it obvious. 'Are you the Sisterhood?'

'We are. For centuries, five of the oldest and wisest Children of Dawan hold sanctuary here at this sacred place. We stand vigil at the edge of darkness itself, and we offer ourselves to those who seek our help or knowledge. We do this in the name of the Architects.'

'Thank you for your hospitality, and your welcome,' Liana said, unsure which individual to address.

'You are injured,' said the figure to her left. It was a man's voice.

'My arm? Oh, it's not too serious, I think. Pardon me if I am being ignorant, but I thought the Sisterhood would all be women?'

'Ideally, yes,' said the one who invited her in. 'However, it has been over a century since a female has selected the Stone of Healing. We must always be five, so Holm is, how would you put it, an honorary Sister.'

'Please approach me, and hold out your injured arm,' said Holm.

Liana stepped forward and pulled up her sleeve, exposing the bloody scrape. The man waved a finger in a small circle until a thin thread of light appeared in the air. With his other hand, he plucked the thread and weaved it back and forth over her injury—like a surgeon would a suture—until the thread of light crisscrossed the whole length of the cut. With a nod, Holm pulled each end between finger and thumb and the wound closed shut. The thread of light faded into nothing, taking any hint of injury with it. He winked at her and motioned for her to return to the centre.

'Allow us to introduce ourselves properly,' said the woman. 'I am Solu.'

'Holm,' said Holm.

The others spoke their names in turn, except one who remained silent.

'And you,' said Solu, 'are Liana Tallan of House Tallan, daughter of Alyssa Tallan, Princess of Moranza, also known as the Old Land.'

'Yes, that's right,' she said, still checking her arm, 'but how did y—'

'We see all,' said Solu.

Liana reasonably surmised Solu was the eldest Sister, but was content to assume for the time being.

'You are here as you bring with you an honoured guest. The *most* honourable of guests.'

'Yes,' said Liana. 'Can you help separate him from me? I would be most grateful to you.'

'Alas, we cannot do this.'

Liana's mood dropped. She needed this being, this Architect, out of her. She grew weary of the heaviness in her head she'd had ever since they'd found their way in. 'Then, pardon me again. Why am I here if you cannot help me?'

'We did not say we couldn't help at all. You are here so that we may help you commune with him.'

'Commune? How?'

Solu didn't reply. The four women, and the man, moved closer around Liana until they joined hands around her.

Everything around Liana was now silent. No wind, no conversation. All she could hear was her own heart as it beat away inside her, and a faint ringing in her ears which had been with her for as long as she could remember. She spun slowly where she stood, looking at their faces. All were aged, grey-haired except for the same amber streak. For all she knew, they could actually be related, so similar were their features. Even Holm, who could be mistaken for a woman unless he spoke.

'Be still. Close your eyes,' said Solu. Then in unison, 'remember the voice of the one within you. Focus. Concentrate.' Liana only heard four voices; one didn't speak, unable. 'Be still, be focused. See them. Call them. Be one with them.'

Liana opened her eyes. The Sisterhood had vanished. The hall she stood in had changed. It looked fresh, new. She looked up and saw a ceiling. A beautiful glass ceiling intricately decorated with ornamental carvings reminiscent of the statues she saw in the Dawanii city.

'Well it is about time!' said the now familiar voice. 'I have not had anyone to talk to for so many hundreds of years now I have lost count. Almost lost my mind, too. Do you know what it is like *not* being able to talk to *anyone*?'

Liana pulled her gaze away from the ceiling and looked to

247

where the voice was coming from. Standing in front of her was a short, mildly overweight man wearing a pure white robe with long sleeves that billowed at the wrists. His hair was a dirty red-brown and brushed back neatly away from his face. He reminded her of her father. Even the eyes were the same.

'Are you Eraidor?' she asked.

'Yes, of course I am. Who else would I be?'

'I don't know. It is possible I am stricken with a form of madness.' Her tone of voice fought back at his indignation.

'Ha. Do you *feel* like you have gone mad?'

'Well, no. At least I hope not.'

Eraidor stepped closer to Liana, examining her intently. 'So this is what you look like? I have only seen you from the inside until now. My last host could not see very well. Not bad, I suppose. A bit plain maybe.'

Liana felt insulted. 'Plain? That's a bit rude, don't you think? Besides, you're hardly the epitome of handsome yourself. You're nothing like I imagined you to be.'

'Dear, I am *exactly* how you imagined me to be.'

'No you're not.'

'Young lady. How I look is entirely decided by the one observing me. To each I am different. No, I look precisely how you wanted me to look, even if it is not what you expected. It comes from deep within you. That being said, I can change my appearance for you if you wish. See...'

The man before her transformed into a young boy, maybe ten years old or so. Pale-skinned with rich ginger hair and wide chestnut eyes, and wearing an appropriately fitted white tunic.

'That's a nice trick,' said Liana, unimpressed.

'Or perhaps, this might be more to your liking...' The boy disappeared and was replaced by a tall, tanned woman in her prime, with straight, light brown hair that flowed beyond her shoulders.

Liana immediately felt conscious that she might be blushing. 'An improvement, I suppose,' she said, hiding behind her words.

The woman disappeared, replaced by the original older man. 'I believe this version of me will suffice.'

'What do you want with me, anyway?'

'Want? I do not want anything from you at all. You merely helped an old and lonely god, and here we are.' He spread his arms wide and turned full circle on the spot.

Liana stepped forward and reached out to touch him, except her hand moved through his arm as though he wasn't there.

'You are seeing only an image from your imagination. I am not really here in this venue. I am still within you.'

'Trapped, the stories say, if I remember them right?'

Eraidor began pacing, slow and aimless. 'Yes, it is true. Many centuries ago. A family feud, you might say. Between me and one of my brothers. Observers might have called it a war, indeed some did. A war which caused devastation all over the world. It threatened to destroy every living thing on this planet. Not *my* fault, of course. I was the one trying to prevent that destruction. I created you. I created all of you and I loved you. But my love was my downfall.'

'How do you mean?' Liana felt dizzy trying to keep him in her sight as he circled around her.

'It was the final fight between us. I sent Sarratenian into oblivion, never again able to harm or destroy.'

He paused before continuing with his story. The expression in his eyes reflected his pain. 'Alas, for my part I was punished. Imprisoned inside a mortal. A human. Even after he died, my entrapment endured. Human life is so short, so fleeting. Each time the person I was... sharing, so to speak, died I needed to find another lest I died myself.'

Liana scoffed. 'Architects cannot die. They're immortal.'

'If only that were true. We cannot be *killed*, but we can most certainly die, given the right circumstances.' Eraidor looked thoughtful as he spoke, as if remembering someone now lost to him.

'How many?'

'How many what?'

'How many have there been? Like me.'

'You are number one hundred and nine.'

That many? 'And were they all as annoyed as I am to find you living inside of them?'

'None of them had any idea. You are the first one who has ever known I am there. For generations, I have only been able to watch. Some of them were kind and loving, their lives filling me with joy as I watched them flourish. Others were... pure evil. Do you know what it feels like to watch someone do the most terrible things? To murder, to... and have no way to intervene, to stop those acts? I did not create you all to destroy each other.' For a god, he really did look as though he was about to cry.

'Why me? What makes me so different?'

'How should I know?' he grumbled. That was not an answer Liana expected.

'You're supposed to know everything. All powerful. All seeing. All knowing. The *Great Architects*!'

'One thing I have learned over the centuries is you humans, particularly the Dawanii, have an overstated imagination of who we truly are.'

Liana expected this person, this god, to be a benevolent, amiable personality. All the stories ever written about the Architects portrayed them—except the likes of Sarratenian—to be kind and merciful. The man standing before her was cantankerous at best. Wouldn't anyone be if they'd not spoken to any other for so long? *Maybe I'm asking too many questions. What else can I say, though?*

'Of course,' Eraidor continued, 'it is only to be expected.

Leave you all to your own thoughts and ideals for too long and you are bound to invent your own stories, eventually.'

One more question. 'How do I get you out? Of me, I mean. I'm really uncomfortable sharing myself, even if it is with a god.'

'You cannot. Well, you can, unfortunately my curse prohibits me from revealing that secret. If I am to be free, then you are to discover how of your own accord.'

'That's ridiculous! Fine, I wish you to be free.'

'I am not a genie, and you, dear girl, are not a bottle.'

Liana huffed. *Answer me this, then.* 'Why me? Why choose me?'

'You were not chosen. There is not a grand design, no prophecy, no divine plan. No, it was entirely accidental. You happened to be in the right place at the right time. It could have been anyone. Indeed, it has been anyone many times. If anything, you were the one who made the choice to save *me.* The real question you should be asking is, why are you the first to be aware of my presence?'

'Go on then, tell me why.'

'No bloody idea.' Eraidor giggled, amused with himself.

Liana's head was hurting. A dull ache of her brain working too hard under the weight of her predicament. 'We're stuck with each other, then?'

'It seems so, yes.'

'What happens now?'

'Live your life.'

'Is that it?' she cried, exasperated. 'Live my life?'

The hall faded back to its previous dilapidated state, and the Sisterhood reappeared, all still exactly where they had been. Liana looked up at the open ceiling and saw the half-moon precisely in the centre. *Half the day! Has it really been that long?* It didn't feel like it.

'Did you find the answers you were looking for?' asked Solu.

'Not in the least,' Liana said, regretting her curt tone.

251

'*Do not blame me,*' said Eraidor, startling Liana. He was still there. '*I am sure as time progresses, we will learn more together.*'

'I thought you'd gone,' Liana said.

'*On the contrary. Now we have connected with one another, I will be with you by your side, so to speak.*'

'I don't like the sound of that. Can everyone see you now?'

'*Only you.*'

'Perfect.' Liana's sarcasm was deliberate.

Solu took Liana by the shoulders and studied her, as if looking for Eraidor inside her. She got so close their noses were almost touching. It made Liana feel uncomfortable—the last person to get so close to her face like that was the palace physician, checking to see if she needed eyeglasses. 'You have been granted a great honour,' she said, still holding on.

'If you say so. I can't say it feels much like one.'

'Oh, but it is. There are those who would offer their very soul to discover the true meaning of their own existence. Many would sacrifice their own lives gladly in the name of the Architects.' She finally let go.

The other four nodded in agreement.

'From what I've seen so far,' remarked Liana, 'it would be a wasted sacrifice. He doesn't appear to know much at all.'

'We have devoted our whole lives to better understand their wisdom,' said Solu. 'Yet, you dismiss them so easily. Why is that so?'

Liana thought about it for a moment, trying to pick her words with care. 'I don't dismiss them. I respect your devotion. Yours, the Tal Valar, and all the Dawanii peoples. It's just that... it doesn't feel *right* that I have to share myself with one of them.'

'You would be free of them if you could choose?'

'Absolutely.'

'*You are not very accommodating, are you?*' said Eraidor. He was still standing—as best as a non-corporal being could—in the circle of five with Liana.

'Why should I be? I didn't choose this. I feel... violated.'

'Bah! You chose, I chose, where is the difference?' said Eraidor.

'Choices are often made for us,' said Solu. 'But they are often for a reason far greater than we can perceive. We do not know why you came together. We do not know why you can see them when so many before you could not. Perhaps, as your bond strengthens, you may learn more.'

'Learn how to be free of him,' said Liana with a brief curl of her lip.

'So indignant,' said Eraidor, shaking his head.

'Don't you want to be set free too? Be able to go and do... godly things?'

Eraidor laughed. *'Of course, especially if all you are going to do is sulk and whine.'*

'So says the grumpy god inside my head.'

'I have good reason to be, as you say, grumpy. You try being on your own for a thousand years and then when someone finally does find me, all they do is complain.'

Liana felt chastised, like a child. As she opened her mouth to reply, the stabbing pain returned to her hand. It was stronger this time, and it made her pull her arm in to her chest. She winced.

'Forgive me,' said Holm, hurriedly stepping forward. 'I was not aware you were injured further.'

Liana waved him away with her other hand. 'No, it's not an injury. Really, I'm fine.'

Holm insisted on looking at what she was trying to hide from them. 'You have touched the raw energy protected by the Origem.' He lowered his head, shaking it gently from side to side. 'This I cannot heal.' Holm retreated backwards to his place in the circle.

'Tell us, child. How did this come to be so?'

Liana recounted the story once more as she examined her hand for herself. The black "spider" had grown again with tendrils now meandering out and along her wrist. The edges of the shadow had a faint purple tinge to them. Whatever it was, was gradually spreading. She gulped and then pulled her sleeve down over her wrist to cover it.

'Then we have much sorrow, and tell you we cannot help. The power will gradually consume you until there is nothing left,' said Solu quietly.

Liana's lower lip trembled. 'What is the Origem, exactly?'

'Ah, now I know this one,' said Eraidor triumphantly. He and Solu spoke next in unison.

'The Origem is all that holds back the raw energy that is the very fabric of the universe. The Architects used that energy to create everything. The first humans were born from it. One man and one woman in our own image.'

Solu continued alone. 'One day, the Architect named Sarratenian came to them and spoke of a fissure, a crack in the barrier that separates this world from that power. With Sarratenian's guidance, the man reached into the fissure and tried to steal the power for himself. The crack widened, and the energy surged through into Rybban like water, flooding the world with power. I believe you call that power magic.

'The man was intoxicated by this magic and nearly destroyed the whole world with it. Mother herself intervened to try to close the fissure with a seal. The Origem. Except that seal is not perfect. Unable to do any more, she decreed that no mortal would ever wield that amount of power again. Thus, any who might try will find themselves consumed by it.'

'That's what happened to the Torn,' said Liana. 'And the same is happening to me, now?'

'Yes,' replied Solu.

'I still don't understand. Was the stone I touched this Origem?'

'No. The Origem is a term often used interchangeably for both the magic itself, and the seal that binds it. That stone was a remnant. The Origem, for need of a better description, leaks. Remnants of the raw magic form around the Origem. A crust, if you will. Over the ages, pieces of that crust break away. Most are absorbed into the world undiscovered. Occasionally, a piece gets lost. Or taken. Those remnants are still potent enough to consume a person.'

Remnant. She'd heard that word recently, though couldn't remember where. 'There must be a way to stop it.'

'There is not. Though...' Solu paused.

'Yes?' said Liana, hopefully.

'The remnant's power should already have consumed you. Something is slowing it down. It may be that Eraidor's presence is affecting its progress. If a solution is to be found. You will find it through him. Your joining, it appears, has given you time.'

'How much time?'

'Days, longer perhaps. It is difficult to foresee.'

Liana looked at Eraidor. 'Is she right? Tell me she's right!'

Eraidor shrugged.

Liana growled in contempt at him. 'Wait, what about my friend, Addan? He had the other half of the stone. When he held it, nothing happened to him at all. He said it didn't even feel anything from it.'

'There are those in this world who magic does not interact with on any level. We don't know why. A small amount of the magic the Origem holds back remains within each and every one of us. Just enough to provide life, and for them, it is nothing more. A few, such as yourself, can learn to draw on that small amount of power, to help them in small ways.'

Liana understood what the woman said. 'Like create light if you cannot see.'

'It could be used for that purpose, yes.'

'But why does it hurt?' The question Liana had always wanted an answer to.

'To remind you of its strength. To warn you against abusing it. To deter you from wanting more. Such power can be addictive. It is a precious gift that is to be careful with, or else be consumed by it.'

Liana shuddered at the thought of becoming like the Torn. 'Where is the Origem?

'We no longer know of its whereabouts,' said Solu.

'It moves.'

'Moves? How can a seal move?'

'It is complicated, and unlikely you can comprehend the answer. I do not mean to insult you. It is merely a fact of human capacity.'

Liana scratched at an itch behind her ear. The day was starting to overwhelm her. Magic had been with her all her life. She *enjoyed* it, and yet now it might kill her. She tried not to think about that part. 'What about the Branding?'

'What about it?'

'Does that use magic, too?'

'Bah! The Branding,' said Eraidor. *'Do not get me started on that ridiculous ritual. Yes, it draws from the magic, but that is a whole other story for another time.'* He put a finger to his lips and pointed at Solu. *'They cannot see me, but I am not sure if they can hear me.'*

'We can sense his presence through you,' said Solu without prompt. 'What is he hiding from us?'

Eraidor pulled a face that suggested he'd made a silly mistake.

'I don't know. He said nothing,' said Liana. It surprised her to find herself defending Eraidor.

Solu may have shown the vaguest sign of offence, but Liana wasn't sure.

All together, the Sisterhood said, 'it is time for you to return. We wish you a safe journey, and we hope you find the answers you are looking for. May the Architects guide you and watch over you, always.' They simultaneously bowed before fading into nothing, leaving Liana alone with Eraidor.

Liana looked at Eraidor questioningly, not expecting the Sisterhood to disappear.

'No idea,' said Eraidor. *'You know, you do not need to use your voice to talk to me. Just think the words and I will hear them.'*

'And you tell me this now?' she said without her voice.

'The Sisterhood understands our nature. Others will not.'

18

PUNISHMENT

A ddan sat on the damp and muddy bank, staring at the trickling water of the stream as it meandered through the village. The attack on the previous day had taken its toll on him emotionally, if not physically. The image of the young girl dying in his arms haunted an already broken sleep. Now awake, he couldn't shake the thought that this whole venture was utterly wrong, and yet he could not escape.

There was another man, like him, who saw the true horror and tried to leave, hysterical and broken. One of the soldiers on strydeback executed him in view of all the other recruits, adding his body to the hundred and nineteen villagers. Addan had counted every last one as they were discarded like animals in a mass grave dug by Companies Three, Seven, and Ten before they were allowed to eat. All of them were innocent, common people living their quiet lives. They weren't fighters. They weren't a threat to anyone. Yet, all had been slain in cold blood.

Somehow, Addan felt responsible, even though none had died by his own hand. He knew that feeling was irrational. Even if he hadn't signed up, the army would have still attacked the village. The defenceless would still have died, and their bodies would still be dumped in a huge shallow grave they didn't deserve.

He wondered if the Dawanii had a ritual for their dead. Did they pray to Aelene to look after their souls in the next life? Did they believe in the Architects at all? Should their bodies have been cremated instead? An endless swirl of dark thoughts and questions drowned his mind. He felt their pain gnawing away within him. Three times he'd vomited. Each time, that pretty young girl screamed at him in his waking dream. He sat alone now, numb to his surroundings. He didn't notice when Milo came and sat down beside him.

'They've been lookin' for ya, the commanders,' he said. Despite everything, he still had his smile.

'Let them look.'

'You'll get disciplined. One of the men from Company Six went for a walk when he should have been helpin' to secure the perimeter. Took a beatin', didn't he?'

'I don't care.' Addan didn't look up from the shallow waters.

'Course you do. Want an apple?' Milo asked, producing two yellow-green fruits from his pocket. He bit into one of them noisily.

'I'm not hungry.' This was only a half-truth. He *was* hungry, but he couldn't bring himself to eat. Meals of slop had been replaced with fruit and dried meats found across the village. The slop, being what it was, should have been enough to make any man gorge on whatever real food he could lay his hands on. Indeed, most of the troops had done so, but he wasn't interested.

'Does ya no good to sulk. Need to get on with it. Why *are* ya sulkin', anyway?'

'I'm not sulking.'

'Yes, ya are. I know a good sulk when I see it, an' ya definitely sulkin'.'

Addan stood up and kicked some loose stones by his feet

into the stream. 'Are you really so blind as to what we've done here?'

Milo looked up at him, mouth full of apple, the juice dribbling down his chin. 'What ya mean?' We came, an' we defeated the enemy. We conquered the village an' now we are preparin' for the next battle. Commander Shaan is bringin' reinforcements an' everythin'.'

'These people were not our enemy. Children are *never* an enemy and should never have to suffer like that girl did. Like they all did.'

Milo wore a nonplussed expression. 'They killed the queen.'

'Not these people.'

'People like 'em. Dawanii people. That makes 'em the enemy, doesn't it?'

'It's not that simple.'

'I'm gonna get more apples,' he said, standing up. Addan couldn't tell if the boy was being deliberately obtuse, or if it really was so cut and dried for him.

Addan sat down again, picking up a nearby stick. He prodded at the mud with no care of what was happening around him. It had crossed his mind—fleetingly—if he should lie face down in the stream and let Aelene take him. *Has my life really turned so bad so fast?* The thought of Liana stopped him. All that kept him going now was the hope he might save her.

'You there!' bellowed a voice. Addan ignored it. 'You, by the stream. Get your sorry hide over here.'

Addan puffed his cheeks and looked to where the shouting was coming from. It was a supervisor; a small man with greasy dark hair and a short patchy beard. He'd told everyone his name, but Addan couldn't remember it now. He remained seated, not in defiance, but indifference.

The supervisor didn't call a third time. Addan felt two arms hoist him from the ground. Two recruits—under orders—had got hold of him under each arm and dragged him, splashing through the stream, and through the grass to where the supervisor waited. Addan didn't resist, nor did he make it any easier for the two men carrying him. They shoved him forward. A cloud of dust billowed as he crashed to the ground.

'Afraid of hard graft, are ya, lad? Or perhaps you think yourself above everyone else?'

'No, sir,' said Addan. He tasted blood on his lips, having bit his tongue as he hit the dirt.

'On your feet.'

He silently counted to five before dragging himself to a standing position in front of the supervisor. He tilted his head to look at him. The poor excuse for a beard hid acne scars underneath the hairs. His nose had been broken in the past, too.

'Name and company number.'

'Addan Stoan. Company Nine.'

'Nine. Tasked with collecting food supplies. Do you think yourself exempt while the rest of your company does their duty?'

'I want no part in it. This is wrong. All wrong. We kill and take what is not rightfully ours? What gives us that right?'

'Right? You talk about rights? What right did *they* have in killing the queen? None, that's what rights. And you signed away *your* right to do as you please when you joined up.'

A crowd was forming around the two of them, probably waiting to see if he would be punished. To some, there are few things in life more entertaining than watching another suffer— so long as it wasn't them doing the suffering.

'Do what you will.'

'Very well, a beating it is,' said the supervisor to an eager audience. Addressing the gathering men, he said, 'two volunteers, if you will.'

Addan wasn't surprised when better part of half the onlookers raised their hands. He returned his attention to the supervisor, not keen to see which two men were picked out.

Most likely two of the biggest. He was right. The crowd fell back, allowing sufficient space, both to get a good view and also so they didn't get caught up in proceedings.

The two men were both a head taller than Addan, and more heavily built. One had a swirling tattoo inked in black on his left forearm. The other had shaved the right half of his head. Both seemed keen. *Wasn't yesterday's brutality enough for you?* The supervisor stepped backwards out of harm's way. 'Ten blows each. No more, no less. No feet—hands only,' he stated, much to the chagrin of the others.

And then it began. Punishment. Deserved. *Welcomed.* Twenty punches. He'd had worse before.

Closing in on him, the man with the shaved head grabbed Addan by the shoulder with his left hand and punched him hard in the stomach. Addan staggered backwards, but kept his footing. Nineteen. Two more punches followed swiftly. Addan barely reacted. *Do your worst.* Seventeen.

A punch to the face. Addan barely caught a glimpse of the tattoo coming towards him, a fist connecting with his jaw, his head reeling. Sixteen. He felt the warmth of blood oozing from a split lip. He spat at the men, but missed them both. Another fist slammed into his side. He could feel a rib crack. His eyes were wet, blurring his vision. Fifteen.

Another fist again headed for his face. Instincts kicked in and he raised an arm, blocking the strike. Did it count? He hoped so. Fourteen.

Another rib cracked, this time from behind, followed by two more punches to the side. He lost his footing and landed on his knees. Eleven. A knee connected with his ear, sending him dizzy. *That's not allowed!* All he could hear was a high-pitched ringing amidst the jeers and roaring of the crowd. He couldn't tell if the supervisor objected or not. Ten.

He was dragged up to standing and took another blow to the face, his left eye puffing up. Nine. *At least my nose isn't brok—*

eight! More hits to the stomach. Seven, six, five. Something snapped, not physically, but still deep inside. Addan's willingness to endure vanished. *Enough!* He caught an incoming fist with his own hand. He looked up and stared into the surprised eyes of the tattooed man, then with a punch of his own, broke the man's nose.

The onlookers erupted with glee. This beating was now a fight. The supervisor tried to intervene, but regretted it instantly as the tattooed man's retaliatory blow missed Addan for a third broken nose. Clutching his face, the supervisor disappeared within the crowd.

Addan put in two more punches before he took one himself. Four. *Was there any point still counting?* Back home, he'd got into his fair share of bar brawls in his time. Always fuelled by alcohol, never feeling the pain until the next day. He'd outfought more than two men before now. Sober, he could manage two, even if they were twice his size. He threw himself at the shaven-headed man, shoulder first, into his midriff. The man fell and took Addan with him.

Both men wrestled to their feet. Addan turned to face the tattooed man, punched and missed. The man stepped backwards, out of the way in time. A sharp pain exploded through Addan's skull, and then it went black.

ADDAN TRIED to open his eyes, but the left one was bruised shut. What he could see through the other was blurred. Someone was standing over him, though. He tried to move, then sit up from his lying position, but his body wouldn't let him. Whimpering in pain, he relented and stayed on his back. He squinted through his good eye, forcing it to focus. After a minute, he saw Milo staring back at him. There was no smile this time.

'I thought ya were dead.'

'Aren't I? It feels like I am.'

263

'Why did ya fight back? That was a stupid thing to do. Ya nearly died, an' the supervisor is *not* happy with ya.'

'No man should have to take a beating. I thought I'd make it a fair fight.'

'Fair? There were two of them.'

'I nearly had them. If I—what happened at the end, exactly?'

'Took a clubbin' to the head. Big stick. Shouldn't have been allowed.' Milo hung his head forlornly.

Addan slowly moved his head to see where he was. He was inside one of the Dawanii houses, but not the one he'd been assigned. As with most of the ones he'd seen, the wooden walls were lined with dry animal skins. Some were plain, while others had abstract patterns or simple images painted on them, presumably with animal blood. The ceiling—all he could see without causing too much pain—was bare, flat, and uninteresting.

'I have water,' offered Milo. 'Ya should have some.'

He hadn't realised how thirsty he was until then. He carefully lifted himself forward to a semi-upright position and accepted a bladder of water from his young friend. The cold water numbed his split lip as he sipped. He tried not to move his arm up too much. The mouthpiece slipped and water spilled down his front. Someone had removed his shirt. There were too many bruises to count, and there were likely more under the cloth strapping someone had wrapped around his mid-chest. He reached for the stone around his neck, relieved to find it still there.

'Did you do this?' he asked. He nodded towards the bandages, immediately regretting it, his neck protesting.

Milo shook his head. 'Rab did.'

'Who's Rab?'

'The man with the tattoo.'

Addan's eyes widened. 'The one who was beating me?'

'That's right,' said a new voice. 'That's my bed you're sleeping in, too.'

Addan instinctively tried to pull himself up to get a look at the man, but moved too quickly and regretted it. A sharp pain under his bandages tore through his chest. 'Why would you help me?' he asked as he gingerly lowered himself back against the bed.

'I was impressed,' said Rab. 'It ain't often I seen a man take a hiding like that without crying and then have the balls to start fighting back. I respect any man willing to, well, be a man. Anyways, no hard feelings, yeah?'

Addan didn't know what to say. 'Sorry about the broken nose,' was the best he could come up with. He still couldn't see the man, so didn't know how bad or not it was.

'No bother. Wasn't the first time. As it goes, I can breathe out the left side again, so you done me a favour.'

'I bet the supervisor is pissed,' said Addan.

'Yeah, he is. He won't be bothering you no more on account of the other supervisors finding out he's been instigating fights, punishments or whatever he's calling them. Shouldn't be doing that.'

'That didn't stop you volunteering.'

'No one else will quarrel with ya either,' said Milo. 'Ya got everyone's respect now.'

Addan took that as good news on the face of it and forced a smile. 'I need to stand up.'

'You should stay lying down for a bit longer,' said Rab.

'I need to piss.' Addan took his time and pulled himself out of the bed, which was little more than a handful of thick-furred skins on a wooden frame. Carefully, he shuffled over to a pot in the corner of the room. Pisspots were the same whichever country you found them in.

Relieved, Addan found that—now he was up on his feet and had the opportunity to gently stretch his aching body a little—

he didn't feel so bad. His scarred leg throbbed like mad. More than a few cracked ribs, a handful of bruises and the mother of all headaches. *I'll live.*

The image of the young girl still weighed heavily on his mind and would likely stay with him until his dying breath, but he now had the will to move forward. He hoped they would soon find Liana—with as little bloodshed as possible—and they both could return home and forget about everything. He blamed himself, of course. Liana had willingly and gladly joined him on this path, but in the end, it was all of his own making. She was the one paying the price, though. He allowed himself to slump—slowly—back on the bed.

'It won't do ya good to lay there all day,' said Milo. 'Now you're up an' still breathin', ya should stay up.'

Rab agreed.

The lad was right. It took every ounce of strength—both physical and mental—to leave the relative comfort of those warm furs behind. 'How long was I out?'

'Oh, a whole day,' said Rab. 'Surprised you didn't die, to be honest. Be grateful you have a soft head.'

Addan knew the man was trying to be funny, but didn't react beyond a wry smile. Milo giggled and playfully punched Rab on the shoulder. Rab wasn't impressed. If looks could kill, Milo would be lying in the mass grave too.

Somewhere outside, a horn sounded, long and slow. The three of them looked at each other quizzically. Addan's sense of time had been muddied by unconsciousness, but judging by the faces of the other two, it wasn't a scheduled calling.

'Suppose we better see what they want,' said Rab as he opened the door and headed out. Milo stood in the doorway to make sure Addan was following behind.

The other members of the dysfunctional army were gathering in the centre of the village, either abandoning their assigned tasks or emerging from huts or other buildings. From where Addan stood, he couldn't see what all the fuss was about, until—a glimpse of a white stryde. Shaan had returned from Moranza. That meant, at the very least, more recruits. It already felt as though there weren't enough resources to go around the two hundred already there. *How many more were arriving?* To him, it felt like an invasion all over again.

He dragged his weight over to the gathering crowd, happy to stay at the rear so he didn't get knocked and jostled, aggravating his already tender body. He could just about see what was happening up front, mostly thanks to the additional height of the strydes. Shaan had indeed returned, mounted proudly on his white steed. Two other strydes stood on either side. One was chestnut coloured, the rider being of the original six. The other was a handsome speckled grey bird that seemed unable to remain perfectly still when commanded. Atop the stryde was a man in full royal uniform. Dark red-brown hair, with a washed-out brown complexion, the family resemblance between Liana and the man was evident. *That's the prince. He came here, to fight? To lead us?*

The horn belonged to one of the taller supervisors, his shoulders barely visible above the mass of bodies all facing front. Almost all were talking amongst themselves, with the occasional sound of laughing thrown in. There was little discipline here in this camp. These men were not used to taking orders, nor had they sufficient training to unlearn any bad habits. They did, however, fall mostly silent when the horn sounded for the second time.

From his stryde, Shaan shouted, 'be silent for your prince, for he wishes to speak to you all.'

Someone near the front gave a cheer, which was quickly stopped as soon as the man realised he was the only one making any noise.

'Thank you,' said the prince, projecting his voice so as many as possible could hear him. He looked anxious and uncomfortable on his bird, as if he didn't really know how to ride it. 'My good friend and loyal advisor, Shaan, has informed me of your bravery and hard-won victory here.'

Hard-won? There was nothing hard about the massacre that happened here. What has Shaan been telling him?

The prince continued. 'Naturally, I am, as I'm sure you all are, deeply troubled by the abduction of my sister, Princess Liana. We must live in hope she is still alive and well, and that we must find her and bring her home.' The crowd murmured their approval. Addan remained silent.

'I have been persuaded to take charge of this operation myself, and that is what I shall do. I may be new to the burden of the throne—and I pray to the Architects it will not be for long —and many of you may not know much about me or what I stand for. But listen here. I will not stand for the murder of my mother. Your queen. I will not stand for the invasion of our great country. I will not allow these Dawanii barbarians and savages to take our women and children. We shall be victorious and we shall set Princess Liana free, no matter the cost.'

The gathered crowd erupted with cheers and applause. Addan feigned approval by lightly clapping his hands so as not to be seen out of turn. He felt like he was missing something. Information he wasn't privy to. The prince talked as though Moranza was on the verge of all out war, but he'd seen none of that. *Had something else happened?* The prince had certainly been misinformed about the true events here at this "outpost" or whatever he was calling it. He feared for what was coming.

19
A PLAN OF ATTACK

'Was that good enough?' asked Cal. 'I don't think that was good enough. I'm not used to addressing large groups of people.' He climbed down from his stryde, his backside sore from riding for so long. Another thing he wasn't used to. It had been a long time since he'd gone far enough away from the palace to require a stryde, and it was the first time he'd been outside the country.

'I would say it was adequate,' said Shaan, who had already dismounted.

Many of the gathered army had already dissipated. The few that remained seemed eager to speak with Cal. None were allowed to approach, though, sent on their way by one of the supervisors. One man, with a face full of bruises and a split lip, was more persistent than the rest, insisting he speak to Cal regarding Liana. He, too, was sent away with the threat of further injury. Cal would have been happy to let the man speak, but Shaan stood between them, moving Cal on to what would be his quarters.

'They are still in training for the most part,' said Shaan. 'The additional five hundred have had less time to prepare. Still,

269

with these numbers it will make up for any lack of discipline. Indeed, they proved most decisive in their first test here.'

'So I see,' said Cal. 'Though I have to say, this place doesn't seem much like a military outpost. I can see the modifications our men are doing, but it seems more... domesticated.'

'Who is to say how the enemy live? It is clearly rather different than what we are used to in Moranza. Everything is made from wood, dirt and rope. Their dwellings are of an unusual design, with no sense of purpose. Rather primitive, you might argue.'

'I suppose you're right.'

The new additions had almost all piled into the outpost, mingling with those already there. Ten more supervisors, each with a stryde, had arrived with them to try to keep everything orderly, though that was already proving difficult. Cal passed by three scuffles between old and new recruits as he and Shaan walked away from the central clearing.

To the left of a cluster of seven huts stood a slightly larger building. Cal struggled to comprehend how they had been constructed. Back home, brick and stone built walls. Here, walls looked as though the trees had melted into them somehow. It made his head hurt thinking about it. The building had only the one storey, as did all of them. The windows, if they could be called such as they were nothing more than irregular-shaped holes in the wooden walls, were covered by animal skins on the inside. He wondered how safe they were to live in.

Inside was just as depressing as the outside. The heavy skins on the holes moved against the outside breeze, and made it dark inside. There were candles—six of them—flickering in the breeze created by them walking in. The smell of melting tallow irritated Cal's nose, so he made a mental note to have someone remove them. It was only a single room with a large, flat surface in the middle resembling a table. A few candle-adorned wooden boxes lined the walls. They too looked like they had been shaped from a whole tree that had been pushed and pulled into shape. Aside from an animal devoid of its body lying across the floor in front of the table, the room was rather basic. Utilitarian, even.

'I imagine there's no problem with dragons in Dawan. Lucky bastards,' said Cal as he considered how he'd never been surrounded by so much combustible material before.

'None that I am aware of,' said Shaan.

'I assume you have a plan for how we proceed from here?'

'I do.' Shaan produced a roll of parchment as if from nowhere. *Did he have that with him the whole time?*

Shaan unrolled the parchment and laid it over the table, using two of the candles to stop it from rolling closed again. It was a map of the known lands. Moranza was labelled on the right, with Dawan—labelled in fresh ink—occupying most of the top left quadrant. Other areas had names drawn across them, including Abbalon, which sat adjacent to Moranza in the bottom right corner. Near the centre, a ragged curved line bisected Dawan and Moranza with "The Divide" written alongside it. Shaan leaned forward and placed his finger on a small X in Dawan. 'We are here,' he said.

'Seems farther away than I expected.'

'The map is not *quite* to scale. It was drawn a long time ago using the old measurements, but it will serve our purpose. As I was saying, we are here. The map shows their largest settlement over here.' He pointed to another spot on the map farther to the north-west. 'I believe that is where were are most likely to find it, if indeed, we do at all. As adequate as a base of operations it is here, you can see there is still a significant distance between here and there.'

'It? Liana, you mean?'

Shaan didn't answer, his focus wholly on the map.

Cal scratched his head as he tried to read the map. 'What are these markings?' he pointed at several small dots in Dawan.

None had names. In fact, only the settlement Shaan had indicated had a label of its own—*Trennale.*

'Other minor settlements, I would imagine. There may be more, or less. Probably more. This map is a copy of an original drawn by Moranzan historians long after the Divide. They had no way of completing it in any significant detail. What landmarks there are came only from spoken tales of the time before it became separated.'

Cal nodded.

'As I was saying, I propose we follow the stream running through our settlement—our base camp—north along here.' Shaan ran his finger along a wavy line meandering through the W and second A of Dawan. 'Then create a second camp here. From there, we will be able to launch an assault on Trennale from here, leaving plenty of distance should their numbers be greater than anticipated, for us to fall back.'

'Will we face any trouble along the way?'

'It is entirely possible. As I say, it is likely not everything on the map is accurate or up to date.'

'Very well. I trust your judgement,' Cal said as he looked up at his friend. Shaan winked before rolling up the map. 'What now?'

'Your choice. If you are hungry, we can eat. If you are tired, your sleeping quarters are in the dwelling next to this one.'

'Neither for the moment. I want to have a look around.'

Shaan nodded in agreement and allowed Cal to leave the room first. No sooner than they had stepped outside, it became apparent something was happening over in the centre clearing. There was a lot of shouting.

'Sounds like another fight,' said Shaan. 'You may need to speak with them all again. See if you cannot instil a touch of camaraderie among the ranks. They do not all need to like each other, but it would make it easier if they did not start killing one another.'

'If you think it best. Come, let's see what all the fuss is about.'

Two of the supervisors shoved men out of the way when they saw Cal and Shaan approach, clearing a path through to the ruckus. Shaan went first, and Cal followed. Both expected to see two or more of the troops rolling on the ground, exchanging blows. Instead, they found a young lad with blond hair and the man with the broken face they'd turned away earlier. Both were standing over an old man in Dawanii clothing, protecting him from the baying throng of thirty men. Two more supervisors had also stepped in to calm everything down. It wasn't working.

Shaan put two fingers to his lips and blew a loud, shrill whistle that made Cal's ears hurt. It was enough to settle the crowd down to a dull roar. The Dawanii man looked scared, dirty and hungry. He cowered under the protection of the man with the black eye.

'What in the name of the Architects do we have going on here?' demanded Shaan.

The blond boy answered first. 'We were clearin' out one of the huts for more food an' we found this man hidin' under a pile of furs.'

'And I'm trying to stop him from being killed,' snarled the injured man as he slapped away the hand of a soldier trying to make a grab for the Dawanii man.

Cal cocked his head. 'You would protect the life of an enemy? Why?'

'Because he's a defenceless old man. There's been enough bloodshed here in this village. I've seen no notion these people were responsible for abducting the princess, if indeed she has been abducted at all. Or the assassination of the queen.'

'It seems,' said Shaan to Cal, but loud enough for all to hear, 'this man is confused on account of his injuries. I am sure all present will agree with me that these people are indeed as big a threat to our own people as any of the Dawanii. I see no reason why this one man, old as he may be, should be an exception.' The surrounding recruits, some still with the body language that threatened the old man's life, sounded their agreement.

'Can we take him as a prisoner of war?' asked Cal. His friend had a point, but the old man *was* unarmed.

'Your Grace, I feel we lack sufficient resources to undertake the responsibility of maintaining the welfare of prisoners. He may only be one man, but be assured, there will be many more along the way. If we were to let him go, he would run right to the enemy and speak of our arrival.'

Cal felt uncomfortable with the choice he was being forced to make. Let the man live and be seen as weak. Let him be executed and forever live with that on his conscience. What troubled him most was how easily his friend reconciled the matter. Shaan had changed since the queen had been killed, and that weighed on Cal more as each day passed.

'Please,' said the old man, his voice was hoarse. 'We did nothing to harm you. I am no threat to you.' His accent was heavier on the vowels than a typical Moranzan tongue.

The crowd chanted, quietly at first, but their calls for blood grew louder. Only the injured man and the boy were advocating for his life. For Cal, the pressure was unbearable. He could feel the sweat beading at his temples.

'But you are a threat,' said Shaan. 'You should have already joined your fellow men under the ground.' He pointed towards the mass grave.

'Then if I am to be slain, I wish to say something to your leader.' He pointed at Cal with a bony finger and beckoned him.

Cal noticed a curious dark scar on the man's palm, like a swirly burn. He stepped forward, closer to the old man, crouching a little, but remaining a safe distance.

The Dawanii man stared at Cal with wholly black eyes— save for a swirl of blue at their centre—as though looking deep inside his soul. 'You find yourself on the wrong side of history. Not everything is as you see it. There is still time for you to put it right, else it will be your ending.'

'Enough,' said Shaan.

Cal stood up and returned to his previous position. *Must I commit him to die?* He wrestled with the decision for as long as he could. All eyes were on him, waiting. He closed his eyes and tried to ignore the knot forming in his stomach. *I need to show strength.* 'Do it,' he said before retreating to the hut on his own. Sweat trickled down along his ears, and the sound of thunder rumbled in the distance as if warning of a storm coming their way.

As he walked, he heard Shaan confirm the order for the execution. Cal drew a deep breath through his nose and swallowed. The condemned man's words lingered in his mind. *Still time to put what right?* The roar of his soldiers echoed through the trees. Cal's thoughts returned to his mother and his sister. All this was for them. *It will be your ending.*

20

EXILE

Addan had tried his best to save the Dawanii man. In the end, he could do nothing. In his attempt to stop the man from being dragged away, he'd taken a boot to the face, knocking him to the ground on his side. What did one more bruise matter? As much as Milo had tried to help appeal to Prince Tallan's better nature, the boy had moved out of the way as fast as the prince had ordered the Dawanii's execution. There was nothing Addan could do now.

The army were thirsty for more blood. Any blood. Addan knew if he continued to fight for the stranger, he may very well have joined him in death.

'I tried, I really did,' said Milo.

'I know you did, lad.' Addan patted him on the knee as he watched the corpse of the old man be carried away by the rest of them. He stayed in the dirt, refusing to be party to any more senseless death.

For the remainder of the day, he went through the motions, doing the work assigned to his company, barely putting any effort into it. He did only enough to keep his mind from drifting back to the girl. He was grateful for Rab—his newest ally—who made sure he saw no trouble from the other men who were picking up his slack. 'I'd like to see you work so hard after you've taken a beating,' he'd said to anyone complaining.

While Company Nine had been tasked with collecting any food they could find—of which they found enough to feed all seven hundred of them for at least three days—it was Company Four who had been put in charge of cooking it.

Meal time arrived with the sound of a blown horn. The pangs of hunger had returned to Addan. He couldn't remember the last time he'd eaten. For the first time in a while, he was looking forward to something, even if it was only food that wasn't slop. However, any sense of interest in what was on the menu soon disappeared when he got close to the makeshift mess hall—whatever it was smelled burnt. *Hopefully they haven't cremated all of it.*

Dinner service descended into disarray almost as soon as a queue had formed. Two hundred men were manageable most of the time with barely more than a minor scuffle. Seven hundred, combined with rumours of the food on offer being toasted to the point of it reaching the next life, was too much for even the strongest men to keep under control. Those at the front picked out the best of it—meals that were only slightly charred—but once word spread that the largely edible food was running out, it was every man for himself. The smaller, weaker men were shoved out of the way by those stronger than them. Addan, too tired to fight, resigned himself to taking whatever was on offer. He didn't pay too much attention to the fighting, not until Milo was thrown from the broken queue lines, tumbling in the dirt.

Addan stepped out of his position and pushed his way to the boy. Milo wasn't badly injured. Maybe he'd have an extra bruise or two by moonrise. Addan helped his friend to his feet and away from the crowd.

'Thanks. I wasn't that hungry anyway,' Milo said as he

pulled a pair of apples from his pocket. He held one out. Addan tried to take it, but Milo snatched his arm away at the last moment. Milo grinned. 'Oh, so *now* ya want one?'

'You're hilarious. Give it 'ere.'

Milo held out his hand again. This time, the apple floated an inch above his palm. He feigned handing the fruit over, content to keep on teasing Addan.

'I have a friend who can do magic like that,' Addan said, trying again to swipe the apple. He missed.

'Kinda useless trick, really,' Milo replied, shrugging. 'Normally hurts my eyes if I do it too much, too, but not so much here for some reason. Fun, though. Don't ya think?' He feigned handing over the apple twice more before relenting.

The disorder subsided with the arrival of Shaan and the prince, along with their supervisors. For all the poor discipline within the ranks, they still knew when it was best to not cause trouble in the presence of those who would serve punishment. The more Addan watched the two men, the more he wondered who was actually in charge. On the face of it, the prince was the leader, with Shaan fulfilling the advisory role. If Addan didn't know any better, he would bet good money that it was Shaan who was in charge. The prince had a demeanour about him, one that screamed indecision and a lack of confidence. Indeed, the majority of the recruits seemed more fearful, more respectful of Shaan than Tallan. Although, that might simply be explained by Shaan having been with them for longer. Something *was* off, though. At the end of it all, Addan didn't care who was in charge, as long as they found Liana.

Once the arguments over the food had receded enough for most to pay attention, Shaan addressed the men. 'Now this base is secure, and our additional forces have arrived and settled in—for the most part,' he said, glaring at a handful who were still fighting over scraps of charred meat. 'We will soon advance towards Trennale. Unfortunately, our maps are not recent, so there is much we do not know about Dawan. Therefore, I have decided to send out two scouting parties along different routes to Trennale before we commit our larger numbers.'

Murmurs of both approval and disapproval rippled through the ranks in equal measure.

'We have the numbers. What's wrong with a brute force attack on their city?' shouted a man from behind Addan.

'Yeah, let's get on with it,' hollered another, with vocal support of several others within his vicinity.

'Take them by surprise,' said a third—a large, burly man with a slack jaw standing directly in front of Addan.

Shaan shook his head, waving a hand, calling for calm. 'In light of one survivor already discovered here, I have to assume there might be more who have escaped, and warned others of our arrival. We need to assume we no longer have the element of surprise on our side. Not least because they started this, and they are surely ready for retaliation.'

'Who's in the scouting party?' asked someone.

Addan had a sinking feeling when Shaan looked directly at him. *Please don't choose me.*

'You there.' He pointed at Addan. 'Name and company.'

Shit. 'Addan Stoan. Company Nine.' He could feel the glare of every other member of Nine boring into him.

'Since you seem to have made it your business here to make a name for yourself, your company will take the northern route.'

Addan cringed. His fellow company members were already cursing his name. He thought about protesting on their behalf, but his body ached too much to care. *Maybe this is a good thing.*

'And for the route west...' Shaan held a finger to his lips, pondering. He turned his head to a supervisor. 'Give me a number.'

'Three.'

'Company Three will take the western route. You are to leave immediately and cover as much ground in a day and then report back here. Do not engage the enemy if you discover them. Map their locations and numbers if you can.'

If Addan didn't like the way he'd been singled out, his fellow company members liked it even less. As much as they were big, brash, and full of themselves, there was a lot to be said for safety in numbers. When it came down to it, in a group of hundreds, they were an army. In a group of ten, they were no more than the thieves, beggars and criminals they'd been in their lives before this. And Addan was in charge of them all.

Milo of course, was willingly on his side. Three of the remaining eight, he had earned their respect for fighting back against the beating he'd taken. The other five had formed their own small alliance within the company. Addan would need to win them over, and he knew that wouldn't be easy.

Except for Milo, Addan had forgotten all of their names. He'd never been good with names. Instead of suffering the indignity of relearning them, he gave them all a number in his mind. Five fancied himself as a contender for company leader. He was one of the hundred or so who had been recruited straight from prison. He matched Addan in height and build, his face gaunt and dry. Although he hadn't heard it from Five himself, Addan had learned his crime had been the murder of his wife. How and why were unknown, and he wasn't keen to ask.

Six, Seven, and Eight all came from the poorest district of the city, and were assigned to Company Nine to replace the three lost in the attack. They were petty thieves, mostly out of necessity to keep themselves from starvation. All were underweight, and older than Addan, though not by much. All had the same dark, lank hair. If he didn't know any better, Addan would think them brothers. Each time Addan spoke, made a suggestion or gave an order, they would all look to Five for approval first.

Four, Nine and Ten, though not happy to be in the scouting party, did at least give Addan enough backing to keep him in charge—for the time being, at least.

Supplies were minimal—barely enough food for two meals each to cover the two days they were to be away. Five did protest, but were told if they wanted more food they'd have to hunt for it themselves. Addan learned quickly the man liked to grumble. It was too cold, too dark. Not enough this, too much that. Underpaid whores complained less than Five did.

As much as he would rather languish in a quiet corner of the camp, brooding over his sorrows, Addan found himself with a renewed purpose as the ten men left the chaos of the camp. He had put Milo in charge of reading the map. Partly to make the boy feel useful—he was the smallest in the group, so prone to bullying by Five and his friends—and partly to diffuse his own level of seniority in the ranks.

Their remit was to follow the river north as far as it went, marking any significant obstacles or places of strategic importance, as well as any inaccuracies. The supervisor had informed Addan the map had been copied from a very old Moranzan text, at least a hundred years old, so it likely couldn't be relied upon too much. Indeed, the camp was barely out of sight when they realised the line of the river didn't match the map. Instead of leading them north, as the map indicated, the river meandered east back towards Moranza.

They followed the bank of the river for a few miles to be sure it didn't turn back in a northerly direction, but it soon became apparent the map was wrong. Very wrong.

'Rivers don't change direction,' said Six, massaging the back of his head.

'I think you'll find they do. My grandfather taught me about it when I was a boy,' said Three. 'Corrosion I think he called it.

Or erosion. Explosion? No, that's not right. Something like that anyway.'

'Whether they do or not isn't important. The map is wrong,' said Addan as he studied the map over Milo's shoulder, trying to find any landmark that could potentially be identified on the paper.

'What do you propose we do about it, oh great leader?' said Five. He looked at his friends, smiling.

Addan refused to bite. 'Two options. We go back to camp now, or we turn back north and continue our mission.'

'I say we go back,' said Eight.

'Agreed,' said Five. 'I say cut our losses, go back to camp and see if we can't get a real map. One that's accurate, like.'

Returning to camp so soon didn't sit well with Addan. He felt they should keep moving north. 'I say a simple vote. Majority wins. Raise your hand if you believe we should return to camp.' Five, Six, Eight, and Ten raised their hands.

'I make that four against six. We press onwards.'

Five clipped Seven round the ear.

'Ow! What was that for?' complained Seven.

'What you think, what for?'

'Sorry, Addan is right. We got a job to do. Don't fancy going back and taking a beating like 'im.'

Addan smiled to himself. It appeared he'd won over one more. He had the majority now and that strengthened his leadership. For the time being, at least.

The farther they walked, deviating from the line on the map, the quieter the group had fallen. In all directions there was nothing but barren, snow-dusted scrubland with a few isolated trees here and there. In the distance to the west was a tree line, which looked as though it was marked in the map, but neither he nor Milo were certain. There hadn't been even a hint of life for miles. Addan didn't want to admit it, but he felt they might actually be lost. Not *truly* lost in the sense of not being able to find their way back to camp, but if he were asked where they were in reference to the map, he did not know.

'I say we turn and head for those trees,' Addan said eventually. 'There's nothing out here.'

Most of the others nodded in agreement. It was too open to stop and rest where they were. Without any shelter from the constant wind, they would soon freeze. At his direction, they all huddled around Milo as he held the map open.

'Does anyone have any notion where we are on the map? Any at all?' asked Five as he snorted the dripping snot hanging from his nostrils back into his head. He hawked it up before spitting it away from the group.

'If those circle things there are trees,' said Three as he stabbed at the map with a finger, 'then why not them be those trees over there?'

'What if they're holes?' said Eight.

'What if what are holes?' asked Milo, cocking his head towards Eight.

'The circle things.'

'Why would they be holes? That makes no sense. No, they're definitely trees,' said Four.

Addan raised his hands in frustration. 'Enough. We'll head for the trees we can see with our eyes over there, and then I suggest we make camp and rest for a while. Can we at least agree on that?'

There was a unanimous silence.

'That's settled then. Come on.'

The trees were farther away than they had first appeared. The snowy landscape hid a slight incline which disguised their true height and distance. Addan hung to the back of the group with Milo.

'Do you really think we're lost?' the boy asked, breaking the silence.

'I'm sure we'll find our way, eventually. There'll be something we can place on the map sooner or later.' Addan tried to sound reassuring, though he wasn't convincing even himself.

Shortly after entering the relative shelter of the woods, the landscape changed. The trees thinned out and revealed the partial remains of a stone building. It was barely more than a wall, one made from rock and stone. It had been constructed using traditional methods, and not shaped into being like every other structure in this land.

He was about to give the order to use the remains as a shelter to set up camp and rest a while, when Seven and Eight pointed out there were more ruins farther ahead. Further exploration revealed they had stumbled upon a long forgotten settlement. Given the state of decay, it had probably been hundreds of years since anyone lived there.

Addan shivered. There was something about the place that felt wrong. He stepped through the broken and worn shells of dwellings and tried to imagine what it might have looked like in the past. It felt more like a Moranzan town than anything he'd seen of Dawan so far. From a time before the Division, perhaps? It certainly looked old enough.

'I say we camp here,' said Three as he pulled at some vines growing up the wall nearest to him. 'No wind here.'

The man was right. How did he not notice the wind didn't blow here? The wind *always* blew. 'Fine,' said Addan. 'Let's gather some wood for a fire and we'll rest here.' Despite the nagging feeling of unease, he saw no reason not to.

It was only after an impressive pile of sticks and twigs had been gathered, Addan realised how unprepared they had been for this expedition. They had nothing to light the fire with. 'That's just wonderful!' growled Five as he kicked the stack of wood apart.

'Now what do we do?' asked Seven.

They all turned to Addan for an answer. He thought through the problem for a few moments, eyes closed, and then a memory appeared from nowhere. A memory from when he was a child out hunting with his father. Rocks. 'I need stones. Sharp ones that look shiny when broken.'

'Good idea,' said Five, spitting more phlegm into the snow. 'Something I can throw at your head.'

Milo was more willing. He scurried off into the trees and returned with a handful of small stones. He handed them to Addan.

'Thank you, these are perfect.' Addan turned them over in his hands, selecting two before discarding the others. 'I need grass, or leaves. They must be dry as possible, though.' Milo hopped off for a second time and returned with a handful of brown weeds. They weren't as dry as he'd liked. With all the snow, bone dry tinder would likely be impossible. He hoped they would suffice.

All the men—except Five, who seemed more interested in kicking the stack of branches apart—watched with interest as Addan got to his knees, held one of the stones to the bundle of dried brush, and struck down with the other stone. The clink of the rocks colliding echoed through the ruins. He struck them again, and again. On the fourth try a spark pinged into the air. One of the men gasped with interest. Addan struck again and kept going, trying to contain the sparks to the dried grass. Eventually a wisp of smoke grew out of the weeds. He carefully blew into it and the smoke gradually became a small orange flame. He picked the smouldering clump up and placed it into what remained of the pile of sticks. He glared at Five, letting him know what he thought of his actions. As the fire took hold, the men all—including Five—gathered the scattered wood and added it to the fire. They all cheered at the small victory, grateful of the warmth Addan had found for them.

With that one small act, Addan had unified his company around him. It allowed him to let down his guard a little. To relax and let go of some of the stress he'd been carrying since he'd left the training camp. There was still the nagging feeling about their surroundings, but for now they were safe and relatively warm.

Five had carried the sack of rations on the journey so far. It was nothing more than dried meat strips, but they were enough to sate any immediate hunger. Addan was surprised when Five handed strips to him first. It was a gesture of respect, and he appreciated it. They all ate in silence for a while until Three asked Seven about the scar on his arm. It was an ugly, jagged red line that ran from wrist to elbow, probably at least a year old.

'Got into a fight once,' Seven said.

'How do you get an injury like that in a fight?' asked Four.

'I missed the guy and put me hand through a window. Sliced it right up.'

There were gasps and even a little laughter at the man's misfortune. And then the conversation turned into a competition, each vying to see who had the best scar with the most impressive story. Most involved a fight or two, with outlandish tales that had they really been true would likely have killed them.

'I got one on ma knob,' said Ten.

'On your knob?' said Five. 'How did you manage that?'

'Not ma fault. I was with ma favourite whore one night, but she had a cold. I said I didn't mind. Felt a bit sorry for her an' paid a bit extra, cos I'm nice and that.'

'Did you piss her off then?' asked Eight, trying to work out how this led to injury.

'Nah. She was doin' 'er job, so to speak, an' she sneezed. Bit right down.'

The company simultaneously reeled in horror, hands instinctively protecting their own crotches.

'I don't believe you,' said Nine.

Without a word, Ten stood up, undid his pants and put on a display.

'Urgh, you can still see the teeth marks!' said Addan trying not to laugh. It was the first time in a long while since he'd found anything funny.

'What about you, you're pretty quiet,' said Ten to Milo as he put himself away.

'I have scars,' he said. He wasn't as cheery as he usually was, but still didn't look that down.

'Well, go on, show us then,' said Four, giving the lad a friendly shove.

'You don't have to,' said Addan, seeing a little reluctance in Milo's face, remembering what he saw back when they first met.

'No, it's fine,' Milo said as he stood up. He turned his back to the group and lifted his shirt revealing not only the horrific red stripe Addan had seen before, but lots of smaller, faded scars around it covering most of his back and shoulders.

'Burn the stones!' said Three amongst sounds of shock and even sympathy from the others.

'Who did that to you, boy?' said Eight. 'Need me to kill 'em for ya?'

'No, he's already dead. I used to be a slave, see? He used to whip all of us, every day, but one day he just dropped down dead,' he said quietly.

'Just like that?' said Ten.

'Yeah, grabbed his chest like someone had put a knife through it an' he dropped to the floor. I been on the streets ever since.' He looked up at the men with a smile. 'It's fine. I'm free now.'

Milo's story dampened the mood somewhat, and ended the line of tales. For Addan, the more he learned about his young friend, the more he admired him. For someone who'd barely made it to adulthood, he'd endured more than most would in their entire lives, and yet, through it all, Milo was one of the happiest people he'd ever met.

'Time to get some sleep I think,' said Six. Everyone else agreed and not another word was spoken until moonrise.

ADDAN BARELY SLEPT. His body was still sore and stiff, his mind still weighing down on him. Every time he closed his eyes, the girl haunted him, pleading with him to save her life. In the end, he sat with his back against a wall, keeping an eye over his company and watching the fire die down until it was smouldering embers.

Seven snored the loudest, unsurprising given the size of him. Three talked in his sleep. Nothing Addan could understand, but the tone of the mumblings seemed rather earnest. Milo barely looked as though he was breathing at all. Addan crept over to his friend and retrieved the map tucked in Milo's belt. Falling back against his wall, he pulled his legs to his chest, and opened the map, resting it between his knees.

He recognised almost all of the marked locations in Moranza. That part of the map was the most detailed. Whoever had drawn it was definitely a native Moranzan. The area that was Dawan was barely more than an outline, with the name written in large letters across it. Someone had marked out the base camp with a red X, the ink recent. Addan traced his finger south and made a small indentation in the paper where he approximated the last place he'd seen Liana.

In the top left of the map, in tiny writing, was the word "Sisterhood", right at the end of a small peninsula. To the south of that, probably two day's walk, if the proportions were correct, was a small mountain with a large black dot at its base. There wasn't a name next to it, but one of the supervisors told him that the dot was most likely Trennale. If Liana was anywhere, she would be there, they told him. Addan hoped they were right.

The map offered no mention of a place that could be this old forgotten settlement. Wherever he and his company were right now, it was unmarked, and that mountain still seemed a long way away.

The sky brightened, heralding moonrise. Addan rolled up the map and tucked it away in his tunic, stood up and stretched the stiffness from his legs, and woke the others. It was time to move. Reading the map as best he could, he'd decided that heading farther into the woods beyond the ruins was the best option. He told his bleary-eyed companions they'd trek until mid-moon before doubling back to base camp. No one argued.

They had barely walked ten paces when Six, who was out in front, motioned for everyone to stop and go low. Addan crept forward past his men and joined Six at the front. 'What do you see?' he whispered.

'Not sure. Thought I saw something move up ahead,' he said, keeping his eyes forward.

'I don't see anything.'

'What is it?' said a voice from behind. Addan wasn't sure if it was Eight or Nine. They both sounded alike.

Six stood up again before immediately shrinking back down. He pointed into the distance. 'There,' he said. 'You see it?'

'No, I, wait, what *is* that?' said Addan, squinting. In the gloom, he could barely make out a shape of something walking slowly through the ruins. Whatever it was, it looked human. 'We should turn back. No contact, remember?'

There was a flash of purple light and a scream rang out behind him. Addan turned. Nine, who had been bringing up the rear, was trying to fight off—what was that? It looked like a man, but it didn't look Dawanii. It towered over everyone and it looked like it was melting. Its arms weren't quite in the right place and the skin on its face hung well below its jaw. The creature cried out a low guttural scream, not one of pain. It was as though it was calling out. Nine was on his back kicking and screaming, trying to fight the creature off as it dragged him through the snow. Everyone else in the company had drawn their swords and, having shaken themselves free of surprise, attacked the monster in front of them.

It barely flinched, even when Three drove his sword through its chest. It kept trying to drag Nine away. And then there was another one bearing down from the left. Two more behind. Before Addan could draw his own sword, he found themselves surrounded. The creatures moved so fast! Three was the first to fall, both arms ripped from his torso by two of the beasts fighting over him like wolves over a lamb. Five and Seven tried to save him, hacking at the creatures with their swords with no effect. They kept coming, unfazed by injury.

Ten tried to escape, running for his life after his sword was knocked from his hand. He had no choice but to run. He didn't get far before one of the creatures hurled a ball of purple light at him, striking Ten in the back. Addan could only watch as the man died with an unworldly cry, but he had no time to mourn. Two of the creatures were closing in on him. Their purple eyes were wide and bright, feral. He rolled away from their grasp, groaning in pain from his injuries, trying his best to focus on surviving the onslaught. Time seemed to slow down for him as he watched his company fall one by one. They didn't stand a chance.

Using a tree as cover, he struck out with his sword, waving it aimlessly in the direction of one of the beasts advancing on his position. He glanced left. Milo was in trouble, on his back, trying his best to scramble away from his attackers. Addan ran for his friend, grabbing him by the tunic to pull him away, but it wasn't enough. A large, tangled mess of an arm took Milo by the neck and held him aloft.

'Let him go!' Addan demanded.

The creature growled low, its eyes empty of emotion. Milo kicked and choked as he tried to prise himself free from the hand around his throat. Then, a crack as the creature flicked his wrist, and Milo's body went limp in its grasp.

'No!' cried Addan as Milo's body fell to the ground. A look left, a look right. Addan was the only one left alive. He screamed, not through fear, but in defiance as three of the ugliest men he'd ever seen moved in on his position. Not one of them had been killed, only his men, his friend.

Addan lunged forward with his sword. A final attempt to save his own life. He struck out at the nearest beast, slicing its arm. It roared in pain and staggered backwards. He swung again but missed. Undeterred, he pushed forward, swinging wildly without skill or form until he hit one of them. It fell, yet did not die. He lashed out again, but then he noticed something —they weren't fighting back, nor were they retreating. They'd stopped. One in particular looked at him with curiosity, his head tilted to one side.

Addan let the sword point fall to his feet, confused, hands still clasped tight around the hilt. His breathing was laboured, heavy, fast. The creatures still didn't advance. He looked around, counting them. Six, no—seven of them. All standing, staring at him, and he didn't understand.

'What do you want?' he shouted. They didn't react. 'What do you *want?*'

The one nearest to him took one step closer and looked down at the sword before looking up at Addan, head still tilted. It made a low growling sound, as if trying to speak, but no words came. It stepped closer. Addan wanted to turn and run, but his legs refused to carry him. He gripped his sword tighter as the creature inched closer.

He studied its features. Whatever the beast was now, it looked to have been human once. The body was misshapen, like it had been ripped apart and reassembled by someone who didn't know what shape it should have been. Veins lined the bare flesh exposed under the ragged pelt it wore, veins that glowed a deep purple, pulsing along the skin. Closer. Less than three paces away now. Addan could smell its breath, rancid, rotting flesh filling his nostrils, urging him to retch. Closer.

The creature was almost nose to nose with him, yet he still could not move, still could not run. *Kill me if you're gonna.* It did not blink, its eyes cold and still. It sniffed. Addan closed his eyes, turning his head away as the stench seeped into his pores. The creature snorted. Addan felt something pull at his neck. The stone. Unable to open his eyes, he felt the creature snatch the leather shoelace, breaking at the back of his neck. After a moment, the smell faded. Addan opened one eye, head still turned, only to see it walking away, the stone clutched in his fist, the others following.

'Is that it?' he shouted. 'You let me live? Why? What makes me so different?' They didn't look back. They kept walking through the ruins until they were gone. Addan dropped his sword and fell to his knees. He looked at the carnage around him. All except him were dead. Streaks of blood melted the snow where it spilled. He crawled over to Milo, the boy face down in the dirt. Addan rolled him over. His eyes were open, but their sparkle was gone. Addan pulled him up to his chest and held him tight for an eternity.

21

MASSACRE

Company Three had returned on schedule, but half a day later, there was still no sign of Company Nine. Shaan didn't appear concerned. Dismissive, in fact. Cal worried. 'Should we send another company after them?'

Shaan shook his head. 'And send them where? They could be lost, or they could have been attacked by the enemy. They are only ten. I do not think it wise to send more men after them. No, we must press on.'

Cal was lying on the bed of furs in the corner of the hut Shaan had chosen for him. It was sparse, but warm. It didn't take him long to realise how much he enjoyed the climate back home. They'd not travelled far from Moranza, but every step so far had been colder than the last.

'You've changed,' said Cal after letting the silence hang in the air for a moment.

'Changed? Changed how?' Shaan was at the table, bent over the map, comparing it to the one updated by Company Three on their reconnaissance. He didn't look up.

'Ever since my mother died. You've been rather... in charge.'

Cal shifted onto his side to face Shaan, propping himself up on his elbow.

'Three have found some useful points of interest. Very helpful indeed.'

'Are you listening to me?'

'Of course. In charge? No, I do not think so. You are the king now. You are the man in charge.'

'It doesn't feel like it, and I am not a king. Not yet, at least. I can't help but feel that going to war was your idea. And you're relishing every moment of it.'

Shaan looked up from the map and looked at Cal. 'War is a decision for the king. I merely advised you of what I thought would be the best course of action to see your sister returned to us safely. That is paramount, is it not?'

'I wish there was another option. Actually, I wish she'd not bloody well run off in the first place.'

Shaan left the map and sat at the bottom end of the bed. He placed his hand on Cal's thigh. 'What is done is done. There is no changing that. You have made the right decision. You *know* you have made the right decision.'

Cal furrowed his brow. *Was it really my decision, though?* 'If you say so.'

'I do say so.' Shaan slapped Cal's thigh twice before standing up and returning to the map.

Flopping down on his back, Cal stared up at the strange wooden ceiling above him and sighed. It was all beginning to get out of hand, and he didn't like it. Why did his mother have to build that damned bridge? Without that, none of this would be happening. He cursed the Architects under his breath. Cursed them for sending his mother visions of peace between the two lands. Look where it had got her—killed by the same people she was encouraged to welcome.

'I think we are ready,' said Shaan, snapping Cal back to the present.

'Ready for what?' He sat up again.

'To move forward. The men are getting restless out there. Too many of them in a small base like this. We need to march on before they all start tearing each other apart.'

'Where do we march to?' Cal stood up and joined his friend by the map.

'There,' Shaan said, pointing to a scrawled mark next to what Cal assumed were trees.

'What's there?'

'Another settlement like this one, as far as I can tell. See how close it is to Trennale? From there we can mount our assault and take what is rightfully ours.'

Cal frowned at his friend's choice of words, then forgot about it, as if distracted. 'Well, if you think that is the best option.'

'If you have a better plan, by all means do tell.'

'No, no. I think you're right. I trust you. Ready the men, then.'

'As you wish, Your Grace,' said Shaan with a bow and a smile. He rolled up the map and left Cal alone in the hut.

He was second-guessing himself, replaying the conversation over in his mind. Had he decided to move out, or had Shaan? *Is this what it's like to lead?* His mother had many advisors in her time. Wise men, religious men, wealthy men—all offering their advice and opinion on the best way to run the country. Was this any different? Did his mother simply choose what was the best advice? Or did she truly make her own decisions? Cal sat back on the edge of the bed and rubbed his face with his palms. His own inexperience burdened him. Only now was he regretting not paying more attention to his mother when he had the chance.

Cal heard a tremendous cheer outside the hut coming from the army—his army. Clearly, Shaan had passed on the news. It came as a surprise how thirsty for blood these men and women were. Was it was from a sense of duty and loyalty to him and their country? Or was it simply for the sport of it, or for the money? Not that there was any money to pay them. He knew to keep that piece of information to himself, at least.

He didn't want to go outside and face them, not yet. He wasn't afraid of them, he simply didn't know what to say to them. He was content to let Shaan rally the troops until they were ready to leave, which wouldn't be long. A shiver ran through him. The cold was a concern, not only to him, but also to the leader of Company Three. Reporting on their return, he and Shaan had been told of the ever-dropping temperature, as well as the darkening sky they had noticed the farther they'd travelled west. There were furs owned and worn by the natives, which had been collected and stored in one of the other huts. Unfortunately, there weren't enough for everyone. Not even half. Cal wondered what effect that would have on morale. Infighting was already becoming more frequent, and they'd not even left the shelter of the camp.

After stealing the last few moments of quiet he could, Cal exited the hut to lead his army to war. One hundred were chosen to remain behind to secure the camp. He wished he had the option to remain with them. *Does that make me a coward?* He hoped not.

Provisions, probably not enough, were loaded onto five wooden wheeled carts to be pulled by four men each— normally such work would be done by cattle, but no one had thought to bring any with them. The Dawanii had kept animals here, but they were too small to be of use. If they were to win, it wouldn't be because of proper planning, Cal considered. He felt awkward as he stood from his vantage point, watching everyone else work. It wasn't his place to help with manual labour. The royal family did not get their hands dirty, his mother had taught him. In any sense of the word.

All told, five hundred and eighty-seven men and women,

plus the supervisors, Shaan, and Cal, marched westwards from the camp. Marching wasn't an accurate word. There was no discipline here. Cal had voiced his concerns about the readiness of the men. Some of the latest recruits had been sent directly from signing up into uniform to join the ranks. It all felt so… rushed. Cal often prayed to the Architects—even if it sometimes amounted to cursing their names when he felt it called for—and prayed now for their blessings and safekeeping on this mission. Hundreds of people surrounded him on his stryde in the centre of the pack. He'd never felt so alone.

Shaan had estimated it would take a whole day to reach the settlement marked on the map. By moonfall, fights had broken out—as predicted—over the clothing keeping the cold out, or for some, the lack thereof. The snow was thicker, and the strydes were also beginning to struggle. Some of the weaker men had collapsed from the freezing wind, eating into their bones. At first, attempts were made to keep them going by carrying them or sharing pelts from the more sympathetic and generous among them. In the end, there was no option other than to leave them where they fell. Left to die alone, frozen into the landscape.

Their deaths only made matters worse for the survivors. More fighting, more stealing, more dying from swords, as much as the cold. The supervisors did what they could to keep order, but there were only eight of them left. They too were too cold to push back.

By the next moonrise, their numbers had been reduced by more than a hundred. Two strydes had fallen, and their bodies were carved up for additional food barely after they'd drawn their final breath. The collective mood was as bleak as the darkened skies. It was a lot quieter now, and Cal felt it wasn't only because of the cold. He tried to ignore that nagging feeling. It was getting harder to concentrate.

With each passing day since leaving the palace, he felt less himself. It was as though a heavy weight pressed against his mind, numbing it somehow. He tried to recall why he was here in this frigid, barren wasteland, and found the memory elusive. Liana, yes, but there was something... else. He looked to Shaan as they rode. He knew to trust him.

Not a single soul had crossed their paths on the journey. Cal had expected great armies of men ready to defend their lands as Shaan—and others—had promised. There was no one. The day before, Cal had thought he'd seen a handful of shadowy figures in the distance. A group of wanderers, perhaps. Or even Company Nine. In the end, he believed it may only have been his mind playing games with him.

Finally, there was a call from the front of the pack. 'Smoke!' yelled someone. Tired, cold and hungry, Cal looked to the horizon. A blue-grey plume rose gently above some trees ahead of them. They had arrived—somewhere, at least. He hoped it was the mark on the map. A newfound energy warmed him and he pushed forward. Soon, the shapes of more wooden huts and buildings came into view. It *was* a settlement, at least.

'I want to approach them with a small group,' said Cal to Shaan.

'Is that a good idea?'

'Maybe, maybe not. If we can avoid further bloodshed, then I would prefer it. It looks to be a village. I don't believe there will be any danger here.'

Shaan shook his head. 'They are your men.'

Cal relaxed a little at the thought of avoiding more death and destruction. He took twenty men with him and advanced towards the settlement. The rest waited behind. *They may not know of our war,* he reasoned. He hoped they would welcome them, offer food and warmth to his charges. He might even find an avenue to peace and negotiation. If this was the settlement marked on the map, they were close to Trennale now. There had to be hope of finding Liana and seeing her home safely. There *had* to be hope.

The settlement looked remarkably similar to the base camp. The buildings were all of the same design and size, and they were arranged in much the same way. There was even a small river. If Cal didn't know any better, he might argue it *was* the same settlement. As they approached, a young boy of no more than ten years was the first to see them. He looked startled and then darted off out of sight. A moment or two later, the boy reappeared with five adults, all wearing thick, dark, *warm* animal skins. They stood close to a hut, looking at Cal and his company with caution.

Cal moved his stryde forward, slowly, towards the strangers. They looked like they'd never seen a stryde before. They eyed it curiously, clinging tight to each other for safety. Cal didn't see any threat in them, though they clearly saw threat in *him*.

'Good day to you,' Cal said, trying to sound both confident and friendly at the same time. 'I am Cal Tallan, Prince of Moranza.'

The Dawanii—three women all similarly dressed with odd stripes of moss green paint in their hair, and two men, older, smaller, also with green paint—didn't move. The boy, hiding behind one of the women's legs, waved cautiously at Cal. None of the adults replied.

'We, my men and I,' he pointed at his company, 'have travelled a long way. In the cold. We are searching for my sister, Princess Liana. Do you know of her? Have you seen her?'

One of the Dawanii women broke ranks and stepped forward. She looked old enough to be Cal's mother. Skin was loosening around the jowls, as if she'd once been fat and then had lost it all. Her eyes were wide and pale. One of the men stepped forward with her. He spoke.

'We request you dismount your beast. Here we respect our animals, and do not burden them in such a manner.'

Cal looked at his men with novel amusement before relenting and stepping down from his mount. 'I mean no disrespect.'

The old woman looked to her companion without speaking. He nodded as if understanding her expression and then turned back to Cal. 'Thank you. Now, please step forward, so I may look at you. Tell me about the one you seek.'

Letting go of the stryde's reins, Cal stepped closer to the pair. He was taller than both of them by quite a margin. The woman barely came up to his chest. 'We believe my sister came to your country and has got lost. We are searching for her.'

'I am Curral. I am Teena's voice. Please speak to her directly and assume I am not here.'

'She cannot speak herself?'

"You are correct. I am Teena. Please state the *true* reason you are here."

Cal looked alternately at Curral and Teena, confused. 'I speak the truth. We came to find my sister, Princess Liana.'

Teena leaned forward, squinting at Cal. "That is not the entirety of your motive, is it?"

'My men could use some warm shelter. We have—'

"Deception! Speak only the truth." The tone of voice was forceful.

That wasn't the response Cal had expected. 'My men are cold and hungry. We have come only to find my sister. Please, if you know anything.' It *was* the truth. He looked beyond the old woman. Other Dawanii had arrived, cautiously interested in the new arrivals.

"Deception! Your words hide your true intent. What is it you are hiding? Let me see." Teena reached forward with her hand, grabbing Cal's in hers.

Cal tried to pull free, but the old woman was strong. So

strong! The company of men closed ranks alongside Cal. He motioned for them to stop. 'Wait. She's not hurting me.' The men complied, wary.

Teena threw Cal's hand away and gasped. She backed away, waving her hands frantically. "You mean us harm! We are in danger! You must go. Leave us now. Please!" She and Curral turned and ran, Teena's arms flailing. Curral screamed for their people to seek shelter, and calling for—Cal wasn't sure what he said—what sounded like "builders."

'I only want to find my sister!' Cal called after them. He watched, dumbfounded, as the Dawanii people scattered in all directions, disappearing into the shadows. 'Did I say something wrong?' he asked no one in particular.

'Dunno, Your Grace. Strange folk, though. I swear he was reading your mind like some kind of fortune teller,' said the soldier closest to him.

Any sign of life in the settlement had gone. Cal barely opened his mouth, ready to order his men back to the main group, when a tree trunk crashed to the ground in front of them. It splintered on impact, sending snow, dust and wooden shards everywhere. Cal's stryde immediately bolted. Before Cal and his men had time to register what was happening, a second lump of wood slammed into the snow, barely missing the group. Shrill cries rang out from deep within the settlement.

'Retreat!' commanded Cal.

The men turned to run. Cal watched as his stryde ran off in the wrong direction, his men running in the other towards where Shaan and the rest were waiting. Except they weren't. They were already charging his way. Another crash of wood behind him. A searing pain exploded from his shoulder. He instinctively grabbed at it and felt a piece of tree embedded near his neck, his hand now sticky with warm blood. *What in all of Rybban is going on?*

Cal broke into a run towards his men. As they charged in his

301

direction, he immediately realised if he didn't get out of the way, he'd be trampled by the oncoming wave of hundreds of angry men, swords already drawn. *Where was Shaan? There! The stryde in the centre.* Cal had no other option but to double back on himself into the onslaught of lumber. His small entourage had already done so. He drew his sword and found himself enveloped in a sea of bodies sweeping him forward into the settlement.

It was too fast. From the moment the first tree crashed down, there wasn't enough time for Shaan to order the troops forward to reach his position so quickly. It was pre-emptive. *Why?* No time to think. He didn't want this. To his right was a large, rough piece of stone protruding from the ground. He ran to it, dodging out of the way of anyone who would bowl him over, and climbed on top. 'Stop! I order you all to stop!' he shouted as loud as he could muster. It wasn't enough. The din of shouting of his charges drowned him out. He kept calling, waving his arms, trying to get them to listen to him. Then he saw Shaan heading his way. 'Shaan, we need to stop this!'

Shaan pulled his stryde to a stop next to Cal's makeshift platform. He grinned at Cal. 'This is war!' was all he said before kicking his stryde back into a run.

A heavy rock fell out of the sky. It smashed at Cal's feet, knocking him off balance and he hit the ground hard. He had to scramble out of the way before he got trodden on. His men were still flowing into the settlement, battle-ready. He looked up. A number of Dawanii were in the trees, throwing heavy wood and stone projectiles down on their attackers. But—he strained to see clearly—they were throwing, but not with their hands. The stones were moving on their own, he was sure of it. He'd never seen anything like it, and wasn't sure *exactly* what he was seeing. He followed a massive log as it flew through the air, crushing three of his soldiers as it landed, unsure if the loud cracking he heard was wood or bone.

Whether he wanted to or not, it was time for him to fight.

Bodies were already creating obstacles along the snow paths that ran between buildings. Projectiles rained down from rope gantries above. Cal not only had to avoid tripping over corpses—most of which were Dawanii—he had to avoid being crushed by anything thrown from above. While he had some limited practice with a sword as he grew up, never before had he spilled the blood of another by his own blade. That changed when two Dawanii—who looked more fearful than angry—came at him with what looked like hammers. Cal easily dodged the first swing, hiding behind his stone platform and using it as cover. The attack was slow and clumsy. He struck back, slicing across the man's chest from shoulder to hip. *I hate this.*

The second man swung low, his hammer punching into Cal's left thigh. His leg buckled, almost losing balance. Pushing up with his free hand, he lunged forward at his attacker, his sword missing the man's chest by a mere finger's width. Cal pulled back his sword for another attempt, another thrust, but took a punch to the jaw before he could fully reset. He tasted blood, biting his tongue as the fist caught him off-guard. Through watering eyes, Cal thrust forward, this time finding his mark. *I'm sorry.*

Farther ahead, Shaan's stryde ran wild and unridden. There was no sign of Shaan, though. Had he fallen? Three more Dawanii died by his sword as he continued forward. Where were they going? What was the plan? The purpose? He felt as though it was all aimless, *unnecessary.*

Glancing upwards, he noticed some of his own men had found their way to the top level, ending the lives of those throwing their deadly debris. Cal had noticed the frequency of wood and rock coming down from above had slowed, which was a relief. His shoulder hurt more now. He could feel the blood trickling down his back, regretting pulling the splinter out. It did feel like some of it was still in the wound. *How bad was it? Not fatal, at least not yet.*

And then it all grew quiet. *Was it over? Did we win?* It didn't feel like a victory. There was still no sign of Liana. He didn't expect her to be here in a random settlement. He had hoped to speak to the inhabitants, to see if they knew anything. He didn't get the chance. Shaan saw to that. Where *was* Shaan? He waded through the dead and dying bodies of Dawanii lying everywhere he stepped. Eventually he found him, sitting casually on one of the logs hurled down from above. There wasn't a mark on him.

'Why?' Cal asked, trying to get his breathing back into a normal rhythm.

'They attacked first,' he said, picking at the only speck of dirt on his pant leg.

'You couldn't have known that from the holding position.'

'Could I not? If you say so. I saved your life back there. War is a fast-moving game.'

'Game? It's not a bloody game.'

'It looks rather bloody to me,' Shaan said, surveying the carnage around them.

'That's not funny,' said Cal. He sheathed his sword and looked over the devastation. So many dead. Women and children, too.

Shaan stood up and put his hand on Cal's shoulder. Cal reflexively pulled away.

'What is the matter?' Shaan asked. 'Should these people not pay for your mother's murder? Do you not want your sister returned safe and well? You shy away when it gets dirty. Well, war is dirty. It is messy. And you need to face up to that. This is what you wanted.'

Cal took a step back. 'I didn't want any of *this*. This was of your making, your doing. I wanted to talk to them, reason with them, but you wouldn't allow it.'

They were interrupted by a supervisor requesting orders. He was addressing Cal, but Shaan spoke for him. He instructed them to search for supplies and enough warm clothing for those who had thus far gone without. Orders given, he turned back to Cal.

'That is not how it was. Yes, I *advised*, but you are the king. The decisions are—and were—yours to make alone.'

He didn't know if it was the heat of battle or the agony of his shoulder wound, but that didn't sound right. His head was foggy, muted, like it had been stuffed with wool. 'I still don't understand how it escalated so quickly. The man I spoke to, he knew we were a threat before we even were. None of this makes any sense.'

'You are injured. Tired. You need to rest before you make yourself ill. A supervisor will tend to your shoulder. I will take care of everything else. Everything will be all right. Leave it to me.' His voice was quiet, soothing.

Cal felt lightheaded, barely able to concentrate. *Leave it to him. He knows what's best.* A chill rose from deep within him, rushing through his whole body. The rumbles of thunder grew closer and more frequent. He felt as though he should fear the oncoming storm, yet there was something else. A sense of something a little too far out of reach. He shook his head, trying to release his mind from the fog that gnawed away at his thoughts. *I trust him.*

Shaan rubbed Cal's back, comforting him. 'Leave it all to me. I have everything under control, now.'

22

A GOD AMONG THEM

On the journey back to Trennale, the twins bombarded Liana with a litany of questions. They wanted to know everything that had happened. What was it like to have an actual Architect within her? Why didn't she look any different, now she could communicate with Eraidor? Did Eraidor have any message for them? What did he look like? As good-natured as they were, by the time Trennale came into view, their incessant questions were wearing her down. Eraidor had to remind her they were still young and not to be so short with them when she snapped an answer without meaning to.

'It's like having a miserable old uncle minding you while your parents are away on business,' she said internally. She was happy she could talk to Eraidor without using her mouth, which meant she didn't have to look like a lunatic talking to the winds every time she wanted to address him.

When they arrived back in the city, Uehan was the first to greet them. He'd anticipated their arrival and walked the path out to meet them. 'I'm so pleased to see you return safely,' he said, beaming. His eyes were now a pure black, except for a small pale blue swirl of light at their centre.

'You've recovered!' said Liana, her relief on full display.

'Yes, it was close, but with all your help, I lived. Aelene spared me and I thank Eraidor for letting me live, and for forgiving me for my ill-judgement.'

'I cannot accept credit where none is due,' said Eraidor, looking the young man up and down, though only Liana could see him. He saw the scar on Uehan's palm, tutted and shook his head. *'The things people do to themselves. I never understood why. It is not my place to intervene, of course.'*

Liana glared at him, though to anyone observing, she was making strange faces to a tree.

'You're blind now?' Liana asked.

'Oh yes, but I still saw your arrival. It's a strange notion, being able to see, but also being blind at the same time. As Nalla told me—sight is not only for the eyes.'

'How can you walk about without--'

'Hitting a tree,' Uehan finished her sentence for her. 'I can see the immediate future all at once. If I foresee myself walking into a tree, or another person, then I will know not to walk in that direction. I find a future where I have no obstacle and follow it. It's rather easy, actually.'

'I'll take your word for that.'

Uehan turned to the twins. 'Your parents are looking for you. They want to tell you to prepare for your Branding at once.'

Both of them bounded off with excitement without a single word of goodbye. Liana wondered if she should feel insulted that she be forgotten so easily, considering what they've been through these past few days. Instead, she smiled at their enthusiasm.

She turned her attention back to Uehan. 'What's it like to see the future?' They strolled through the city as they talked.

'Strange, but interesting. It doesn't work like you would think it works. The future is forever changing, so it is impossible to see very far ahead accurately. The closer to now, the clearer I can see what is to come. Also, I can't see *everything* that is about to happen either. I have to know what I'm looking for.'

'How do you mean?'

'He means he may or may not know if you are going to trip over that rock.'

'What ro—' Liana caught her right foot on a flat stone protruding from the dirt. It took every effort to keep herself from crashing to the ground.

'I apologise,' said Uehan. 'I should have warned you about that. Even though it is a gift, it still takes practice to focus on the right future.'

Ember barked, as if to mock her. 'I don't know what you're laughing at,' Liana said. 'You weren't any help either.' Ember bowed her head.

'What's Eraidor like? Is he wonderful? I hope he's wonderful.'

'He's not what I thought he'd be. To be honest, he's rather moody.'

'Now, now.'

Uehan frowned. Clearly that wasn't the answer he expected.

'Do you want a race?' asked Liana. 'To your home.'

'Why? Are we in a hurry?'

'Oh, I want to see a god run, that's all.'

Ember was up for the challenge too, running off ahead. Liana had noticed the animal seemed to understand more of what she was saying the longer they spent together. Uehan, despite his recent change, was pretty swift on his feet, leaving her trailing behind. Liana had imagined seeing Eraidor huff and puff beside her as he tried to keep up with them. It annoyed her no end when he simply floated, motionless beside her as she ran through the city.

'That's cheating,' she said.

'*I do not see how. I am within you, remember? I do not need to run. I simply... am.*'

The city centre was buzzing with activity. It became evident to Liana very quickly that a Branding was every bit a community event. Torches had been lit and placed outside of every building, lighting up the whole city against the dull sky. The torches trailed up the mountain too. Considering the number of trees, Liana was impressed nothing had caught fire. Naked flames still made her feel uneasy. A lifetime of fear was difficult to overcome. The whole scene reminded her of the aftermath of a dragon invasion back home, but without the destruction and cries of despair. Here, everything was planned, each torch in a uniform position and distance from the next. She watched the flames dance in the wind, appreciating the beauty of it all.

Uehan's mother was also pleased to see Liana's return. Aranan, still disdainful about his brother's betrayal, barely acknowledged her. He only nodded before leaving the room. Helela insisted Liana stay with them for as long as she was in Trennale, for which she was grateful. She had given little thought to how long she would stay. Her mind had been occupied by other, more pressing concerns.

Liana had been given a fresh change of clothing, which she appreciated. When it came to getting undressed in the privacy of her room, it was only then she realised things weren't exactly private anymore. 'I don't want you looking at me,' she said aloud.

'*Does it really bother you that much? I created all living things, remember? To hide your nature in front of your creator seems rather illogical.*'

'I don't care. I don't like the idea of you watching, or looking, or even having a little peek. There's plenty of dirty-minded men, and women, back home. I really don't appreciate one of them being inside my head.'

'*Very well, I shall avert my eyes.*'

'Thank you.' Liana undressed and was surprised by the number of bruises she had picked up along the way. *No wonder I ache so much.* The Sisterhood healer had done a fine job on her forearm; that felt as good as new, better even. Had she known about the other injuries, she would have asked for their healing too. She tried to ignore the spreading shadow. The tendrils had only grown by an inch or two since she left the Sisterhood. The mark tingled a little. As long as it stayed that way, she could put it at the back of her mind for now. *How much time do I have, though, really?*

She kept one eye on Eraidor, who stood conspicuously in the corner facing the wall, pretending to count the number of cracks. Something told her it might all be an illusion and he could maybe see out the back of his head. She was well aware of how beautiful she was. Not out of vanity, but because of all the attention she'd had ever since she started becoming a woman. She'd even caught her brother stealing a glance once, even with his proclivities. Curiosity got the better of him, he'd said. Years of attention left her a little paranoid when it came to men sometimes.

Presentable again, she left her bedchamber, still feeling uncomfortable with Eraidor's omnipresence. There had to be a way of freeing him. There *had* to be. Even he hinted of a possibility, but any solution had to be her discovery and hers alone. The thought of having to live out the rest of her life with a deity within her would likely drive her to insanity, probably sooner rather than later.

Helela had made a meal for them all. A simple meat broth with some brightly coloured vegetables Liana didn't recognise. There was something resembling bread in a bowl in the middle of the table. It all smelled wonderful, and most importantly—it was hot. Charred rabbit could only carry a woman so far.

After the meal, Uehan's mother asked a question Liana

hadn't expected. 'Would you like to paint your hair in our tradition?'

Liana thought about it for barely a moment. 'Yes, I think I would like that very much.' It had been many years since someone else had touched her hair. Not since her favourite waiting maid had died. She had fond memories of sitting in front of her, having her hair brushed while talking, usually mocking the men in their lives. She missed those days dearly.

Uehan's mother produced a bowl of water and a white stone cup containing a red powder. She invited Liana to sit on a chair, then instructed her to lean her head back into the bowl. The water was warm and smelled of petals. She savoured every moment as Helela massaged and washed away all the dirt, along with the stress of the past few days.

'Why do you colour your hair this way?' asked Liana, more to stop herself from drifting off to sleep, but there was genuine interest too.

'It is a long held tradition. Every settlement and tribe has their own colour. The colour represents our devotion to the Architects, and all the gifts they provide for us.'

'I do find their little rituals fascinating,' said Eraidor.

'What do you mean?'

'None of this is from our own instruction or direction. They come up with everything themselves. Hundreds of years ago, they used to leave out piles and piles of fruit as offerings to us. Every single day. The fruit would eventually rot away. Why would we need food? We do not need to eat. It seemed to make them happy, though. Such a waste of good food, really. Eventually, they stopped. Most of them, at least.'

'It doesn't do any harm though, does it?'

'No. I simply find it fascinating. Not everything they do in our name is well-meaning, however. Many times I have witnessed murder in my name. In the name of all the Architects. That hurts. No human was given the right to kill another, especially on our behalf.

Humans can be so hateful towards each other, and often for the most trivial of reasons.'

Helela finished rinsing the excess dye before using a large square of cotton cloth to dry Liana's hair. She then handed her a decorated, round plate made of metal that showed her reflection.

Liana looked exactly like a Dawanii now, which amused her. She was growing to like these people. Everything was so much simpler here. Little was expected of her, and everyone worked together for a common good. They were a proper community, and everything Moranza wasn't, where most people only looked out for themselves. Ember approved of the new look too, sniffing at the colouring before licking her cheek.

'Come. We are to join everyone to celebrate the twins' Branding.'

Not everyone appeared to approve of Liana's new look as she and Uehan's family walked to the amphitheatre. The majority did, but some—mostly other women—tutted and shook their heads. Some were more discreet than others. They knew she was an outsider, and a new colour of hair wouldn't change that.

'Pay no heed to them,' said Uehan. 'They mean you no harm, really.'

'I'll have to take your word for that.'

'I like that you are one of us now.'

'One of you? I'm not sure that I am. I'll likely only stay until after the Branding, then I really should leave for home. I have my own family there, for better or worse. They'll be missing me, I'm sure.'

Uehan looked disappointed.

'Don't be sad. I promise I'll come back and visit. Maybe you can come to Moranza and see *my* home.'

'I think I'd like that. But...' His expression changed from sadness to concern. He looked down.

'But what?' Liana gently used a finger to lift his chin so she could look at his face. The blue swirls in his eyes looked eerie in the half-light, with tiny flickering orange reflections of the torches dancing within them.

'I don't know. I feel something. When you said I could come to the Old Land, I saw a dark shadow. It told me I would never see your home.'

'The boy might be right. I feel something... out of place.'

'Like what?'

'Time will tell, I think.'

'It might be my imagination,' said Uehan. 'Time will tell, I think.'

'Interesting!' said Eraidor.

Uehan's mother was saying nothing, but Liana saw the look on the woman's face, and it was a look of worry. Liana looked at Ember. She didn't look worried at all, but then again, what would a worried cinderfox look like?

The amphitheatre was already alive with activity. Orratan, accompanied by his assistant as always, noticed Liana and broke off his conversation with a woman not quite his age. He came over to greet her.

"My dear, Liana." He took hold of her by the shoulders and squeezed gently. "I see Uehan's mother has been taking care of you. If I may say, it suits you," he said, referring to her new hair colouring.

'Thank you. She thought it might allow me to feel less conspicuous.'

The amphitheatre was filled with laughter and excitement, all witnessed by the ring of giant Architect statues encompassing them. Some Dawanii from other nearby villages and tribes had come to witness the ceremony. It was easy to tell who the visitors were solely by their hair. Some had a red stripe, others had yellow or green, or even a combination of two. Even though they were all there for the twins, a significant

313

amount of attention was on her, and it made her feel uncomfortable.

It started with a man from—she was told—a small village close to the city called Tumm. He was around her age, slightly shorter, and had a bright yellow stripe of hair running from ear to ear around the back of his head. He spoke with a strangely deep voice. 'It is an honour to be in your presence.'

'Thank you,' said Liana tentatively.

'I believe he means me,' said Eraidor.

'Oh.'

'Please, if I may,' said the man. 'My daughter has a terrible affliction. One so awful even the healers are unable to cure. I fear she may die very soon. I beg for you to help her.' He fell to his knees, hands clasped together.

'I'm so very sorry to hear that,' said Liana in her best sympathetic voice.

'Can you do anything for him?' she asked Eraidor.

'I cannot. Not least in my current predicament. Even if I wanted to help, there is a strict non-interference edict. Prayers go unfulfilled, questions are unanswered. Crimes go unpunished, and virtues are unrewarded.'

'You'll allow her to die, then? That seems rather cruel, don't you think?'

'I would not expect you to understand. These matters are far more complicated than any human mind could possibly fathom.'

Others had noticed the pleading man and gathered around Liana. They too hoped she—through Eraidor—could cure their ills or grant their desires. Liana tried her best to placate them, but the tugging on her hands, her legs, the pushing and shoving became too much. All had their requests. Men, women, even one young child who only wanted to ask for her pet rabbit to be brought back from the dead, all made their pleas. Liana quickly became overwhelmed.

'Please stop!' she cried. *'What do I do?'*

Before she got an answer, Orratan broke through the circle, took her by the hand while, at the same time, fending off anyone who got too close. He ushered her through an animal-skin door that led to a quieter area.

"May I apologise on their behalf? Some of them are really quite desperate, and clearly their emotions have got the better of them. To know they are truly in the presence of an Architect is a powerful thing indeed."

'Thank you for helping. Eraidor said he's not willing to help them.'

'That is not entirely true. Not all is clear cut as you believe it to be.'

Liana spoke aloud. 'Yes, it is. You said specifically that you won't interfere. *Won't*. That means there is a choice. Why shouldn't you help them?'

'I also said I am not presently in a position to help. Within you, I am powerless.'

'That's an excuse. You're not the only Architect, are you? So why do you, as a collective, let them suffer so?'

The assistant tapped Orratan on the shoulder to get his attention. She whispered something to him and he nodded in return.

"I believe, to intervene would eventually do more harm than good," Orratan said.

'He is right. He has quite the adequate grasp of matters for a mortal man. We learned very early on in humanity's existence the mistake of helping them with their every ill or whim. Let them have it all, we thought. Be kind, be generous. Be merciful. It only took a century or so to realise how wrong that was. Nobody died. They should *have died. Of old age, disease, but they did not. They kept on living well beyond the limits of their bodies. In the end it was quite a mess.*

'Then there were the prayers. Allow one person to have what they desired often meant someone else would suffer instead. Then they

315

would pray for their suffering to end as well. And so on, and so on. It became impossible. So we had to step back. Leave you all to your own selves. Of course, on occasion we might give someone a little push in the right direction, sometimes for their own reward, other times for the greater good. Fate, if you will.'

'I still don't think it's right,' said Liana, addressing Orratan. She turned her back on Eraidor, not that it did any good. He simply floated back into her line of sight. *'Will you leave me alone for just one moment?'*

"I will speak with them. I'm certain they will understand. Most of them, at least. Though, you must be kind and accept there will still be some who will make demands of you during the remainder of your stay."

'I will try my best. Thank you.' Liana bowed a little in gratitude.

"I will leave you alone here for a while. Please do come and rejoin the celebration when you are ready." Orratan returned Liana's bow with one of his own before leaving Liana alone with Eraidor once more.

'I'm starting to regret saving your life,' she said, looking around and noticing Ember wasn't by her side.

'That is not true in the least.'

Liana sighed. 'No, it's not. I'm frustrated is all. I want my life—need my life back. How do I stop this power consuming me? How do I get you out? Surely you wish to be free of me also?'

'Of course I do. I have yearned for so many lifetimes to be free. To go where I want. Be in two places at the same time, should I wish.'

'Why won't you tell me how to release you, then?'

'As I have already said. I cannot.'

'Why?' Her frustration threatened to turn into anger. She paced around the room, wishing there was somewhere to sit down. Aside from a window looking out over the ceremonial grounds, the room was empty. She considered that a waste of a perfectly good room.

Eraidor didn't answer her as he gazed out of the window. *'Such a strange ritual, if you think about it.'*

'Don't ignore the question. Answer me! Why can't you tell me how to be free of you?' Her face became quite hot.

'Because, if I tell you, we will both die.'

His words hit her like a stone. 'What do you mean, "die"? Don't be ridiculous.'

'This is my curse, remember?'

'What about me? Why am I made to suffer?'

'In all truthfulness, I do not know. It is most irregular that you are aware of my presence at all. There is no precedent.'

Liana settled down a little, more out of exhaustion than satisfaction. 'Not even a hint? Point me in the right direction?'

'No. My release is predicated on a specific condition being met by my host. Since they are ordinarily unaware of my presence, they could not be coerced or otherwise influenced in finding the key. The mere fact you are aware of me does not change that. Also, remember that my presence is also what is keeping you alive. Do not be so eager to be rid of me until we find a way to solve that conundrum.'

A thought entered Liana's head at that moment. 'In all the hundreds of years, not one of the people you have... known, has ever done what is required to free you?'

Eraidor actually looked sad. He shook his head slowly. *'Alas, they have not. Until then, I remain trapped. Perhaps forever.'*

Liana felt a sudden resolve growing inside her. 'I promise I will figure it out.'

'I know you will try, but I have low expectations.'

'Has anyone told you, you can be really condescending sometimes?'

'No. It has been a thousand years since anyone has told me anything.'

Liana growled. 'Well, it's true. Don't underestimate me.'

23

THE BRANDING

The twins' parents were possibly the nicest, kindest people Liana had ever met. Both were rather small, barely reaching Liana's chest. Tima, their mother, was nearly as wide as she was tall. She had soft grey eyes that reflected a lifetime of wisdom and love. Derrum, their father, was barely more than bones, and nimble on his feet. His eyes were also grey, but much lighter than Tima's. If they stood side by side and Liana squinted, their combined form resembled a much older version of the boys.

Liana seemed more worried about the twins' future than they did. Of course, she knew next to nothing of their ways, of their beliefs. What she did know, was the mathematical outcome of their Branding meant one of them was likely to die.

'*Do not interfere,*' said Eraidor.

'*I wasn't going to say anything.*'

'*You were. And you may very well be right, but it is not our—your—place to say what is on your mind.*'

'May I ask a question?' Liana said to the parents as they stood looking at the monument that would soon decide their sons' future.

'Yes, of course,' said Tima as she ran her fingers along the stonework.

'I said, do not interfere.'

'If only the first-born may undertake the Branding, how are both of them allowed? Surely one of them was born before the other?'

Derrum laughed. Liana raised an eyebrow.

'It's a funny story,' said Tima.

'No, no,' said Derrum. 'Let me tell her.' He sat down on the outer stone ring, only for Tima to clip his ear. He stood up again immediately. 'When they were born, we lost track of which one was which, on account of them both looking the same. We were only expecting the one child. Who wouldn't be? We still don't really know which one is which. Both have been the other so many times. You might even say they're both the same person in a way. So, when it came to the Branding, the elders decided they both could participate if they chose to.'

Liana didn't really understand why it was a funny story. If she were a twin, she'd definitely want to know which one she was. 'But what about—'

'Liana, I mean it. No good will come of this.'

'Fine.' '—you both, did either of you undergo the Branding when you were their age?'

'I was permitted, though I chose not to,' said Derrum. 'Sometimes I regret my choice, but I like life the way it is now. I'm content.' He took his wife's hand in his and squeezed it, staring wistfully into her eyes.

'I had an older sister, so I couldn't.'

'Had?' The word escaped Liana's mouth before her brain could stop it. 'Oh, I'm sorry.'

Eraidor tutted and shook his head.

'Oh there's nothing for you to be sorry about. This is the way of the world.'

The conversation was interrupted by the abrupt appearance

of the twins, both full of energy and excitement. They were wearing different fur tunics to everyone else. The only ones Liana had seen so far were all of a uniform colour, including her own. The twins were wearing coats of mixed colours in a patchwork of patterns. Small individual pieces of fur, each the size of a hand, all stitched together. Ember was with them. Someone had tied a matching scarf around her neck. She seemed very proud of it.

'Do you have a preference?' Liana asked.

'Preference for what?' the twins said together, while hugging their parents in turn.

'Careful.'

'If you could choose your own stone, specifically, which one would you prefer?'

'Oh no, we aren't permitted to choose ourselves. Eraidor chooses for us.'

'That's not what I mea— never mind.' Liana hoped someone would change the subject, quickly realising—finally —it was perhaps best not to ask.

'Is that right? You choose?' she asked Eraidor.

'No, I do not. Never have. No interference.'

There were a lot of people gathered to witness the Branding, with most stood in a large circle around the monument. Liana tried to count them, but was interrupted and directed to stand by a very tall, very well-built man with a long black beard flecked with grey. She smiled at him politely as their eyes met. She had to assume he smiled back as she couldn't see his mouth through all the facial hair.

From where she now stood, she had a good view of the proceedings. She was a little off-centre, so the kneeling area was only a slight head-turn to her right. She would be able to see the twins' faces as well as the important part of the ritual— plucking an orb from the fire itself. The fire wasn't lit yet. She presumed its ignition would be a part of the overall ceremony.

'*I have always found their customs and rituals most intriguing,*' said Eraidor. '*Even if they are quite appalling at times. I remember a long time ago, they used to throw those who they suspected of being in the early stages of becoming Torn into the Great Lake.*'

'*To kill them before they turned?*'

'*If only. No. As I say—suspected. If they floated, they were deemed to be beyond saving and were executed. If they sank, they would be considered free. Except they usually drowned. It took them decades before they figured out their folly.*'

'*Sounds awful.*'

'*Indeed. And before you think too little of the Dawanii, the Moranzans had their own fair share of ridiculous notions in their history too.*'

'*Like what?*'

Before Eraidor could answer, Orratan, who was now standing at the mouth of the monument with his assistant beside him, called for everyone's attention with the clap of his hands. The sound he made echoed around the amphitheatre as though a hundred hands had all clapped at the exact same time.

"Welcome everyone on this joyous and momentous occasion. And a special welcome to Haal and Eelan as they prepare to enter adulthood and undertake the Branding."

The entire room erupted into a rhythmic chanting, except for Liana and Eraidor. Liana attempted to join in after figuring out the tempo, but by the time she did, everyone had fallen silent, leaving her own "ooh ah" lingering in the air like a bad smell. She shrank back a little against their stares. Orratan looked at her and offered a sympathetic wink.

"It is now time to light the Flame of Life." Orratan turned to face the monument, closed his eyes and began to chant, moving his hand in small circles over the orbs. A tiny flame popped to life in the centre. Slowly it grew until it created a column of flickering light, casting a purple hue over everyone present, their shadows dancing behind them.

With the fire created to his satisfaction, Orratan turned around again to face the twins. "If Haal and Eelan would please step forward."

The boys gently nudged each other forward, neither wanting to be the one in front—a shyness within them Liana had not seen before. Orratan gestured, encouraging them to him. He patted each on the head as soon as they were within reach.

"Have you decided who is to go first?"

Haal and Eelan turned to each other, their expressions suggested they were having a last-minute psychic conversation with one another. Eventually, they nodded. 'I will be first.'

Liana wasn't sure which boy had spoken. She thought by now she'd learned who was who. Now, in the shimmering fire-light, she couldn't tell them apart.

"Eelan will go first."

The chanting started again, louder this time. Liana pretended to join in. The fear of not knowing how long it would last and getting caught out a second time got the better of her. As the chants filled the air, Orratan was talking to Eelan, though their words were drowned out by everyone else. Without prompt from anyone or anything, the chanting stopped in perfect synchronicity.

Eraidor feigned a yawn. *'All this noise is so tiring.'*

'Do Architects get tired? Do you even sleep?' Liana asked.

'Not in a sense you would comprehend.'

Eelan knelt down in the gap between the stones. He closed his eyes and mouthed words to himself. He could have been speaking, but Liana was too far away to tell for sure. Everyone else started singing. The melody was deep, almost to the point of vibrating the statues around them. It was calming and peaceful. Liana didn't understand a word, as it was not in the common tongue.

'What are they singing?'

'It is an ode. To me. I do not like it.'

'I think it sounds rather nice.'

'Not the tune. There is nothing wrong with that if you enjoy that sort of thing. It is the words. They are praying to me to watch over the boy, to make him grow strong and wise. To bestow on him the gift truly meant for him.'

'And what's wrong with that?'

'What is right with it? I have no hand in their rituals. Never have done. They designed this whole spectacle on their own.'

'I'm beginning to wonder if there is any point to you at all.' Liana kept her attention on Eelan, pretending she couldn't see Eraidor out of the corner of her eye.

'Point to me? Show a little respect if you please.'

'Respect? What for? You won't help them. You belittle their rituals, their beliefs—all for you, I might add. You refuse to help me, to help yourself, and you want respect? Ha!'

'Your words hurt me.'

'Good. Do something about it then. Earn your respect, and if you can't, at least show them some respect.'

Eraidor didn't say anything more. The singing was growing to a crescendo. As much as Liana was unfamiliar with their cadence of chanting, she did know music and the way melodies were constructed. She surmised it was nearly time for Eelan to make his choice. She was right.

Eelan leaned forward with his right arm outstretched. He reached into the fire and screamed. Liana looked at his parents for their reaction. No parent would enjoy seeing their child in pain, but the only expression on their faces was one of pride. Eelan pulled his arm from the fire, a stone orb held tightly in his hand. He turned his wrist so his palm faced upwards, the orb resting between his fingers. Eelan offered it to Orratan, who picked it up and revealed the symbol. "Healing."

The chanting resumed for a third time and Liana found herself joining in, confident she was learning its rhythm. *'What sense is healing again?'* she asked Eraidor. It was a peculiar notion to be chanting with her mouth and talking with her mind at the same time. It wasn't quite the same as daydreaming, but it was close.

'He will lose his ability to smell.'

'Ah, that's it. Doesn't seem too bad of an exchange, if I'm honest. Out of all of the choices, smell seems to be the best one to lose. Especially as you can help others when they are ill.'

'The ability to smell is as important as the other senses. Food will never taste the same, for example. So much flavour is found in the nose. Also, for a reason I have never understood, it makes them more prone to becoming ill themselves. Minor ailments, mostly. And while they can heal others, they cannot heal themselves, nor be healed by others with the healing hand. They will spend the rest of their lives being more cautious.'

'I'm beginning to think I believe you.'

'Oh? About what?' he asked.

'About this ritual. No Architect would be so cruel, surely?'

'They have learned to find a balance when using the Origem. To take it all leads to the Torn. To ignore it is to turn their back on the nature of the world. I may not like it, however, I created them with their own free will. I do wish they would not attribute it all to me.'

'I could tell them it isn't you.'

'No! Absolutely not!' Eraidor almost combusted. Ember definitely noticed—she looked right at him.

'Fine. I won't. There's no need to shout.'

'Their beliefs are the result of hundreds of years of dogma and experience. Tell them the truth and it will only serve to destroy them. I have seen it happen before and I do not want to witness it again. Promise me, no matter what you see, you will not interfere.'

Liana held her hands up, which got the attention of a few people close to her. She dropped them again. *'No interfering. I won't say a word.'*

'No matter what.'

'No matter what,' she repeated.

The chanting stopped. Liana managed to close her mouth at almost the same time as the others. Eelan had rejoined his parents, hugging them both and showing them his fresh burn mark on his palm. It was Haal's turn. He seemed a little less nervous having watched his brother, and stepped forward with a newfound confidence.

Haal took his kneeling position, and the singing began again. At the right moment, he placed his hand into the fire. It was his turn to scream in pain, though barely for a moment. Hand still in the fire, he fell silent. He pulled his hand halfway out and then back in again. Liana looked at Orratan, and then at Haal's parents. Although they didn't look worried, their faces suggested something was off.

Eyes closed, Haal removed his hand all the way, an orb in his grasp. As had his brother done before him, he offered the orb to Orratan, who took it and showed it to everyone. "Death." Haal didn't even flinch.

When Liana heard the word she couldn't stop a yelp escape her mouth. Her fears had come true. She looked around at everyone else. None appeared shocked or sad. Rather the opposite. There wasn't any elation or enthusiasm like they'd shown towards Eelan, though there were many nods of acceptance.

'This is their way,' said Eraidor with a curl of his lip.

'It's wrong, just wrong.' Liana felt her eyes getting hot.

Haal examined his hand, holding it with the other as he walked back to his family.

The chanting resumed. This time Liana didn't join in. Every fibre of her body wanted to scream out at the injustice she perceived. She knew she couldn't. She knew it wasn't Eraidor's will that he had been chosen to die. *Was it really so important they believed it?*

'*You must not interfere, Liana. I know you want to. You will only cause them harm if you do.*'

Liana had never fought so hard against her urges in her whole life. She tried to think of anything she could do or say that wouldn't break their tradition. Their beliefs. In the end, she found nothing. She forced away the tears, controlled her breathing, and let the chanting finish without her participation.

The fire subsided into nothing as the air fell silent. It was over. The circle of witnesses broke, with every man, woman and child present taking their turn to offer their blessings to the twins. Liana hung back and watched on. Ember stood loyally by her side, leaning into Liana's leg as if to console her. Orratan, once he'd spoken to the twins, noticed Liana and came to speak with her.

"I know you are sad. I can see it in your eyes. I don't truly expect you to understand our ways. Please know that this is a great honour for Haal, I promise."

'How long does he have? Part of me expected him to die right after you declared his orb.'

"He has until moonrise. Aelene will call for him then."

Liana nodded, though she was unsure whether it was a good or bad thing his death was still a while away. How does anyone reconcile knowing when their life will end beforehand? In the few instances where she'd contemplated her own mortality, she'd decided she would rather die in her sleep, preferably as a very old woman. Waking up dead, her mother called it.

'He must be scared, though?' Liana said.

"Must he? Why do you believe that?"

'I would be, I think.'

Orratan smiled. "Ah, I see. Your empathy is admirable,

though misplaced. As all who have gone to meet Aelene, he will do so gladly."

'What do you—the Dawanii—believe is in the next life?'

"We don't know. I'm not certain anyone living does. All we know for sure is Aelene will look after you when this life ends. We will know what is next only when it is our own turn."

'Is he right?' she asked Eraidor.

'Ah, now that would be telling, would it not? The truth is, death has many meanings to many different people. Ultimately, death is the greatest mystery of life. Even to Aelene.'

The sound of music filled the air. Liana followed the sound to the far side of the amphitheatre. Two women and two men played wooden instruments that looked very similar to the flutes they had in Moranza—except Moranzan flutes were made of metal. The tempo of the music was upbeat, celebratory. Some of the children present danced along, innocent and playful as oft children are.

"You should offer your good wishes to the twins yourself. I'm sure they would appreciate it."

Liana hesitated at first. She didn't know what to say to either of them, but especially to Haal. There were still a number of people gathered around the pair. Liana hung at the back, not eager to speak. She allowed everyone else to say their piece first. Eventually, she was the only one left. By then, a feast had been brought out and people were mingling amongst themselves.

'Liana, there you are!' said Eelan, taking her by the hand. 'Did you enjoy the ceremony?'

Such a simple question, but already she struggled with what to say. 'It was very nice,' was all she could manage.

'I think I will miss you,' said Haal. 'You are a very interesting woman.'

'Are you truly not sad?'

Haal bent down and gave Ember a scratch behind the ears. Something Liana had learned the cinderfox liked a lot. 'No, I don't think so. I will miss my brother, and my family. Eraidor has decided I am ready to go with Aelene on my next journey, and that can only be good.'

Liana looked at Eraidor, but said nothing to him.

'I will miss you, too,' said Eelan to his brother. 'It will be strange not to see you every day. Still, I have a new important calling in life.'

To Liana, the change in their lives was massive. To the twins, and everyone else, it seemed so... trivial. No different from losing an old toy. A toy you loved and treasured all through your childhood, only to lose it one day and simply move on with life. She wished the boy had chosen a different stone. Which reminded her. 'I saw you hesitate, choosing your orb.'

'Yes,' said Haal. 'I touched the first one, and it felt cold, as though it wasn't for me. Something told me I should choose another, so that's what I did.'

'So, if you had stuck with your first choice, you wouldn't die today?' said Liana.

'This orb or that orb. It does not matter. He chose the one he did. Do not sow doubt in his mind.'

'You're right, but Eraidor made the right choice for me,' replied Haal. 'He is with you, so you know it to be true.'

Liana smiled weakly before pulling the boy into a hug, fighting hard to keep the tears away. *'I know you didn't choose this for him,'* she said to Eraidor. *'How can I let him die when I know it's all a lie?'*

'You must. I do not like it any more than you do. Pull yourself together. Be happy for him, or at the very least, let them believe you are.'

She let go of Haal, took a step back, and forced her smile wider. 'I'm glad to have met you. I will remember you always.'

'I am glad to have known you too, Liana.'

With a nod from both of them, the twins left her alone and

went off in the search of food. Liana wasn't feeling hungry. All told, she'd rather go back to her room and cry for them. She'd never known pain like it, not even when her father died. That was different, though. It was the way of life. You are *meant* to grow old and die. Even if a sickness takes someone early, as it had done her father, it's still natural. To knowingly—willingly—give up your existence so young. It tore away at her.

'*How will it happen?*'

'*Aelene will come and take him away,*' Eraidor replied.

'*That doesn't really explain it to me.*'

'*Aelene will come for him. His body will fall still and his spirit will go on to the next life. His family will then burn his body and return it to the Origem.*'

By the time moonrise came, most of the guests had left. The only ones remaining were the twins and their family, Orratan and his assistant, Uehan and his mother, the musicians, and another six Liana didn't recognise. The twins were dancing to a cheerful tune. They held each other's hands and spun in a circle, skipping to the beat of the tune. It was then when Haal fell to the ground, almost pulling Eelan down with him. The music stopped briefly before resuming with a slower melody. It wasn't a melancholic tune, nor was it a happy one. The twins' parents knelt down beside their fallen son with Eelan next to them. Everyone else gathered around in a loose circle, ready to observe his passing. Liana stood with Ember next to Orratan.

While Haal's family were saying their final goodbyes, the room turned dark. There was a light coming from somewhere, but Liana couldn't see its source. Before her eyes, everyone faded into the darkness except for Haal, herself, Ember and Eraidor. '*What's happening?*' she asked.

'*How interesting. It seems you shall bear witness.*'

'*I don't understand.*'

A figure emerged from the darkness. A tall woman wearing a white fur cloak with a large hood stood—almost as though

329

she were floating—where Uehan had been standing. Her attention was on Haal at first, but then she noticed Liana and looked surprised. *'Oh, this is most irregular, most irregular indeed. You should not be here. It is not your time yet. No, no, no. Not your time.'*

Liana stared at the woman, her mouth trying to move, but no words came. She had a light olive complexion, high cheek bones and pale yellow-white eyes looking out of very thin eyeglasses that had an even thinner silver frame. Liana had never seen someone so beautiful.

'Liana, this is Aelene,' said Eraidor.

'Oh, look who it is,' said Aelene, overacting a pretence she hadn't seen him. *'We have all been wondering where you got to. How long has it been now?'*

'Too long.'

'Too long indeed. Have yourself a good little predicament right there, eh? Hiding out in this dear little thing.' She pointed a slender finger in a circular motion at Liana.

'I am not hiding. It is a curse.'

'Yes, I can see why it would be,' she said, tilting her head forward, looking over the top of her eyewear.

'What's that supposed to mean?' Liana whispered to Eraidor

'Ignore her. It is me she is trying to insult. Not you,' he replied.

'You should consider yourself lucky, young lady. Very rare, very rare indeed for someone to regard me when it is not their time. Quite the honour, you might think? I could make an exception and look after you both. You and the boy. No? Well, I do get bored sometimes. Take someone early, let another stay beyond their... expiration, shall we say?'

'Did you make him choose the Orb of Death?' asked Liana.

'She speaks! No dear, I am far too busy to involve myself in their little games. I merely clean up the mess. Respectfully, of course.'

'Of course,' echoed Liana, one eyebrow raised.

There was a sound of a deep exhale from the ground. Liana looked down to see Haal sitting up. *'Is it time?'* he asked, looking up at Aelene, then Eraidor, and then to Liana. He frowned. *'Did you die too?'*

'Not unless she wishes to,' quipped Aelene with a mischievous giggle.

'No,' said Liana. *'I'm only here to say goodbye.'*

'Oh.' Haal pulled himself to his feet. *'Well, goodbye then.'* He smiled and took Aelene's hand in his. He looked at Eraidor. *'Thank you for my life. Please look after my brother for me.'*

Eraidor bowed his head at the boy.

'I will see you again, Liana, my dear. In the meantime, I shall look after this one. Stay safe.'

Liana felt hot tears burn on her cheeks as she watched Aelene turn and lead Haal away into the darkness. *'Goodbye, my friend.'*

As they faded away, the world around Liana returned from the darkness. Eelan and his parents were still crouched around Haal's lifeless body. She didn't know why, but it surprised her to see him lying there, his face now pale, yet peaceful.

'She's not how I imagined,' she said to Eraidor.

'Of course not. That was how Haal saw her. She was there for him, not you.'

Uehan broke the silence, clearly panicked. He was pulling at his hair behind his ears, his expression fearful.

"What is it?" said Orratan.

'Danger. I see danger.' He stepped up to Liana and looked into her eyes. 'Your people are coming here. Danger. No, no, no. They mustn't. We are not prepared. They are coming!'

24

ALONE

Addan lost the feeling in his fingers a long time ago as he did his best to dig a grave for his friend. The only tool he had was a tree branch. He'd gone through several of them, all eventually breaking as he tried to carve out a final resting place for the only friend he'd had left out here in the frozen wastelands of Dawan.

Milo looked so small now, devoid of life. Devoid of that smile of his, of everything that made him who he was. The boy truly believed being here in this strange land, surrounded by the death and brutality of it all, was a better life. How bad had life got for him back in Moranza, before all this? Addan would never know.

In truth, he barely knew him. It had only been a few turns of the moon, yet there was more life, more hope, in that young man's eyes than in others three times his age. And now it was gone. For what? Nothing. As far as he was concerned, there was no hope left. Little to live for, except Liana. She was the only reason he kept going.

The hole he had dug was barely a foot deep when he concluded he could dig no deeper. A pitiful attempt, all things considered. It would have to do, and he hoped the ground was cold enough to keep the smell of death away from any foraging animals that might undo all his work.

Milo's body had already begun to stiffen when Addan carefully placed him in the shallow grave. He had little option but to use his feet to scrape the dirt, ice, and snow over his friend. To bury him. It felt disrespectful in a way, like kicking sand at a desert vole, or something like that. Not his face, though. Addan couldn't bring himself to do that. He knelt down in the wet mess of icy dirt and used his hands for that part.

He had no coins to place on Milo's eyes, as would ordinarily be required. He hoped the Architects wouldn't punish the boy for that, given the circumstances. Would the Architects even accept him into the next life now? The boy *had* killed, hadn't he? Addan wasn't in the habit of praying to them. He'd found it didn't make much of a difference in his life if he did or did not. Here and now, somehow he thought it right he should say something.

'It wasn't his fault,' Addan said, still kneeling. He looked into the sky, to the tiny twinkling lights. Some of the old stories claimed these lights were the Architects themselves. Maybe they were, maybe they weren't. Still, he picked one apart from all the others, one with a blue-green hue that looked brighter than the others. He spoke to it.

'He was only a boy, and he was kind, and brave. He suffered enough in this life, so please look after him. I have no coins to offer as payment for his passage, but please accept his soul into the next life, whatever that may be.'

There came no reply. The only sound was the persistent whistle of the wind as it turned the air around him. It was getting colder now he had stopped moving, the burial complete. He could lie down right here, next to the grave, go to sleep. Sleep would come so easily if he allowed it. He was so tired and alone.

He rolled on to his back and stared silently at his little blue-green light as it flickered above him. The sky was so dark here without the moon. It felt like he was floating in a sea of nothingness. He could no longer feel his toes, his hands already numb. *I think I should rest now. I've done all I can. Forgive me, Liana. I tried, I really tried.*

As his eyelids grew heavier, he caught a glimpse of something in the sky. A thin streak of bright white light moved fast in a diagonal line above him. It lasted no more than two heartbeats before it fizzled into nothing. *What was that?* It was a curious sight, and it made him sit up and take notice. Where did it go? Did one of those lights fall from the sky?

There goes another! As bright as the first, a bright line tracing itself high up in the air before, again, vanishing into nothing. If they were truly the Architects like the stories said, was this some sort of sign? Were they trying to tell him something? There was no way to know. It was enough, though. Enough to push him on. He would not give up. He would not lay down and die. He would not forsake Liana.

Addan dragged himself to his feet and fought to stay upright. There were no more lines of light in the sky, only the thousands of dots there had always been.

'Goodbye, my friend. Be at peace now,' he said to the small and unremarkable grave. Then he turned away and moved one foot in front of the other to continue his search for Liana.

With each small, laboured step, he gradually regained some of the feeling in his extremities. He could feel the snow beneath his heels, which was enough for now. He considered if he'd ever feel his toes again. He decided he could manage without his toes. What he needed was light. The map he carried, now stiff and frozen itself, was next to useless without the moon or some other light to read it by. If it wasn't for the snow underfoot, he doubted he'd be able to see anything at all.

He was lost.

He had passed what he thought was the last line of trees a long time ago, and now there was truly nothing around him. He couldn't stop, not for a moment. If he stopped walking, he feared he might not be able to start again. It had already taken everything he had left within him to leave Milo behind. He no longer felt the cold. He'd gone well beyond that point, and couldn't tell if he was shivering anymore either. Hunger had also come and gone. There were still rations in the satchel he carried, but they had frozen and were no longer edible. He had to keep moving, even if it killed him. If he were a gambling man —which, in all honesty, he was—he'd get good odds for never seeing moonrise again.

His body grew weaker, yet his mind was alive with thought. With nothing else around him, the voices inside his head were the only company he had left.

'You should give up,' came the words in his mind. Over and over. 'Give up. There's nothing for you here. There's no use in suffering like this.'

'I won't,' he said.

'Just lay down, go to sleep. It will all be over. No one would blame you. You tried, you really did. It's time to rest now.' The voice sounded like his own, though muted, flat. It tormented him, yet soothed as he fought against it.

'I will *not* give up,' he shouted through gritted teeth.

'She wouldn't think less of you if you stopped now. Liana would forgive you, you know she would. It's over. It's time to stop. Rest. Sleep. *Die!*'

'I've seen Aelene take so many. I will *not* give her the satisfaction of taking me too. Not yet. I have to save her.'

A vague shape of a figure stood in front of him, his vision blurred by the frozen winds. Was it real? Or was it only in his mind? The figure spoke with the same voice. 'So many of those around you, those who knew you, have died now, haven't they? All those lives you touch, they all die, don't they?'

335

'Not my fault,' Addan whispered. 'I tried...'

'Yes, of course. You tried. Always the one of good intention, aren't you, brother?' The voice changed a little, deeper, yet still familiar. The shape standing before Addan coalesced into the figure of a man he instantly recognised.

'Renni. Is that you? It can't be you. You—'

'Died? Yes, brother. I died. A terrible death. You weren't there that day, and you should have been. Where were you, Addan? Where were you when I needed you?'

'I'm sorry. It wasn't my fault. How could it have been my fault? I wasn't to know.'

'You should have been by my side. If you were then you would have been there to save me. You left me to die, Addan. You left me to die. I was scared, Addan. You abandoned me.'

Addan reached out to his brother and stumbled to his knees. Tears rolled down his cheeks before freezing against his skin. 'I'm sorry, Renni. I wish it could have been different. I wish I had died that day and not you. You didn't deserve to die.'

'None of us did.' The voice sounded different. Pitched higher, layered, as if two spoke at once. 'You left us to die and Aelene came for us.'

Addan squinted at his brother, but it was no longer him he saw. The vision of his brother melted away, morphed into that of another. A girl. *The* girl. He reached out to her, one hand to the ground, and wept.

'Why did you let me die? I was so scared,' said the girl. Even now, her face was bloodied and a large splinter of wood protruded from her abdomen. Her eyes were narrowed, accusing.

'I tried to save you. There was nothing I could do, it was too late.'

'*Why* did I have to die? I'm only a child. Why did you come? Why did you kill me? Kill us all?'

'I didn't kill you. I didn't kill any of you. It wasn't meant to be like this. None of this was meant to happen!'

'Yet it did. And you let me die alone.'

'You were not alone. I was there, at the end. I'm sorry. I really am sorry!' His weeping had erupted into full sobbing. He threw his hands in the air and screamed. A raw, guttural scream that tore through the wind and into the void. 'Why must I be tormented like this?' he shouted at the sky. The tiny speck of blue-green light was still there above him. He screamed at it. 'I'm sorry! What must I do?' His shouts reduced to a whimper, his shoulders moved up and down with every breath. He felt broken, helpless.

'That's it. Ya can rest now. It's over. Sleep. Aelene will come for ya. It's what ya deserve.' The voice had changed again, and the girl faded into the darkness, replaced by the young boy he'd buried. He looked happy. Clean. Alive.

'I don't want to sleep,' said Addan as he rubbed away at his damp eyes. 'I have to keep going. She needs me.'

'I needed ya,' said Milo. 'Ya were my friend, an' then the monsters came.'

'I couldn't protect you from those *things*.'

'I know.' Milo smiled. The same grin he always had. He spoke softly. 'It's time to rest now. Ya look hungry. Here, would ya like an apple?' He produced a perfect red apple from his pocket and offered it forward.

Addan's mind was slowing, as if his head was being held under water. Milo moved in and out of focus as Addan reached out for the fruit. He was hungry now, so, so hungry. As he touched the apple, it turned from red to brown, to black before disintegrating into dust that carried away on the wind.

He gasped as the boy's skin changed colour. Thin purple lines traced from his fingers along his arms and across his face. The smile vanished, his lips drooped. Addan recoiled as Milo's body contorted and twisted in impossible ways. 'No!' cried Addan.

'It's too late,' said Milo, as his jaw distended. 'The monsters came for us an' this is what I have become, an' ya're to blame. Ya were my friend, an' they came. They took me. Made me one of them. All who know ya die, Addan. All who know ya. It's time to stop now...'

Milo's voice trailed away into nothing and the image of him disappeared with it leaving Addan alone once more. He leaned forward and pressed his head into the snow. He pounded at the ground with both fists until they bled. He tried to scream, but no sound came.

'I will not die,' he said, barely audible to himself. He pushed up from the snow. It wasn't as dark now. On the horizon ahead of him was a lighter area that separated the sky from the ground. The moon was rising and a new day was coming. Somehow, from somewhere deep within him, he clawed at the last vestiges of strength he had left.

'Why must I suffer so? I am a good man. I will not stop. I will not quit. I will not,' he growled as he forced himself back on to his feet once more. 'I will keep going until my final breath. I am coming, Liana. I will *not* die today.'

25

ABOVE EVERYTHING

U ehan was almost hysterical. He kept screaming, 'they're coming. We're not ready! No, no!' over and over until he fell, exhausted, to the floor. Even then, he still clasped his ears and hair, rocking back and forth, repeating himself.

"A foreseer's first true vision can be somewhat overwhelming," said Orratan, seemingly unsure of what to do with himself. Haal's lifeless body still lay not two paces away from where Uehan sat. Eelan had knelt down beside his friend, trying to comfort him, still him. It wasn't working.

'He said we are in danger,' said Tima. 'What does that mean? Who's coming?' She had moved away from Haal just before Uehan collapsed from fear he might have landed on her. Derrum held her close, silent. Stoic. Everyone looked at Liana.

'Don't look at me like that. I don't know any more than you do,' she said. *'Do you know what he means?'*

'In the literal sense, he has seen your brethren arriving here in the city, and their presence will be a threat to these people,' said Eraidor.

'Why would they come here? My people aren't a threat to anyone.' She walked over to Uehan and bent down opposite

Eelan. 'Tell me what you see.' She held his hand and squeezed gently.

'They're coming.' There was pain in his voice.

Liana looked at Eelan. 'Is there anything you can do to help him now you are a healer?'

Eelan shook his head. 'It is not a pain I can heal. I have seen this before, and it should pass quickly.'

'They're coming. We will all die. They come to kill.' Uehan snapped his head up to look Liana right in the eyes, and then scrambled backwards out of reach. 'They come in your name!'

Orratan looked at Liana, scrutinising her. "What do you know of this? Speak the truth and I shall know."

'I'm sorry, I really don't know what he means. My people have no reason to quarrel with Dawan.'

"If what he sees is true, there must be a reason for it."

'You can tell if someone is telling the truth or not. So, is he?'

Orratan turned to Uehan, who was still on the floor, rocking, mumbling. "It is difficult to tell, when one is talking about the future. What is yet to come does not always prove to be true. However, I feel *he* believes it to be the truth."

Liana watched Uehan. It was almost like he'd reverted to how he was before. 'Are you sure he's not... broken? If something went wrong for a second time...'

"He is still adjusting, yes. The gift is not something that suddenly just is. The body, and especially the mind, needs to rebalance. Now think, Liana. Why would they come? Why would they seek to harm us?" Even though the voice was not his own, his companion was remarkably good at tone. The notes of concern were evident.

'Maybe they are looking for me. He said they come in my name. That must be it. I have been gone for too long now, and I didn't tell anyone where I was going when I left, except for my friend who came with me.' Addan—it was the first time in a while since she'd thought about him. *Did he seek out my mother? Tell her I was here?*

Orratan pressed a finger to his lips, holding his elbow with his free hand. "Plausible. Though I fail to see how that would account for the apparent threat they pose."

'Addan escaped the fighting. I told him to run. If they thought I was in danger here, they might believe they have come to rescue me.' She sat on the edge of the monument, thinking through any and all reasons why the Dawanii should feel threatened. There was the attack by the gabbalins, which she still didn't understand how, or why it happened. Nor did she know why the gabbalins were so interested in the stone she had stolen.

"There's more. A piece of the puzzle is still missing. Why did you travel to Dawan to begin with?"

'We were following a woman. We stole the stone, and she stole it from us and came here.'

"Keep going. I can feel you nearly have the answer. What is it? Why did you choose that day?"

It felt like Orratan was reaching into her mind, pulling the facts out of her, piece by piece. 'My mother, the queen, wanted me to attend a formal event. A delegation from here were invited to discuss opening a dialogue between our peoples after we built the bridge over the Divide.'

Orratan looked confused. "An invitation? We received no such invitation. You are the first from the Old Place to visit this city in our lifetimes. We also sent no delegation. Yet—I see no falsehood in your words."

'This is rather curious,' said Eraidor. He had been slowly mingling, listening, unnoticed by everyone except Liana.

'Do you know something I don't?'

'No, not exactly. I do have a feeling something else is at play here.'

'Like what?'

341

'*I cannot say.*'

'*Cannot, or will not. Another of your silly no interference rules?*'

'*You wound me, Liana. I cannot say because I do not know. Find a way to separate yourself from the others and we shall find out together.*'

'I don't know then,' Liana said. 'I think the time has come for me to go home. If I am the cause, or will be the cause, whatever, then I should go. I truly wish you all no harm, and I cannot place you in danger.'

"Very well. Though I fear it will not be so simple a solution."

'I'm not sure I have any other choice.' She stood up and pulled her fur coat down straight. 'May I be excused? I need a few moments to myself.'

Orratan narrowed his eyes, but agreed.

Outside the amphitheatre, Liana stopped, looked around, and sighed. Her adventure was ending. It was time to go home, but why? Uehan foresaw a threat from Moranza that involved her somehow. "They come to kill," he had said. *Why? What has my mother done?* Liana turned to Eraidor, the godly man forever at her side, wanted or not.

'I need to know what's happening. If it's about me—for me —then I need to know so I can help stop it.' She was alone, so felt she could speak out loud. The constant internalising of speech exhausted her.

'*You once asked me if I perform miracles. While this is not a miracle in what you would consider the true meaning of the word, I can do something. Now, I need you to close your eyes and focus.*'

'Focus on what?'

'*Up.*'

'Up?'

'*Close your eyes and imagine yourself in the sky looking down on yourself.*'

Liana frowned. 'I'm not sure where you're going with this.'

'*Trust me. Now, close your eyes and concentrate.*'

She took a deep breath and exhaled slowly through her nose. *I may as well humour him.* She closed her eyes and tried to picture herself above the trees, looking at herself standing in the snow, feeling like a fool. Nothing happened. At least she couldn't see Eraidor, but she could still feel his eyes boring into her. She screwed her eyes tighter, trying to force whatever was meant to manifest. Still nothing. She exhaled and opened her eyes. 'It's not wor—'

'*It is a* little *higher than I had anticipated, but we can fix that.*'

Liana was stunned to find the ground beneath her feet missing. Not only was it missing, so was everything else. She found herself floating in the darkness of the stars with nothing around her except for Eraidor.

'*Turn around, look.*' Eraidor pointed over her shoulder.

With nothing beneath her feet, it felt odd at first trying to reorientate herself with no ground to purchase below her. She swung her arms in an attempt to spin herself around as though she were swimming. It worked a little. After a few more swings, much to Eraidor's amusement, she had turned enough to see a massive red ball of fire. It was the largest thing she'd ever seen, and it was so beautiful, mesmerising and terrifying all at once. 'What is *that?*'

'*You are looking at Father, the sun.*'

'Haha, no, that's not possible. Father is nowhere near that big.'

'*Turn around a little more, see what else is here.*'

Liana twisted herself further and saw another sphere. Not as huge as the red fireball, but still large enough. She recognised it. 'That looks exactly like Mother.'

'*It is Mother. Now look there.*' He pointed to the left of the moon.

Against the backdrop of the sun, the moon was moving slowly from left to right from her perspective. Something was emerging from behind it. Another sphere gradually came into view. Half of it was completely dark, the other half glowed hot in the face of Father.

'That is our home. We call it a planet. You call it Rybban.'

'Impossible!'

'Not impossible at all. Well, for almost everyone, yes perhaps you are right, but for you? You get to witness the marvel of our creation.'

'So I can fly now?' Her tone was flippant.

'Ha, no. In reality, we are still standing exactly where you were. What you are seeing is all in your mind. Not to say that it is imaginary. This is all quite real. We created all of this. Father is a star, like all the others you see in the dark skies. Your home, the planet circles the sun and Mother circles the planet. Understand?'

'I... think... so.'

'Allow me to speed this up for you a little.' He waved his arm slowly from right to left. All three spheres moved rapidly away until they were much smaller. Father was at the centre, glowing brightly still, with marbled patterns rippling across its surface. Rybban moved around the sun in a perfect circle, with Mother circling the planet. It was like a well-choreographed dance in the night sky.

'Mother turns differently to Rybban,' she stated, pointing to the moon, making small circles with her finger.

'Indeed she does. In the early days of existence, Rybban turned just the same as Mother, but during one of our own wars—there were many of those in the beginning—there was an accident, and the planet... for want of a better word, broke.'

'Oh?'

'Yes, so one side is always facing the sun, and the other is forever in darkness. In between, there is a small, narrow ribbon between light and dark, where conditions are just right enough for life. That is how we named it, though it has been corrupted since then, courtesy of some of your historical texts to read as R-y-b-b-a-n. It sounds the same, so I suppose it matters little.'

'It seems like an awful waste of space if we can only live in a little bit of it.'

'True. We did discuss it. Whether we should try and get the old girl spinning again. After a few hundred years of arguing, we deemed it unsafe to do so.'

'Why would it be unsafe?'

'On account of everything and everyone on it being flung off.'

'Ah, that wouldn't be good.'

'Precisely. Anyway, enough of the history lesson. We must return to the purpose of this little jaunt.' Eraidor snapped his fingers, and they fell towards Rybban. Its size grew until it replaced the darkness with a perfect view of the "ribbon of life."

All the moving out and in around the planet made Liana feel a little sick to the stomach. As they settled at a spot closer to the surface, the view became more familiar to her. In between the light and dark sides, she saw what looked like the most detailed and colourful map of her home she had ever seen. It looked almost identical to the maps she would find in the books her mother liked to keep and study.

She was still too high up to make out any people, but she could see the mountains with their clouds swirling around their peaks, and a dark smudge where her home city should be. What the maps didn't show her were the lands and islands both to the north and south of Moranza.

'There is more to Rybban than just Moranza and Dawan,' Eraidor said when she questioned them. *'The ribbon encircles the whole planet. The world you know and in which you live is only a small part of it.'*

They fell closer still. Now it really *did* feel like she was flying. The darkness of the empty space between the three spheres was gone and there was only the land and sky above. A thin edge of Father still shone on the horizon, slowly disappearing the lower they went. In mere moments they flew over her city, heading west towards Dawan. From her vantage point, the city looked smaller than she had imagined. The Divide, however, looked much larger, like a giant had taken a knife and cut right through the earth. A gaping wound in the world.

'I need you to focus again, Liana. Who would be in Dawan? Where would they be? Find them.'

'I don't know. My mother? My brother maybe?'

'Try to find them.'

Down they went, lower until they were barely above the treetops. Everything was moving so fast now, it was dizzying. 'Why is there no wind?'

'Remember, you are not really here.'

Everything slowed down. Ahead, was a group of people. Hundreds of them. Some of them were wearing the queen's colours. 'There,' she said, pointing at them. She and Eraidor circled around the swarm of people before landing a short distance in front of them. They weren't marching, but they were moving with purpose. As the army grew closer, Liana thought she recognised one of the men on a stryde near the back of the group. She squinted to counter the moonlight reflecting on the snow, focusing on his features. There was another man, farther in front on another stryde. She *knew* him. It was Shaan, riding tall and stern, leading the throng of people forward. She looked back at the first rider. Yes, yes, it was her brother. Her heart lifted. 'It's Cal, my brother.' She hopped up and down, waving at them with both arms, trying to get his attention. Nobody saw her.

'Your brother had come searching for you,' said Eraidor.

'It looks like it. I'm unsure why he needs so many men to help. It looks like an army of soldiers, but we've never had an army. There hasn't been a need for one for centuries.'

The first line of the approaching army was almost upon their position. *'They look miserable,'* remarked Eraidor.

'They look cold and tired.'

'*Indeed. They have come a long way. All for you it—*' Eraidor was looking at Shaan.

'What is it?' asked Liana.

'*Impossible! I know that man. How is he here?*'

'Who, Shaan? He's my brother's advisor. Friend, well I mean, advisor friend. I've never liked him that much. He had a thing for me, once. Then he became involved with Cal. After tha—'

Eraidor interrupted her, his face filled with horror. '*I see the danger now. Oh dear, young Uehan was right.*'

At that moment, Shaan turned his head and looked in their direction. Liana thought he could actually see her, the way he stared. Then she realised it wasn't her he was looking at—it was Eraidor. He raised a hand in a wave, smiled and said, 'hello, dear brother.'

Immediately, Liana found herself whipped away from the army and was once again flying above the trees. 'Hey, stop!' Take me back to Cal at once!'

'*We must return to ourselves immediately.*'

Liana felt the urge to fight back. She wasn't done. There was something else she needed to see. She willed Eraidor to stop. And they did.

Eraidor was surprised by the sudden inertia. '*How did you do that? You should not be able to push against me in that way.*'

'You don't control me. I won't allow it.' *Is this the key to getting him out of me? To fight back against him?* She looked up, away. Something—someone—was calling to her. It was faint. 'We are not done here yet.' She took a deep breath and closed her eyes. *What is it? What else do I need to see?*

When she reopened her eyes, they were moving again. Faster. The trees fell away until there was only a barren snowscape below. Then, a speck in the distance. *There.* She concentrated hard, ignoring Eraidor's protests. The speck grew into a figure, the figure of a man staggering in the snow. He was alone, defeated. Broken.

Liana knew who it was even before she saw his face. It was Addan. She called out to him as she stopped beside him. He didn't hear her. 'What happened to you?' she whispered as she watched him push himself forward. 'Are you looking for me? I'm here, Addan. I'm right here with you.' She reached out for his hand, but it simply passed through her own like it wasn't there.

'*You cannot do anything for him,*' said Eraidor. His voice was quiet, but there was a hint of annoyance within it.

'I can't leave him here like this.'

'*I say it again, Liana. You are not really here.*'

'Yes I am. I can see him, see his pain.' She turned to her friend. 'Addan, I will find you, I promise. Be strong for me. I'm coming.'

Addan stopped and his head jerked upwards a little. 'Liana?'

She gasped. 'Addan, I'm here! Can you hear me? Addan!'

His head dropped again, and he trudged onwards, one small step at a time.

The world spun around her so fast it blurred into a wash of grey and black. In an instant, she was back where she started in her own body. Her head was spinning and she almost lost balance. She managed to keep herself upright with the help of the wall beside her. 'Take me back!' she demanded.

'*No. It will not do you any good. There is nothing you can do for him.*'

'I have to help him. I'll go the long way round. On foot. I can't leave him out there alone.'

'*You have forgotten about your brother's army.*'

'Oh, I've not forgotten,' Liana said, fists clenched. She could feel her blood pumping through her body so fast.

'*What do you propose to do about it?*' It was a valid question.

'Me? I'll...' she trailed off as her thoughts caught up with her. Her fingers relaxed a little. Addan and the army were so far apart. If she went to Addan, the army would surely reach Trennale before she could return. If she went to Cal first, then Addan would likely die from the cold. Then she remembered Shaan. He *looked* right at Eraidor. He could see him. What did he say? "Dear brother." She glared at Eraidor. 'How could Shaan see you, and why did he call you his brother?'

Eraidor lowered his head and turned away. *'The man you know as Shaan is not a man. His true name is Sarratenian.'*

Liana recognised the name, and it took her a few seconds to remember where she knew it from. 'Wait. You mean he's named after the Architect of Ruination? I don't understand.'

'What I am saying is, he is *the Architect of Ruination.'* He turned back to face Liana. *'It is time you knew the truth.'*

She felt a cold bead of sweat run down her spine. She folded her arms in front of her. 'I'm listening.'

'You were taught my entrapment in humans, such as yourself, was a punishment. That is not the whole story. I know you have heard of the old tales of the fights between Architects that ultimately led to the creation of what you call the Divide. The truth is, I was the one responsible for that. Myself and Sarratenian.

'We fought, like all siblings do—that is not a uniquely human thing. It is natural in any living creature. Human, gabbalin, dragon... god. However, such squabbles do not often end with such catastrophic consequences. It was not entirely my fault. Sarratenian loves nothing more than to cause chaos, to destroy anything good, anything beautiful. He particularly enjoys seeing mortal beings suffer. Not out of malice or hate. To him it is merely sport, in the same way a child would pull a leg from a spider. For only the sake of seeing what would happen.

'He does it because he knows it tortures me. I created you. I created all life, and I love you all. That part is true, and the torment is very real.'

'So he would start a war for no other reason than to make you angry?'

'Something like that. I fear I caused all this. At the end of our last fight, I banished him. I opened a tear in time itself—something I am not permitted to do in the laws that bind us and all of reality—and pushed him into the future. The Divide stands as a permanent scar of that day. I thought I had banished him for millennia, until long after all civilisation has came and went, and there was no living thing left for him to torment. Evidently, I did not send him far enough.'

'Then he seeks revenge.'

'Yes, though I fear there is more to it than that. Something else...'

'Like what?'

'I am uncertain. Yes, he means war as that is his nature, but that desire may hide another goal.'

As fantastical as his story was, it did make sense. In the realm of her having an actual god residing within her, anything was possible. *One more question.* 'Who punished you?'

'Amser, the Architect of Time. It is such a sensitive thing, time. Break it and it can destroy a star. You were—I was—lucky to only cause a small schism; the Divide. It could have been so much worse. So Amser imprisoned me inside the ones I loved the most. My gambit worked, though. Before the Divide, this world knew only war and destruction, famine. Desolation. Sarratenian's influence permeated everything.

'In his absence, there has been nothing but peace in this world. For all this time Sarratenian effectively ceased to exist, until now. Now, I fear what his return might mean for you all.'

Liana remained silent after he finished speaking. What was there to say? 'I still need to help Addan,' she said after a while.

'You need to remain here in Trennale. These people will need you to help defend them. Do you see, Liana? Fate has brought you here. Fate has brought us together. You must stop him. The lives of the many are worth more than the life of only one.'

And therein lay the problem. For her, it was an impossible

choice. How could she stop a god? *Stop a god?* 'Hang on. Why does it have to be me? Why don't *you* stop him? You are not the only Architect, right? I've read the religious texts. There's so many of you. Where are they?'

'The answer is threefold. I do not know where they are. They would not necessarily know Sarratenian has returned. And I am still imprisoned, therefore I am helpless.'

Liana growled to the point of screaming at the sky. 'I want you out! This is *not* my fight. It's yours. I didn't ask for any of this. What is the point of you? What is the point of a god who cannot be a god? I wish I had never saved you!' She stopped herself from saying more. She was panting, her heart racing. 'I can't do this,' she whispered. 'I need to find a way to rid myself of you. What if I find Amser and plead for your freedom?'

Eraidor shook his head. *'He is bound by the rules as much as I am. Only you can set me free. I would dearly love to tell you how. What I said before is true—to tell you is to kill us both.'*

For the first time in her life, she felt completely helpless and alone. 'I need to speak to Nalla.'

Nalla knew Liana was coming. Of course she did. Orratan had offered to accompany her, but she declined. 'How do I choose?' Liana asked. 'I need to save my friend, but how can I?' She'd told the old woman everything Eraidor had recounted. Nalla sat by her fire, expressionless throughout. She didn't give Liana any indication of surprise or foreknowledge. She only listened.

'Tell me, Liana. At what point did you decide you were alone in this?'

Liana raised an eyebrow. 'What do you mean?'

'I mean,' said Nalla, 'if Sarratenian is coming here to attack us, do you believe we would sit idly by and allow that to happen?'

'No, but I have seen their numbers. There's hundreds of them.'

'We will do what we can to defend ourselves. Whatever the cost may be.'

'Can you not see the outcome? You have the gift of future sight, don't you? You must know how this all ends, for better or worse.'

Nalla shook her head. 'You are mistaken. The mark you see on my hand is not what you believe it to be.' She held out her palm to reveal a nondescript mark that didn't match any of the symbols Liana had seen on the stones.

Liana scratched the back of her neck, confused. 'I don't understand.'

'There is much to come that cannot be foreseen. I have *some* knowledge of the future, though it is not in the way you would comprehend. Let me simply say, a lifetime of experience allows for some insight, as imperfect as that may be.'

'Tell me what I should do. Can you tell me that, at least?'

'I cannot influence your decision. It is yours to make and yours alone. What I can tell you is I have every confidence you will make the right choice.'

'You're beginning to sound like Eraidor.'

Nalla laughed a little. 'The Architects are wise. They too should be listened to, even if you do not wish to hear them.'

Liana paced around the cave. The low ceiling meant she could only move a few steps in any direction. It was better than not moving at all, as restless as she was. An idea formed in her mind. 'Would you permit me a stryde? I can cover more ground quickly with a mount.'

'No, we cannot allow that. We forbid it. We do not use animals in that way.'

She threw her hands in the hair. 'You wear their furs and you eat their meat, but riding them is forbidden? That makes no sense.'

'To you, perhaps. To us, animals are sacred and we treat them with honour. We only kill what we need and for their

352

sacrifice, we ensure we make use of every part of them. Nothing is wasted. What we will not do is treat them as slaves. We do not ride them, and we do not work them.'

'If you must save him, then I have a suggestion,' said Eraidor.

Liana was trying her best to pretend he wasn't there. An impossible task. 'What?' she asked aloud. Nalla somehow knew she wasn't addressing her.

'Have you not noticed your affinity with the creatures you meet? You have such a strong bond with Ember. You can communicate with her, and she with you, no?'

'Of sorts. What's your point?'

'He means,' said Nalla, 'ask Ember to help you.'

26

RESCUE

Eraidor had showed Liana how to get to Addan almost instantly in her mind. On foot, however, it would take hours. She knew she'd wasted so much time already with her indecision. In the end, it wasn't really a choice at all—she couldn't allow Addan to die out there alone. When she had trekked up the mountain to see Nalla, she'd left Ember with Orratan. When she exited Nalla's cave, Ember was waiting for her outside, alone.

'That should prove the bond you both have beyond any doubt,' said Eraidor.

Liana crouched down beside her furry friend, stroking her behind the ears, blue fire rippling between her fingers. 'Are you willing to help me?'

Ember bowed her head as if to say "yes," then pulled back onto her hind legs and pushed herself bigger. The blue fire burned brighter, flowing out a hand-span from her body. The small cinderfox swelled in size. Liana wondered how big Ember could get before reaching her limit. She daren't ask.

Liana carefully climbed onto Ember's back. She'd ridden a stryde once, almost. It had barely gone ten paces before she fell off and vowed never to ride one again. Cal, of course, had found it hilarious. Even her mother found it amusing. She had tried to hide it behind regal concern, but Liana had seen the mirth in her mother's eyes.

It was time to go. Liana grabbed Ember's fur around the neck, possibly too tightly, but there was no complaint. She held on tight, too afraid to fall. Ember moved forward, slowly at first. Liana found it difficult to keep her balance, but they both quickly settled into a rhythm. Before she had left the cave, Nalla reassured her that defence preparations would begin immediately, though she warned Liana not to delay her return. She had to make it back to Trennale before the army arrived.

Indeed, before she'd reached the outskirts of the city, people were already gathering with a sense of urgency over the threat approaching them, perhaps only little more than a day away. There was no time to waste for any of them. Liana took one last look back before nudging Ember into a run.

The animal was fast. Liana had never covered ground so quickly—her jaunt outside the planet in her mind notwithstanding—and she didn't like it. Until now, the fastest she'd ever gone was in a stryde-pulled coach, with all the shelter and protection it provided.

Ember didn't stop or tire, or even slow down at any point along the way. She kept on running, understanding the urgency of their journey. The more Liana learned about this cinderfox, the closer her bond felt to her. From the very first moment Ember had stopped that direwolf, Liana knew the cinderfox would protect her with her life. How long ago was that now? It felt like a lifetime.

The trees, once densely packed together, faded away behind them as they headed out into the open wastelands. They were getting closer to where she had spotted Addan the first time. She looked ahead, searching for him. The wind, made worse by their own speed, stung her eyes. It was hard to see. Warm tears rolled from her eyes before freezing on her cheeks as the cold air whipped past her.

'How do we find him?' she asked. 'He won't be where we saw him last.'

'I doubt he will have got far. He was walking in the direction of Trennale, so we should find him if we stay on this path.'

Ember kept running through the snow until there was nothing. The landscape was empty, not a single point of reference anywhere in any direction. Liana asked for the cinderfox to stop. Despite her not running herself, keeping balance was tiring her. She dismounted and immediately rubbed her face with her hands, trying to clear the wet glaze over her eyes, to bring the world back into focus. 'Can you see anything? Can you see Addan?'

'Alas, I cannot.'

Something caught Liana's attention out of the corner of her eye. She spun round and brought a flat hand up to her brow. There was something there, way off in the distance. She walked towards it. Ember kept pace with her as she broke into a run, trying to make out what the object was. As she grew closer, Liana slowed down to a stop as she realised it was only a brown-grey rock protruding from the snow. She slumped against it, crestfallen. Slamming her fist against the hard surface, she screamed in frustration. 'Where are you?'

'We will find him,' said Eraidor.

'Are you sure about that? Can we try that fly above thing again?'

'I do not believe there is any need for that. Look.' He nodded upward behind Liana's shoulder.

She pushed herself away from the rock and turned around. There was another dark shape ahead. Not a rock this time—it was moving. Slow, but definitely moving. Liana ran, ran as fast as her legs would allow. Her heart lifted as she realised she had found him. He was still alive!

'Addan!' she shouted.

He looked up in her direction and stopped walking. 'Liana? You're not real, you're only an illusion. Why must you torment me like this?' He was agitated, delirious.

Liana threw her arms around him and held him tight. 'It's really me, Addan. I've got you. I've got you. Everything will be all right now.'

Addan looked up, and their eyes met. 'I was meant to save *you.*' He started to cry and buried his head into Liana's shoulder.

Liana looked up at Eraidor. 'He's very cold. We need to get him warm, but I don't know how we can out here.'

They took what shelter from the wind they could offered by the lone rock she'd mistaken for Addan. Ember squeezed her way between Addan and Liana. The cinderfox pushed them apart and rounded on Addan, and nudged his legs out from underneath him. She allowed him to fall gently onto his backside before curling around him. Ember's blue flame grew and turned green and then a soft yellow. Liana could feel the warmth herself.

Liana looked at the cinderfox. 'Had I known you could do that, I'd have asked you to keep me warm on the way here too.' Ember blinked as if to say "you never asked," before moving a front leg away, making space for Liana to join her friend.

The warm fur of the cinderfox was better than any fire. Any hint of cold melted away as she nestled in under Ember's paw and pulled Addan closer to her. He was shivering still, though it was settling down as the heat soaked into his bones. She brushed his hair from his eyes as the frozen strands glued to his brow melted. He was awake, whispering to himself, words she couldn't quite make out. 'You're safe now. We'll rest here for a while and then we'll take you back to Trennale.'

'Yes, Trennale. I must go there. I need to save Liana.'

'No, I'm here. Here with you right now. Everything's all right now.'

Addan turned to look at her, his eyes wide and unfocused. It was like he was staring right through her. 'Liana? I love you, Liana,' he said. His head fell forward, unconscious.

'I know you do,' she said, still stroking his hair.

'We should not remain here for too long,' Eraidor said, breaking the silence. Ember lifted her head from the snow and glared at him.

'I agree with Ember,' said Liana. 'I know we need to get back to Trennale, but he needs to rest, and clearly, so does she.'

'Thankfully, I do not need rest.'

'Feel free to head back by yourself. You won't have any argument from me.'

'Do you really despise me that much?' he said, pulling his hands to his chest and pouting to emphasise his melodrama.

'Despise? No, I don't despise you. I would like nothing more than to be free of you, but I don't have to hate you to want that.'

Eraidor didn't say anything more. He turned his back to the group and looked out over the wilderness.

LIANA WAS unsure if she slept at all, but Addan woke up with a start, bringing her out of her own thoughts. 'Addan, you're awake. How are you feeling?'

'Where are we?' he said. He was more alert than when Liana had found him, but he was still quiet.

'The middle of nowhere. I saw you on your own out here, so we came to rescue you.'

Addan attempted a laugh, but it prompted a brief coughing fit. 'I was supposed to rescue you.'

'We need to get back to Trennale. Cal and Shaan and their army are on their way there themselves. They mean to attack them, because of me, except... Addan, Shaan is not who he claims to be.'

'I don't understand.' Addan slouched backward into Ember as if remembering something. 'You don't know, do you?'

'Don't know what?' Liana unconsciously pulled away from her friend a little.

'The queen is dead.'

Those four words crushed Liana like a falling rock. She scrambled free of Ember and turned back to face Addan. 'No. That can't be true. She's not dead. Tell me you're lying.' Tears were already wetting her cheeks.

'I wish I were. It was the same day we met Dess and came to Dawan.'

'How?' she said, wiping her face with the back of her hand.

'The Dawanii.' Addan looked exhausted still. 'The delegation came to meet the queen, but they killed her.'

'Why? That makes no sense? I don't understand.'

'With you missing too, they believed you were abducted. I tried to talk to your brother, but each time I did, Shaan blocked me.'

'I fear Sarratenian is behind that also,' said Eraidor.

Liana looked at Eraidor, but didn't respond to him. She was more concerned with what Addan had to say.

'I tried to come back for you, but the guards on the bridge wouldn't let me back over.'

'How are you here, then?'

'I joined the militia.'

A short, sharp burst of laughter escaped Liana's mouth. 'You? Joined the militia? That has to be the stupidest thing I've ever known you to do, and I've seen you do some really stupid things. Wait, what militia?'

'I was drunk. It seemed like a good idea at the time.' Addan shifted his weight to a more upright position, his back supported by Ember's under belly. 'It was decided there should be an immediate retaliation for the queen's assassination, and for your rescue. They recruited anyone and everyone willing. And let me tell you, most of them aren't nice people. The whole thing was chaotic from beginning to end.'

'*Sarratenian wanted a war, so he found a way to orchestrate one.*'

'This ends now,' said Liana as she pressed her fingernails into the palms of her hands. 'Ember, let's go. Addan, are you strong enough to ride?'

'*What are you doing?*' said Eraidor, concern very apparent in his voice.

'*I'm going to find Cal. Show him I'm alive and we can put an end to this.*'

'*No. We are to return to Trennale. Nalla and Uehan have seen what is to come and sees that as the correct course of action.*'

'*I don't care. Nalla said herself the future is always changing. This is all because of me, so I am the one who must make it right.*'

'*You are not the cause of this. Sarratenian wants blood, and it is for me, not for you. Showing your brother you are still alive will not change anything.*'

'It might. I have to try,' Liana said aloud. She climbed onto Ember's back and instructed Addan to take a position in front of her so she could help keep him upright. Ember adjusted her size larger to accommodate the extra weight.

'Who are you talking to?' asked Addan.

'It's a long story and I'm not sure you'd believe me. We need to go, now.' She clapped Ember's shoulder to say she's ready, and the cinderfox launched into a run.

'*Stop, Liana, stop!*' Eraidor's protests fell on deaf ears.

'*Make me,*' she said defiantly. In that moment, she felt herself go rigid and was thrown from Ember's back. She landed hard, her back to the ground and her eyes staring at the sky. She tried to get up but couldn't move.

'For your own sake, and for everyone else's, I cannot permit you to do this.' said Eraidor as he looked down on her.

Ember had stopped and doubled back. All three of them were looking down on Liana as she struggled to move any part of her body.

'What have you done to me?'

'Have you not noticed? The more time we have spent together, the more connected we are? I am not just inside you, I am a part of you now. Well, not completely as yet, but we are becoming as one.'

'So I'm your prisoner now? No, I won't accept that.' She pushed against the feeling that was weighing her down.

'Prisoner? Not at all. It is not a voluntary thing on my part. We are entering a new co-existence. A connection I have felt with no other before you. I surmise the Origem energy coursing through you is responsible. Rather interesting, no?'

'I want you gone. Get out of me. GET OUT OF ME!' Liana screamed and pushed, fighting back against the pressure. She felt something give and she could move. She stood up quickly. Nothing had changed. Eraidor was still there, still inside of her, but she had regained control, for now.

Addan looked confused and concerned. 'Are you all right?' He put a hand on Liana's shoulder.

'I'm fine. Let's get moving.' As she remounted Ember, she glared at Eraidor. *'You don't control me.'*

With Addan back on the cinderfox too, they set off for a second time in the direction of where Liana had last seen the army. It wasn't long before a mass of footprints in the snow told them they were on the right track.

Eraidor didn't speak, but Liana could feel his constant pull, willing her to stop. She fought back, like they were both pulling opposite ends of an invisible rope, vying for control of her very being. What started out as a heavy feeling in her head before she even knew of Eraidor's presence was quickly becoming a complete envelopment of her soul. *What's the secret? How do I free myself?* She had a nagging doubt in her mind. Was he really not telling her because it would kill them both as he suggested, or was it for a more self-serving reason? Was Eraidor a good god? The stories said so, but that's all they were. All she knew is she had to find a way to set herself free.

Addan pointed to something ahead. Liana looked over his shoulder towards the horizon and found what she was looking for. There they were. Hundreds of men heading for the city. She guessed they were no more than half a day away now. She was growing tired, not only from the riding, but also from keeping Eraidor from taking over.

As they grew closer, unseen, Liana realised in her haste she hadn't planned what to do once she caught up with them. She wasn't in any position to fight if they were inclined to attack. But they wouldn't do that, would they? She was who they were looking for. They were approaching the army from behind. Was that a good idea? She thought not. Liana reached out to Ember and asked her to circle wide so they would meet head on. It was quite a detour, running far enough wide so they wouldn't be spotted. Shaan was leading the army. He should see her first.

'*This will not achieve anything,*' said Eraidor as they rounded the group of marching bodies.

Liana asked for Ember to stop. They would wait, standing, for them to approach. It would give them a small amount of time to rest. She felt Eraidor's pull relax a little. It was up to her now. She stepped down from Ember and stood by her side, unarmed, and waited.

They were perhaps only one or two hundred paces away when one of the men at the front of the pack noticed something was in their path. Liana watched on as Shaan raised a hand, ordering his charges to halt, which they did in a synchronised manner. Shaan, on his stryde, moved forward towards their position alone. Behind him, her brother was atop another stryde somewhere in the middle of the pack. Less than twenty paces separated Liana and the army, with Shaan standing exactly central between the two parties.

'So good of you to join us in person this time,' said Shaan, addressing Eraidor. He winked at Liana. 'How are you finding my dear brother? Good company?'

Liana spat at the ground in front of her. 'Did you kill our mother?'

'The Dawanii killed your mother. Cal and I witnessed it ourselves. You should have been there.'

This wasn't the Shaan Liana knew. This version was more cocky, more arrogant, if that were possible. 'That's dragon shit and you know it. I've spent time with the Dawanii. They didn't send a delegation to our city, so whoever it was that killed our mother, it wasn't them.'

'Sarratenian, you may drop the pretence now. You are fooling no one,' said Eraidor.

Shaan dismounted and took a step forward. 'All right, yes, I confess, I arranged the whole thing. I killed the queen, the stupid old woman. She had no clue how to run a city, let alone a whole country.'

Liana felt the rage boil up within her. 'Why?'

'Because I can, because I wanted to. For a year I listened to her, to you, and to Cal, bless him.' He turned and glanced a look back at Cal. 'You all have no idea how small you are. Look around you, there is nothing. Your world is empty. At first, I offered encouragement to fire your imagination, yet it fell on deaf ears. I grew bored, tired of waiting, so I thought, why not start a war?

'War is the mother of invention, to turn a phrase. It has been centuries since you have had a good old war with lots of blood and bodies, and that is all your fault,' Shaan said, jabbing a finger in Eraidor's direction. 'Though I am sure your punishment is far worse than mine, dear brother. For me, it was all over in an instant. One moment I was there, and then I was here, a thousand years apart. Centuries have passed and humanity has made no progress at all, except everyone got soft and lazy. No innovation, no invention, and no desire to better yourselves. There is nothing left but apathy for your own lives. It is quite maddening. This is not the world that was meant to be.'

'Well, I'm here and I'm alive,' said Liana. 'There's no need for war, no need to fight. If I can see Cal, then he will see me, and see you for who you really are and we can end this.'

Shaan laughed. 'He is not in charge here, I am, and you are insignificant. I will wage war, and I will watch you all burn. Poor old Eraidor, he cannot do anything, he is powerless, help-less. I could release him from you, little girl. Yes, I could do that for you, but then I would have to kill your brother as the price to pay. Look at you. All wrapped up in your own little life, playing your games with your friend there. Yes, I see you, Addan Stoan. The man with nothing special about him at all, yet wants to be saviour to all. I really thought you would be dead by now. I assume that is what happened to all the others? Did you kill them yourself? No, I do not think so. You value life too much, crying over that girl, and pleading for the life of an old man. You did not even know their names.'

Addan made to step down from Ember, but Liana raised her arm and motioned for him to stay put.

'I want to speak to my brother,' she said, firmly but quietly.

'Yes, why not? Let us bring your brother. I have my brother here, so it is only fair you should have yours.' Shaan put his fingers to his lips and blew a whistle, which made Liana's ears hurt. She watched as Cal made his way on strydeback through the still army. She went to run to him, but Shaan sidestepped, blocking her. 'No, no, you may stay exactly where you are.'

Cal pulled up beside Shaan. 'What's going on? Who is this girl holding us up?'

'Ah, see how he does not even recognise you? I will admit, you do look rather different now that you are one of them.'

'It's me, Cal. It's Liana. You have to stop this. Shaan isn't who he says he—'

'My sister is a prisoner of your people. Have you been sent to negotiate for her freedom?'

'No. I promise you it's me, Cal. I came to tell you to stop. To show you I am alive. There's no need to search anymore. I am here. I want you to take me home.'

Cal didn't reply. All he did was stare at her, and she wished she knew what he was thinking behind those eyes. Something had changed in him. Everything had changed in him. His posture, his tone of voice, everything. It was like she was looking at a different man entirely. She looked at Shaan. 'What have you done to him?'

'I have done nothing other than help him become the man he was meant to be. A king brought to rule.'

Liana frowned. *King?* It was a word she hadn't heard before. 'I never liked you. From the very first moment you arrived at the palace, I knew there was something *wrong* about you.'

'And yet you did nothing about it.'

'What could I do? You found favour with the queen, and you found your way into his bed. There was no talking to either of them about you.'

Shaan laughed. 'You may be right. I wonder, though. If I had come to the palace as a woman, would you have disliked me so?'

'Don't flatter yourself.'

'It could have been yours, Liana. Instead, you chose to involve yourself with those far beneath you. You ask what I have done to your brother? Ask what you have become yourself. Look at you. You are not worthy of the privilege you were born into. Such a shame, really.'

365

'Is this girl to escort us to Trennale?' asked Cal. 'Does she know if Liana is safe?'

'*I'm* Liana!' she shouted, punching a fist at the air. 'Cal, *look*. Look at me. It's me. I'm standing right in front of you. Stop this madness and let's go home.' She took a step closer to him. The stryde he was on snapped at her with its long neck and razor sharp beak. Ember growled in return.

'This girl is of no consequence, my dear friend. Another lost soul in the wilderness. Pay her no mind. Come now, Trennale is not far. We will find what we are searching for there.'

'I'm right here!' Liana raged. She formed a ball of white light between both her hands and willed it to grow. Pain seared through her head as the light grew brighter. When she could no longer hold it, she threw it at Shaan. All it did was fade into nothing before it reached him. He laughed. Cal looked at her blankly.

'Feeble,' said Shaan. 'You think because you have found a way to use the Origem, you can control it. It makes you feel powerful, but now you see the truth. You are nothing. Insignificant. And I grow tired of it.' He dismounted from his stryde and drew a sword.

Addan climbed off Ember and drew his own blade. Ember growled and moved forward in front of Liana, defending her.

'*There is no need for this, brother,*' said Eraidor.

'And yet, you are powerless to intervene.'

Shaan lunged at Liana, but before he could strike, Addan threw himself forward and deflected the sword away with his own. Ember pounced, making to bite at Shaan's sword hand only to be struck hard on the nose. The cinderfox yelped and regrouped alongside Liana, her blue fur fading back a little.

Liana tried again to imagine as much of her magic as she could. The light she created fizzled out before she could do anything with it, as though Shaan was blocking her somehow. All she could do was back away, stay out of his reach. She looked at Cal pleadingly. All he did was observe. There was no emotion in him. He was wholly indifferent to what was happening in front of him.

'He will not help you,' said Shaan. He held his sword forward, pointing it directly towards Liana's face.

She glanced at the group of men. Shaan's army. None of them had moved an inch or reacted in any way since their encounter began. Their silence made her feel uneasy. Not so long ago, they had all been ordinary people from her city, and now they were ready to go to war. How did this one man, god or no, have so much power over them?

'You need to turn and run,' said Eraidor. *'You cannot win against him. Not here.'*

'You should listen to him. My brother is a wise old thing. He thinks I would not strike you down right here as that means I would kill him, too. Surely one god would not destroy another? Would he?' Shaan grinned and moved the tip of his sword around in small circles at Liana's face. He feinted forward, barely a few inches.

Addan reacted to the move. He struck with his sword from above his head, slamming his blade into Shaan's. Liana flinched and tried to stop her friend from continuing. It didn't help. As he brought his sword down a second time, ready to slice at Shaan himself, he was flung backwards in the snow by an invisible force. He groaned as he landed, the sword thrown free from his grasp. Liana ran to him, the sound of Shaan's laughter hanging in the breeze. She exhaled when she saw he was unharmed.

In her mind, she imagined the power of the Origem burning within her and willed it to form in her hands. Nothing happened. Frustrated, she pulled herself to her feet and tried again. *This has to work!* A bright, ball of flaming energy formed in each hand, glowing hot, burning. All her life she feared fire, and now she summoned it willingly.

'*Liana, no,*' said Eraidor. '*You cannot fight him. He will destroy you. Do not think he will stop because I am part of you.*'

'*I have to try.*' She threw one hand forward, and then the other, aiming the fire at Shaan, missing both times as he deftly stepped out of harm's way with inhuman speed.

'Now, now. There is really no need for this. I will let you all go, for now. Consider yourselves fortunate that I do not wish to harm my brother. He is all that saves you now. If I were you, I would heed his advice and run.'

Liana tried again, growling as she pulled the fire from within her. Once more she missed her target.

Shaan sighed. 'Very well, if you insist.' He pushed both fists forward, slamming them into Liana's chest. She toppled backwards into the snow, winded.

'*We need to run!*' insisted Eraidor.

Liana could feel him pulling on her again, and she knew he was right. There was nothing more that any of them could do. She watched as Shaan raised a hand in the air. A signal to his army. In lockstep, they all advanced. She scrambled over to Addan and helped him to his feet before dragging herself and him onto Ember's back. Together, they turned their back on the army and Shaan. Liana turned her back on her brother. Ember ran.

After a safe distance, Liana afforded herself a glance back. They weren't giving chase. She could still see Shaan at the front. He gave her a wave. 'See you again soon,' he said. She heard him clearly, despite the distance.

Now they were heading back towards Trennale, away from immediate danger, Liana felt less pulling from Eraidor. *How long before I won't be strong enough to resist him at all?* The gradual consumption was as concerning to her as Shaan's advance on the city.

'Do you want to tell me what's going on?' asked Addan, breaking the silence as they crossed the wastelands. He had the same place in front of Liana as before, but she didn't have to struggle to keep him balanced this time now he'd warmed up. In fact, he was feeling a little *too* warm.

Liana told Addan everything that had happened to her since she last saw him, with interjections from Eraidor along the way, which were neither helpful nor wanted. It wasn't easy having a three-way conversation when one of the parties couldn't see or hear one of the others. Addan, in turn, told her about his time in the army. At least Eraidor didn't interrupt *him* as he spoke.

By the time Addan reached the part in his story of walking alone after the Torn attack—the one part Liana had her own experience of—she noticed he was speaking slower and getting words mixed up.

'I couldn't save any... of me, I mean... them. Milo... especially. He did... n't deser—' he slumped forward and fell silent.

Liana told Ember to stop so she could check on him. She lifted his head up. Sweat poured down his face, his eyes closed. He was so hot to the touch. 'He has a fever,' she said, remounting Ember. 'We need to get him to the city now.'

'Too much time in the cold, I fear.'

Liana glared at Eraidor and instructed Ember to run as fast as she could.

27

THE GIRL UNKNOWN

C al wanted to destroy the Dawanii now. It was a constant thought that occupied his every waking moment since they destroyed that village. Cutting them down as they defended their home felt... satisfying somehow. It was like a fire raging within him, quelled at the sight of the bloodied, battered corpses. Lives ended by his own hands. It felt good. Really good. *The Dawanii will—and should—suffer the consequences of their actions.* He will find Liana, and he will return to Moranza victorious. He owed everything to Shaan, of course. The man was everything to him. Shaan was strong. *Decisive.* Everything he had aspired to be his whole life.

The image of his mother, the queen, lying in a pool of her own blood at his feet was permanently etched into his mind. It's what drove him now. He looked to Shaan as they rode atop their strydes, leading the army onwards towards Trennale. Shaan was confident they would find Liana there.

He hated everything about Dawan. The cold and the snow. The darkness. Why was it the farther they travelled in this forsaken land the darker it got? It made him feel miserable.

Even his new army—Shaan's army—had grown quieter since they left the makeshift base camp. There had been so much noise in the beginning when he had first arrived. Now? Now, the lowest members of society marched through the snow in near perfect silence.

'How anyone survives in this awful land is beyond me,' he grumbled. He was talking to himself, though Shaan did hear him as they rode side by side. The strydes didn't like the cold either. There were only a dozen left now. The supervisors didn't complain that they had to walk. No one complained anymore.

'I have always found that people seem to have a knack for adapting to the world around them, for better or worse,' said Shaan.

'This is definitely worse.'

This was all Liana's fault. If she only shared in his sense of duty and responsibility, he wouldn't be here. If she had only stayed for the welcoming ceremony. Shaan had said she should consider herself fortunate. The Dawanii might have killed her as well that day. Cal still didn't understand why they had committed that terrible act. Why did they declare war on Moranza, unprovoked? Shaan didn't have an answer for him, and so far, he hadn't found one here. He put all his faith and trust in Shaan, and hoped he would find the answers he was looking for once they reached Trennale.

As the throng of hundreds of men moved as one through the white desert, Cal found himself in the middle of the pack. His stryde, as thick with feathers as it was, seemed to seek out the warmth provided by the surrounding soldiers. Cal himself, sat several feet higher than everyone else—except Shaan, who was leading from the front—and had no shelter from the winds. The ever-winds swirled and scattered the dusty snow, lashing at his cheeks.

He thought about dismounting, continuing on alongside

the bird. That would mean walking, which seemed to him like a worse option. The Dawanii fur coat the supervisors had found for him offered some warmth, but not enough. It had an earthy smell to it, which he didn't like. And he despised the thought of it having a previous owner. A Dawanii owner. That owner was probably dead now, and he took comfort in that. He pulled it tighter round his neck with his free hand, clinging on to whatever heat he could.

After what felt like too long, with little change in scenery to make it feel like they were making any progress towards their destination, Shaan ordered a halt. Cal watched as his friend broke forward to greet two dark figures ahead. They were accompanied by what looked like to him a large white tamewolf. *Who were these fools to be out in this desert alone?* As he clicked his tongue to signal his stryde to move forward to join Shaan, he felt something grab his ankle.

One of the soldiers—one of the few women in the ranks— had a hold of his boot. The woman was still otherwise facing forward, an empty expression on her face. It was an odd sight. He tried to shake his ankle free, but the woman's grip was solid.

He recognised her. Her blonde hair had darkened and matted with blood and dirt, and her clothing matched all the others around them. He knew her name. He'd spoken to her briefly as they crossed the bridge. Noelle. A farm-worker from the outskirts of the city. She had nothing left in her life after her husband and young son had died in a dragon attack last year.

'Release me,' he said, looking down at her. She didn't move. She looked dead ahead, her arm aloft and holding his boot. He tried again to kick her away. None of the other soldiers intervened or reacted in any way.

He glanced back ahead. Shaan was still engaged with the strange travellers. They were too far away to hear anything said between them. The hand at his ankle tugged.

'What is it you want?' he demanded, growling.

Noelle slowly turned her head—only her head—and looked up at him. Her eyes were dark and sunken, and there were tears welling underneath them. 'Where's my boy?' she whispered. Her voice sounded empty.

'You told me he died. Remember?' He didn't know what else to tell her.

'He did? Oh. Tell him I love him, won't you?' Then she turned her head back to face front and let go of his leg.

Cal frowned, confused. He looked at several of the others, darting glances from head to head. They were all silent and unmoving. A whistle from up ahead grabbed his attention. Shaan wanted him to join him.

He clicked for the stryde to move. The soldiers around him stepped out of the way without direction or even any acknowledgement of his presence. They simply moved, still facing ahead. Only facing ahead. Why did that bother him? His mind felt heavy. It had done for a while. Something was off and whatever it was, was too far out of reach to put his finger on. He hated the Dawanii, though. He knew that much. And he trusted Shaan. Completely.

Cal approached the small group. The animal wasn't a tamewolf. In fact, he didn't know what it was. Curiously, it looked as though it was on fire. One of the two strangers, a man, was sitting astride its back. The man looked familiar.

The other was a girl with half her hair painted a different colour than the other. Dawanii. That was all he could see of her features. The rest of her face was out of focus somehow. Whoever this girl was, she was agitated.

'What's going on? Who are these people?' Cal asked. He dismounted and joined Shaan by his side. Both strydes took the opportunity to rest, lying down in the snow and tucking their long wiry legs underneath their feathers.

'They are of no importance to us,' said Shaan.

The girl shouted something, animatedly. Cal didn't recognise the words. Something inside nagged at him, telling him he should understand. Shaan replied to her. Cal didn't take in what he said. Whatever it was only made the girl more angry, to the point Shaan pulled out his sword and pointed it at her.

The man with the animal—who didn't look like a Dawanii —leapt forward with his own sword and attacked Shaan. Cal was relieved when his friend easily outmanoeuvred the stranger and sent him crashing to the ground. Cal felt as though he should have intervened. Should have defended Shaan. *Why didn't I?* Then he was distracted by the burning animal. It growled at him and Shaan. *A truly strange creature. Magnificent in its own way. I should like one as a pet once I return home as king.*

Cal watched as the girl ran to her companion. She was still ranting at Shaan. Why couldn't he see her face? He rubbed at his eyes in case ice or grit had somehow got in them. It didn't help. *That animal looks like it would make a great pet.*

A flash of yellow caught his eye. The girl's hand glowed as if it were on fire. She threw that fire furiously at Shaan, but he escaped her attack unharmed. Cal wondered if the girl had some kind of magical power about her. One that could disguise her face and control the elements themselves. *Perhaps I should do something to help. Why is it so dark and cold out here?*

The girl stopped shouting. She said something quieter to Shaan, and then they—the two strangers and that beautiful beast—turned away and ran.

'Come, let us be on our way,' said Shaan.

'I don't understand. What happened? Who were they?'

'Dawanii scouts. They demanded we leave their lands or we are to face the consequences.' Shaan clicked his fingers and his stryde wearily stood up. Cal's did the same.

'Did they say anything about Liana? I couldn't understand what they were saying. Could you?

'It seems our assumption is correct. They have her in Trennale, and are refusing to negotiate. They wish only to speak to the queen.'

'They killed her already.'

'It appears they do not understand Moranzan hierarchy. Their customs are quite different to ours. They are nothing more than primitive savages, in my opinion. Nevertheless, it changes nothing. We continue to Trennale as planned and they will know our fury.'

By the time Cal had remounted his stryde and taken up his position within the army, his already blurry recollection of the encounter with the two strangers had faded. He hated the Dawanii, he remembered that. And the white, fiery animal that wasn't a tamewolf or direwolf. *One of those would be a fantastic pet, wouldn't it?*

The army marched onwards, slowly, silently. Shaan led from the front. He didn't check his map, yet he knew where he was going. Cal trusted Shaan. Completely. He loved him. He knew his friend would find his sister, and together they would defeat the enemy. They would crush them and make them regret the day they killed his mother.

In the distance the top of a mountain came in to view at the horizon. The moon broke through a clouded sky and it wasn't so dark anymore. Still cold though, and not as light as back home. This war will be swift, he knew that. Shaan told him that. Shaan knew what was right. He trusted him and he loved him.

'We have found Trennale,' declared Shaan. He pointed to the mountain.

'Liana is there?'

'Yes, you will find your sister there at that mountain, and you will find vengeance. We will both find what we came for.'

For a moment, Cal's mind cleared of all the fog and the cold. He knew what must be done, and knew he had the strength to defeat this evil that stood before them. As long as Shaan was by his side, he knew. He knew they would see victory on this day. He knew the Architects would look down upon them and see these people, these *bastards*, crushed and defeated.

He loved Shaan. He trusted him. Completely.

The time for victory had arrived.

28

THE STORM APPROACHES

By the time they made it back to Trennale, much had changed. A wall of fallen trees, foliage and all, was partially constructed already. There were three routes into the city, unless one was to climb over the summit of the mountain. The largest entrance, the one they were approaching, was blocked by a large barrier of wood and leaves, save for a narrow gap roughly ten paces wide. Liana was impressed by how quickly the Dawanii were making progress with their defences.

Two men carrying a huge pine tree, bereft of its roots, nodded to the returning party as they passed by. Liana hadn't decided which gift she would choose for herself, had she been one of them and took the Branding, but she decided she would be content with superhuman strength. She wondered what it would be like not to feel anything, though. Orratan had told her it wasn't only the physical sense of touch that was lost, but the emotional sense too, and the latter scared her more. Maybe a healer would be better? She definitely didn't like the idea of being deaf, even though she couldn't remember what power was bestowed in return. Had Orratan told her? Maybe, but helping Uehan at the time had been more important. Something to do with protection? She'd ask him again if they ever get the chance. In the end, she was glad she wouldn't be Branded. It did make her more appreciative of her senses, though.

Safely through the defensive wall, it didn't take long before she saw a familiar face. Two, in fact. Uehan and Eelan rushed to greet them.

'Your friend is sick,' said Uehan. 'I saw it just before you arrived. I brought Eelan, he can help.'

They both helped Addan from Ember and laid him down on the ground. Liana sent Ember off to find food for herself, the cinderfox returning to her natural small size the moment she was clear of them.

'He's too hot,' said Eelan, his concern undisguised.

'Can you help him?' asked Liana.

'Yes, I think so, but it will take time.'

'How much time? It won't be long before Sarratenian reaches the city.' She refused to call him Shaan any longer.

'Help me take him to the caves. It's where we're evacuating anyone not able to fight.'

Liana and Uehan each took one of Addan's arms and held it around their shoulders. Neither were strong enough to carry his weight on their own, and with anyone actually capable of that feat already engaged in defence construction, the best they could manage was to drag him. Liana was sure he wouldn't mind a few bruised toes if he got the help he needed.

Aside from Nalla's cave, Liana had not seen any of the others. She'd expected to find a number of holes dug into the mountainside much like the old woman's abode, but she was wrong. There was only the one entrance which sat slightly above ground level. As they approached, many people—mostly young children with ancient looking guardians—filtered past her and into the hole in the mountain. Uehan led the way up the shallow slope and into the cave. Liana thought it would be incredibly cramped with all those vulnerable people crammed into such a small and narrow space, but after a dozen or so paces inside, the claustrophobic corridor opened out into a huge cavern. Her jaw dropped.

'You didn't tell me about all this,' she said.

The large empty space had room for hundreds of souls, maybe even a thousand, if she had to estimate. There was a large open space below, accessed by either of two sets of steps carved into the perimeter. Stalagmites, some twice the size of an adult, grew in a haphazard pattern on the stone floor, the space around them occupied by the Dawanii—were they refugees? Citizens was probably more apt; it was still their home, after all.

The stone steps were uneven, steep and well trodden, so they took their time carrying Addan down them. A young girl, no older than seven or eight, ran up to help them as they neared the bottom. She was a pretty little thing, and Liana smiled at her as she grabbed a handful of Addan's pant leg. It wasn't much help, really, but it was appreciated all the same.

Eelan, who had followed behind, asked for Addan to be leant up against one of the stalagmites.

'Shouldn't we lie him down?' asked Liana as she released the arm from around her neck in tandem with Uehan.

Eelan shook his head. 'Seated is better. He will recover faster this way.'

Liana deferred to his better judgement, even if it was different to anything she had learned about treating the sick and injured back home.

'I'll be fine here with him. You should go back out and find Orratan to see how you can help.'

Before Liana could reply, there was a shout from someone on the far side of the cave. She, along with almost everyone else, looked to see where the sound came from. On the opposite set of steps, a young man was shaking his fists and seemed extremely angry. It was Aranan and he was heading right for

Liana. Aranan's voice carried around the entire chamber, holding everyone's attention as he pushed his way through them.

'This is all your fault!' he shouted as he shoulder-barged an older man out of the way. 'She is not to be trusted. First, she arrives here on her own, learns of our ways and gains our trust, and then she brings her armies to destroy us all.'

Liana didn't know what to say. She stood with her mouth slightly open as the embodiment of fury itself headed her way.

Uehan stepped into the space between them. 'It's not true. She *is* a friend to all of us.'

'It's all right,' said Liana as she raised her arm to stop him. 'I can speak for, and defend, myself.'

Aranan stopped short of tackling Liana to the floor. He was seething. Behind him, a number of others were moving themselves closer, their body language suggesting the young man might have a point.

'I can assure you I knew nothing of this. I did not seek you out. My friend, your *brother*, Uehan found me and brought me here. Until then, I did not even know of your home.'

'Lies. Who is to say you are not Sarratenian himself? You claim to be blessed with the presence of Eraidor, but I have seen no evidence of this. No one has. We only have your word, and I for one, do not take you at your word.'

'Are you sure there is nothing you can do to show yourself to anyone but me?' Liana asked Eraidor.

'Alas, no. Until I am freed, I cannot demonstrate anything.'

'You have no brand, and I have caused no harm to you, so why would you believe me to be a liar? Orratan has already seen the truth of my word. Does that not satisfy you?'

Aranan didn't reply.

'Is there another here with the Brand of Truth who would listen to me, to allay your fears?' At first there was no response from the crowd, but then a girl a little older than Uehan stepped forward.

'You can determine what I say is the truth?' Liana asked her.

The girl nodded and spoke with her hands.

'She says to look her in the eyes and speak your words. She will know if you are truthful,' said Eelan.

Liana nodded and did as she was directed, repeating her story to the girl. When Liana finished, the girl tilted her head to one side slightly as if pondering what she had heard before turning to the not-quite-so-angry-now Aranan and nodded. Liana had expected some sort of grudging apology, but he simply sniffed and went back the way he came.

Liana thanked the girl before turning her attention back to Addan and the others. 'Whether I'm truthful or not, it is clear I am not welcomed here by everyone.'

'Pay him no mind,' said Eelan, looking up from beside Addan. 'Aranan still resents his brother for taking away what was rightfully his.' Uehan hung his head, acknowledging his guilt. 'Addan will be all right, I believe the worst has passed, but it will be a while before he wakes up.'

'Thank you for your help,' Liana said. *'And thank you for your help too,'* she said to Eraidor.

'I have not helped.'

'Precisely my point.' Liana felt a pushing sensation from inside her, and it was getting stronger as time passed. There was a battle brewing within her and it was beginning to feel as though she was on the losing side. She pushed back, but it was tiring.

Liana looked around at all the others gathered in the cavern for any further signs of discord. To her relief, there were none. Most were grouped together in their own family units, their faces etched with fear over what was to come. An old man, bald but with a painted scalp in the same pattern as if he had hair, smiled weakly at her. She smiled back at him before self-consciously averting her eyes. She resolved to stay and help them, whatever it took. It was a feeling that took her by surprise. Throughout her life she'd shunned her responsibilities to her own people, yet even though she barely knew the Dawanii, there was a compulsion within her to protect them, to stand up for them. She wondered how much of that was her own conscience and how much was Eraidor's influence. *Am I in control anymore?*

It took her a while to find Orratan once she left the cavern. She felt uncomfortable leaving Addan so soon after finding him, but there was nothing she could do to help him for now. Eelan would look after him, and that gave her comfort.

Orratan was in the amphitheatre alone. Even his companion wasn't with him. He smiled at Liana when he saw her and invited her to sit next to him on the edge of the monument by tapping the space beside him. The pair sat in silence for a while as Eraidor glided around the perimeter, looking at the intricately detailed statues representing the Architects lining the walls in turn.

It was the first time since rescuing Addan that Liana had stopped. The silence was comforting in a way, with only a soft, distant ringing in her ears left. The world was so *noisy*. Everything from the wind, the wildlife, the human interactions—a constant connection to everything, a reminder that no one is truly alone. It was the calm before the storm, she knew that, but for this brief moment, she was at peace. She thought of her mother, and regretted not being there in her last moments. *I should have stayed,* she thought, wiping away a tear.

Ember padded in with a chicken in her jaws. It was dead and plucked raw. *Where did she find that?* The cinderfox looked pleased with herself as she lay down on Liana's feet and devoured the bird, bones and all. It made Liana feel hungry, though the uncooked chicken wasn't at all appetising.

'I tried to stop them,' Liana said after a while, when the urge to break the silence became too much. 'I thought if I could show my brother I was alive and well, it would all be over, but I was wrong.' She closed her eyes and breathed in deep through her nose and sighed.

Orratan put his hand on her knee and squeezed as if to say, 'it's all right.'

'If anyone were to ask me, not so long ago, if I believed in the Architects, I would have told them no. To me, they were only stories, old stories. Now, but now, I have one inside me fighting to get out, and another with ambition to destroy us all.' She turned and looked at Orratan, who looked a little sad.

She looked over at Eraidor, who was staring at the statue of, if she was right, himself. *'What do we do? How do we stop him?'*

Eraidor turned around. *'His power comes from the control and manipulation of others. Without that, he is nothing.'*

'So we must kill them all, my people, his army?' The thought made her feel sick to the stomach. Was there no alternative? She'd already tried to convince him to stop, but that didn't work. Either way, he was still advancing on Trennale and it all felt so *inevitable*. She had a feeling gnawing away inside her that she, along with everyone else, was in a game. A game where Sarratenian and Eraidor were the players and everyone else were the pieces.

'Can't you do anything to stop him? He can see you, and you can talk to him. Change his mind somehow.'

'I was the one who banished him, and he wants his vengeance. I sincerely doubt anything I could say would dissuade him,' Eraidor said, holding his hands together in front of him.

'So we all must suffer, must die, for your petty squabbling? Where's the fairness in that? None of us asked for this, none of us deserve this!'

Eraidor did look guilty, his eyes giving him away. *'If I were of myself, then I would be able to stop him. Or at least try.'*

Liana stood up, angry. 'Then tell me how to release you!' Orratan jumped a little, startled.

'I cannot, I have told you I cannot. You must come to that yourself. It is the only way.'

'So this is all on me then? I don't accept that, I won't accept that. How dare you lay this all on me. What right do you have? What right do you have to preside over the pain and destruction to come? You profess your love for humanity, for your own creation, but yet you refuse to help. You would sacrifice us all for your games?'

'I am not certain you understand what true sacrifice is.'

'What in the name of you all is that supposed to mean?'

The door to the amphitheatre opened, interrupting the silent argument. It was Uehan. He stepped inside, his head bowed a little. 'They are close,' he said.

Already? Liana thought.

Orratan nodded before standing up and pulled straight his fur coat. He motioned for Liana to follow as he made to leave the room.

'You too,' said Liana to Ember. The chicken was gone except for a small sinew dangling from the corner of the cinderfox's mouth.

Trennale was eerily quiet. Anyone vulnerable was safely hidden away, and those able to fight, to defend, were somewhere along the new perimeter wall. Liana was unsure how strong that wall would be, considering it was mostly whole trees hastily stacked one on top of another. Parts of it looked like it would collapse at any moment. The pathway Liana had used both times she'd entered the city was now completely sealed off as had, she was told, the other two ways in. The city was now cut off from the outside world, for better or for worse.

'How many people do we have able to fight?' Liana asked Uehan.

'A little over three hundred. Eighty have the strength brand. They will be at the front.'

That didn't sound like many, especially spread out along the wall. Liana wasn't sure how many men Sarratenian had, but it was definitely more than three hundred.

'What other weapons do you have? They will break through the wall, so what then?'

'We have no weapons. Some have made tree branches shortened into batons. Others have tools used for farming, small hunting knives, perhaps.'

Liana swallowed. They didn't stand a chance. They were outnumbered and practically unarmed. Their hopes rested on eighty men and women with the ability to hurl large, heavy objects at the enemy, and that was it. It pained her to consider them as the enemy. Those were *her* people advancing towards the city. She was queen now her mother was dead, something she hadn't realised until that moment. But what could she do?

She turned to Eraidor. *'They're all going to die.'*

29

TORMENT

It was dark, so very dark, and all Addan could hear was screaming. The screaming of men as their flesh was ripped from their bodies by creatures who looked like patchwork dolls put together by a blind man. He lashed out with his arms, trying to push away his attackers, their glowing purple veins dancing around in the darkness like string in the wind. Someone was calling his name. 'Addan, please help me, Addan.' It was Milo. He sounded so scared.

Addan scrambled around, tripping over himself as he tried to get away, trying to save his own life, but he couldn't abandon Milo. He needed his help. He stilled, only for a moment, as he listened for where Milo's pleas for help were coming from. There—ahead on the right. *I'm coming*. He stumbled his way forward, avoiding the purple streaks trying to block his way, to kill him.

'Addan, help.'

He was close now. The screams of the others, his company, grew quiet as their cries turned to death. Milo was still pleading for his life, one of the attackers bearing down on the boy. Addan could barely see, but there was enough light from the snow to

386

guide him. Addan charged the creature, crashing it and himself to the ground. He scrambled free from the monster and took hold of Milo as he lay curled into a ball in the cold, wet snow.

'It's all right, my friend. I have you now. You're safe with me. I will get you out of here.' Addan turned the boy to face him, except it wasn't Milo he saw.

'I begged for my life and you did nothing. *You let me die!*' screamed the first Dawanii girl he'd met.

'No! I tried, but I couldn't save you!'

And then the darkness had gone. Addan coughed and spluttered as his surroundings changed around him.

He was in a cave, surrounded by hundreds of frightened people. Dawanii people. They were mostly women and children, with a few ageing men among them. His body ached as he tried to move, to straighten his back. *Where am I?*

As he tried to block out the memories of the past few days that haunted his dreams, he realised there was someone sitting next to him. He turned his head and was surprised to recognise the face. It was Dess! Or was it Yra? He couldn't tell. Even seated, the woman towered over him.

'Which one are you?' he asked, clenching his teeth in a grimace as he shifted his weight to get a better look at the woman. She was wearing Dawanii clothing, of sorts. Something was off, but he couldn't figure out what, exactly.

'What an odd question,' replied the woman. 'There is but one of me. I would think there is only one of you, too. How about ten of you? That might be fun. Confusing, though. How would you know which is you is which?'

Addan regretted asking. 'I only meant, you look like someone I met before. Two actually. One was called Dess, and the other, Yra.'

'Oh my, how marvellous. It has been such a long time since I have seen my sisters. How are they? Did they look well?'

'You must be Mo.'

The woman grinned and clapped her hands like a happy child. It was a peculiar sight. 'They spoke of me. I am so happy they have not forgotten their only sister.'

'Only? There's three of... never mind. What's going on? Why do I keep seeing versions of you? How many of you *are* there?'

'We are but only three. Did they not tell you? We are the Fates. Some have accused us of being Architects. I suppose, in a way, they are right. More like cousins, I like to think. Less serious.'

Addan scratched his head. 'What do you want from me?'

'Want? Oh yes. I think I remember. My sisters and I had a discussion about this a long time ago. Before you were born, in fact. I was supposed to say something to you. Ah, yes. You need to go to Dawan.'

'This *is* Dawan. I think.'

'Oh, yes, of course. We agreed Dess would see to that. Good. If you know of Yra too, then I need to... yes, tell you to be brave, ignore those nasty voices in your head. And, yes. To tell you it was not your fault, and you are important in what is about to happen. We knew Sarratenian would return. He *is* tiresome, do you not agree? Anyway, be brave. I have said that already. You will know what you need to do when the time comes. Got it? Good. Well done.'

The words poured from the woman's mouth like a river. Addan struggled to keep up. 'Why me?' His head hurt.

'No idea. We did not choose you. Our purpose is only to guide those who need our direction. The whole world has a path to follow. Fate, see? We exist to ensure everything and everyone stays on that path. Occasionally, we have to nudge people along a little. So, consider yourself nudged.' She punched him in the shoulder.

'Ow!'

'Oh look,' she said. 'What is that over there?'

Addan looked to where Mo pointed. He couldn't see

anything other than the bare rock of the cave. 'There's nothing the—' he turned back to Mo, but she was gone. 'Huh?'

'Hush, be still, you're safe here,' said a voice. A young man with dark hair painted half red crouched beside him.

'What's going on?'

'It was simply a dream,' said the man. 'You are among friends. Liana brought you here, but you developed a fever. I helped heal you.'

'I, uh, I don't understand. Who are you? Where is Liana?'

'She's not far. My name is Eelan.'

Addan leaned forward, still fighting a cough, and looked around. 'I need to find Liana. I need to save her.'

Eelan gently pushed Addan back, preventing him from standing up. 'You need to rest. You need to recover from your ordeal. Please do not worry about Liana. She is quite safe, I assure you. Here, drink this.' He handed Addan a leather pouch.

The water in the pouch was cool, and it soothed his chest as he drank it all, spilling a good amount down him. He was hungry, but he wasn't in any mood to eat, and wasn't sure if he'd manage to keep it down if he tried. Though he felt better, every bruise and scrape on his body called out to him each time he moved, reminding him they were still there, but he couldn't stay sitting down forever. What was he leaning against, anyway? Some sort of rocky spike poking up from the equally stony floor, from what he could tell. There were others like it here and there, and upside down ones on the cave roof. If the cavern was a mouth, then these were the teeth.

Carefully, and in spite of Eelan's protest, Addan dragged himself to his feet, ignoring the spinning sensation and dancing motes of light in his vision. 'Can you take me to Liana, please?'

Eelan finally relented, but not without a few words Addan didn't quite catch. He followed the young man up some steps, cursing each one for the pain they inflicted on his back and legs, through a narrow carved corridor and into the open air.

Addan found a familiarity with his new surroundings. The aesthetic was certainly Dawanii, but there was something different here than in the smaller village he'd seen. Bigger, yes, but that wasn't all, but he couldn't quite work out what. Eelan led the way. It was darker here than anything he'd seen previously. The only light came from small fires on the ends of long sticks planted in the ground here and there. Their orange glow made everything feel warmer than it truly was.

When he saw Liana, on one of the platforms strung between the trees, high above the buildings, he broke. A powerful wave of emotion rushed over him. It was so strong he started to cry and he couldn't do anything to stop it. Every moment, every injury, every thought—both dark and light—hit him all at the same time. And there she was, his friend, watching him as he reached the top of the platform. For one single moment, all the pain melted away as he threw his arms around her, but only for a moment.

'You should still be resting,' said Liana through his shoulder. Addan released his hold. 'You look... dreadful.'

'I feel it, but I couldn't not see you. It's been so long.'

'Don't you remember us finding you? Us trying to stop Sarratenian from attacking?'

Addan tried to think, to remember, but it was nothing but fog and pain. 'No, I don't. I was walking alone, everyone had been killed by these *things*, these creatures.'

'Torn,' said Eelan.

'But after that, I don't remember.' Addan paused. 'Who's Sarratenian?' *Mo had mentioned that name too.*

He listened to Liana as she explained everything to him. She sounded like she'd already told him once, but he'd forgotten it all. He felt bad for that, but it did feel good hearing her voice again.

'I need to tell you something,' he said, once she was done. 'Remember Dess? There's three of them. Dess, Yra—she helped me find my way back to the bridge—and Mo. I saw Mo just now in the cave. I think. It may have been a dream, I'm not sure. Anyway, she said they were Fates, and, it's all very strange. She said they meant us to come here. Something to do with Sarratenian.'

Liana nodded along with his rambling, and then looked to her left as if acknowledging someone invisible. 'I sometimes wonder if we have any free will at all,' she said, glaring at, presumably, the Architect she spoke of. It was hard to tell.

'I see them,' said another young man. He was standing on the edge of the platform behind Liana, looking out across to what looked like a pile of fallen trees. The man looked familiar to Addan, but he couldn't think how.

From their vantage point high above the huts below, they could see out beyond the mass of trees. Large swathes of open land, pocked with holes where those trees once stood, stretched into the darkness. Liana had explained, but to him it seemed fanciful that someone could tear a whole tree from the ground as if it were nothing more than a weed. Yet the evidence before him was undeniable.

Looking over the scarred landscape beyond the wall, a shadow of movement in the distance was coming their way, just as Liana's friend had said. The shadow grew larger, taking form as what little light there was filled in the detail. It *was* the army he had once been a part of, but there was something different about it. It wasn't until they were close enough to see their faces he realised what that difference was—they were all marching in an orderly, disciplined way. They were as one now, and a far cry from the disorganised meandering progress he'd once been a part of. *What's changed?* They now looked like a proper military unit, and that made him feel uneasy.

Roughly fifty paces out, they stopped marching. And then nothing. All the men and women, led by the man he knew as

Shaan simply stood and watched, unmoving. 'What are they doing?'

'I'm have no idea,' said Liana as she scratched her head. She turned away, her attention taken by the one he couldn't see.

'It looks like they are waiting for something, or someone. Maybe for us to attack them first?' said the Dawanii man.

'Uehan, do you see anything ahead?' asked Liana.

Ah, that was his name!

Uehan frowned and shook his head. 'It's unclear. I see them attacking, breaking through the tree line, but it is hard to say *when*.'

Addan huffed a little. 'Then we should attack first. The longer we let them stand there, the more likely it is they attack first and take the advantage.'

'You're right,' said Liana, 'but the decision is not ours.'

'Then whose is it?'

Before anyone answered him, there was the sound of movement from the army. Addan and the others all pivoted to look at the same time. The enemy was separating into three smaller groups. Two of which split away in either direction along the tree barrier and out of sight.

Addan felt almost as broken on the inside as on the outside. Bruised, battered, tortured. How did he have the will to carry on, to keep fighting? That strength *had* to come from somewhere. He looked at the others with him in turn. All of them looked so scared.

'The advantage is lost,' said Uehan. 'Now they have splintered, it will be harder for us.'

Addan found himself in agreement with him. Why haven't they attacked their enemy? He looked across to the other platforms. Large hunks of rock had been piled in several places within easy reach of the Dawanii who stood between them. He was familiar with the rocks, almost a little *too* familiar. Those men and women were ready to defend their home, but they, too, were waiting for something, or *someone*. Who was in charge here?

'Why aren't we doing anything?' Addan said. Not that he was eager to fight, far from it. He'd seen enough bloodshed to last many lifetimes, but the longer they all did nothing, the more nervous he felt.

The middle group of the army marched forward and disappeared behind the makeshift barrier, their only line of defence. The outer leaves of the wall shook. It was time.

30

A MEETING OF MINDS

Liana felt rather unwell as she looked out over the city from where she stood above the strangely shaped Dawanii houses. The wind blew as it always did, and tree branches above her head swayed in the breeze. It was the only movement she could see. The Dawanii were prepared, as well as they could, for what was to come. Now, an anxious calm fell over the city, and they waited.

The enemy on the other side of the hastily built tree wall were just as silent. The only sound was the snapping of wood as they pulled at the defences. *The enemy.* They were *her* people, her subjects. They used to be, at least. Except now, they were about to attack the innocent. For what? There hadn't been a war in almost a thousand years. In a matter of days, the world had turned in on itself and she was frightened of what was to come.

She saw the scared expressions on the faces of those around her. The trembling of a people who had done nothing except accept her as a friend, as one of their own. She felt guilty, like it was all her fault somehow. She had brought this war to their homes, their families. The men with swords on the other side of the wall, she didn't know them. They were not her people anymore. That was not *her* army.

Ember brushed hard against her leg. Liana looked down at her friend. The cinderfox didn't look scared, like she knew everyone else was. Yet the expression in her bronze eyes told Liana she would give her life to protect her, whatever was to come.

'*Why is he doing this? What can he gain from destroying these people's lives? They've done nothing,*' Liana said to Eraidor. The man—the god inside her—stood stoically at her side. He'd been quieter than usual since they returned to the city.

'*He is angry. For what I did to him, and for how the world turned out in his absence.*'

'*So? What gives him the right to do this? Because he's a god? It's not right. Not right at all.*'

'*In the past, for many generations throughout history, there has always been war in one form or another. It is within human nature to fight and to take. To kill and destroy each other, often for minor reasons or none. Until I sent him away as I did, he was always there to encourage that darker side of you all.*'

She turned and looked at him. '*Why? Why is there a god whose only reason for being is to make war? I don't understand.*'

'*No, I would imagine you do not. It is his nature. Although... Although I fear there is another motive at play here. He has chosen this place, specifically.*'

'*Why?*'

Eraidor didn't answer, which frustrated her. What else was being hidden from her? Addan spoke of Dess—the Fates, a name she hadn't heard of before today. *Was this all some grand design?* She asked Eraidor again, why? He wouldn't say.

Liana huffed and turned back to the Dawanii gathered below. There were men and women in equal number, all ready to defend their homes. Most were armed with nothing more than sticks. *They're all going to die,* she thought.

'I have to do something. I have to try and end this before it's too late.'

'I do not see how you can. Sarratenian will not stop until he has what he wants.'

She thought about what she could do other than help them fight. She was no warrior. None of them were, really. Could she kill if it came to it? She didn't know. Yes, she'd killed that gabbalin, but that was through luck rather than judgement.

'I need to speak to my brother,' she mumbled.

'Did you say something?' asked Addan, who was a few paces farther along the gantry, standing next to Eelan. Liana didn't know how many healers they had like Eelan. Whatever the number, they would soon be needed. She didn't answer her friend.

'I need to reach Cal. If I can get him to see reason. Maybe... if I can get him to stop, order the army to go home somehow.'

'I fear Sarratenian has too much influence over him. It may already be too late. You would be wise not to consider him as your brother any longer. Sarratenian has complete control over them all.'

She shook her head. *'I refuse to accept that. Can you take me to him? Make me fly to him like last time?'*

'He would not see you. You would not move from where you are standing. When I took you above the world, it was merely a projection.'

She pointed at Addan. *'He heard me, though. I spoke to him and he answered me. You saw it.'*

'He was close to death, delirious. It was merely a coincidence that he spoke your name when you called out to him in that moment.'

Liana grabbed Addan by the sleeve. 'When you were alone, walking through the wastelands. Did you really hear me?'

Addan frowned. 'I can't remember. Maybe?'

'Think, Addan. It's important. Did you hear me calling you? I was there, and I told you I was coming to save you. Remember?'

He scratched his head. 'Possibly... yes. I think I do remember something.' His expression changed from a look of concentration and deep thought to one of pain. 'It wasn't my fault,' he whispered.

Eelan stepped in. 'He's still not well. I'm trying the best I can for him. He shouldn't be out here. Let me take you back to the cavern where it's safer.'

'No,' insisted Addan. 'I need to be here.' He looked at Liana. 'I'm sorry. I think I heard you, but I can't say for certain if it was real or not.'

Liana smiled at her friend and released his arm. She turned back to look out beyond the tree wall, trying to pick out which one of the figures on the other side was her brother. There— next to one of the strydes. *That's him, I'm certain of it.*

She closed her eyes and tried to focus on him, willing him to hear her. *'Cal. Can you hear me?'*

'You are wasting your time,' said Eraidor. She ignored him.

'Cal. It's me. Liana. Listen to me.'

There was nothing. She opened her eyes, and the man was still standing where he was, not even looking in her direction. A thought entered her mind. She removed her glove and looked at the black scar on her palm. Its tendrils were etched deeper now, and the purple edges were more pronounced. The raw energy of the Origem was eating away at her and it scared her. *Could I use this power somehow?* She took a deep breath in through her nose and focused on the energy trying to consume her. *'I need to speak to him. Take me to my brother.'*

Eraidor raised a hand as if to stop her. *'There is nothing yo—'*

The world spun, and everything around her blurred. When everything settled again and she'd regained her sense of balance, she found herself surrounded by darkness. There was no light at all, yet she could still see herself.

'Hello?' she ventured. She was alone. No Ember, no Addan. *No Eraidor!*

The darkness changed. It grew lighter, and she found herself on a rocky plateau. Everything was grey and there was no wind. She wasn't cold either. In the distance, there was a flash of lightning in the sky, followed by a dull rumble of thunder. She'd not seen a storm in years.

The lightning flashed again, yet there was nothing to see. It was only her, on a plateau in the middle of... nothing.

'Hello?'

'Liana, is that you?' The voice was quiet and distant, coming from behind her.

She turned towards the voice. There was only the darkness. 'Cal? Is that you?'

'Yes, I'm Cal. I've been searching for my sister. Have you seen her?'

Liana edged forward carefully until she saw a shadowy figure ahead of her. Although the darkness obscured his features, she recognised the figure as her brother instantly. She ran closer. Cal was sitting on the lifeless surface of the plateau with his legs tucked under his chin, arms wrapped around them. Another bolt of lightning lit up their surroundings, and she caught a brief glimpse of what looked like hundreds of other people. Silent and unmoving. She was sure they *were* people, but she could be mistaken. Whatever it was she saw was hidden by the gloom that surrounded her and her brother.

'It's me. I'm here, Cal. Wherever here is. I need your help. I need you to call off the army. Don't go to war. These are innocent people, and they're scared.'

'I can't,' said Cal. His words were muffled as he talked into his sleeves.

'You can. If not for them, then do it for me. Tell Sarratenian to stop this madness.' She bent down beside him and lifted his head so he could see her. He looked terrified.

'It's not that I don't want to. I can't. He has control. I trusted him. I let him do this and I can't stop him. I'm sorry.'

The sky lit up around them. Brighter this time, and the lightning felt closer. The low rumble of thunder now crackled in the air. There was still no wind. Another flash, and another. Liana caught a better look at what was around them. They *were* men. There was no doubt now. Hundreds of them, all perfectly still and silent, stood as if they were guarding them both.

'Where are we?' she asked. It was strange not seeing Eraidor standing near her. He'd know what was happening. After all this time, wishing he wasn't forever in her company, wishing that she was free of him. Now he wasn't there, and she wished he was.

Another flash of lightning. Different this time. The thunder boomed right over Liana's head and the gloom of her surroundings stayed bright. It wasn't quiet anymore. The audience surrounding her and Cal were no longer silent. A wall of pure anger and vitriol erupted. The men, once still and lifeless, were now shouting and screaming. For all their noise, she couldn't understand their words.

Liana shook her brother by the shoulders. 'Cal, what is this place? Do you know where we are?'

'You are somewhere you should not be,' said an unfamiliar voice from behind her, clear above the din. Except it wasn't an unfamiliar voice at all. It was Cal. She stood up and spun round.

The man standing in front of her *was* her brother. She turned back to also see him still sitting hunched up on the ground. *There were two of him.* She looked back at the second one. He didn't look frightened. In fact, he looked anything but. This Cal stood tall, confident and imposing. Both wore the same uniform. His looked sharp and clean, contrasting the dishevelled attire of the Cal cowering behind her. Liana did not recognise the man standing before her. He may look like her brother, but it was not him.

'Who are you?' she demanded. 'What is this? What's going on?'

'It is me, Liana. Cal. You should not be here. You need to leave at once.'

'I'm not going anywhere.' She turned back to the Cal she recognised and once again brought herself to his level. 'Cal. You need to stop this attack. Let me help you.' She tried to pull him to his feet. As she did so, the baying crowd of men around her grew louder in protest. They didn't move from where they were standing, which was something. She did feel intimidated by them, though.

'He cannot help you. He is not in control here. I am,' said the one standing.

'Then tell me what it is you want? Why have you come here?'

'I have come to rescue my sister.'

'*I am* your sister!' She marched over to this version of Cal and stared him in the eyes, not more than a step away from him, her fists clenched. He didn't back away or flinch at all.

'Do you not think I know my sister? You are not her. Look at you, with your coloured hair and animal furs. You are a Dawanii imposter.'

'I promise you, I'm not. It's me, Cal. It's really me.'

'Lies.'

Thunder and lightning continued to split the air around her. There was no rain, no snow. This storm that grew ever closer was dry, which made it feel worse to Liana somehow. She didn't know what to do or say.

'The Dawanii,' continued the Cal standing before her, 'must pay for what they have done. I will have my vengeance.'

'Vengeance? For what? It wasn't the Dawanii who murdered our mother. They're good people.'

'I witnessed it with my own eyes,' he spat. 'She welcomed them and they slayed her in cold blood for it.'

'No,' said Liana, fighting to hear herself over all the shouting and the thunder. 'That's not true. It may have looked

400

like it was the Dawanii, but it was Shaan. Sarratenian. He killed her. He admitted it.' Her voice cracked as she spoke.

'I saw it too,' said the broken Cal. 'He's right, it was the Dawanii. You weren't there, Liana. Where were you when we needed you the most?'

Liana turned. *He called me by my name!* A breakthrough. As small and defeated as this version of her brother was, he at least could see through her change of appearance. She went to him. 'Yes, Cal. It's me. Fight this, stop this all from happening. I need you to be strong.' Once again, she tried to pull him to his feet, and again she failed.

She had to try a different approach. Whatever had happened to her brother on the ground, he was in no fit state to fight. It was up to her. She had to take on the version of Cal standing over them. Fight him, if necessary. She reached for the energy to form in her hand only for nothing to come. Nothing at all. She had no weapon here other than her words.

'I am queen now,' she whispered. She stood up straight, as tall as she could make herself and stared him down. 'I am your sister, and I am your queen. You will listen to me, recognise me. I command you to end this.'

Cal laughed and offered a clearly fake bow. 'My sister, who would be heir to the throne, abandoned her city, her people, in their darkest hour. I say she is no queen at all. *My* sister, the one who always refused her duties. *My* sister, the one who preferred the company of commoners. *My sister!* The one who—if she really is standing before me now—has made her bed with the Dawanii savages who murdered the queen? No. She is no heir. She has no claim to the throne or crown. *I* was the one who was always there. *I* was the one who always did my duty, come what may.'

'Oh please!' Liana interrupted. 'You didn't care about the crown. No man has ever worn it, nor have they sat on the throne. All you have been interested in is other men. Anyone who turned your head. And then Shaan arrived at the palace. He had you wrapped around his finger and you fell for it. Well, not I. I see right through him now. This,' she held out her hands showing the army sneering and shouting around them, 'is all his doing. Can't you see that? This isn't you, Cal. He's got inside your head.'

Cal struck her across the face with the back of his hand. 'Lies! Lies of a common whore who thinks herself to be worthy of the crown.'

Liana raised a hand to her cheek. It didn't so much as hurt as surprise her that her own brother would strike her. He'd never done that before. Ever. She knew in that moment that the man standing before her was not the Cal she knew, if it were him at all.

'It's all true, I promise you. If you won't see reason, then it will be down to me to stop you,' she said, backing away out of reach. It still made little sense to her where she was. A strange, violent sky above, a hoard of men surrounding her and two men, each her brother and yet strangers to her. There was no way out. The Cal on the ground refused to move, locked away in his own despair. The other, arrogant, loathing.

'This isn't real,' she muttered to herself. 'It *has* to be a dream of some sort.' If that were the case, she reasoned, then she would need to find a way to wake up. To escape back to the world she knew. There was no other way but through. She picked out one of the soulless, nondescript men that surrounded her, counted to three and ran at him shoulder first. As she was about to make contact, she lowered her head and hoped she had enough strength to barge him out of the way. She hoped momentum would carry her through.

Nothing happened. There was no impact, no crash of her shoulder into the man's chest, or any other part of him. She stumbled forward, right through her target, as if he wasn't there. Forcing herself to stop running, she turned around, only to find herself right where she started. The cowering Cal was still on the ground, the other with his arms folded across his chest, laughing.

'This can't be happening,' she said. 'What is this place?'

'This is not a *place*,' said Cal. He unfolded his arms and walked the perimeter of the men around them. 'This is me. You are in my head, and I think it high time you left. You are not welcome here.' He positioned himself so he was standing over his weaker self and grabbed him by the hair.

'Let go of him,' demanded Liana, taking a step towards them.

'Do you like this pathetic version of me so much, you would defend him?'

'Yes, he is my brother, of course I would.'

'And me? Would you defend me? Am I not also your brother?'

Liana's head hurt. Never had she been made to consider if she would defend her brother, would protect him. Neither of them had ever come close to being threatened with their lives before. Now, as she considered it, there was no question. Yes, she would defend him, with her life if it came to it. But what of this other Cal? Were they both the same man?

'I don't want to fight you,' she said. 'Please, stop this madness and let us go home.'

Cal let his other self go, shoving him to the ground. He snarled. 'Pathetic, both of you. We are coming, Liana. The Dawanii will suffer, and I will be king. If you dare stand in my way, then you will fall with them. Now, get *out!*'

The sky exploded around Liana in a bright white flash, accompanied by the loudest crack of thunder she'd ever heard. It was almost as if she had been struck by lightning directly. She covered her ears with her hands and screamed in pain. And then all the noise stopped. When her sight returned as the light faded, she found herself back on the gantry. She felt dizzy and reached for the nearest rope and missed. She crumpled to the floor, but felt herself caught by the arms of someone.

'Liana, are you all right?' the voice belonged to Eelan.

'Yes,' she said, as she shook off her disorientation. She looked up to see Eelan and the others all standing over her with concerned expressions. Even Ember looked worried for her. 'I'm fine.' She allowed her friends to help her to her feet.

'*What happened?*' said Eraidor.

Liana actually found herself glad to see the Architect standing before her. '*I spoke to Cal. I was inside his mind, I'm sure of it.*'

'*It appears your bond with the Origem is growing stronger. To reach out and touch another in such a way should be far beyond any mortal. Even the Dawanii, with their way of harnessing the power of the Origem, can barely manage more than exchanging thoughts.*'

'*It was the strangest feeling. It was like I was actually there. Inside his mind. Sarratenian, he has control of him, but I saw two of my brother. I don't understand how.*'

'*There is still some strength left within him. He is fighting against Sarratenian's control over him.*'

'*But what does it mean?*'

'*It means,*' said Eraidor, lifting his head a little, '*that hope is not yet lost.*'

31
WAR!

The tree wall seemed to Liana like a mad idea at first, but as the attackers tried to breach the defences, she realised the ingenuity of it. There was no way to scale it, and no way to tear it down without it collapsing on them. Finding a way through the myriad of branches and leaves would take time and would allow anyone making it through vulnerable to being picked off by the Dawanii one at a time. She could hear them on the other side. Not voices, but the snapping of branches and the rustling of leaves as they tried to make their way through. It had crossed her mind if they might try to burn it down, but that would take a long time before even that would make the barrier passable.

'Do you think they will break through?' she asked Uehan.

He nodded. 'I have seen it. We *will* have to fight.'

'Then I want to help. I can't idly watch from up here. I know I am not responsible for this, but I am part of the problem, so I want to be part of the solution. I cannot allow Sarratenian to destroy you all.'

'*You cannot stop a god,*' said Eraidor.

'*There must be a way.*'

405

'I will also stand and fight,' said Addan, stepping forward.

'You are not in any fit state to fight,' said Eelan.

'My wounds are healing and I do not hurt as much. I will fight.'

'I have an idea,' said Liana. 'Uehan has seen that they will breach the wall, so I think we should help them. I need to find Orratan.' Before anyone replied, she pushed past and made her way down to the ground and ran towards the amphitheatre. She hoped he was still in there. Ember ran ahead of her and blocked her path. *No? He's not there? Where?* Ember barked and ran off towards the wall, then veered right towards the second pathway.

Liana found Orratan, with his assistant, talking animatedly with two other men she didn't know. He carried a broken piece of tree branch. *Is that the best weapon he can find?* Much like at the main path, a number of those able to fight were gathering, ready for when the defences were eventually breached.

'We need to break down the wall,' she said in a half-whisper between heavy breaths. Running wasn't something she liked to do often anymore.

Orratan turned to her with a look of dismay. "Break it down? You cannot seriously suggest such a thing."

'Listen to me. Uehan has already foreseen they find a way through. If we stand here and wait for that to happen, then they all come through and we are outnumbered.' She held out her arm, indicating for them to walk away from the wall, making sure nobody on the other side had any chance of hearing them speak.

"What is your proposal?"

'We push.'

"Push? Push what?" Orratan and his companion both looked bemused.

'They're on the other side, climbing, breaking branches, trying to find a way through. All of them, right now. If we push, collapse the wall on *their* side. The weight of the trees will either crush them or trap them. We won't be able to stop them all, but it might be enough to balance the numbers, enough to give us a chance.'

Orratan tapped his lips with a finger. Liana could almost see his mind working through her plan.

'I think it is as good a plan as any. It will not stop Sarratenian himself, though,' said Eraidor.

'We'll get to that part when the time comes. If we can't stop his army first, then we may as well surrender now.'

"I need to discuss this with the others. I cannot make this decision on my own." Orratan stepped away.

'Can we look through the wall? I want to see what is happening.'

'We can, but Sarratenian will see you too.'

'I don't care what he can or can't see.'

'Very well.'

In a blink, the giant hedge swooshed around her and she was on the other side, with Eraidor still standing next to her. She was right. The men and women under Sarratenian's control were slowly and methodically working their way through the branches. Climbing, breaking away smaller sections to open up larger gaps. The trees were so densely stacked, even a rabbit would struggle to find a way through. There wasn't enough room for all the hundreds of soldiers on the wall, indeed most stood stock still awaiting their turn to advance.

Liana turned and looked at Sarratenian, on his stryde at the back of the group. He *did* notice them, she was sure of it, though he did not engage. There was no sense of urgency on his part. If he truly was immortal, then he had all the time in the world.

Behind Sarratenian, Cal sat atop his own stryde. He looked nothing like either version she had seen inside his head, if that was where she truly had been. Instead, she saw the brother she had always known. He looked nervous. Anxious, even. His body language told her everything she needed to know. He didn't want to be there, she was sure of it. Did he really believe she had been abducted? Did he now know the truth as she had spoken it? There was no way to tell. She had to hope that when the time came, she would be able to get through to him. The real him.

'Enough,' she said. 'Take me back.' Liana opened her own eyes and found herself back within the city. Orratan was walking back in her direction.

"We agree," he said. "Toppling the wall in their direction has the best chance of success. We will defend ourselves against however many remain."

Liana felt the pain in her right hand move along her arm. Turning away from Orratan, she removed her glove. The black smudge covered her palm completely now, and the thin tendrils had spread to her fingers and were making their way up her arm. As the edges of the tendrils glowed purple, she felt their energy burrow into her.

Eraidor shook his head. *'You must fight it.'*

'I don't know how.'

'Trust in yourself. The Origem is too powerful for any one person. You must not allow it to consume you. The Origem exists only to give life and meaning to the entire world, not just its inhabitants. To everything beyond the world, too. Rybban is such a tiny piece of everything.'

'Did you create the Origem? I mean the magic, not the seal itself.'

Eraidor shook his head. *'No. The Origem was here long before the Architects. There has been many a discussion among us over the eons about whether the Origem created us also. No one knows for sure. None of us remember a time when we were not... alive, I suppose you would say. It is much the same as you do not remember a time before your own life.'*

'The Origem may be your *god, then.'*

'In a manner of speaking, I suppose you might be right. Either way, using it as a weapon will only cause you harm. Each time

you draw on it willingly, it accelerates the process that consumes you.'

'*Right now, it seems better than being killed in a war.'*

'*It may seem that way, however, I assure you it is not.'*

Preparations were almost complete, with the strength branded Dawanii all co-ordinated along the trees opposite the soldiers position. Liana felt a hand on her shoulder. She turned to see Addan and Uehan. They exchanged glances, silently affirming their readiness for what was to come.

"Stand back," said Orratan.

Anyone who wasn't charged with pushing moved back well out of the way should the wall collapse in the wrong direction. Liana held her breath as she watched the strongest Dawanii push at the trees. Nothing happened at first, but then came the creaking of wood as it gave way to the pressure. One of the trees at the very top disappeared from view followed by a crash on the other side. She expected to hear the enemy scream. Nothing. Only the sound of snapping wood.

One by one the trees fell away. The sound they made was so loud it echoed off the mountain, announcing to the world the attack had begun. Dust and snow spray kicked into the air creating a cloud that obscured Liana's view. At least one tree had fallen inward. She could make out a Dawanii man pinned under a large branch. It was a strange sight to watch him heave it from his chest and throw it aside as though it were nothing. He *was* injured, though, with bright red blood oozing from a gash in his bicep. He didn't seem to notice as he ran back into the cloud of dust and trees.

"Don't run to them. Wait for them to come through to us."

It fell quiet for a moment. The wall had fallen, the trees had stopped moving. For a brief instant Liana held hope they'd defeated them all in one go, but that hope evaporated along with the cloud of debris ahead of her.

The debris cloud settled and through the dust, the shadowy

figures of the survivors emerged from what remained of the wall. At first, there were only a few, but that quickly developed into dozens. How many had died or were trapped? There was no way of knowing. She hoped for many, but already it proved not enough.

The front line of defence tackled the first of the soldiers through the wall. They threw their large rocks and stumps of trees, trying their best to knock them down. There were too many of them—tens of sword-wielding attackers swelled to hundreds too fast. As effective as a flying boulder to the head was at killing, it was too slow a method to prevent them from being overrun. As the army breached the trees, they fanned out in every direction. Liana drew on the energy devouring her hand.

She had no other option. Eraidor protested, as did Orratan once he realised what she was doing. Liana imagined a ball of fire in her hand and hurled it at her nearest target. The young Moranzan soldier evaporated into nothing.

Orratan looked terrified and backed away. Eraidor shook his head in sorrow.

There was no time to think as the silent, crazed hoard charged forward. Liana didn't wish to kill, not if she could help it. The sight of the man being turned to dust horrified even her. She took to attacking the ground at the enemy's feet, to slow them down. It wasn't working. Before she could imagine more energy in her hand, the gap between them had shrunk so much there wasn't any option but to fall back or be struck by the blades of her own people.

Orratan had drifted away to Liana's right as he fought off the first of many swords seeking to kill. He was still only armed with nothing more than his tree branch. It was less an effective offensive weapon, but did an adequate job of keeping him alive —so far, at least.

Addan was the only one to have a sword, but he was not a

swordsman. Liana knew he had a taste for a fight, but that was with his fists and usually after a night of heavy drinking. He was doing the best he could, but had already taken a fresh cut to his right arm while defending himself from two men at once. But to Liana's surprise, it was Uehan who was at the best of it.

In her peripheral vision, Liana watched as her young friend, blind by eye, weaved in and out of the enemy with a club stick in each hand. He anticipated every move, every swing, parry, or lunge. Watching him fight, she understood. He saw more now than he'd ever done before the Branding, she was sure of that. Single-handedly, Uehan was keeping them all alive.

Liana continued to step back while trying to keep close to her group. She didn't want to lose sight of anyone. It was becoming more chaotic with each heartbeat. There was no end to the numbers coming through the defences. *Had none of them died at all?* Her idea had clearly failed, but it wasn't the time to dwell on regrets. She continued to fall back with the others until she felt a jolt through her entire body and stopped.

'What is happening?' she asked Eraidor, who had been standing like a serene island alone in a stormy sea. An observer and not a participant. And then he disappeared. *'Where did you go?'*

'I am still here. You can feel me now—our bond is growing stronger. It is why you no longer feel the pain of the Origem's power when you wield it. I can help slow its progress, for a while, at least, if I wield it with you.'

'I don't like where this is going.' Still fixed to her position, Liana formed a fireball in her hand, except it wasn't her decision to do so. It was *her* body, *her* arm held outstretched, but it was not her will. She could feel Eraidor pulling at her muscles. They tingled as they controlled the bones underneath. She felt herself twist, releasing her ball of energy, her hand now pointing to a blank-faced soldier coming her way. She hadn't seen him until that moment—had Eraidor not

411

turned her, she would surely have been struck down under the enemy sword.

'I thought you said the Architects cannot harm us humans,' she said as she fought against Eraidor to regain control of her legs. She wanted to turn and run. Her companions were already out of sight behind her, except Ember, who remained stubbornly at her side.

'In ordinary circumstance, perhaps, but had I not... intervened, you would have died and I along with you.'

'That's not as comforting as you make it sound.' Liana tried to step backwards, but Eraidor was pulling her to her left. She pushed against him, but it was like moving through mud. *'Let me go!'*

'I cannot. You need to trust me to help you, to ensure we both survive this. Our bond is too great. I can no longer pass another host. If you die, I die.'

Despite his words, Liana pushed with every last bit of strength she could find to regain control of herself. To anyone else paying attention, it would look like she was having some kind of standing seizure. Eventually, in time to jump out of the way of a sword thrusting towards her stomach, she regained control of her limbs. She turned around, scanned the area for her friends and ran to them.

'You should not fight me,' said Eraidor, still invisible to her.

'Then don't try to control me. I am my own person, and I thank you to keep it that way.'

'We must work together.'

'I don't want to work together. I want you gone from me!'

'So you keep saying.'

Liana didn't reply to that. Now was not the time for arguments. She was in control again, and that was all that mattered at this moment.

Despite the efforts of her small group, and the rest of the Dawanii fighting alongside them, they were becoming overwhelmed. Liana couldn't help shake the notion that there appeared to be more enemy fighters than she had seen in formation when she had tried to persuade Sarratenian from attacking in the first place. *Where were they coming from?* For every one they managed to kill, there were two more behind, ready to continue the fight.

There were too many of them and they were too close. She tried imagining more light, as much fire as she could muster. She stared at her hand, willing more energy to her palm, but nothing happened. Eraidor was interfering. She could feel it. *'Release me! We'll both die if I can't make my own decisions.'*

'You have to stop using it now. It is becoming too much for you to endure, even with my help. I can feel it tearing you apart.'

'I have to! I need to use it.' She could feel the Origem calling to her, but knew he was right. She was no good to these people dead. *I need another option.*

A young-looking soldier made a lunge for her and would have been successful if Ember hadn't intervened. Her faithful protector pounced forward, tearing at the man's throat, yet he did not scream or cry as he took his final breath. Liana saw an opportunity and rolled forward and snatched the blade from the dead man's hand as he hit the ground.

The sword was light, and the hilt felt cold as she wrapped her fingers around the hilt. The blade itself was bent slightly near the middle as a testament to its poor, cheap craftsmanship. It was better than nothing. The tip proved still sharp as she buried it into the stomach of yet another soldier, slicing through the flesh with surprising ease. She winced as the man fell to the ground, dead. As she stepped back, she was slammed sideways, sending her to the ground shoulder first. It was Addan—he'd pushed her out of the way of an attack she hadn't seen. Addan dodged the sword and punched the soldier in the face, square on the nose, before wrestling the blade away and turning it on its former owner.

Still, they had to fall back. Addan helped Liana to her feet. There was no choice left but to run. The Branded Dawanii were fighting valiantly, but they were outnumbered and brute strength was not enough to prevail over the sheer number of enemy soldiers flooding through the defences.

'What do we do?' shouted Liana to no one specific. There wasn't a reply. All were too busy trying to keep themselves alive as best they could.

'What do we do?' she shouted again as she tried to block another sword swinging her way. Her defence wasn't successful enough to prevent a cut to her arm. She yelped as the pain ran up to her shoulder.

'Run! We run!' Uehan replied.

It was the only thing they *could* do now, and Liana wasn't going to argue. Run where, though? If they sought refuge in the cave under the mountain, that would only lead the invaders directly to the most vulnerable of the city-folk. There wasn't really anywhere to hide, not that hiding would do any good. They still needed to defend the city—somehow. 'Up the mountain?' she suggested. There was no confidence in her voice. Her last suggestion, which was adopted, turned out to be less than successful.

"Yes," said Orratan through his assistant. "We will then at least have the high ground."

There was only the one path leading up the side of the mountain, with many dwellings scattered along the way. They should all be unoccupied by now, but Liana hadn't seen Nalla since before the attack started. She had to hope the old woman was safe somewhere else.

The five of them, Uehan, Eelan, Addan, Liana, and Orratan, with his assistant, and of course, Ember, scrambled along the path behind the cover of the Branded who were doing their best to hold back the silent enemy. Liana guessed there were fewer than half of them left now. Bodies of both sides were growing in number, scattered in the snow and dirt.

Liana looked back towards the wall, the view of the city improving the higher they went. The soldiers were still pushing their way through the trees. No sign of Sarratenian though. Only the hoard of people who not so long ago were her mother's subjects—her subjects, now. She was their queen, but she felt like nothing of the sort. All her life she'd shunned the idea that one day she would rule over all of Moranza, and now that time had come, she wanted it even less. As she ascended the mountain, she felt so far removed from her old life she wondered if there were any way back at all.

Above them came the sound of falling stone, crashing against the rock face. They all looked up at the same time. Liana cowered as debris and small pieces of rubble rained down on them. A cloud of dust spilling out from high above obscured where the fall originated, but Liana had a sinking feeling something wasn't right.

'Dragons!' shouted Eelan, pointing at a dark, pulsating cloud way above them.

'What?' said Addan.

'Dragons,' said Liana. Their appearance couldn't have come at a worse time. She had seen them off once, and her first thought was to raise her hand and try to fend them off a second time, but she paused. She turned to Orratan. 'I can try to scare them away again,' she held out her hand, exposing the black and purple scar tracing along her skin, ready to summon more energy.

"I can't stop you. You know the dangers of the Origem's power and yet you wield it anyway."

'What choice do I have?'

Orratan shook his head. "Do what you must." He turned away from her, returning his focus to the onslaught below, and

415

taking cover behind whatever he could find as he made his way farther up the mountainside with the others.

Despite Eraidor's protests and Orratan's warning, Liana imagined a ball of light, ready to throw it at the swarm above her. It looked different this time, unlike any swarm she had seen before, either here or back home. It had definition, a shape, like when you look at clouds as they roll through the sky and see a face. They hadn't attacked—yet; there were no shards of ice raining down upon them. This constantly moving formation seemed like it was observing them.

As Liana readied the energy in her hand, Eraidor spoke. *'There is another way.'*

She could feel him pulling against her harder again. It was a constant battle of her own now. The fight for control over her own actions. *'What other way?'*

'Speak to them. Ask for their help.'

Liana let slip a single 'ha,' at the notion. She dismissed the light in her hands.

'Why not? You already understand the strength of the bond between you and Ember. Who is to say the dragons are any different?'

Ember looked up at Liana, as if to say, 'I can hear you both.'

'And say what to them? Please don't attack us, by the way, I'm sorry for nearly killing you the last time we met?' Liana looked down as Ember pawed at her knee. Eraidor was right—the bond between them was unlike anything she'd felt before. She'd assumed it was because of her current situation with Eraidor. After all, they had both come to her at the same time. But what if it was more? What if Ember had nothing to do with Eraidor? It was worth a try. *How, though?*

She could feel Eraidor trying to pull her farther up the mountain path. He wanted her to get closer to the dragons. She followed the path with her eyes as it snaked up the mountain, zig-zagging through the sharp lines of the rock. The path seemed to stop some way short of where the dragons were gathering. Would that be close enough? It was worth a try, so she broke into a run. She pushed past Uehan and Orratan and made her way upwards. Every time the path turned back in the opposite direction, she glanced downward. The army was overwhelming the base of the mountain. Many the Dawanii still alive were now trapped at different points along the mountainside. There was no way back down now. The Branded were doing their best to slow down the enemy's progress, but the advantage of the high ground wouldn't be enough. Liana pressed on upwards until the pathway ran out.

She was close enough to make out individual dragons as they flew through the air, creating patches of dark and shadow. In a way, it looked beautiful, and she wondered how they knew where to turn without hitting one another. The sight was mesmerising and frightening at the same time as the cloud of dragons pulsed in and out of itself. One minute it looked like a blotch of nothing in the sky, and then the next it looked almost like its own being with legs and a head. It was as if it were trying to pull itself into a new shape. She couldn't tell what exactly, though there was definitely a tail.

The wind was stronger at the end of the path, whipping her hair across her eyes. She no longer felt the cold, though. Ember, of course, was less than two paces behind her. The cinderfox howled at the dragons. It wasn't aggressive, more of a "hello, we're here."

The pulsating cloud moved closer to her. It looked like an inverted teardrop for a moment before a tail formed from the pointed end, along with two wings that stretched out either side. Thousands of tiny dragons, each capable of injury and destruction, coalesced into one single giant of a dragon. A perfect replica of their smaller selves. Liana could still see each individual dragon, but overall, the beast they had become looked more like a shadow in the sky. It was magnificent!

The huge dragon-shaped swarm hung in the sky at the edge of the mountain, flapping impossible wings as Liana held out her arm to it. She didn't know why she did that, but it felt right somehow, like trying to coax a bird to feed from your hand. The creature looked at her through the eyes of hundreds as if appraising her.

'Talk to her,' said Eraidor.

'How do you know it's a her? There's thousands of them.'

'She is a phalanx—one that is made of many, and that many is female. Can you not tell? I can tell.'

'If you say so.' Liana looked up at the dragon and whispered. 'I mean you no harm.'

The phalanx didn't react except for a change in expression. This form, created from countless miniature versions of itself, didn't have eyes as such. Yet there was a distinct narrowing of the ridges around where the eyes should be. It was a curious sight to behold, both hypnotic and dangerous at the same time.

Liana glanced down at the chaos below. The army was making steady progress up the mountain. Time was running out and there was nowhere else to go. Her only hope was in the air before her. 'We need your help,' she said, looking back at the phalanx, her arm still aloft.

The phalanx didn't reply, though she didn't really expect it to speak. Ember didn't talk either, but her connection to the cinderfox meant there was a form of communication and understanding between them that was more than simply a pet understanding simple verbal commands.

'Can you feel that?' said Eraidor.

She almost said no, but there *was* something. It wasn't words or language at all. What she felt from the beast was akin to an emotion. A single thought appeared in her mind.

HURT

To Liana, it was as clear as if someone spoke actual words to her. The feeling of guilt within her was immediate. 'I'm sorry for hurting you.'

QUESTION

She thought for a moment. Did the phalanx mean, "why?" 'You were attacking the city and its people.'

FRUSTRATION

'I don't understand what you are trying to tell me.'

FEAR

'Yes. The Dawanii were very afraid. I thought I was helping to defend them from you.'

NO

US

To Liana the words felt like two independent thoughts, not just the one. She didn't understand at first. She cocked her head. 'You are afraid of the Dawanii?'

YES

'Why?'

DEATH

Liana spoke to Eraidor. *'Do you understand what they—she— is trying to say?'*

'I believe she is trying to say these Dawanii are a threat to the dragons in some way.'

TRUTH

In her time in the city, Liana had not heard anything about anyone attacking the dragons first in any way. As she thought about it, she realised there had been very little talk about the dragons at all. Not even in the aftermath of the attack she herself had witnessed. The sound of voices below reminded her this was not the right time for these questions.

'Will you help us? You can see the city is under attack. We have no way of defeating Sarratenian without your help. Everyone will die.'

NO

Liana clenched her fists. 'Please! Whatever trouble there has been between you and the Dawanii, I will try to help resolve. I need your help first. There is no need for everyone to die.'

No thought presented itself this time. There was nothing. Then, the phalanx pulled back its head and roared so loud Liana staggered backwards. It wasn't the roar of a single voice. Every small part of the whole cried out at once, the sound reverberating off the mountain face. Behind her, Addan was calling her name, barely audible above the chorus.

The phalanx cried out a second time, and before she had time to react, the form of the dragon shattered into a murmuration of thousands and enveloped her. She spun around in time to see Addan as he called to her. All of her surroundings became a blur as swathes of tiny blue dragons whirled around her. She could barely make out her friend running towards her, reaching out, but there was nothing he could do. And then the ground fell away.

32
ON THE EDGE

For the first time since he made the drunken decision to volunteer for the army, Addan wanted to fight. The Dawanii weren't his enemy, and he had known that ever since that brutal slaughter of an innocent village. Now, he stood alongside them, ready to put his life on the line for them. He wondered if they would still stand beside him if they knew what he had been a part of. None had died at his hands, but he was as guilty as any of those who were pushing their way through that wall of trees.

He recognised many of their faces. He caught a glimpse of the shaven-haired man he'd fought cresting the wall, but it wasn't the same man. None of them were. There was no life within them, and Addan couldn't comprehend why. They were always such a noisy, vocal group, but now they attacked in total silence. The only human sound was from the Dawanii, and more often than not, those voices were of fear and pain as they fought and died.

Liana had given him the sword she'd plucked from the dead hand of a Moranzan soldier. He'd lost his own sword at some point along the way, probably during the attack from those

421

terrifying half men, half—something creatures. The sword had a bend in the middle, but it was better than trying to fight his former comrades off with only his bare hands. They were losing the battle, though. He could feel it. Outnumbered, outmatched, the Dawanii were being forced back towards the mountain.

Addan kept close to Liana, not wanting to let her out of his sight a second time. She seemed different now, more assured, hardened. Occasionally she shouted at the other nearby Dawanii, other times it seemed she was talking only to herself. And the cinderfox—that curious creature who never left her side, but leapt to her defence any time she was under threat. He wondered if it was the same one that saved both their lives from the direwolf. That felt like such a long time ago now.

'Dragons!' one of the Dawanii in their little group shouted. Addan's mouth had fallen open when he looked up at the largest swarm of dragons he'd ever seen high above them.

Liana bolted away along the path, leaving him behind. He tried to run after her, but the old man grabbed him by the elbow to stop him. For someone so old and small, he was surprisingly strong.

"Let her go." The woman with the old man did the talking —yet another thing Addan had trouble getting his head around.

'What is she doing?'

"I am uncertain, except, I think, she is doing what she thinks is right."

Addan jumped in surprise as a small rock smashed into pieces at his feet. It had come from below. He looked down to see his old army counterparts were now themselves throwing whatever they could find at them, their swords almost useless as the Dawanii climbed out of reach. Their projectiles weren't much of a threat, though they did force their targets to take cover behind whatever they could find. One of the Dawanii men took a rock to the head, causing him to bleed. Addan raised an eyebrow when the man barely flinched and continued on as though nothing had happened. What he wouldn't give to not feel pain at all right now.

The image of the girl who pleaded for him to save her haunted him still, as did the agony of losing and burying his young friend. Eelan had done something to help lift that dark veil that engulfed him. Although his pain was still there, deep down, his will to stand and fight had returned. For how long, he didn't know.

How close to death had he come? There were several occasions along the way now when he would have gladly allowed Aelene to take him on a new journey. Thanks to these people, she would have to wait for another day. Despite the terror and destruction below, he resolved himself to survive. No, not only survive—to live.

Addan turned his attention back to Liana, who was now well above them. She had stopped and it looked as though she could go no farther. The swarm had morphed into something different. Something new. He rubbed his face with his hands, unsure of what he saw. Hundreds, or maybe even thousands, of minute beasts had become one giant dragon hovering in the sky. A pair of huge wings flapped as if holding it in place, and a long tail hung below, flicking at the rocky surface of the mountain. This new creature, made of a thousand more, stared at Liana. There were no eyes as such, merely a suggestion of anger on a face that didn't seem real. Liana held out a hand to it. *What was she doing?*

The beast was large enough to make a small meal of her, yet she was reaching out to it with her arm as if she were offering to feed a stryde. Addan felt the urge to get closer to her. He pushed past the old man. He wouldn't be stopped this time. He weaved his way through the other Dawanii, who were mostly paralysed with fear. A dragon above and an army below, they were trapped with nowhere to go. The path wound around corners, making it difficult for Addan to keep Liana in his sight. He hoped he could get to her in time. In time for what? And what could he do once he reached her? That was something he would have to figure out once he made it.

He turned the final corner and as Liana came into view, there was an ear-splitting scream, low in pitch and angry. It was unlike anything he'd heard before. A thousand tiny dragon voices all screaming at once, so loud maybe the whole world would hear it. From where he was, he couldn't see the dragon, except for the shadow of a tail flicking against the moonlit sky. Liana was still reaching outwards. He ran to her and shouted her name. Liana dropped her arm and turned. She looked surprised to see him.

The amplified scream came a second time, somehow more frightening than the first. Addan gulped as the dragon's head appeared behind Liana. It looked so real, yet as if an illusion at the same time. Its features—the eyes, mouth, nose—were so abstract. A mere suggestion of what a dragon should be when made up of countless tiny versions of itself. Was this one dragon, or many? Both and yet somehow neither. 'Liana, watch out!' he called as he pulled himself to a stop, skidding on the loose shingle of the path.

Before Liana could react, the dragon burst into thousands and enveloped her completely, and then she was gone, the dragons retreating. Addan rushed forward as close as he dared to the edge without falling off himself. Neither Liana nor the dragons were anywhere in sight. He collapsed backwards to the ground under a wave of emotion that wanted to suffocate him. After all he had endured to save her, after all the distance travelled, it was for nothing. She was gone. The air fell silent except for the sound of his own heart as it tore apart inside him, beat by beat. He could barely breathe, but didn't care. Images of Liana flashed before his eyes, of the time they first met. She'd saved his life that day, not that she knew. The grief over his brother's death had been too much for him to bear alone. He saw their first adventure together hunting for dune rats near the Eastern Plains, and the moment he fell in love with her when one ran up his leg, making him scream. Oh how she laughed! That beautiful, beautiful laugh. Liana's face blurred and faded, only for Addan to see the girl again.

'You couldn't save her, either. Everyone you touch, everyone you love, dies because of you. I died because of you,' sneered the girl.

'Stop it! Just stop it! Go away! I tried to save you all, I really tried and I couldn't...'

'What is the point of you carrying on? You are no use to anyone. Why not join us? Come and fly with us.'

Addan's vision darkened around the images of Liana, the girl, his brother, and now Milo too. Their words, their suffering, their deaths, all taunting him, haunting his mind. He pulled himself on to his knees and crawled forward towards the edge. *Why not end it here? They're right, they're all right. They all died because of me.* His palms rested on the very edge of the path. Small stones and grit gave way under the pressure, spilling out over the side to the ground below.

'Close your eyes now, Addan. Close your eyes, it's time to sleep,' whispered the voices in his head. He shifted his weight and pulled his hands up from the ground, ready to let go of it all, but as he took in a final breath, something caught his eye in the distance. Addan hesitated, the air still held inside his lungs, and the darkness in his mind lifting enough to keep him from letting go. Hope. Something in the near distance moved across the sky. Addan squinted, fighting the voices from his mind as he concentrated on what he could see. Wings. He could see wings! It was the dragon, he was sure of it—and it was heading his way. He watched it fly closer, his breath still held. And there she was, clinging to the back of the mass of dragons that had become one single creature. She's alive! As he punched the sky, releasing the air from his lungs, the ground beneath him gave way.

No! I want to live! Addan scrambled backwards as the dirt beneath him slipped away. *This is it, isn't it? This is the end. I'm sorry, Liana.* As he felt his weight fall forward, something lurched him backward, pulling him away from the edge, to safety. He fell onto his back, hitting his head on the ground. Looking down at him was Eelan and the old man. Addan panted as the realisation hit him he wasn't about to die. His heart was racing and his limbs were shaking as he was helped to his feet.

'It's all right, friend, we've got you,' said Eelan reassuringly.

'And the dragon has Liana,' replied Addan.

33

TAKE FLIGHT

The sudden speed of movement through the air made her feel sick. Her stomach felt as though it was fighting to escape through her mouth. The cold air rushed by her faster than in any storm, making her vision blurry and her face sore. All around her, in every direction, were dragons. They were falling with her—except—she wasn't falling. She was flying.

'Put me down!' she demanded, flailing her arms at the dragons zipping around her. She couldn't reach any one of them. There was enough space between the creatures to see the ground rushing up towards her. She gasped in fright and the air burned her lungs. Then they changed direction. Left first, then up into a spiral.

'This isn't right!' she shouted. 'I'm sorry for hurting you. I didn't know any better. Don't do this, please!' She didn't know if they could hear her breathless pleas or were ignoring her. The sickening feeling faded, but only because it felt like she was about to lose consciousness. She was already losing the feeling in her arms and legs.

CONSIDER

Consider? Did that mean they were thinking about helping

her, or whether to kill her? She tried to keep her eyes open, to keep herself awake. Pleading wasn't working, that much was obvious. In a last ditch effort before she passed out, she stiffened her body. Drawing on the last of her strength, she closed her eyes and projected her thoughts onto the dragons. *'You will help me.'* It was a demand, not a request. The dragons screeched and roared around her. This time, she *was* falling. She had been released from the swarm and was now in freefall. Her back was to the ground and as she flailed freely in the sky, she watched the pulsing cloud of dragons grow smaller as she fell away.

'I'm sorry,' she said to Eraidor.

'Do not give in. If you want us to live—fight!'

Liana sucked in what might be her final breath and projected as loudly and as forcefully as she could muster. 'YOU WILL NOT LET US DIE!'

It seemed to take forever for the ground to meet her. How high had these dragons taken her? She closed her eyes, ready to meet her end. Something broke her fall. Opening her eyes again, she found herself between the steady beating wings of the phalanx. Fully formed and solid. She pulled herself onto her stomach and clung on any way she could. The swarm of tiny dragons had all interlaced with one another. No longer separate, they were as one. Solid. Each individual creature was now like its own scale covering the whole that was meant to be. The soft blue colouring shimmered in the moonlight, almost metallic.

A burst of energy rushed through her veins as she realised she would live, and the pull of unconsciousness faded away with every flap of this new dragon's wings.

OBEY

Liana couldn't help but laugh. A laugh of nervous relief. She looked around to get her bearings. *The mountain must be behind us.* She didn't dare to turn around to check in case she fell off. Keeping hold of the phalanx was difficult, and she wished for some kind of saddle like a stryde would wear. All she could do was dig her heels in, hoping it wasn't hurting the animal. There was no indication either way.

The phalanx arced through the sky, turning back towards the city. Liana still couldn't see the mountain—until she looked down. They were so high above its peaks. It all looked so small. The whole of Trennale barely occupied one side of the mountain, and all else nothing but trees. Looking farther west lay the edges of darkness, far beyond the point where it was too cold to survive.

HOME

Liana felt as though the word was more than a statement. 'You want to go home?'

YES

'Where?'

BETWEEN

Between what? Liana didn't understand.

OUTSIDE

The emotion felt more insistent as they circled the mountain. An image flashed through her mind, as if a memory was being pushed through. It was indistinct, and not much more than a swirl of red light and random shapes. It reminded her of the dragons from back home; the ones that created fire. The ones she knew and feared so much. Did the answer lie with them? Her thought was interrupted.

ABOMINATION

'What is? Tell me, I don't know what you are trying to tell me.'

RED NOT OF US

She shook her head in frustration. Answers would have to wait. She needed the phalanx's assistance here and now. 'I promise I will help you, though not until we are safe first.' Liana pulled at the dragon-shaped scales with her right hand, urging a change in direction back towards the city. Beneath her, she felt the phalanx's torso swell before it belched out a ball of liquid that quickly solidified into ice. She watched it fly through the air towards the base of the mountain where the Moranzan soldiers were still attacking. She was still too high in the sky to make out individual people, but the ice shard looked to be headed right for a large group of attackers. As the phalanx glided lower, past the mountain peaks, the projectile slammed into the ground. Around the impact, everything crackled as the ice consumed it before shattering in an explosion of its own. Tiny-looking bodies scattered in all directions, blown from the centre of the blast.

Liana felt a sudden sense of unease at the apparent success of the assault. They *were* her people, after all. She watched as those outside the reach of the icy explosion continued to advance without reaction. *This isn't the way,* she thought. They were all under Sarratenian's control, and she knew he needed to be their focus. She needed to find him.

'Can you see him?' she asked Eraidor.

'No, though I expect we will find him outside the boundary. You will notice he does not participate directly in the harm of mortals. Such as it is forbidden for us to do so, though there is nothing to prevent the manipulation of humans from inflicting harm on themselves.'

Although that notion was of little comfort to Liana, the outcome was the same—too many people were dying today, and she had to stop it. The phalanx veered to the right towards the uprooted trees as if it had heard Eraidor. The beast flew lower and roared at the people fighting hand to hand on the ground. The only ones in fear of the phalanx were the Dawanii. The Moranzans barely noticed its presence.

Soldiers were still breaking through the wall in an endless procession. There was no one left on the ground to defend the city, having all fallen back towards the mountain, so they swarmed the city unabated.

'Can you do something to stop them from getting through the wall?' she asked the phalanx as they swept over the tops of the taller buildings.

PREVENT

The phalanx arced round until it was flying parallel to the makeshift wall and spat out glob after glob of liquid at the upturned trees rapidly. Unlike the singular balls of water demonstrated thus far, these did not freeze instantly. They were still liquid as they hit the branches at regular intervals, each exploding in a cascade of icy rain. That rain solidified on the trees until it closed all the gaps between the leaves and branches, making it wholly impassable. Some of the soldiers became trapped in the ice, half their bodies protruding, flailing, as they found themselves captured in a frozen prison. None of those already through the wall turned back to help.

Liana was impressed by the ingenuity. She feared it wouldn't hold them for long, but it was something, at least. She asked the phalanx to crest over the boundary. It was time to find Sarratenian and put a stop to it all. The phalanx rose upwards over the tree line, revealing the pock-marked ground on the other side and there he was—standing in the centre of the clearing as an observer to his own will. Her brother was alongside him. 'Hang in there, Cal,' she said as they swung around back towards the city.

Sarratenian looked up at them as they circled above him, but otherwise didn't react. Liana thought she saw a smile, but it may have been a trick of the moonlight. She commanded the phalanx to attack him, an easy target there by himself. It seemed *too* easy. The creature complied, heaving her chest and spitting out an icy ball, perfectly aimed at the rogue god below. The ice slammed into the ground exactly where he stood, erupting in a spray of snow and tiny shards of glassed water. Liana slapped the phalanx in celebration for a shot well made, but her joy melted into despair as the misty debris cleared to reveal Sarratenian still standing exactly where he'd been and completely unharmed. Not even Cal reacted to the explosion, he too unscathed.

In a flash of anger and frustration, Liana clenched her legs tight on the phalanx's body and let go with her hand to imagine her light. She pulled back her arm and threw a ball of energy at Sarratenian, followed by another and another. All three vaporised as they hit an invisible barrier before they reached Sarratenian. He didn't even step out of the way.

'Set me down,' demanded Liana. The phalanx complied, descending from the sky until she was low enough for Liana to jump off, landing on her feet in the snow. The phalanx continued on, flying back above them, but staying overhead, circling, waiting.

'I demand you stop this now!' she shouted while keeping a good distance away from Sarratenian.

The Architect turned to face her. 'Demand? Who do you think you are to speak to a god in that manner? You do not have the right to demand anything from me.'

'It's not just me. I have Eraidor within me and he demands it too.'

'Ah yes, my old brother, my friend and foe, the Architect of the People. The one you humans all revere so... enthusiastically. It is a rather unfortunate position he finds himself in now, though, is it not? Trapped inside the body of a mortal. It is curious that you know of his presence, but there was always something about you. You were the reason why I came to the palace to begin with. Of course, I was rebuffed. So strong-willed, but your brother was less of a struggle to manipulate.'

Liana imagined more light energy into her hand.

Sarratenian laughed. 'The Origem is a great power, yet you wield it so clumsily. There is potential, though. Yes, there is. I saw it within you. Tell me, why did you persist with toying with magic even when the pain of it told you to stop? Almost everyone stops. Almost.'

Liana opened her mouth to answer, but paused. Why *didn't* she leave magic alone, like everyone else? 'I don't know.'

'Of course not. I could have taught you, if you had let me. But you disliked me so, not at first, not *quite* from the beginning. I suppose your connection to the Origem stopped you in some way, subconsciously perhaps.'

'What is it you want? Is it me? You said yourself when you came to the palace, your interest was with me before it was Cal.'

'You think too highly yourself. It is most unbecoming. You are nothing special, merely a means to an end.'

'What end?'

'To right the wrongs of the past. Not *my* wrongs, but yours, your people's wrongs. Imagine my despair when I found myself here after almost a millennium and nothing had changed. What progress have you all made in these last thousand years? I will tell you—none. The world is almost exactly as it was when I left. I should have been here, to push you all forward. To grow, to flourish. That is *my* role in the world. You think me evil, but nothing is further from the truth.'

Liana turned to the wall. There were, by her approximation, a hundred soldiers left on this side of the ice, maybe a few more. Silently, they chipped away at the icy barrier, trying to find a way through. 'And what about them? How can you claim not to be evil if you force them to kill, to allow innocent people to die?'

'Innocent? Hardly. Most of them were lifted from prison, and the rest from poverty. I have given purpose to their miserable lives. It is for the greater good. Humanity has stagnated in my absence and I will change all that. Once I have what is hidden here, I will set right the world for the good of you all.'

'*Can't you do anything, say anything to stop him?*' Liana asked Eraidor.

'Ah, yes,' said Sarratenian, breaking away from where he

stood. He slowly and deliberately stepped towards them. 'My dear brother. I am sure he would wish to stop me, to fight against me. We have fought for eons over many things. But you cannot, can you? Here you are, trapped inside this girl, fated to only but watch. Are you not bored yet, brother dear? How many lives have you lived in since I have been away? Fifty? A hundred? What terrors, what banality have you witnessed?'

Liana could feel an anger bubbling up within her that was not her own. And then she spoke, but the words were not hers. 'I have witnessed many things, yes that is true. I have learned so much about my beloved creations. In spite of their flaws, for which there are many, they have the capacity for love, for kindness, for growth. You say nothing has changed. You are wrong.'

It was an uncanny feeling, and Liana didn't like it. She circled slowly in a mirror to Sarratenian, but it was not her intention. *'What are you doing?'*

'What I must. I apologise, but you must feel us becoming one. You cannot stop him on your own. Only I have the power to end this.'

Liana fought back, pushing against Eraidor, but he was growing stronger and it was near impossible to regain control of her own body. She was feeling what he felt, his thoughts overlapping hers. Her heart raced as fear welled up inside her. She felt trapped, a prisoner of her own self.

Sarratenian laughed. 'Look at you both struggle so. She is a strong one, no? I saw that in her the first time we met. I am not at all surprised she turned out to be the one who broke the barrier to know you were there. Tell me, will she work out the secret to your freedom, do you think? No? You know, I think she might, given enough time. Time you do not have.'

'Why can't you tell me? I can't carry on like this,' she said. Her strength was waning with the near-constant fighting over her own ambulation. For a moment, she regained control of her legs and forced them to stop. She felt no malice or ill-intent

from Eraidor, only a sense of righteousness, a will to stop his brother, and there was no relent from him.

'He cannot,' said Sarratenian. 'I could, but I will not. If you knew the secret, then it would be impossible for you to... extricate yourself. I care not for you, Liana, but my brother deserves that you try. No. It is far more fun to watch, it really is. Are you are clever enough to discover the answer alone?'

Liana felt her scarred hand twitch. It felt hot, yet it did not burn. Eraidor raised her hand in a quick, smooth motion and flicked her wrist towards Sarratenian. A bolt of pure white lightning exploded from her palm, missing Sarratenian's head by no more than a finger.

Sarratenian's expression changed from one of glee to annoyance. 'Now, now, play nicely.'

'*What was that?*' demanded Liana.

'*The Origem is capable of so much more than you would dare imagine. The pain you feel when drawing from the Origem is its own way of preventing the abuse of that power. I can unburden you from that pain. I feared the Origem would consume you. As I become more of a part of you, I see that I can protect you. Through me we can defeat him.*'

'Stop it,' she said out loud. 'I didn't ask for this and I don't want to be a part of this. I forbid you to use me in this way.'

Sarratenian laughed again. 'Oh, poor little Liana. The one who sought adventure, and the one who denies her responsibilities. You never could play nicely with others, could you? Not even your own brother.' He turned to Cal, who was still upon his stryde, watching on in silence. 'Tell me, have you always been so self-centred? Is a sacrifice for the greater good beyond you?' He continued his wide circular walk, keeping opposite Liana like the slowest of all dances. 'That being said, had you been more responsible and listened to your mother and stayed like a good little princess, you would have died alongside her. That was the plan. Still, it all worked out in the end.'

Liana wanted to scream, but no sound came from her mouth. She wanted to fall to her knees, but her body was not her own and Eraidor wouldn't allow it. Inside her mind she felt a prisoner crying out into a void of nothing.

'Breathe,' said Eraidor. 'You will be no use to either of us if you lose consciousness.'

Liana forced the words out between laboured breaths. 'How, though? Architects cannot kill. Eraidor said...'

'Is that what he told you? We have rules, yes. Although, what are rules if they cannot be broken? We cannot force you humans to do anything against your own nature. But, should we so desire, and I so, so desire very much, we can manipulate those suppressed and hidden, how should I put it? Proclivities, yes, that will do.

'I cannot make a man kill another if he refuses to do so, but if that man wanted to murder, then he could be... encouraged. And that was all I did. A thousand years may have passed since your two lands were one, true. That does not mean there is not some latent animosity deep within.'

'Why?' Tears were running down Liana's cheeks. 'If you wanted us dead, surely there must have been less elaborate ways?'

'Oh, thousands of them. Few that would provoke a war, and war was necessary to find what I need to restore the world to what it should have been. The smell of blood and battle. Beautiful, do you not think so? You would have gone to war for your brother, wouldn't you? He was not so keen. So he needed an extra incentive. Strange though, that on the very day I was to have you killed, you decide to leave of your own volition. Very strange indeed. No matter, we are all here now. One big family, reunited.' Sarratenian looked at Cal and gave a bow. Cal offered a thin smile in return.

'This isn't a war,' said Liana. 'This is slaughter. The Dawanii are peaceful people and aren't any threat. My people too. We didn't want war either.'

'Encouragement, Liana. None of these people would be here if they truly did not want to fight. Remember that.'

'The Dawanii most certainly don't want to fight. They're completely innocent in all this. They don't even have any weapons.'

'Innocent? Hardly. How much do you really know about these people you have become so fond of?'

'Well enough.'

Sarratenian pointed to the sky. 'Ask them about your pet up there. You will see they are not all they make themselves out to be.'

ASSISTANCE

Liana looked up at the phalanx and took the thought as an offer of help. 'Yes,' she said.

The phalanx immediately turned nose down with her wings outstretched and dived towards the ground. She screamed, then heaved her belly before spitting out a stream of ice directed at Sarratenian.

Liana pulled herself back out of harm's way. She didn't have to fight with Eraidor this time—he was more than willing to do the same. It was a new feeling, her and Eraidor working together. If she fought against him, it felt like wading through mud all the way up to her neck. If Eraidor simply allowed her to do as she normally would, it was no different than if he wasn't there at all. With both of them pushing to achieve the same aim, that felt more... powerful.

Snow kicked into the air as the ice projectiles slammed into the ground, making it difficult for anyone to see. Liana lost sight of Sarratenian. She could feel Eraidor trying to use her power again. This time, instead of protesting, she leaned into it and moved as one with him. She could feel what he was feeling, thinking what he was thinking, and it all made sense. There was a pure energy flowing through her, and she knew what she had to do.

He was ahead of her. She could see through the snow cloud, her vision now stronger, as though she was seeing through two pairs of eyes. She knew what Eraidor wanted her to do and without thought or premeditation, she threw out her hands creating a bolt of energy in Sarratenian's direction. It was hard to tell if it struck the god, but it did hit *something*, sending a cascade of sparks into the air in all directions.

She ran forward, spurred on by Eraidor, unsure if she was moving her legs or he was. It didn't matter. All she had to do was allow herself to let go and move as instinct directed her. All those years of painful manipulation of magic—the Origem, as she'd come to know it—made sense now.

The phalanx continued to circle and attack with her ice. Liana, with the power and strength of a god pulsing through her veins, launched volley after volley of pure Origem energy at Sarratenian. It wasn't enough, though. Sarratenian deftly deflected every shot as he emerged from the clouds of snow and dirt surrounding them all. Liana watched as he turned to his men, still trying to breach the wall of trees and ice, and made an elaborate gesture in their direction.

The hundred soldiers stopped and turned on command. They ran without voice or soul towards Liana. She no longer felt scared. Her breathing was calm, her heartbeat slow and steady. She threw another bolt in their direction, hitting one of them square in the chest. It killed the man outright and sent half a dozen more in his immediate vicinity to the ground, but the rest kept coming unabated.

'There's too many of them,' she said.

'I agree,' replied Eraidor. 'Call her back. We need to retreat.'

Liana reached out to the phalanx, who immediately swooped down and landed beside them. Quickly, Liana scrambled onto the beast's back and they were in the air again before she could grab a firm hold, almost falling off the opposite side. As if the phalanx knew, Liana felt the weight of the animal shift beneath her, stopping her from falling off.

They flew higher. As Liana looked down, she realised she couldn't see Sarratenian. They circled around the clearing for a while, but he was nowhere to be seen.

The ice wall exploded, with debris cascading in all directions.

'There!' she pointed to an area within the city limits. Many of the buildings were destroyed, and the dead from both sides were scattered in the dirt and snow. From where she stood, Liana watched as Sarratenian and Cal rode their strydes into the city with their remaining soldiers. They were heading for the cavern.

She scanned the side of the mountain. Those who had retreated from the ground assault were now holding the line on one of the cross-paths. Among them, were Addan, Ember, and the others. All were still standing, to her relief. The phalanx knew what Liana needed from her and sent a small barrage of ice at the remaining silent attackers, who were trying to make progress up the mountainside. Two direct hits would buy her friends the time they needed. It was all the help she could offer right now. Cal and Sarratenian had to be her priority.

The phalanx swooped low to the ground and screamed at the advancing men. Both strydes screeched in surprise. Cal was unseated, crashing to the ground awkwardly. Sarratenian held steady and brought his mount under control before coming to a halt. The army around them also stopped.

Liana commanded the phalanx to set down on the ground, blocking the way to the cavern. She didn't dismount. 'I can't let you do this!' she shouted. The phalanx roared as if in agreement.

'You continue to surprise me, Liana,' said Sarratenian. He dismounted his stryde, which turned and ran away through the remains of the ice-tree wall to seek its own freedom. The other pulled free from Cal and chased after its companion. Neither man showed concern.

'Look around you. There's nothing left for you here except the innocent and defenceless. What more do you want from these people?'

'You are quite right. These backward people did not put up much of a fight in the end, did they? A thousand years of nothing. No history, no war. No *progress*. Rather sad, really. Do you not agree?'

'There's nothing wrong with that. Why should there be war? Why should the world burn? Because you say so?' She could feel the phalanx struggling beneath her, as if it were feeding on her anger. 'Well, there's nothing left here for you. No one to fight back. No one to wage war. So what now, Sarratenian? What now?'

Sarratenian took a step forward. 'Now, dear girl, I get what I really came for.'

34

WE WILL DEFEAT THEM

Lightning crackled in the sky around the mountain as Cal watched his army tear through the defences of the Dawanii settlement. These people were weak, just like all the others on the way here, and soon they would be victorious. Shaan said it would be glorious. He loved Shaan and trusted him.

Once, he had been scared. Scared to leave everything he knew. The evil Dawanii had killed his mother and taken his sister. He was king now, and he would lead a new, united nation. Moranza and Dawan would be whole again, for the first time in a thousand years. Shaan said it would be the greatest era mankind would ever know. He loved Shaan and trusted him.

Yet here was this girl, a Dawanii, standing before them atop a great beast of a dragon. She claimed she was Liana, but he knew that not to be true. Shaan told him so. She *did* look familiar to him, somehow. The dragon cut an imposing sight in the sky, though he was not scared of it. Why wasn't he scared of it? The beast was hundreds of times larger than any dragon he had seen. Terrible creatures that destroyed everything they touched. Such terrible, tiny creatures. They had razed his city to the ground time and again over the centuries. Not this one, though. This dragon was different, and he wanted it.

Lightning lit up the darkened clouds above, and the dragon roared and reared against the shadow of the mountain behind it. The girl on its back shouted at him and Shaan.

'I can't let you do this,' the girl declared. She looked so small on the dragon's back. Insignificant. Inconsequential. Yet she stood in their way. How dare she stand in their way.

A memory inside his head gnawed away at him. A dream. He had a hazy recollection that Liana had come to him, to try to stop him. Why did he remember that? It felt real, yet it was only a dream. He couldn't recall the last time he'd slept. He knew dreams only came when you weren't awake, and he'd been awake for so long now. Where was Liana, really? Not here, not on this dragon. He knew that.

He turned to Shaan who stood next to him. He looked so strong, so self-assured and powerful. This girl would not stop him. She could not stop them. They would defeat the Dawanii and he would rule them all. He would claim the dragon as his own. Shaan spoke and he clung to every word.

'Now I get what I really came for,' Shaan said. Cal knew what he meant. The true purpose of why they were here. To claim true power. A power once lost.

A handful of Dawanii men and women joined the girl and the dragon. Most had already been killed and these few remaining were no match for his army. Shaan raised his arm, signalling for his men to ready for attack. They fanned out in a line around them both. They were ready. Silent. Loyal.

'What else could you want from these people?' the girl asked.

'The Dawanii hide a secret. I have come to claim it and put right my injustice.'

An image appeared in Cal's mind. A bright swirling light

suspended in the air. Except it was more of a tear, a fissure in the space around it. A memory, one that was not his own. He knew this was Shaan's memory, and he shared in it and understood. He could feel immense power pouring from the tear and he knew the Dawanii were hiding it from them. Shaan wanted it, and so did he. This girl stood in their way, so she had to be removed. He could feel Shaan's thoughts as if they were one. There was no fear anymore. He trusted Shaan, and he loved him. He would die for him and he would kill for him. He knew he had to kill this girl. For him.

The dragon roared and bucked before taking to the sky amidst the thunder and lightning that grew louder and closer. Shaan nodded and Cal gave his army the order to attack. It would be easy to wipe out these few remaining Dawanii savages. Cal drew his own sword and ran with his men.

Cal had a taste for blood now, and he liked it. The first Dawanii man fell with a single cut from his sword. It was too easy. A shard of ice smashed into the ground near him, exploding into dust, missing everyone. He looked into the sky and saw the dragon circling. There was nothing he could do about it, though he knew he didn't have to worry. Shaan said the dragon was his concern. Words were not needed to hear him.

These Dawanii were a curious people. They could throw stones with only their minds. Those that had been sent forward to fight, at least. They could make the ground churn up at their feet and trees bend to their will. If he had that kind of power he would be unstoppable and feared by all who witnessed him. Despite this strange ability, they were still falling, still dying at the tip of his blade. They were no match for him and his army. *You will all bow before your king!*

'Where is it?' demanded Shaan. 'Where is it hidden?' He did not fight. There wasn't any need for him to. The beautiful chaos and destruction revolved around him and he did not flinch. Cal could feel the bond between them grow stronger the more time passed. He knew what Shaan was looking for. He knew what it looked like, but not its name. He would help him find it.

'Give us what we are looking for,' shouted Cal to the girl on the dragon in the sky. He knew she could hear him, although he didn't know why he knew that.

The girl didn't reply, only driving the beast down to swoop past them. The giant wings pushed the ever-wind in the opposite direction, creating a swirl of dust and snow around him. He swung with his sword at the dragon's tail as it went by and missed. Not even close.

Then it all went dark. Silent. *What's happening? Where am I?* There was only him and the blackness of nothing. Except. A figure in the distance coming towards him. He knew who it was immediately.

'Liana?'

'Yes, Cal, it's me. I need you to listen to me. You need to stop this before it's too late.'

Faint flashes of lightning far off in the void fractured the darkness as she approached him. A sense of lightness washed over him as though a weight had been lifted. Memories returned. Memories of a time forgotten. A time when he was with his sister when they were younger and happy. He felt scared. Why was he scared?

'Liana? What's happening to me?' He pulled his arms to his chest and bit on his thumbnail.

'It's Sarratenian. He's destroying everything. He's manipulating you, and I need you to see it. I cannot stop him, not without your help. Please, Cal, you need to be strong for me and fight him.'

'I can't. He's too powerful. I'm sorry.'

Liana took hold of him by the shoulders and squeezed him tight. 'You have to fight it. You have to try.'

'It's too late,' Cal said. And then his sister was gone. The storm and the sound of war returned in an instant. He looked up at the dragon as it bore down on him. The girl on its back called to him. Should he know her? He thought for a moment he'd seen Liana there, heard her pleading with him, but the notion evaporated. He turned to Shaan, who looked at him with a smile. He loved him. The dragon was heading right for him.

A blinding flash of light erupted right at the moment Cal thought the dragon had hit his friend. He shielded his eyes with his arm. The dragon screamed, crying out. The bright light dissolved into a thousand pieces around them. Not pieces. Dragons. So many miniature versions of the larger one. They darted through the air in all directions before dissipating into the sky, leaving only the Dawanii girl alone in the snow. She was already on her feet, brushing herself down, readying herself to fight.

'What have you done with it?' demanded Shaan, who hadn't moved from where he stood before the dragon attacked him.

'Done with what?' asked the girl. She turned her head and looked as though she was talking to someone who wasn't there.

Cal stepped forward and pointed his sword at her. 'Tell him or I will end you right now.'

'I don't know what he means. Cal, please. You need to stop this.'

'You know me? How do you know me?'

'It's me. Liana. I need you to remember me, Cal. Recognise who I am.'

'Where is the Origem seal?' growled Shaan. 'I know it is close by. I can feel it. I can see its power. Tell me where it is.'

The girl didn't answer.

'Tell us what we want to know,' said Cal. He jabbed at her with his sword. She was unarmed as best as he could tell, though that wouldn't stop him from killing her. A stray thought deep within him told him he *shouldn't* kill her. He didn't know why.

'No, I don't know where it is. I haven't seen it,' she said. A second later, she cocked her head as if reacting to something unseen beside her. Shaan reacted in the same way. It was as if there was someone else there. *What can't I see?*

'Kill them all,' said Shaan.

The fighting around them had continued all the while. The Dawanii had taken down a good number of Cal's army, but very few of the enemy remained now. And the dragon was gone, destroyed by Shaan. Such a shame—he wanted that beast for his own.

Cal took his sword in both hands, ready to strike down the girl. She pleaded for her life as he raised the blade above his head. He hesitated. *Why don't I want to do this?* Breathing deep, he brought his sword down just as something slammed into his side. He only caught a glimpse of white and blue as he fell to the ground. A sharp pain tore at his arm as teeth pierced his skin. He cried out as he realised his plight, pinned down by the weight of the creature he'd seen earlier. The one he wanted for himself. He rolled over, and the animal released him before it took a position beside the girl. It growled menacingly at him.

He tried to scramble for his sword, but the pain in his arm was too much. All he could do was cradle his damaged limb, blood trickling through his fingers. He looked to Shaan, but he wasn't there. He scanned the immediate area. *There.* Cal stumbled to his feet, still clutching his arm. The girl and her animal had already gone after Shaan, leaving him behind. She was shouting at him. Something was in her hand. Something that glowed a bright white, crackling, fizzing. *What was that?*

'Shaan!' he shouted, trying desperately to warn his friend. Barely a whisper left his lips.

Somehow, Shaan must have heard him as he turned round to face the girl. She pulled her glowing hand back and threw a ball of bright white light at Shaan. It appeared to strike him in the chest, a direct hit, though nothing happened. Shaan was unharmed, and he simply smiled at her. The strange white wolf animal stood by her side, snarling, barking. He had to do something to help.

Cal ran at the girl directly from behind. She didn't notice him coming at her. He leaned forward with his shoulder as he made contact, and the two of them crashed to the ground. The girl yelped in surprise. The animal immediately came to her defence, biting into his ankle. Cal screamed out in pain and tried to kick the beast free.

'I don't want to hurt you,' she said. *Why not? I'd like to kill you. Argh!* The white wolf with the angry blue fire tore at his leg, relentless in its attack. Cal kicked out with his other foot, which connected with the animal's head. Finally, it released him, and he rolled away and got to his feet as fast as he could. It was difficult to put weight on his injured foot, and he was sure it was bleeding. *Bastard animal!*

He found himself standing behind Shaan. Had he stepped in to defend him? He couldn't be sure. It was two on two. The girl and the beast facing off against him and Shaan.

'Tell me where it is,' demanded Shaan.

'I don't know what you're talking about. I really don't,' protested the girl. She made her hand glow again, ready to throw another ball. Except it wasn't a ball this time. With both hands she stretched the light apart, creating a ribbon that arced wildly as if she were controlling a lightning storm of her own. She lunged forward and pushed.

'No!' she screamed and the world turned white. A blinding flash engulfed him, pain searing through his chest. And then, nothing. Silence. Darkness.

Cal became aware of a ringing in his ears. It was barely anything to start, until it became an unbearable high-pitched scream in his head. In the distance, somewhere in the blackness of wherever he now was, a muted flash of lightning lit up the space around him for barely a second. And then it was dark again. He thought he saw a shadow, in that brief moment of light. Someone there with him.

'Cal, I'm so sorry. I didn't... I wasn't...'

He recognised the voice. His sister. Liana. He tried to step forward, closer to her. There was nothing beneath him. He called to her.

'I'm here. Don't go, Cal. I need you to be strong for me.'

The darkness lifted—only a little—and there she was, standing before him. She was crying, broken, reaching out to him with her hand.

'What happened?' he asked, taking a step to her. 'Where are we?'

A retreating storm rumbled in the distance. Far, far away now. It had been closer, he was certain of that. He remembered the storm. A raging tempest that had gone on forever.

'Inside your mind. I am here with you. Stay with me, let me help. Be strong for me and I'll take you home.'

'What happened?' he repeated.

'He moved, Cal. He moved out of the way, and it was too late for me to stop. Oh, what have I done? What did he let me do?'

Cal followed her gaze to his chest, except there was nothing there other than a smouldering hole tinged with purple-white light. He touched the edges with his fingers and the light tingled against his skin. *This isn't right. Should I be scared?* 'Did I die? Am I dead, Liana?'

His sister took hold of his hand and held it in hers. Tears rolled down her cheeks, and he knew then, the truth.

'I'm sorry,' she said. 'It's all my fault. I couldn't stop him.'

'You have nothing to be sorry for. It was my choice, my decision. I let him in. I was weak. You... you were always the strong one, Liana. I was jealous of you in a way, and I was blind.

Blinded by my own ambitions, and frustrated by the hand I was given. He saw that in me and used it, twisted it. I wasn't strong enough, I know that now. I loved him and I trusted him, but now I see the truth of him.'

Liana squeezed his hand tight, her lower lip quivering.

'Go,' he said softly. 'You have to stop him. For me, and for our mother. I can go no farther, but you must continue.'

'I don't want to go.'

'You cannot stay here. My time has come, and that's all right. I knew there was no way back for me once the storm came. The truth is, it was over for me the second our mother died. He had me in that moment. That was my true end. Not here, not now. Please don't blame yourself.' He pulled his hand free from hers. 'It's time.'

'I promise I will finish this.'

The darkness returned and she was gone. All that remained was the high-pitched ringing in his ears, it too fading to nothing. The storm was gone forever now, and he closed his eyes.

35

CONFRONTATION

Addan had been mere inches away from falling to his death. Only moments before, he wouldn't have cared. All had seemed lost, with little reason to continue on. The thought of Liana dying meant it would have all been over for him. He was only here for her and for nothing else. He had signed up to serving in a false war, against an enemy who had slain the queen, solely to find her. Now that he had, he found himself on the opposite side of that war. If it wasn't for the young Dawanii man called Eelan, he would be dead, having fallen from the edge of a mountain by accident. It would have been a fitting end to an unfortunate existence.

Liana was alive, and so was he, and he vowed to fight on. To live. As he tried to still his breathing and regain composure after being hauled back from the brink of death, he watched the cloud of dragons in the sky and prayed she would be all right.

Eelan knelt over him and, with both hands holding his head, he frowned and then nodded. 'You need to rest,' he said. 'I cannot heal your mind on my own. You need sleep.'

Addan brushed him away. 'I'll be fine. How can I sleep or even rest when we are under attack like this?'

'It is not your war to fight,' said Eelan.

'I know. I still want to help. This war is wrong and should never have been started. We were told that the Dawanii killed our queen, and that Liana had been abducted by you. I thought it was my fault. I abandoned her when I should have stayed. I should have protected her when the gabbalins attacked your people, but I ran like a coward.' Addan lowered his head in shame.

'Yes, now you see the lie. We are honoured to have you fight alongside us if you wish. We are so few now.' Eelan looked out over the city below, where most of the fighting had taken place.

Addan stood up, retrieving his sword from the ground as he did so. His back twinged with pain, most likely from where he'd been pulled away from the edge of the mountain. He rotated his hips to stretch it out. Looking around at his surroundings, he tried to work out what to do next. They were at the end of the carved pathway. It was impossible to go farther upwards, and the Moranzan army was still advancing from below. They were trapped, and the only way out was to fight.

Who was leading this group? Not the old man who didn't speak. Nor the woman who was with him. The other two were too young and one of them was blind. Was it really down to him? Would they listen to him if he gave them orders? He'd had a hard time getting his own company to listen to him, and they were all dead now. *That was not my fault.*

'We can't stay up here,' Addan said. 'It won't take too many of them to overwhelm us and force us off the edge. We need to get to safer ground before they get here.'

'He is right. Here we stay, here we will die,' said the young blind man.

Addan surveyed the way down. The path zig-zagged all the way. He picked out a wider plateau below them. The Moranzans hadn't made it that far, and it looked like a safer place to take a stand than where they were at the moment. He spoke his mind to the others, and they agreed to follow his lead back down the mountain.

As they reached the plateau, a number of Moranzans had found their way to that level at the same time. They approached silently with an empty look in their eyes. Addan recognised some of them from the village, but most of them had likely come from the additional contingent that had arrived with the prince. He wondered where the prince was now. He'd not seen him in a while, not that it had been anyone other than Shaan—Sarratenian—in charge.

He held his sword out in front of him while urging the others to remain behind him. The Dawanii were unarmed, so it was all down to him to despatch the enemy in front of him. Quiet voices gnawed away at the back of his mind, telling him he should surrender. Telling him that there was no point fighting. He fought to bury the whispers, to ignore them. Now was not the time to give in. He had to fight. He had to survive.

The first two Moranzans attacked together, trying to take Addan on either side. He ducked the first blade as it swung at him high, as if aiming to remove his head. He brought his own sword round in a sweeping motion, slicing into the leg of the second man. Any ordinary man would have cried out in pain, yet there was no reaction at all aside from the man falling to his knees.

Addan couldn't stop to understand why. The first soldier had already adjusted his stance to strike again, this time lunging forward. The Moranzan sword missed by a mere inch. Addan turned on his heel and grabbed the man's sword arm, and pulled it up behind his back. With his own blade, he slid it into the soldier's side, aiming upwards into his ribs. The man crumpled to the ground as silent as he'd ever been.

Blood dripped from his blade as he withdrew it from the corpse. Before he could swing around at the next attacker, Eelan pushed him out of the way of another sword he hadn't seen coming. *That's the second time he's saved my life.* 'Thank you,' Addan said, as he regained his footing. Eelan simply nodded in reply before picking up the sword of one of the dead Moranzans. Addan allowed himself a small smile, knowing he wasn't fighting alone any more.

The Moranzans kept coming, one after the other. It was down to him and Eelan to defend the others. The old man and the woman kept their backs to the rock face. A sensible move, so no one could sneak up from behind them. The blind man stood in the middle of it all, chanting to himself. He moved and dodged as if he could see at least something, even landing a punch on the nose of one soldier who managed to get by Eelan.

Back at the training ground, Addan despaired at how inept his fellow comrades had been, not that he had much in the way of fighting skills or training himself. Here on the plateau, he was grateful for their lack of skill. Even though they were being controlled somehow, merely doing the bidding of Sarratenian, they moved slowly and predictably. The only advantage they had was their number, and that was what had cost so many Dawanii lives. Their shouts and cries were lessening as time went on and more of them succumbed to the onslaught. Addan wondered how many would be left once all was said and done. Not many at all, he guessed.

The soldiers kept coming and his sword arm was tiring. There was no grace or poise in his moves against the enemy. Through it all, it had come down to little more than hacking away at limbs and bodies in the hope they would die before he did.

'Give up,' said a voice inside his head. The girl again. 'You cannot win here. There is no need to try. Lay down your weapon and accept your fate.'

Addan tried to shake the voice away. He had to keep his head clear. The voice persisted as he stepped left to dodge another attack. This time he was too slow, and the blade of the looming soldier sliced into his left arm above the elbow. He cried out in pain. His instinct was to grab at the wound with his other arm, but there was no time. This soldier was more relentless than the others. Addan tried to defend with his sword arm as this man punched and kicked, swinging some kind of axe in any and all directions. The man was screaming, though there was no sound. The look on his face was pure hatred locked behind black, lifeless eyes. Addan stumbled backwards, unable to fight off this onslaught.

'It's over,' said the girl. 'You cannot win this.'

She was right. She had always been right. He couldn't save her, he couldn't save himself. This might really be the time he died. He closed his eyes and held his arms up across his face in a final effort to defend himself as the axe swung over him. The axe didn't come. A huge weight fell on him and knocked him off his feet. The axe-wielding soldier fell dead, pinning him to the ground. He pushed a limp, dead arm away from his face to see the blind man grinning, a large rock stained with blood in his hands.

'I may be blind, but that does not mean I cannot see,' he said. He wasn't looking *at* Addan, more like somewhere beyond him.

Addan heaved the corpse from him, ignoring the searing pain in his arm. There was so much blood now it was hard to tell how much of it was his or his attackers'. He tried to stand up, ready to take on the next one. To his surprise there were none left. Between him and Eelan, and the blind one's intervention, thirteen Moranzan soldiers lay dead at their feet.

Eelan staggered over, exhaustion evident, and took his injured arm in his hands. 'A small wound. Easy to heal.' He closed his eyes and weaved a thin line of light through the cut until it faded away.

'I will never not be impressed by how you manage to do

that,' said Addan. Although the pain had gone and the wound healed, his sleeve was still sticky with blood.

"Thank you for your assistance," said the old man through the girl. Another thing he couldn't get used to. The Dawanii way of life was so different to the one he knew. He didn't know much about history. A small memory tucked away in the corner of his mind told him they were once the same people before the Division. The more he learned about the Dawanii, the more he realised they were no longer the same. They still spoke the same language, though the inflections and cadence had changed somewhat. And they didn't call it the Division. What had the old man said? Cataclysm. On the whole, he liked these people, and they had accepted him into their lives with ease.

'If only they knew what you have done,' said his brother inside his head. 'Tell them you have killed their own. See how they treat you then. Kill you on the spot, wouldn't they?' Addan's brother had never mocked him that way when he was alive. He knew the voices weren't real, yet they continued to taunt him and he couldn't figure out how to stop them. Would they be with him forever until they got their wish? Until he died?

'We can't stay here,' said Eelan as he kicked dirty snow at one of the corpses. 'More will come, and I need to help the wounded.' He turned to the old man and the woman. 'Orratan, we need to get you to the cavern, to safety.'

Orratan, yes, that was his name. Addan was certain he would forget it again before the day was over. Names had always eluded him. He looked out over the city for Liana. All he saw were burning buildings and dead bodies. There was no sign of the dragon creature, either. What a beast that had been. He hoped beyond all hope that Liana had survived somehow. What would he do if she was gone? He sighed and wiped his face with his hands. Now was not the time to worry about after. They had to get through the day yet.

He offered an arm to Orratan's companion, to help her step over the bodies strewn in their way. It seemed like the right thing to do. She smiled at him as she accepted his invitation, though it was an odd sort of smile, as if to suggest it was a strange thing to do. She didn't speak unless it was on behalf of Orratan, though, he'd noticed. He was certain he'd not been told her name.

The blind one grew panicked all of a sudden as they made to leave the plateau. 'We are not safe here. He comes! He seeks answers, searching for the secret that cannot be told!' He cowered, clutching at his hands while staring at the sky. *This boy is more troubled than I am,* he thought. Addan guessed he was maybe a similar age as Milo had been. So many young lives caught up in all this destruction. Eelan barely looked any older himself.

"Come, we must hurry," said Orratan.

It was too late. Addan looked to the path leading farther down the mountain. A figure was approaching them with haste, a figure he recognised immediately. Shaan. Sarratenian. Whatever he called himself. He was marching with purpose, a stern look on his face. He held no weapon and had no other men with him. The man looked exactly as he had done when Addan first laid eyes on him—untouched by battle, his uniform was pristine and not a hair out of place. Addan pulled his arm free of the woman and readied his sword once again.

'Ah, it is the brave warrior turned traitor,' said Sarratenian as he approached the plateau.

'Come no further,' said Addan, gesturing with his sword.

Sarratenian looked beyond Addan at the others. 'Defending the worthless lives of these backward people until the last. I should commend you, really. However, you are standing in my way. I advise you step aside, or you will die alongside your new friends.'

'Where's Liana?'

'Dead. A shame really. She had such determination, such spirit.' He looked out to the city. 'You will find her along with her brother. Once this is all over, if there is anything left of the world, perhaps you might like to bury them together?'

Addan felt his blood boil as he digested the god's words. He lunged forward in an attempt to drive his sword into Sarratenian's chest, to stop him here and now. The blade glanced to the side as if striking an invisible wall, causing him to lose his step. He looked on, confused. It should have been a clean hit. How had he missed? Steadying his footing, he tried again. Sarratenian had already moved past him. A strike to the back then. Cowardly, but his only option. It too, failed to land.

Sarratenian ascended the plateau and immediately singled out Orratan. 'Where is it? I know it is here, and I demand you tell me where or I will raze the entire city to the ground until I find it.'

Orratan, of course, didn't reply. His companion tried to speak on his behalf, but she stuttered her words. "I know not of what you speak." She and Orratan tried to back away in tandem.

'Lies!'

Addan caught Eelan's attention. They looked at each other and shared a nod, silently agreeing they should try to attack Sarratenian together at the same time while his attention was on Orratan. It was their only chance. Addan gave a signal and both of them ran at Sarratenian from either side, their swords trained on their target. Addan made sure of his attack by holding the hilt of his own blade with both hands. There was no way he could miss a third time. Before he knew what had happened, he found himself with a mouthful of dirt and snow as he crashed to the ground.

'I commend your persistence,' said Sarratenian, standing over him. 'Try as you might, you cannot harm me.'

Addan felt a pressure in his mind, a darkness, as though

457

Sarratenian was reaching into his brain and squeezing it tight. 'Rest now,' said a voice. It was Milo, lying there with him in the dirt and darkness. The girl was there too, and his brother. 'You can do no more to help. You have failed, as you have always done,' they all said together. 'Close your eyes and sleep now. You are defeated.'

36

THE ORIGEM

She shook Cal's lifeless body, willing it to move and sobbed. *I've failed him.* Ember leaned against her, placing a paw on her leg.

'*Liana. You need to move. Now!*' demanded Eraidor, his voice urgent.

She pulled her head away from Cal and looked at Eraidor, once again visible to her. Wiping away tears to clear her vision, she saw him pointing frantically behind her. She swivelled on her knees to see three of the remaining Moranzan soldiers heading her way. They ambled quietly, steadily towards her, their faces devoid of any expression or emotion. Their blood-stained swords readied for attack. They were coming for her and closing the gap fast. She hurriedly looked around her. There was no sign of Sarratenian. *Where has he gone?*

Liana lowered her brother carefully to the ground. As she looked at his face, his eyes still open, a deep sense of anger boiled up inside her and erupted. She rose to her feet and screamed at the approaching soldiers. The glow in her hand ignited into a ball of light that felt so hot, so raw and powerful it felt as if it would tear her apart. She hurled it at the soldiers with enough force all three vaporised on the spot.

Hatred and anger overwhelmed her. Eraidor protested loudly, trying to cool her down, but she ignored him. She spotted another lone Moranzan and ended his life. *For Cal. For my brother!*

Breathless and vengeful, she searched for others. She would kill them all. They would know her fury. There were no others. Only a handful of Dawanii remained, and they looked terrified of her. Even Ember looked on, wary. Sarratenian was gone and her brother was dead. She collapsed to her knees and screamed at the moon, her arms fallen by her side.

'This is not the way. Do not let your pain consume you,' said Eraidor quietly.

'Leave me alone.'

'I cannot. Nor should you be alone. I fear for what you are becoming. Part of that is my fault and I am sorry. Though, you must take responsibility for your own actions. Sarratenian may have held power over those people, but their lives were not yours to take in vengeance.'

'They would have killed me first had I not.'

Eraidor didn't reply. He was right, though. Something was happening to her, and she didn't like it. Why *did* she kill those men? Yes, they were about to attack her. She could have run away to the mountain, to safety. It wasn't them who killed Cal. No, she had done that. He died by her touch. She looked at her blackened hand. The power it contained frightened her now.

Liana stroked at Ember's fur as the cinderfox brushed against her leg. 'I shouldn't have come here. I shouldn't have stolen the stone. All of this is because of me.'

'If you had stayed, Sarratenian would have killed you already. Tell me, why did you want the stone in the first place?'

She tried to steady her breathing. 'I felt it calling to me. When I first held the necklace in my hands, there was a connection. It felt alive somehow. I tried to ignore it at first, but I couldn't get the thought of it out of my head. I knew I needed it somehow. Like it was a part of me.'

'And you now know what it is.'

'The Sisterhood said it is a piece of the Origem itself.' She felt its power flowing through her as if the stone was still in her hand. Every beat of her heart radiated pure energy through her veins. It was both scary and intoxicating at the same time.

'Yes, and no,' said Eraidor. 'It is a fragment, a remnant of the power beyond this world. The Origem seal was meant to prevent it coming through. However, the seal is imperfect. It weakens the barrier that protects this world from the magic. As the power seeps through the rift the Origem creates, small fragments solidify into a form you would recognise as the stone. Not unlike how lava from an erupting volcano hardens as it cools.

'A thousand years ago, Sarratenian sought to destroy the Origem completely, and let the world flood with magic. It would have destroyed everything, and now he is attempting to do so again. Can you not see, Liana? It is your destiny to stop him. The Origem calls to him, as it does to you.'

Liana didn't have the strength to fight anymore, though she knew she couldn't stop. If she did, she would end up as dead as her brother, and the Dawanii would surely be destroyed. What could she do about it, though? Why had it all fallen on her shoulders? She looked at her blackened hand. Time was running out for her. She knew that.

The fighting between the Moranzan army and the Dawanii defenders continued around her unabated. The Dawanii were losing, that much was abundantly clear. She thought on Eraidor's words and knew he was right. The only way out of this was to find Sarratenian and stop him once and for all. Where had he gone?

Ember whined and scratched Liana's leg with her paw, trying to get her attention.

461

'What is it?' Liana asked.

The cinderfox yawned with a squeak and looked at the mountain, and then yapped once. Liana squinted to try to see what Ember was seeing. There wasn't anything specific that looked different to how it had been. Ember, though, grew more insistent that there was something wrong there.

'Do you know what she means?' she asked Eraidor.

'No, however, it is evident to me that your friend here wants you to go there with haste.'

Ember barked excitedly, as if she was confirming Eraidor's supposition. Liana still didn't understand, or even know for sure, how the cinderfox could see and hear Eraidor. She had no doubt it was the case, though.

Liana picked herself off the ground. There wasn't much of an option, and without a clearer plan of her own, discovering what had got Ember so agitated seemed the best thing to do right now. She clenched her teeth and ran towards the mountain, trying her best to stay clear of the fight still raging between the Dawanii and Sarratenian's army.

When she got to the plateau, what she saw made her freeze on the spot. Sarratenian was there, his arm outstretched and Orratan hung suspended in the air in front of him. The old man was struggling to breathe and his legs were flailing, his whole body writhing as he tried to free himself. His assistant was on her knees, pleading with Sarratenian to let him go. It was the first time Liana had heard her speak when it wasn't on Orratan's behalf since the day she first met them.

Farther behind Sarratenian were Eelan, Addan and Uehan, all watching on in horror. They were all too frightened to do anything to intervene. Ember barked furiously at Sarratenian.

'Tell me where it is,' demanded Sarratenian of Orratan.

'Release him at once,' shouted Liana, readying her weapon. 'He cannot speak, so he can't tell you anything.' She turned slightly to address Eraidor. *'I thought you told me Architects can't hurt humans directly.'*

'We cannot. That is to say, none of us do. Sarratenian has always followed his own rules, and only follows the edicts we created when it suits him. It appears that currently, those rules do not.'

'Please let him go,' said the woman. Then her posture stiffened a little. "Let me go and I will tell you what you wish to know."

Sarratenian cocked his head towards the woman, an eyebrow raised in curiosity. Then, he flicked his fingers forward. Orratan fell backwards with some force, landing against the rock face of the mountain. He choked and wheezed as he fought to catch his breath.

Liana exhaled, relieved at his release, though that relief was short-lived. She gasped as the woman was lifted from the ground in Orratan's stead.

'How interesting,' said Sarratenian as he held the woman in the air without touching her. 'You both are connected through the mind. He speaks through you, an ability granted through manipulation of the Origem. Tell me, how has someone who is not of our kind achieved this?'

Through strangled words, the woman answered. 'We offer ourselves to the Architects. We offer tribute and they bestow their power upon us.'

Sarratenian turned to look at Liana. No, he wasn't looking at her, he was looking at Eraidor. 'Is that so? Tell me, brother. Why do we give these feeble creatures such gifts?'

'We do not,' said Eraidor. *'They only believe we do. They have found a way to harness the Origem themselves. This is not our doing.'*

'Ah, so they *do* have what I seek.' He turned back to the woman, who was still struggling any way she could to extricate herself from his grip. 'There is a powerful artefact I have been searching for and I believe it is here in this city. You will tell me where it is, or I will destroy you all and everything in this place until I find it myself. Save yourself the misery and tell me. What I seek is what gives you this ability you claim is a gift. It is not a gift. It is stolen.'

A collective realisation rippled amongst all who were watching, except for Addan. 'What does he mean?' he asked. He had not moved from where he crouched the whole time since Liana had arrived at the scene. Eelan stood next to him as if defending him.

'The monument,' whispered Liana. 'He wants the monument.'

'He will destroy this city with or without what he desires,' said Uehan. 'I see it all now. He means to tear apart the world. To release the full power of the Origem. Yet, I now foresee no future beyond that.' The young man was wringing his hands, staring into nothing. Ember yowled at his words. It almost sounded like human speech.

'I have to stop him,' said Liana. She felt she had to do something. If nothing else, she had to get him to let the woman go. 'I will take you to what you are looking for.' It was her only gambit. 'First, you have to release her.'

At the same moment, Addan leapt to his feet and screamed before charging at Sarratenian like his backside was on fire. Sarratenian deftly sidestepped the attack. Addan lost his balance and fell heavily to the ground.

'The man who yearns to save everyone, yet manages nothing. You keep trying so hard. I am sure you would find yourself more comfortable back at home in a bar, perhaps? No? Actions have consequences, and I feel none of you appreciate my true power, or the gravity of the predicament you find yourselves in. Allow me to demonstrate.' He turned, bringing his arm in a circle to point out over the edge of the mountain. The woman moved through the air at the same time until she dangled precariously over the city below. Sarratenian hurled the woman to her death.

'*Sarratenian, brother, what have you done?*' gasped Eraidor.

Liana and the others all cried out in horror. Eelan, Addan and Orratan all turned their heads away, unable to watch. Liana saw it all. She watched helplessly as the woman crashed against the rocky surface some distance below her. There was no way anyone could survive such a fall.

'Why?' she demanded, her voice wavering. 'I already agreed to show you what you are looking for.'

'Because I can,' he snapped. 'For nearly two years, I have watched you all live out your pitiful lives, and it is pathetic. You do not deserve the right to live. I will bring this world to an end and start over. I will do it right, and it will be glorious.'

Liana felt a rage pulling at her from the inside. It was a feeling that had been developing ever since she had tried to save that old man. Ever since Eraidor came to her. The feeling grew stronger, like it was changing her somehow, as if there was a force desperate to devour her. 'I've changed my mind,' she said. 'I will not help you. I will *end* you if it is the last thing I do.'

The feeling of fury within her radiated throughout her body. She fed on the energy that was trying to consume her, drawing on its power. But there was something more. Eraidor had something to do with it, she was sure of that. A combination of them both. Until now, she had done whatever she could to fight the might of the Origem as it tried to consume her. She had pushed against Eraidor the whole time too, a battle within herself of both god and magic. *What if that wasn't the way?* What if she accepted it? What if she truly let them both in, beyond merely letting Eraidor guide her actions? She closed her eyes and took a deep breath.

'Liana, you're burning,' said Eelan.

'It is as I saw!' said Uehan. 'She is with Eraidor and he is within her. I see hope where there was none before. The end is yet to come. She is here and she will save us, and yet also break us.'

Liana opened her eyes and looked at her hands as she held them out in front of her. A thin purple-white flame rippled over her skin. It looked almost like Ember's fur. She looked down at the cinderfox, who yapped with excitement back at her. 'What's happening to me?'

'If I did not know any better, I would say you are becoming a god,' said Eraidor.

'Impossible!' cried Sarratenian.

Liana held out her blackened hand, and then her other. She could feel the purple tendrils tracing their way all through her body. She didn't feel scared. It felt right to let it take her. She trusted it.

'How incredible.'

'I feel... I don't know how I feel. Powerful. It's as though I am part of everything. I am standing here, and yet I can see the whole world at once. Back home. The Sisterhood. I can feel myself standing on the surface of the sun and yet I am still here. I can...' she raised her hand and pushed it forward fast in Sarratenian's direction. For the first time, her actions had an effect on him. He stumbled. It wasn't much, barely making an impact, but it was enough to startle him.

'No human should have this power,' he cried. He fought back, mirroring Liana's push on him. All she felt was a breeze.

Liana moved forward, making to grab hold of Sarratenian. He shoved his way past her and leapt over Ember before hot-footing it down the mountain.

'You cannot stop me!' he shouted as he ran. 'You are an abomination and you will be destroyed. I will find what I came for and I will start this pathetic world over.'

Orratan ran to Liana. He mouthed words, but there was no sound. He no longer had his assistant, and she could see the intense pain in his eyes. He used his hands to make shapes and symbols.

Eelan watched the movements and spoke. 'He asks, what has happened to you? He asks if this is Eraidor's doing?'

'I don't understand it myself. Ever since I have known he is within me, I've felt different. Like something has been growing inside me. And now...'

'Does this mean you have the power to stop him?' asked Addan.

'I really don't know.' She turned back to Orratan. 'What is the monument, really? It is what Sarratenian wants, I'm certain of it.'

Orratan looked guilty all of a sudden. After a pause, he spoke again with his hands.

'He says,' said Eelan, 'inside the monument is a remnant of the Origem, like the stone you had. It allows us to receive our gifts from the Architects.'

'Sarratenian would have no interest in a mere remnant,' said Eraidor. *'It has to be the Origem itself. All this time and it is right here. How did I not see it? The Origem is the very fabric of everything. It has the capacity to destroy. All of time and space. Energy and matter are all contained within it. Before even our own beginning, there was the Origem. It was all that existed in the universe. Everything is born of it. If Sarratenian tries to wield it, it will do more than reset the world as he believes. It could destroy everything, including himself.'*

'Why would he risk destroying himself?' asked Liana as she flexed her hands and fingers, watching the glow dance on her skin.

'He seeks to be the ultimate god of everything,' said Uehan. 'I foresee all futures and also none of them. He does not believe it will destroy him. He only sees a world where everything is as he plans it to be. He must be stopped. Yet... I see no future where that is possible. Not even with you, Liana.'

Liana swallowed. Was this really the end? The battle for the city continued to rage on below. This war had now become a fight for everyone, for life itself. Every living thing in the world and beyond now depended on her, all blissfully ignorant of their impending demise. Even with all this new power coursing through her body, she felt nothing but dread and fear. Not for herself, but everyone around her. She looked at each of her friends as they stood before her, each seeing her as their only hope. Uehan's words weighed heavily on her. She would do whatever it too—*argh!* Intense pain seared through every inch of her body, radiating outward from the pit of her stomach to her head, her hands. Everything burned all at once. She fell to the ground and screamed.

'What's happening to her?' asked Addan, panicking.

'The power consumes her,' said Uehan. 'It is too much for her. Too much for anyone. This isn't right at all. I see her death, yet I see her outlive us all.'

Liana tried to fight against the pain. She reached out with her hand towards Eraidor. 'Help me,' she whimpered.

'I am not certain I can any longer. No human was ever meant to have this power. You will need to fight to control it. Do not let it overwhelm you. Focus. Imagine the energy as an object and push it from you. Control it. Do not let it control you.'

She fought to slow her breathing, to remain calm. Every sinew and bone burned with the power that sought to tear her apart. The whole world spun around her. She could see her parents, standing over her as they did when she was an infant. Her brother. The Council. Moranza. The whole world and the stars. She felt dizzy with the whole of her existence coming at the same time. And then it slowed down.

Her heart rate quelled, and the spinning stopped. 'I understand it all now,' she said. 'I know everything. The beginning, the end, and all that is in between. I have to stop him, and only I can.' The pain didn't subside, but she no longer suffered it. It was the strangest feeling. She knew she was in complete agony, yet it did not hurt. She stood up.

Before any of the others could object, she ran as fast as she could down the mountain path. The momentum carried her, bowling over anyone who got in her way. Silent Moranzan soldiers trying to fight their way up crashed over the path's edge as Liana shoulder-barged them out of her way. She had to get to the amphitheatre before Sarratenian could claim his prize.

She knew she was too late before she reached the amphitheatre. The huge ornate entrance was destroyed. Fractured stone and wood were scattered across the threshold. Tentatively, she stepped inside.

'Go carefully. However strong you think you may be feeling right now, I promise you it is nothing to how strong he is,' said Eraidor.

'If I don't stop him, who will?'

She trod lightly as she made her way through the corridors to the amphitheatre. It was a huge building, one she had only been inside of twice. It felt different now, somehow. Lifeless. Cold. The open arena was at the back of the building, and when she found it, she was surprised to find it exactly as it had been when she was last there. The effigies of the Architects lined the perimeter, all looking down from on high with their solemn expressions. In the centre stood the monument. It too, was untouched. If Sarratenian had designs on what it contained, then he wasn't here yet. The air was still and tasted stale. There was no wind here. It was as though they had stepped out of time itself.

'Not all is as it seems,' said Eraidor as he walked around the monument, inspecting it.

'Indeed it is not, brother.'

Liana scanned the area, looking for where the voice was

coming from. He was here, but she couldn't see him. Something moved in the shadowy alcoves between the Architect statues. More movement caught her attention at the periphery of her vision. Moranzan men—*her* men, standing silently in the darkness. They waited, swords in hand, watching. There was still no sign of where Sarratenian actually was. He *was* here, though. From her position near the monument, she found herself surrounded. There would be no way out without killing these men. A way out was not what she sought, though. For now, she ignored them.

The monument, with its three twisting fingers, loomed over her, imposing, lifeless. *'Do I destroy it?'* she asked.

Eraidor shook his head, still walking around the structure, examining some of its finer markings. *'The monument itself is more than decoration. What Sarratenian seeks is what is contained within it. If you destroy the structure, all that will remain will be the Origem itself. If anything, you will only be helping him with his goal.'*

Liana sighed. 'What do I do then?'

'Die,' came Sarratenian's voice. 'It is already too late. You cannot stop me. Therefore, it would be best if you simply... ceased to be.'

'I'm tired of this,' yelled Liana. 'Show yourself. If you want the Origem, then come and get it.' She shifted her position, looking around sharply, trying to ascertain where her enemy was. And then she saw him. Standing between the statues of Wisdom and Dreams. He was staring up at one of the other statues.

'You know,' he said, 'I think this one does capture my likeness rather well. Do you not agree? Maybe a little less cheerful.' He paused to gauge Liana's reaction. 'No? Quite right. I hate it.' The ground shook. Dust and debris fell from the walls and then the statue that represented him exploded, sending shards of rock in all directions. Liana shielded her eyes with her arm.

'I won't let you do this,' she shouted. She imagined the energy forming her hand. Nothing happened.

'You need to think differently,' urged Eraidor.

'Differently how?'

'You need to think like a god. You are the power now.'

Liana concentrated and imagined hurting Sarratenian, imagined stopping him. She narrowed her eyes to a frown, teeth clenched, and held out her hand towards him and pulled. The statue of the Architect of Dreams, depicted as a young girl wearing a long flowing dress made of ribbons, toppled forward to land on Sarratenian where he stood. The statue broke apart as it hit him and he staggered under the full weight of it.

As the cloud dissipated, it became clear it had little effect. 'You are growing stronger, I will admit that,' he said. 'Although, you are still nothing more than a child learning how to walk for the first time. It is impressive, but ultimately, you will fail.'

She pulled again, this time tearing down not only the statue of the Architect of Wisdom, but also the wall behind it. The impact vibrated around the whole amphitheatre. The noise hurt her ears, yet she felt no pain. She heard him laughing above the sound of crumbling stone, and then an invisible force slammed into her. She fell backwards, skidding across the ground until she found herself at the feet of the statue of the Architect of Life—Eraidor himself. It too didn't look anything like the being standing near her, though the perspective was different from between its carved stone feet. As she stood up, she realised that she hadn't been injured. Her only feelings were that of the agony of the remnant burning away inside her. That pain was not the same.

Sarratenian, undeterred by the rubble, made towards the monument. The lifeless structure glowed as it had done during the Branding ceremony. With a crackle, a small lilac flame flickered into life within the centre and quickly grew until the whole arena was bathed in a shimmering purple light that matched

471

her own. The shadows of the remaining statues moved and danced as though they too were alive.

She knew she had to do something to stop him, even if she wasn't sure what he was trying to achieve. She scrambled over the ground and tried to get between the monument and Sarratenian. Already cast aside once with such ease, she needed to find a way to anchor herself. She dug her heels into the dirt and imagined a way to stop herself being pulled or pushed away.

'Move,' commanded Sarratenian. He pushed at her a second time, yet she did not yield, her feet firmly fixed to the ground.

Liana tried to concentrate the energy in her hands again. A ball of light or fire, anything. Something to use against him. Nothing came. *What is the point of having the power of a god if I can't use it against him?* she thought, frustrated. She needed to think differently, Eraidor had said. How would a god fight another god? She thought back to all the stories she had read as a child. *Maybe...* She looked up to the sky hoping to see thunder-clouds. All she saw were stars. No help there. *The monument!*

She turned to the monument. If Sarratenian had the power to control it, then perhaps she could do the same. She stared into the purple flame and tried to see beyond it. If she could touch it with her mind, make it do what she willed it to do, then maybe... The air in the room exploded as she reached into the flame and pulled it out like a ribbon. The flame spiralled as she moved it in shapes, back and forth, with a gesture of her hands until it wrapped around Sarratenian. She imagined the flame as a rope around him and pulled her hands towards her chest. The ribbon of purple fire tightened around him until he couldn't move.

'Yes!' she shouted at her own success. This man, this god, was now her prisoner and he couldn't do anything about it. Somehow, she expected him to scream and shout at her, but he didn't. He was too quiet. Was he... smiling?

The fire bonds melted into nothing, leaving only the flickering flame within the monument. Liana looked on in horror. It wasn't enough. She knew then she couldn't defeat him.

'It was a valiant effort, I suppose,' said Sarratenian. He stretched his arms and neck as if loosening the body after a long sleep in an awkward position. 'I have already told you, your power is merely an illusion. A *delusion* even. Now, if you do not mind.' He motioned with his right hand and once again Liana found herself seated on the ground.

'*Get up,*' said Eraidor. '*You have to keep trying. You have to find a way.*'

'*I can't,*' she whimpered. '*I'm injured.*' She looked down to see a shard of broken statue protruding from her side. Blood oozed around it, soaking her furs. Even without pain, she realised how bad the wound was. She needed Eelan or another healer, but she was alone. She pulled free the fragment and tossed it away. It came out so easily. She tried to imagine her healing the wound itself. The hole in her abdomen remained.

'*Then all is lost.*'

All Liana could do now was watch as Sarratenian stepped up to the monument. The Moranzans all stood sentry, perfect in their silence as he touched each of the three curved stone spires in turn. As if they were made of paper, he pulled them apart and they fell to the ground, shattering on impact. The fire grew further, unbounded, until it was twice its original size. And then it went dark. There was no flame. No shadows moving across the walls. No sound other than Liana's own breathing and the sound of blood rushing through her ears. Nothing.

Except.

A minute speck of purple light where the monument once stood.

'Behold the Origem,' said Sarratenian, unseen.

The tiny mote of purple light cast no shadows anywhere.

'*Something is wrong,*' said Eraidor. Liana couldn't see him either, nor herself. Surely she should be able to see something?

'Why can't I touch it?' said Sarratenian with anger in his voice.

The purple mote pulsed. Only a little at first. The pulse grew brighter and faster until the world around came into view again. Then there was a whining sound coming from the light, low in pitch, but getting higher until there was an intense burst of pure energy around it. When Liana's eyes adjusted, the mote had settled into a pulsating ball of light that moved from purple, to green, to red and blue. All the colours she could think of all took their turn to shine before settling into to a rich indigo. It was beautiful.

'Why can't I touch it?' Sarratenian repeated.

She could see him now, as clear as if the moon shone down upon him. He was reaching out for the Origem, but an invisible force stopped him from claiming it for himself.

'*The Origem protects itself,*' said Eraidor with triumph in his voice.

Sarratenian turned his head towards Eraidor and growled in disgust.

Something else caught Liana's attention. Beyond Sarratenian in the periphery of the hall. The Moranzans were moving forward slowly towards the light as if they were attracted to it. Thin lines of light threaded through the air, each one connecting to a soldier at the head. There was something different about them, though she couldn't quite see what. It wasn't until the first one—the one closest to her left—staggered by her that she noticed a purple line tracing its way along its face. She'd seen it before somewhere. It took less than a second for her to remember where. Torn!

She watched on in horror as the Moranzan men approached the ruins of the monument, their bodies glowing as the purple veins spread through their bodies. And then their bodies changed and distorted, as if they were melting with every step. Sarratenian cackled again.

'They are absorbing the power of the Origem. It is changing them. This is how the Torn come to be,' said Eraidor. *'You need to get out. Now.'*

37
FINAL BREATH

Addan couldn't stand by and do nothing any longer. The voices in his head continued to tease him, taunt him. Liana wasn't dead as Sarratenian had claimed, and that thought alone was enough for him to have the strength to carry on in spite of what the voices told him. None of this was his fault. He had tried to save the Dawanii girl, and it was already too late when he found her. There was nothing he could do to save Milo either. His guilt over his death was that he didn't die along with him. Why didn't those terrible creatures kill him too? It was the stone. He had to believe he was spared for a reason, and that reason was to save Liana.

What about his brother? He wasn't even there on the day he died when the first iteration of the bridge collapsed. Instead of working, he'd got drunk. So many people working on the bridge died that day. He should have been there, but if he had, surely he would have died too. In truth, he would never know. None of this was his fault. He knew that now.

'I have to go after her,' he said to Eelan and the young blind man, his name forgotten, again.

Orratan grabbed his arm as he tried to leave. He made some

476

gestures with his hands, with a pained expression on his face, tears in his eyes. Eelan translated. 'It is too dangerous for you. There is nothing you can do to help. Liana has the power of a god within her now and she is fighting to stop another god. She may very well not survive her trial either. If you go to her, your death is inevitable.'

'What would you have me do then?' asked Addan, exasperated.

Eelan watched Orratan's hands. 'We cannot stop you. Please know that we will not be able to protect you either.'

'The Origem is discovered!' cried the blind one.

Addan turned to Eelan. 'If you don't want to help me, fine. At least show me where to find her.'

Eelan thought about it for a moment and then nodded. 'This way.' He gave Orratan's hands a squeeze, acknowledging something unspoken between them before he led Addan from the mountain into the city, swords at hand. Curiously, the young blind man followed right behind. Addan tried to fathom how someone who was blind could make their own way through the chaos and cleanly step over obstacles such as the dead unaided. As he made his own way closely behind Eelan, he came to the conclusion it was best not to think about it too hard. Nothing was right here and the sooner he accepted that, the less of a headache he would have. Liana had to be his sole focus now.

He wasn't sure if it was the cold that made his mind numb, or if it were all Eelan's doing. He was grateful to his new friend for his help to keep the voices and the visions away, but there was more to it than that. He felt as though his head was wrapped in a thousand layers of bandages, smothering every thought he had, both the good and the bad.

So much had happened since he resolved to save Liana, so much had changed. He had changed. Liana had changed too. He barely recognised her now, and not only because of the way she dressed. He had always seen her stubborn side, often ignoring it in the vain hope that one day she would turn to him and realise she loved him as he had always loved her. Now, it was clear to him her only goal was to save the world. The Liana of old—his best friend and partner in crime—would have laughed at the very idea of being a hero, a saviour to the world. Yet here they were.

He still didn't understand entirely what was happening, how this all came about. A war between men and the gods—the Architects. Like most, he'd never seen an Architect before, and he was supposed to believe that the man he knew as Shaan was actually Sarratenian, Architect of Ruination. Not only that, but Eraidor, the Architect of Life was *inside* Liana, trapped. And so it was a battle of the gods, a fight between family—siblings —and he and the other mere mortals were simply caught up in their warring.

Eelan led him through the remains of the city with the blind man keeping up with them both. The fight continued on, though there were more dead than still living on both sides. Wounded Dawanii tried to shelter where they could, and there was the occasional Moranzan soldier wandering aimlessly without thought, searching for someone to attack. He wondered if he'd have become like them if he'd not been sent on the scouting mission. Was that good fortune, or by design? Shaan himself had sent him away. Why? Something was keeping him alive, he was certain of that. Keeping him alive to save Liana. The Fates? Or something else?

There were no signs of the dragons either. All in all, it was a sorry state of affairs. As they turned another corner, ahead, the sound of collapsing stone and wood rumbled through the breeze. Addan knew that was where he would find Liana, and he hoped it wasn't too late.

They stopped at a courtyard to a large temple-like building.

Most of the front wall had collapsed in on itself. Dust particles still clouded the air around it.

'You don't have to come with me,' Addan said to Eelan. 'Thank you for bringing me this far, and for all your help.'

Eelan shook his head. 'This is my home. I will stay with you. You still need my help.'

The young blind man pushed past them both and climbed over the rubble and disappeared into the building. *What is he doing?* Addan ran after him, as did Eelan. Inside the building, it was eerily quiet. Debris from the ceiling fell in small amounts as the aftermath of the destruction settled. Ahead, there was a strange purple light. Addan was convinced he heard a voice, one that wasn't in his head. A woman. Liana. Yes, he was sure it was her, somewhere ahead in another room.

Eelan urged caution as the three of them moved through a dark corridor until they came to a gap in the wall, partially covered with an animal skin curtain that had seen better days. On the other side, Addan could definitely hear talking. He peered through a gap in between the skin and wall. What he saw first made him take a step back.

'What is it?' asked Eelan in a whisper.

'Torn. They are consuming the full power of the Origem. The world is at an end. We are too late,' said the blind one, his name still elusive. He stood to the side with a hand pressed against the corridor wall as if feeling for something.

Addan readied his sword and hoped these Torn creatures would fall under the steel the same as any man. He knew Liana was in that room. He pulled away the skin curtain, ready to take on whatever was on the other side.

Never had his imagination created such terrible creatures as those advancing towards them, with their melting flesh and burning eyes. They evoked such a sense of pure terror simply by being there. Then there was the smell. Rotten, decaying air assaulted his nose. Even the help of Eelan was barely enough to stop him from being overwhelmed. Addan knew the Torn were as deadly as they looked. He tried not to think of how quickly they had ripped through his company. His companions—Milo —their lives snuffed out in seconds. He had survived though, and every moment since, part of him wished he hadn't.

These Torn moved differently. Slower, more awkward. Still silent. Addan could hear his own heart beating in his ears as he readied his sword. The numbness was gone for now. He should at least have been afraid, but it wasn't fear he was feeling, it was anger. All the emotion, the experience and the torment he had witnessed—and suffered—ever since leaving the city boiled up inside him. Once suppressed—kept bubbling underneath the surface with the help of Eelan—it was now free and surging through him. As he caught sight of more Dawanii men and women coming to defend their home, Addan lunged forward with his sword and screamed.

With his first swing he missed his target completely and almost lost his balance. He recognised the Torn as a former young man from the company adjacent to his—barely—there was hardly anything left of his face that resembled his former appearance. He never knew his name, not that he'd have remembered it anyway. Whatever this man was now was far removed from what he once was, and that distance was growing with every second as the body became more distorted. The second swing of his sword connected with the Torn's right arm—raised to block it. The blade tore through the skin of the forearm with steel meeting bone, yet the creature brushed the sword aside as though it was nothing.

Addan pulled back, took his sword with both hands, and held it to his side before thrusting it forward at the creature. The tip of the sword pierced through the Torn's chest where he knew the heart was and yet nothing. It was a fatal blow. It *should have been* a fatal blow, yet the creature still stood, its blazing red eyes tearing into Addan's very soul. For a moment,

Addan did nothing. He held the sword at the Torn's chest in disbelief it was still alive. He glanced to his left at Liana.

She was near the centre of the arena, burning with Origem energy as she confronted Sarratenian. She hadn't seen him or the others arrive yet, her attention solely on the Architect she was determined to stop. He tried to call to her, but his mouth was too dry to shout.

Addan blinked, returning his attention to the Torn creature coming at him. As it clawed at his shoulder, he shoved forward and sent the creature staggering backward, releasing it from his sword. Yet it did not fall. Pain sang out from a fresh scratch, which made his eyes wet with tears.

The creature snarled silently, its contorted face bearing yellowed teeth that dripped with thick saliva. Even without words, Addan knew it was taunting him. He slashed his sword wildly in large arcs in front of him in an effort to keep some distance between them. What else could he do? *How do you kill what can't be killed?* He turned to run. Run away as fast as he could, but there wasn't anywhere to run. He was surrounded by a mix of swinging swords, spilling blood and the living corpses of those who would destroy him and his friends. There was no clear way out.

Ahead, Eelan was engaged in a hand to hand tussle with a Torn that was missing an arm. Even with that advantage the young Dawanii was clearly struggling, barely able to keep the creature from biting at his ears. Addan wanted to run away, but how could he run if that meant leaving everyone else to die? There was a sense of inevitability to it all. Run, hide, and maybe live. Or stay, fight and likely die? What would be the difference? Sarratenian would be victorious either way. *I cannot be a coward.*

Addan drew a deep breath and pulled from whatever power it was that Eelan bestowed on him. Everything seemed to move in slow motion, only for a moment, but for long enough to pull himself together. He exhaled, raised his sword high above his head, and ran at the one-armed Torn.

'Move out of the way!' Addan shouted to Eelan as he bore down on the Torn. Eelan glanced over before throwing himself backward, out of the way of Addan and his raised sword. As Addan closed the gap between him and his target, he pulled his sword down in a shallow diagonal sweep to connect with the creature's neck. As the blade made contact, to his surprise, the metal sliced right through the flesh and out past its throat in one fluid motion. He turned with the blade so as not to lose his balance. He looked up in time to see the Torn's head roll from its shoulders and on to the stone floor with a satisfying thud. Red-purple blood sprang from the neck of the creature's torso before it collapsed to the floor.

Addan, panting, watched the headless corpse, expecting it to stand up, but it merely laid there twitching. He kicked it hard, but there was no reaction. It was dead. *It was actually dead!* 'Cut their heads off!' he screamed to anyone who could hear him.

He smiled at Eelan, who smiled back, a small moment of victory shared between them. Eelan's smile quickly vanished, his eyes opened wide in fear. Addan reacted to the unspoken warning by spinning round on his heels only to face another Torn barely a step away. Before he could raise his sword arm, he felt a blow to his cheek as the Torn's right fist struck him, sending Addan crashing to the floor. His ears rang and his eyes lost focus. He tried to find his feet but couldn't, falling back to the floor for a second time.

Someone grabbed underneath his armpits. Immediately he tried to struggle and break free, but relaxed when he saw it was Eelan. Addan, with help, scrambled to his feet. The two of them lunged away from their attacker, pushing themselves out of its reach. It was Eelan's turn to stumble, catching a toe on a raised edge of a cobble. He was still holding on to Addan by the arm, and in his fall, he nearly took both of them crashing, but somehow they remained standing.

Addan steadied himself. A quick survey of the room to get his bearings told him they were losing this fight. Even with a new sense of momentum now they knew how to kill the Torn, there were too many of them. He counted three headless Torn corpses, but there had to be at least a dozen dead from their own number. They needed a miracle if they were to live to see another day. Addan looked to Liana.

She was too far away, engaged with the Architect. They both were shouting at each other as they fought their own battle. He considered what he could do to help her. He could try pushing his way through the myriad of Torn and Dawanii, but he realised she was holding her own. Out of everyone fighting, she was the only one who appeared to have an advantage.

A Torn solider stepped forward, blocking his view. Addan brought his sword up and hacked into the creature's neck, but his aim was too low. His blade struck collar bone and the force of the impact reverberated along his sword arm into his shoulder. The Torn was undeterred. It leaned into the sword, now wedged between its bone and flesh, pressing in towards him. It took two tugs with his full weight behind it for Addan to extricate his weapon. He was tiring now and suspected the others would be feeling the same. The Torn didn't look tired, though. *How much more can I take?*

Addan mustered up as much strength as he could find for another swing. This time his steel found its mark, and the head dropped, with the body following behind. Enemy blood spattered Addan's face and clothes, but he was too tired to care. He used the crook of his free arm to wipe his face before searching for the next target. Then he felt something snap inside him.

The world around Addan went dark. The figures of those around him—Dawanii, Torn, Liana—became mere shadows in a grey-black haze of nothing. What he could still see seemed to slow down to an almost stop, and all he could hear was the sound of his own heart thumping within him. Even that had slowed right down. Thump. What had happened? Thump. Was he dead? Thump. The darkness closed in around him. *Thump.*

'It's too late. You couldn't save me. Why wouldn't you save me?' The voice was inside his head and he recognised it immediately. The voice in the darkness. *Her* voice.

Addan shook his head furiously to clear his mind, but the voice did not stop. The darkness, the shadows, the torment all kept coming at him with a relentlessness that tried to overwhelm him. He tried to see, but he could not. He screamed as loud as he could to block out the voice, but she would not be silenced.

A second voice joined in. Their voices overlapping, creating a chorus of torment. The girl, and his brother. *'It's all too late. You should give up now. You cannot save her, just like you couldn't save us. It's all your fault. The blame is all yours. You let us die, and now you must too.'*

'No!' screamed Addan. 'It wasn't my fault. I know it wasn't. You cannot blame me. I tried. I really tried!'

'You are destined to fail here. There's no point in trying now. Give in to the darkness. Come with us. You cannot save her. You were never the hero. You aren't worthy of being a hero. You let us die. A true hero would not have let us die.'

Addan turned and looked for a way out of the darkness. He needed to find Eelan, but he couldn't feel his presence anymore. Something told him he had to find a way out of the darkness himself. But how? He remembered what Eelan had taught him. Take deep breaths. Slowly. Focus. Find something to hold on to.

He breathed in deeply and closed his eyes. The voices persisted. They were laughing now. Exhale. Calm down. See through the darkness and find the light. Find a way out. Breathe. Eyes open.

The darkness receded, and Addan found himself back in the

madness of battle. Immediately he became aware of a painful feeling in his right hand. He looked down and saw he'd had gripped his sword so tightly his knuckles were white. He tried to relax his fingers but couldn't, his hand paralysed with, what? Fear? Guilt? He searched the arena for Eelan. There was no sign of him. Torn continued to bear down on what was left of the Dawanii. Liana was still fighting with Sarratenian by the broken remains of a stone sculpture with a pulsing bright light at its centre.

It was the cinderfox who drew Addan's attention next. The curiously beautiful animal who, since he'd found Liana again at least, was never far from her side. Except now it was hunched over the body of a man near the rubble of a collapsed statue. Addan couldn't see who it was but inside, he knew.

The voice of the girl inside his head giggled. *'Another you couldn't save.'*

'Shut up!' Addan demanded as he pushed his way over to the body, avoiding Torn along the way. 'Why is it for me to save you all? It isn't my fault. It's not my responsibility to save everyone.'

'Yet you used him to save yourself and now look what you have done.'

'I didn't ask for any of this!' As Addan reached Eelan, the cinderfox looked up at him. There was a look of sadness in her eyes as she sat protectively over the fallen young man.

Addan crouched down beside Eelan. Blood was pooling underneath where his friend lay and he knew in that moment there was nothing he or anyone else could do to save him.

'I'm sorry,' Eelan whispered. The words caught in his throat making him cough.

'You're a healer. Tell me you can heal yourself. Tell me you can do that.'

Eelan tried to move, but what energy he had left was waning fast. 'We cannot heal ourselves. Only others.' His eyes were wet and the colour was fading from his cheeks. He reached up with a hand to Addan, trying to touch his face. Addan took the hand and held it to his own cheek.

'Thank you for trying to help me,' Addan said, his words barely making a sound.

'It's who I am.'

The side of Addan's face felt hot from the touch of Eelan's hand. The voices in his head quietened ever so slightly. It was one final act of healing, Addan knew. The last vestiges of strength transferred in a final show of friendship. The heat dissipated and Eelan's hand fell limp in Addan's, and with no other words, Eelan closed his eyes and breathed his last.

As Addan carefully lowered Eelan's arm, the cinderfox nuzzled into him as if to offer comfort. Addan absently stroked the back of her neck. The darkness was already returning, and the voices reminded him they weren't too far away. Any last help Eelan had given him would soon be gone, and he would have to face his tormentors alone.

It took a growl and a shift in position by Ember for Addan to remember where he was and the chaos that surrounded him. He turned on his knees and followed the cinderfox's stare to a Torn soldier coming at them. The creature ambled with a limp, dragging a footless leg across the stones leaving a smear of blood in its wake. The impediment barely slowed it down as it closed the distance between them.

Addan pulled himself to his feet as fast as he could, then realised he'd laid his sword down when he tended to Eelan. There was no time to grab it. The Torn was almost within arm's reach. Addan had no choice but to throw himself to one side out of the way. He landed awkwardly, twisting his knee in the wrong direction forcing all his weight onto his other leg.

The voices in his head laughed at his pain.

'Stop!' he cried. Was this his life now? A constant tormenting reminder of everyone who died? He'd always blamed himself for his brother's death, but the young Dawanii girl? There was nothing he could do to save her. And now Eelan had died. Would his voice join the chorus of his guilt-wracked mind? Something had to change. He had to find a way out. But how?

He noticed the blind man grappling with a Torn soldier, struggling for his own life. He looked so small and utterly terrified. Addan felt helpless and acutely aware that he was unarmed as he caught the attention of one of the larger Torn.

To his left, around six paces away, lay the body of a Dawanii man. In his hand was a sword and Addan had to get it. He was unsure if he had the time to retrieve it before the approaching Torn would cut across his path. There was no choice—he had to try. Pushing off with his good leg, he launched himself forward, dropped his head and fell into a roll towards the fallen Dawanii. He came up an arms-length short of where he needed to be, and with the Torn almost upon him, he scrambled forward on all fours until he could reach the blade. He wrestled it free from the dead man's grasp before rolling onto his back. As he looked up, the Torn was barely two paces away, looming large over him and blocking everything else from view.

There was no time to pick himself up from the floor, and there was no way the sword would reach the creature's neck. Addan shivered. *Is this it? Will I die this time?* The voices in his head continued to taunt him, but he refused to listen to them. He refused to give in. The Torn closed in on him and all he could do was slash his new sword around wildly while trying to push himself backwards with his heels. He succeeded in only slicing through the already tattered leggings of the Torn, scraping thin lines through flesh that oozed purple-red blood.

It was over. Addan resigned himself to his fate and closed his eyes. He lowered his sword and awaited death. And he waited. Nothing happened. Then, a snarling, growling noise made him look. The cinderfox had come to his aid and was tearing into the neck of the Torn that would be his killer.

The cinderfox ripped chunks of distorted flesh from the Torn, yet the creature still made no sound. Its mouth did open as if it were screaming, but there was no cry. Addan watched as it tried to free itself from the jaws of the cinderfox, both now rolling on the floor locked in a fight for survival. He got to his feet and went to swing at the Torn's neck, but hesitated. Their wrestling meant there was no clear line. Strike wrong and he could easily decapitate the fox by mistake. The animal seemed to know, though. She caught Addan's eye and released the Torn from her mouth, her white fur spattered with the blood of their enemy.

Addan took the opportunity as it was presented and pulled his sword down in a single fluid motion with whatever strength he had left. Sharp metal met with already butchered flesh and the head rolled away from its owner. Addan's whole body trembled, and he was out of breath. He looked at the cinderfox, who appeared satisfied with the kill.

The last vestiges of Eelan's healing powers ebbed away from him as he looked for Liana. He called out her name.

'Stay away!' she shouted back. The bright light from the glowing orb that hung in the air obscured her from his sight. He followed her voice and found her on the ground, propped up by her elbows with Sarratenian looming over her. She was injured, blood seeping from a large wound in her side.

Addan stepped through the scattered dead to get to her.

'You need to run, Addan. You need to get out of here,' said Liana.

She told him to run. Again. The last time he ran he thought he had lost her forever. This time he would not run. This time he would stand his ground. He was *not* a coward, and he would not give in to the voices inside his head. 'I'm staying, Liana. I have to save you. I *need* to save you.'

'I don't need rescuing.'

Sarratenian laughed. 'The young hero comes to the aid of his dear friend. How noble.'

'It won't work. You can't save her.' It was Milo's voice he was hearing now.

'I have to try.' Addan fought to ignore the endless torment as much as he ignored the gradual darkening of the world around him. Time was running out.

He watched the evil god take hold of Liana, hoisting her into the air as if she was nothing. *No, I won't let her die!*

He charged, aiming to tackle Sarratenian to the ground. What else could he do? He lowered his head and reached out to throw his arms around the Architect as he sprang forward. It was enough, barely. The god, surprised by the attack, released his hold of Liana. She hauled herself to her feet as Addan rolled on the ground in her direction, separating himself from Sarratenian before he could react.

Addan watched Liana reach for the energy inside her. She glowed brighter, her entire body bathed in a pale white light. She looked *infinite*. At the same time, Sarratenian made his move, going in for the kill. He was faster than her. Without hesitation or thought, Addan closed his eyes, screamed, and threw himself at Liana, shoving her out of harm's way, taking the full force of Sarratenian's assault in his back. He collapsed to the ground and groaned as the air left his lungs. He wasn't sure if the laughing he could hear came from Sarratenian or the voices in his head. He didn't care. He'd saved her, and that was all that mattered. Everything he'd been through had been for this one moment, he knew that, and he smiled. Hot lightning flooded his body as a burst of energy tore through him, and the laughter fell silent.

38

THE END

Death had not come for Liana in that moment. Addan had thrown himself forward in the space between her and Sarratenian, and given his life to save hers. He gasped in pain and crashed to the ground at her feet. *What has he done?* Blood pooled underneath him as he tried to raise a hand to her. He whispered something, but she couldn't understand what he was trying to say.

Liana looked up at Sarratenian. Even he seemed surprised at what had happened. She screamed at him. Barely a sound escaped her mouth, her rage was so visceral. She looked back at Addan, her friend. If Sarratenian chose now to strike her down then so be it. In that moment she no longer cared. The Architect didn't attack, choosing instead to claim his prize. She pulled Addan closer to her. 'Stay with me, Addan. Please don't die.'

She looked up at Eraidor, the useless god who was always there, yet might as well not. 'Where's Eelan? I need Eelan. He can help him.'

'... dead...' Addan said. His voice was so quiet.

It felt to her that time paused very briefly, only for an instant, as she took in that revelation. Both twins dead. First

490

Haal and now Eelan—her only hope of helping Addan extinguished also. 'No, no, no. I'll find a way. Just hang on. Please. Come on, Addan. Stay with me.'

'I couldn't... help... them,' Addan coughed. Blood bubbled from the corner of his mouth. 'They said... said... said I couldn't.'

'Hush, don't try to speak. Help will come.' She squeezed him tightly to her, desperately trying to deny the inevitable. She promised to help, but there was none on offer. All she could do was watch as the life faded from her friend—her best friend.

It was only in those last few seconds she realised the truth, but as the small black dots in his eyes relaxed, she knew it was too late and he was gone. The colour of his eyes was so, so green. So beautiful. It tore at her how she had never *truly* noticed them before. Regret. Sorrow. *Rage.*

Liana could barely contain herself long enough to lay Addan on the ground before launching herself at Sarratenian. Injury be damned. She would end this here and now. An incendiary anger welling up inside her spilled over. She barrelled into Sarratenian as he tried again to claim the power of the Origem for himself.

Uehan was in the background, defending himself against the Torn. No easy feat without the ability to see, yet he was surviving. Liana felt she should help him, but if she didn't stop Sarratenian they would all be dead soon enough. She staggered across the amphitheatre, trying to put herself in between Sarratenian and the Origem. There had to be something she could do with her newly acquired powers that would be strong enough to stop him. How though? How do you defeat a god?

She had to believe she was stronger than him. It was the only way. How did the Dawanii create their homes and their structures? She imagined the ground swelling up around Sarratenian. She reached out with her hands and imagined sculpting the earth beneath his feet. The walls shook and crumbled, and then the ground moved. She willed the stone flooring upwards and it obeyed. A vortex of dirt and stone whipped up around Sarratenian, almost lifting him from the ground with it.

'You cannot stop me. It is already too late. Can you feel the magic flowing into this world? Can you? I will start this world anew, and make it right.'

Liana *could* feel it. It reminded her of warming her hands at the hearth in Uehan's home when she first arrived here. Different, though. It wasn't actually heat she felt coming from it. She imagined the energy from the Origem pouring into her, and then channelled that energy into her vortex around Sarratenian.

'*You must stop,*' cried Eraidor. '*Your body cannot take any more of this. It will destroy you.*'

'If it kills me to defeat him then so be it.'

'*If you die, then so do I.*'

'Then help me. For the sake of everyone, help me.'

'*I am helping. If I were not within you, you will have already burned to your death. I am all that is keeping you alive.*'

Sarratenian was trapped in a swirling mass of debris and stone. She could already feel she wouldn't be able to hold him for long. It allowed her time, though. Time to consider what else could be done. She had to destroy the Origem itself. How though? A scream to her right caught her attention. Uehan. He was in trouble. She couldn't let him die, too. Yet if she released her concentration on the vortex, Sarratenian would break free of it almost instantly.

'I need more help,' she said through gritted teeth. 'I can't do this alone.'

She pulled at the ground around Sarratenian, trying desperately to create as much disruption as she could. As a result, the walls shook violently and more of the statues collapsed. The cacophony of stone smashing against stone filled the space around her. Two of the Torn fell trapped under the rubble. Liana counted at least three more still standing, two of which were attacking Uehan near a pillar against the right wall. She had to get to him.

Releasing her control of the vortex, she moved to get closer to Uehan. She imagined a fireball in her hands, willing it to form. She felt the energy of the Origem within her moving through her arms and out through her hands. A ball of white hot fire grew at her fingertips and she hurled it at the Torn closest to her. Immediately on contact, the creature that was once a man of her own city incinerated to dust.

The second Torn barely acknowledged the demise of the other. It bore down on Uehan who was trying his best to dodge the onslaught. The Torn creature was trying to grab hold of the young man. It carried no weapon. It seemed to want to tear him apart, limb by limb. She was too far away to get to him in time. As she imagined another fireball, agony surged through her arms. It felt like her veins were about to explode, pulling the flesh from her bones. Until that moment, she had felt immune to the pain she knew her body was feeling. Something had changed inside her, no—that wasn't it. The pure energy of the Origem inside her was changing, growing.

'It is too much! Your body will break apart,' cried Eraidor anxiously.

'I can't stop it. I can feel the whole world, everything. It burns!' The fireball formed in her hands, though it couldn't grow as large as the first one before it became too intense to hold on to. She threw it at the other Torn. It didn't have the speed or reach of the first one, as if she no longer had the strength to propel it to where she needed it to go. The white hot ball of light landed at the feet of the Torn. Was it enough? It didn't look like it until... the leggings the creature wore ignited. Slow at first, then the fire spread until the ex-human became a living torch. Still, it did not scream.

Liana slumped backwards, cradling her injured side. Uehan was out of immediate danger and that had to be enough. She could feel the energy consuming her from the inside out and wondered how much time she had left before it ended her life, taking Eraidor along with her. Clenching her jaw, she forced herself to continue. For as long as she drew breath, she vowed not to give up, not while Sarratenian was still a threat to this city and everything beyond.

Eraidor continued to protest. He was so impotent amidst all the chaos. While everyone else fought for their lives, he only stood, seen only by Liana and Sarratenian, unable to do anything else other than speak.

The vortex Liana had been desperately trying to hold together shattered, though not without total failure. Sarratenian was sent backward, away from the Origem with enough force to knock him over. He landed at the foot of one of the few remaining statues that had yet to crumble. It barely took any time at all for him to get to his feet, unharmed.

'How does it feel to witness all this power, brother? How does it feel knowing you can do nothing to stop me?'

'*Sarratenian, I implore you to end this madness. What do you hope to achieve if everyone is dead?*' said Eraidor, stepping through the rubble to him.

Liana watched the two gods together as she tried to catch a breath and bring the power tearing her apart back under control. She realised that if she did nothing, the feeling of her skin burning didn't get any worse, though it did not subside. *There has to be something else I can do.*

'Oh dear, poor Liana. Look, brother, see how she struggles with the powers only meant for us? She *is* strong, though. How much longer can she keep you alive, do you think? I wonder what it will be like when a god dies. Never happened before, has it? Something new for the world. I should ask Aelene if there is a next life waiting for us too. I would say she is a little busy right now, though.' He tilted his neck left and right as if to stretch out some stiffness in his muscles.

'I should have made sure to have sent you right until the end of time, the end of everything.'

'Ah, but you did not. I am grateful to you, I truly am, brother.'

The thin, string-like ribbons of light continued to extend from the rift, each one connected to a Moranzan soldier, corrupting them, making them Torn. It was a terrible sight to watch as their bodies distorted and melted as the energy from the rift altered their very being. They were no longer human. Liana wasn't sure if they were even still alive. Their eyes burned wildly like molten metal spheres. They moved awkwardly as they bore down on their prey. The Dawanii did their best. Even with their own powers, they succumbed easily to these monsters.

The ribbons of the rift latched on to the Dawanii now too. Liana watched, horrified, as they also changed. Purple lines appeared on their faces before tracing their way throughout their bodies. The Dawanii *did* scream in pain as the raw power of the rift coursed through them.

Something caught Liana's attention. Something small atop the rubble watched over the devastation that unfolded. One solitary dragon perched on the broken head of one of the Architect statues. Its wings were tucked close against its body and its head was cocked to one side. Liana tried to reach out to it. 'We need your help.'

The dragon tilted its head to the other side and looked right at her. She was convinced it heard her plea, yet it did not move.

'Where are the others? I beg you, please. Will you only watch and see everyone die?' she pleaded.

The dragon blinked and then flew away. Liana's heart sank. *It's over, then.* She observed the situation around her. There were more Torn than Dawanii now, and those who hadn't died or been taken by the rift would soon meet their end. Sarratenian himself stood on a mound of broken statues, practically dancing. His hands moved through the air as if to music, pulling on the threads of light connecting the rift to the Torn like puppets on string. He cackled to himself at the orchestra of battle before him. Eraidor could do nothing other than watch. Liana saw the hurt in his eyes and shared in his grief.

The two of them were almost the same being now. How much of her own self was left? It was hard to tell. Ever since she had tried to save that old man's life, she had felt herself eroding away, piece by piece, and she fought it every step of the way. Now, it was too much to bear.

Above her came a screeching sound and immediately her heart lifted. She looked up and saw the small wings of a solitary dragon flying in circles above her. Then another, and another. In mere seconds the whole sky was filled with hundreds of dragons creating their patterns in the air. There were more than she'd seen before. More than had taken the form of the phalanx that showed her what it was to fly. They swarmed and the sound of thousands of beating wings hummed and buzzed, vibrating through the breeze.

ASSIST

'Yes!' cried Liana. 'He must be stopped. Will you help us?'

HOME

Liana didn't know what they meant, but she could feel their emotion and their willingness to at least try to stop Sarratenian from destroying everything. The dragons descended until Liana was surrounded by the flying creatures. It was hard for her to see anything through the blur of wings and tails.

'Can you destroy the rift? If we can stop these threads, the things turning people into monsters, we might stand a chance against Sarratenian.'

NO

She was surprised and confused by the response. What did they mean, no? Were they here to help or not? Surely Sarratenian couldn't control the dragons, too?

HOME

The swarm coalesced and took the form of a larger version of itself. The shape was vague and ill-defined, yet awesome and beautiful at the same time. It flew higher, clearing the way around Liana. Sarratenian was still there, but the threads of light coming from the rift had faded. Whatever the dragons had done had some effect, at least. The Torn were still Torn, and they continued to attack anyone who was not one of their own. Sarratenian shouted angrily as he fought to draw more power from the rift. Only small and ineffective tendrils protruded from the still glowing fracture between worlds.

Liana, emboldened by the abrupt change in fortune, summoned as much strength as she could and imagined the ground swell up around Sarratenian once again. She could feel the energy tearing her apart as she staggered closer to him. *I will not let him win.* She imagined herself as one with the dragons, imagined them feeding on the power within her, for them to help defeat the god who would destroy the world for nothing more than his own sport.

She connected with them, and she understood.

HOME

'Help end this and you can to go home. I promise,' she whispered. She no longer needed to raise her voice for them to hear her. And then the strangest thing. She felt herself leave her body and looked down at the destruction below as if she were one of the dragons. Sarratenian was trying desperately to regain the control he had lost. Uehan was fighting against the Torn, unable to see, yet still anticipating every attack that came his way. The few remaining Dawanii tearing up the ground themselves and fighting for their lives. She saw it all. And she saw more. Everything.

All at once, she saw the very dawn of time. The creation of her planet, her home. Every planet and star as they gathered in clusters of millions and more. They too, were part of many

497

other clusters in a vast expanse of everything and nothing. She witnessed the beginning of time itself, and its end. Eons passed in a heartbeat and a mere second lasted for eternity. She knew everything the Architects knew. She was a god. And she knew how it all ends.

She knew how to defeat Sarratenian, and she knew it would be her end as well.

Instantly, she found herself returned to her own body. The massive phalanx of many dragons flew low above her. She could still see as they saw. Her skin glowed pure white and fizzed against the air. Her agony was so intense now, yet it did not feel like true pain. Ever since she first discovered magic she had fed off the pain it caused her. All the headaches and torture in her bones told her to stop, time and time again. She had ignored it, even dared it to hurt her. Now she knew. The pain was the magic and the Origem was the pain. And now she commanded it. *She* was the pain.

Liana stood firm, digging her heel into the ground. She breathed in and counted to three. The dragons knew what they had to do, and together they acted as one. Liana ran. She ran, surefooted and fast—injury be damned—closing the distance between her and Sarratenian. The phalanx burst into her individual beings and flew fast around Liana and Sarratenian, cutting them both off from everything else around them. It was only the two of them now. Liana pulled back her right arm and closed her fist around a roaring ball of fire and Origem energy, and as she reached her enemy she slammed that fist into him. Everything turned white. Blinding. Silent except for a high-pitched ringing that echoed against the swirling wall of dragons.

Sarratenian growled loudly, shouting. He fought back, pushing Liana away with both hands. She staggered backwards, her fall cushioned by the air the dragons and their beating wings made.

'I will not be stopped,' shouted Sarratenian.

'It's already over. I have seen it. No longer will you cause such misery. You will regret the day you met me,' Liana replied. She was already standing, ready to attack again.

'I am the only true god here and you are nothing. You cannot stop me. Look at you, barely alive in that feeble body of yours. This power is not meant for you.' He lurched forward and grabbed her by the arm and yanked her to him.

Nose to nose, Liana grunted and punched her way free. *Is this how it is to be? All this power and it comes down to an old-fashioned fist fight?* She struck him on the nose and he howled. The look of surprise on his face said he'd never been attacked in this way before. He snarled and reciprocated. The bridge of her nose shattered, and she laughed. She fed off the pain now. It only made her more determined. Head down and forward, she charged him.

The two of them wrestled for dominance. He was strong, stronger than her, but she had landed on top of him, handing her the advantage. She pulled him forward towards her and then pushed, cracking his head against the rocks with such force they broke around him until there was a man-sized hole in the ground.

HOME

Liana looked up at the revolving wall of dragons. The pattern had changed, and the wall was moving. She knew she needed to move with it. They were leading her and Sarratenian somewhere. Closer to the rift. She could feel their collective thoughts urging her to move out of the way lest she get swept up in their momentum.

The power within her felt absolute. Eraidor was still there with her, yet it had been a while since she had seen or heard him. Was that a consequence of absorbing his power and that of the Origem? It really felt as though they were one now. Perhaps she didn't *need* to hear him. It crossed her mind that she actually *was* him now. Or maybe he was her. Or something new entirely. A hybrid human god.

She knew how this ended. She grabbed Sarratenian by the hair and dragged him kicking and screaming along the ground. He reached for anything he could gain a purchase on, but he only pulled rock and earth along with him. She ignored his protests. She knew she was stronger than him now.

'This ends here,' she said. 'You came here searching for the rift. Searching for its power so you could destroy this world and the people living on it. Well, I give the rift to you, *Shaan*. If you want it, you can have it.' With his hair still in her hand, she grabbed him by the neck with the other and lifted him from the ground and pushed him head-first to the mouth of the rift. He screamed.

She fought as he struggled to free himself from her grasp. His eyes lit up like miniature fires as the pulsating energy of the rift reached out to him with the same tendrils that had claimed the Torn.

The dragons roared as the rift grew larger. It threatened to not only consume Sarratenian, but take Liana with him. *I know*, she thought. She knew that to destroy him was to destroy herself also. She had no choice. She pushed, but somehow Sarratenian broke free and they both fell away from the rift.

And then the dragon wall evaporated, surging upwards. The circular wall turned into a funnel and one by one, the dragons flew into the rift. Liana knew. Home. The rift was where the dragons belonged. It was where they came from, brought into this world centuries ago, and now they could return. Hundreds and then thousands of the minute animals filtered through the opening, but that was not their final act.

'You are free now. Thank you for your help,' Liana whispered. With one last effort, she took hold of Sarratenian and lifted him up and offered him to the dragons. He screamed as they enveloped him, forming a giant dragon claw clutching him in their grasp. He looked so feeble compared to them. This fist of dragons took him with them, into the rift, to whatever existed on the other side.

It was over. Sarratenian was gone, consumed by the rift, taken to the other place outside this world. The tendrils extending from the rift had gone also, no longer offering a connection between the void and the Torn. Everything fell silent. The rift pulsed softly as if nothing had happened. Liana looked around her. There was almost nothing left, such was the scale of devastation. Only one Architect statue remained standing. She didn't recognise which one it was.

The remaining Torn had stopped their attacks and now stood almost like statues themselves. It took her a moment to locate Uehan. She found him on the far side of a large pile of rubble that had once been a wall. He was prodding at a Torn corpse with his finger as if making sure it was dead. Liana stepped over to him. Loose stones and rock moved clear of her path as the power still coursed through her body. When she reached Uehan, she noticed something still troubled him.

'You can relax now. He's gone. We're safe,' she soothed.

Uehan shook his head. 'He is not gone. He will return and the world will still end. You will still die and yet you shall live on. I see both the past and the future, all at the same time. It hurts.'

'I see it too,' she replied, though she considered how different it would be for her than him. The whole world still burned inside her mind and she knew the power of the gods was eating away at her and soon there would be nothing left of her. She wondered if Eraidor would survive, or if they both would die. She had succeeded in her task, despite what Uehan was saying. Sarratenian was gone, and she saw no future where he would return.

She was wrong.

An unnatural cry filled the air from behind her. She

whipped her head around. The rift crackled and spat, growing angry once again. Within it, a ghost-like image of Sarratenian's face appeared.

'He returns!' declared Uehan, clutching at his temples with both hands. The blue swirls in his darkened eyes stared into the sky.

How? She could see everything, or so she thought. The dawn and end of existence. Yet Uehan had seen something she hadn't. *I need to stop him. I don't know what else to do.* For all her knowledge imparted to her by the power of the Architects, she envisioned no way to stop him.

'If there is anything left of you, Eraidor, talk to me. Tell me how to stop him once and for all time.' She reached inside of herself. She still felt him. Eraidor did not reply, not with words, at least. A feeling. A thought stirred in her head. A notion. A solution.

'I have to destroy the rift completely,' she said to Uehan.

He looked horrified, releasing the grip on his hair. 'You cannot. To seal the rift is to deny us of the Architect's gifts. We will be without. Everyone. You cannot do this. Find another way.' He was trembling.

Liana considered his words. *"We will be without."* All the knowledge of existence poured through her mind like a torrential rainstorm. She knew what he meant. Was there no other way? Her mind raced as she tried to find another option. There was none. She rested a hand on his shoulder. 'I have to do this.'

Uehan's lower lip quivered. 'You can't. It will end us. End our way of life.'

At least you will have a life to live, she reasoned. The knowledge of the Architects told her their gift, as Uehan called it— their abilities—came from the Origem. The power that seeped through the tear in the very fabric of reality. To close the rift would cut off that power from everything. Everyone. Including anyone like her who could make spheres of light or make objects move without touching. It would all be gone. How devastating would that be, to rip away their very beliefs, their religion? *Better that than to die.*

Liana knew Uehan had seen this future and she could see how frightened he was of it. 'You know it is the right thing to do,' she said to him. She looked back at the rift. Sarratenian's form was gaining more definition, the rippling tear between worlds growing to fit his form. She had to do it now. There was no more time for reasoning.

She left Uehan, pulling free as he made a final grasp to stop her. She didn't look back. How would she close the rift? The knowledge didn't have an answer for that. It was all down to her, and only her. She hobbled to the rift amid the screams of Sarratenian as he fought to free himself, to return to this world.

Summoning the power within her, she could feel her body failing. The unfelt agony called to her, begging her to stop. This final act would kill her, she was certain of that. No other choice, though. She imagined the rift closing and pulled at the edges, willing them to close. Nothing happened. She stared into the other-worldly gaze of an angry god that desperately wanted her to fail. She would not fail.

There had to be a way. *Think, Liana. Imagine.* What did the rift remind her of? What was it? A tear in reality. An injury. A *wound.* A memory flashed in her mind of her time with the Sisterhood. She remembered the wound on her arm and how they healed it, weaving Origem energy across her injury like a surgeon with a suture, pulling the ends tight and repairing the cut as though it had never happened.

Liana imagined.

She summoned a thin ribbon of light between her fingers. As she held out her hand, the delicate strip of energy danced and swam around her wrist. Into that thread she poured out every last drop of energy she had within her and slowly moved her arm back and forth across the furious image of Sarratenian. Liana crisscrossed the wound with her suture of light until she was satisfied. Two loose ends dangled on either side. One for each hand to pull tight and cut off the Origem's power forever.

This is it. This is my ending. She took hold of the threads and closed her eyes. Sarratenian screamed in front, Uehan cried from behind. With the last spark of power inside her she pulled. The silent agony turned into pain, real and unbearable pain. She felt it all, right until the end.

39

THE BEGINNING

'Come on now, wake up.' The voice was distant and quiet. Familiar.

Liana opened her eyes and tried to sit up. Immediately, she felt dizzy and sank back. 'What happened?'

'It is over.'

She rubbed at her eyes and tried to force down the nauseous feeling. As the blurriness faded, she saw Eraidor standing over her. 'You came back,' she said. 'Where were you?'

'I was there, I promise. Now, however, I am not.' He smiled at her.

'What do you mean?' As she spoke, she realised something was different. Something had changed. His voice wasn't coming to her internally anymore. She could actually hear him, through her ears. She felt different, too. Like a weight had been lifted somehow.

'The path we shared has come to its end. In defeating Sarratenian, you have freed me from you. My curse is lifted.' He sounded prideful.

Any disorientation she felt evaporated, and she was on her

feet in less than a second, her injuries healed. All of them. The man—the god—that had been part of her being for so long now looked different. He looked real. 'I thought you'd be taller,' she remarked, smirking. Her expression changed. 'How though? What did I do? It can't have been simply by defeating Sarraten-ian. You said you thought he'd been sent to the end of time. If that had been true, you would have been trapped forever. So, what was it?'

'Ah, the secret. Yes, I should imagine you would like to know. Strictly speaking, you died. My punishment was always to move to a new host at the end of their life. That never changed, even with you. The only way I could be freed was if my host sacrificed their own life for another. Willingly, and without expectation. Closing the rift required so much power it was fatal. You knew it would kill you. You felt it. Yet you did it anyway.'

'Everything would have been destroyed if I didn't. There wasn't a choice.'

'There is always a choice, my dear Liana. You chose to help my previous host. You chose to save your friend when he was close to death in the wilderness. You are not as selfish as you would have yourself believe.'

'How am I alive, if I died?'

'My gift to you. Call it... an intervention.'

Her thoughts turned to her friend. 'Addan,' she said, glumly. 'He died, trying to save me. He was more a hero than I could ever be.'

'Hmm, maybe, maybe not.'

Liana looked at her surroundings. Dawanii and Moranzans —what few of them were left—milled around looking lost, they themselves taking in the devastation around them. Those who had become Torn were returning to normal. They still didn't appear quite human, but they were no longer fated to die, or worse. The monument was completely destroyed, as was everything else except for one lone statue. A woman, carved as though she was covering her eyes with both hands. 'Who is she?'

'You know, I am not familiar with that likeness,' Eraidor admitted.

'I believe the statue is me,' said a feminine voice.

Liana turned to see Aelene approaching through the rubble. She stepped over everything with perfect grace and balance, not once stumbling. Her hair was different than when Liana had last seen her. In fact, her whole appearance was that of a much younger woman. *Whose imagining of them was this?* 'Why are you covering your eyes?'

'I cannot say for certain. Not very flattering though, is it?'

'A reasonable likeness,' said Eraidor.

'Ah, brother, dear. I see you have extricated yourself. Well done you,' she said condescendingly. She looked around at the aftermath of the battle with disgust and tutted. 'So many dead. Do you not think I have enough work to do without you adding more to it? I am a very busy woman.'

Liana agreed, as well as feeling guilty for her own part in the bloodshed. With all the power she had, she should have found a way to stop Sarratenian sooner. She tuned out of the conversation Eraidor was having with Aelene, her attention concentrated on the fallen. How many had lost their lives? She started counting the bodies, but quickly stopped as her feelings overwhelmed her.

'Have you taken all their souls away already?' Liana asked.

Aelene clicked her tongue. 'I may be an Architect, but you cannot expect me to work miracles. I am not only taking care of these poor people. There is a plague in the south also demanding my attention. Do not fear, all will be helped along their way in due course.'

'I only meant—'

'Yes, I can be in more than one place at the same time.'

'No,' said Liana, more insistent. 'I wanted to know if you have taken care of my friend. I wanted to say goodbye to him.'

Aelene huffed and rolled her eyes. 'Where are they?'

Liana scanned the area, looking for Addan. She couldn't see him. Where had she been when he had saved her? There. She scrambled over the broken remains of one of the statues to a body lying face down in the dirt. She recognised the clothing and didn't need—or want—to see his face. She silently pointed to him.

Aelene glided over, her long white dress caressing the rubble as she went. 'He is still here,' she said. 'Come along, young man.' She extended her arm over Addan and made an upwards motion.

As it had done when Liana had witnessed Haal's passing, her surroundings darkened until all that was visible was herself, Addan's body, and the two Architects. A figure resembling the man she knew pushed himself away from the corpse and stood up. His feet were hidden, as if he was standing inside the body. He looked perplexed.

'I'm so sorry,' Liana said as she stepped to him. She opened her arms to embrace him, but then remembered he had no physicality to him. Not any longer. She tucked her hands into her armpits, arms crossed.

'Huh?' Addan looked around him, and then down at the ground. 'Ah. Shit.'

'You will not have long,' warned Aelene. 'Say what you need to say. Places to be, people to send to the next life.'

Liana looked at her and scowled before turning back to her friend. 'Why did you do that?'

'I couldn't let you die. I promised myself I would protect you. I shouldn't have left you back in the forest. I was a coward, Liana. I should have stayed. When I couldn't find you, I promised myself I would find you and I would save you. They said I couldn't. That everything was all my fault, even though it wasn't.'

'Who's they?'

'The voices. It doesn't matter, they've gone now too. I couldn't save them, but I knew I could save you, and that's all that matters to me.' He wore a smile on his face, not one of self-satisfaction, but one of pride.

'Well, you always were an idiot,' Liana said, fighting back tears with a laugh. 'Thank you, though. I mean it.' She looked to Aelene. 'Does he have to die? Tell me you have some way he can live. I can't let him go. He doesn't deserve...' she looked back at Addan through wet eyes.

'He is already dead,' Aelene said coldly. 'I can no more bring him back to life than you can turn yourself into a flower.'

'No, of course not,' Liana conceded.

'Time for you to go now,' said Aelene to Addan. 'If all these souls have to wait too much longer, it is going to get very messy around here. It is of no help to anyone to dally.' She reached out to take him by the hand.

'This is goodbye then,' he said. 'As this is my last chance to say it. Then, I love you, Liana. I always have, ever since we first met.'

'I know, and I love you, too,' Liana said. It *was* the truth, but she loved him as a brother, nothing more. He didn't need to know that in his final moments, though, except...

Fighting back the tears was far harder than fighting a god, and she wiped her eyes with her arm. When she looked again, Addan and Aelene had gone. Her shoulders shook, and she released all her emotions at once like a waterfall breaking a dam. 'Goodbye,' she mouthed as she crumpled to the ground.

She felt something wet in her ear, which startled her out of her sorrow. It was Ember. Liana dug out a smile and stroked the back of the cinderfox's neck. The blue flame in her fur rippled softly around her fingers.

Liana then realised Ember wasn't alone. Orratan had arrived, and so had Uehan and Helela. She was relieved to see them all still alive. Orratan helped her to her feet.

'The Origem's light has gone,' said Uehan softly. 'It was as I saw. By closing the rift, all magic has gone from this world.'

Liana nodded. She could feel it. Or, more precisely, she couldn't. With a raised hand, she tried to imagine a ball of light. Nothing happened. No light, and no headache. She had taken the knowledge of all creation into her mind. Now, she couldn't remember that wisdom at all. None of it. Gone forever. She looked to Eraidor.

'The young man is correct. The rift allowed the Origem's energy to trickle out into this world. It has done so for a thousand years, filtering into everything that lives. The Dawanii learned to harness it and build it into their religion. Others, like you, only had the faintest of notions it existed. Most, well, it had no effect on their lives at all. Now the rift has been sealed, and everything you knew as magic has gone.'

'Uehan is still blind, though,' Liana said.

Eraidor nodded solemnly. 'Yes, and that will always be so. And it is the case for all of them.' He paused, thoughtful. 'I can, however, restore their senses.'

'How? If there is no Origem.'

'I am an Architect. We are not mortal, and therefore we are not bound by the same laws as you.'

Liana nodded. His words were of some comfort to her. If they had lost their abilities permanently, at least they could see and speak once again. She wondered how their lives would change now. There'd be no more Brandings. No one to heal their ailments, or build their unusual houses. She thought about the Sisterhood. What would their purpose in the world be? *I've broken a whole civilisation.*

'Do not be hard on yourself. What you did had to be done. If I have learned anything over the centuries, it is that these people are resilient, and they will adapt. It is better to live and learn renewed, than to die ignorant.'

Those who were still alive and able to walk had gathered around, surrounding them at all sides. Somehow, they had understood that this new figure standing among them was Eraidor himself. Liana couldn't work out how, exactly. She took a step back to let him address everyone.

'Sarratenian, the Architect of Ruination has been defeated, in no small part because of your bravery here today. I share in your sorrow for those who gave their lives this day. Be assured, they will all be cared for by Aelene as they walk their path to the next life.

'The rift has been closed. No longer will you be able to touch the Origem. I will grant you all the return of the gifts you offered to us in tribute when you undertook the Branding.'

As Eraidor raised his arms, as if ready to perform his miracle, Liana was surprised to see Orratan step forward and stop him. The old man made shapes and gestures with his hands and fingers. Liana didn't understand what he was trying to say, though Eraidor smiled and nodded.

Stood beside Liana, a Dawanii woman of an age around ten years older than her, spoke Orratan's words. "I thank you for your generosity and your warm words. Respectfully, I wish to decline your offer. Though I may not be able to rely on the Origem any longer, I do not ask for my voice back. My inability to speak is part of who I am. I have been this way my entire adult life, and I cannot imagine it any other way now."

The woman paused briefly as Orratan looked around him before he continued on. "Of course, I do not speak for everyone else stood here. They are free to decide for themselves. Everything happens for a reason, and we are who we are. The world has changed now. There are many other villages across Dawan who will not understand what has befallen them today. We will go out, and we will unite, and we will live on."

'Of course,' said Eraidor. He bowed to Orratan before taking his hand warmly.

'What about you?' Liana asked Uehan. 'Don't you want your sight back? It has only been gone a short while.'

Uehan smiled and shook his head. 'It would not be right. I stole my Branding from my brother. I have learned there are other ways to see, and while I may no longer see the future, I will find my way. Please do not worry. How it is, is right.'

Liana wondered if she would feel the same if she were in their position. True, she no longer had any power of her own, such as it was. Aside from the pain, she hadn't given anything up in return for that power. She had lost her brother and her best friend, though. And she would give anything to have them back in her life. Anything.

As the gathered crowd dissipated, Liana thought of home. She was queen now, and not a single person back in Moranza would be aware of what happened here. From what she understood, they believed the Dawanii murdered her mother, and she would need to explain that wasn't the case at all. She imagined the look on the Council's faces when she told them. The Tal Valar. Now *they* would want to know everything, and they would especially want an audience with Eraidor.

'What will you do now?' she asked him.

'Hmm, now I think about it, I would like to go swimming.'

'Swimming?' His answer was not what she expected.

'Oh yes, I used to be quite fond of that. Then, I think I will travel. It will be a novelty to go where I wish to and not where someone else wants to. Once, one of my hosts took it upon himself to go meditating at the edge of a cliff. Two whole years he stayed there! I was so bloody bored.'

Liana giggled. She looked down at Ember. 'Well, I suppose I had better take you with me, though I don't know what everyone else will make of you.' The cinderfox let her mouth hang open before making one of her squeaking yawns. Then she padded over to Uehan and curled up around his feet. She looked at Liana with an expression that told her, 'I'll look after him.' Liana smiled and shook her head. 'Yes, quite right too,' she said.

EPILOGUE

Liana stood outside Nalla's cave, and looked out over Trennale. In the two days since she had defeated Sarratenian, the Dawanii were already rebuilding their lives and their homes. Despite all the devastation that had taken place, they had welcomed the remaining survivors from Moranza as if they had always been friends. No, not friends, *family*, just as they had done when she first arrived with Uehan.

For their own part, the Moranzans had little memory of what had happened. They knew they had signed up to go to war, but beyond that, they had forgotten the rest. Out of the hundreds who came with Sarratenian, fewer than fifty remained. Any fight they had within them had faded along with Sarratenian's influence over them.

It was time for her to return home now. Not that it felt like home any more. She wanted to stay here. In her short time with the Dawanii, she had felt a kinship. Finally, somewhere where she belonged. She would come back, though. Often. Uehan had made her promise. It was the easiest promise she had ever made.

The half moon of midday hung in the dark cloudless sky

and the wind blew as it always did. The world continued on, as it always had, and now always would. Sarratenian was gone. She hoped permanently, though a small doubt scratched away at the back of her mind. Maybe one day he *would* return, though hopefully not for another thousand years. She and everyone she knew would be gone by then. Except maybe Nalla. That woman already looked like she was a thousand years old and could easily live for a thousand more.

Liana accepted a clay pot of warm tea from the oldest person she had ever known, stood beside her side at the entrance to her cave.

'I'm all alone,' Liana said, contemplating all that had happened. 'My brother and my best friend. My mother, too. All gone.'

'You are only as alone as you choose to be. Yes, you have said goodbye to the ones you love. We all have, and you will do so again many times in the future.'

Liana sipped on her tea, thinking on the old woman's words.

'You still feel guilty,' Nalla said after a while.

'Yes.'

'You shouldn't. Everything that has come to pass did so for the right reason. Your path was determined for you a long time ago, before you were born, in fact.'

'What do you mean?' Liana knew what she meant, or at least she thought she did. She thought back to what Addan had told her about Dess, and the others he said he met. *The Fates.* Dess had led her to Dawan, there was no doubt about that. Did they mean her to find Eraidor? Did they already know that she would, and then with his help, find a way to save the world from Sarratenian? Her head hurt as she tried to understand all the possibilities, and that, maybe, free will wasn't real.

'It is no coincidence, you standing here with me, now. This was always meant to be, but at the same time, none of this was meant to happen at all. The world has been out of balance ever since the Division. It still is. The world is still broken, yet to mend it, a wrong from the past needed to be set right first.'

Liana frowned, confused.

'Your story does not end here. In fact, it has barely begun. You may believe yourself to be alone, and you mourn your losses. Let me tell you this. The future is forever changing, and the past is not as permanent as you believe it to be.'

'I don't understand.'

'No, you don't, but one day you will. Time is a curiosity that very few understand. I saw a future where Sarratenian won his desire, and yet here we are. Here I am. I am still here when perhaps I should not be. Destiny is a strange thing, Liana. Everyone has a path, though not all paths run straight.'

'Who *are* you? Are you an Architect?'

Nalla laughed and hit Liana in the leg gently with her stick. 'No, no. I am as human as you are. Perhaps somewhere deep inside, you know who I am. Or perhaps not, not yet. One day you will discover the truth, but you have a long journey ahead of you, and y—'

The old woman stopped talking and staggered backwards, clutching at her temple, her eyes tightly closed.

'What is it? What's wrong?' asked Liana, bending down beside her.

Nalla opened her eyes and relaxed. Whatever pained her seemed to be passing. 'Change is coming. I need you to remember. I need you to remember all that has happened here. It will be important that you do. The time has come. Time is crucial to your future and to your past. Our past. Our future. Do not forget, Liana. Do not ever forget.'

And then Nalla vanished.

THANK YOU - PLEASE READ

After almost two years of many sleepless nights thinking about this world and the characters within it, this novel is finally complete and in your hands.

Liana came first, watching a curious ritual play out around a camp fire, an invisible voice calling to her for help. Everything else you have read was built around that idea. Rybban? Where did that idea come from? I'll tell you... Isaac Asimov. He had an idea he called "Ribbon World", where life could only exist in the thin line between light and dark of a tidally locked planet. Sci-fi, yes of course. What a great setting for a fantasy world, though. Don't you agree? Anyway, I hope you enjoyed reading it as much as I enjoyed writing it.

I would like to take this opportunity to say thank you for picking this story up and spending your valuable time reading it. There are literally millions of books to choose from, and you chose this one! It means a lot to me, really.

If you enjoyed *Orchestra of the Gods*, please consider leaving a review on Amazon, Goodreads, or wherever else you choose to share your thoughts. And tell a friend! Reviews are one of the most powerful things you can do as a reader. They help inform other readers like yourself to discover the books that they will enjoy reading.

I am now turning my attention to the next book in this series, and I hope you will come back and visit Rybban again in the not too distant future.

Also, please don't forget that you can sign up for my newsletter via my website damien-buckley.com/mailing-list—a novella set before this story is coming soon and the ebook will be exclusive to newsletter subscribers. What's it about? Well, you'll have to wait and see. I will say, a few familiar faces will make an appearance.

Thank you once again,

Damien Buckley

2nd April, 2025.

Printed in Great Britain
by Amazon